SALVATION IN THE SUN

The Lost Pharaoh Chronicles Book I

LAUREN LEE MEREWETHER

Edited by
SPENCER HAMILTON

LLMBooks Publishing

Copyright © 2018 Lauren Lee Merewether

ISBN: 1523205881
ISBN-13: 978-1523205882

For Mark

EXCLUSIVE READER OFFER

Get the first story of
The Lost Pharaoh Chronicles Prequel Collection
for FREE!

Visit www.laurenleemerewether.com
to receive your FREE ebook copy of
The Mitanni Princess.

GLOSSARY

CONCEPTS / ITEMS

1. Chief royal wife – premier wife of Pharaoh, Queen
2. Commander – second-in-command of Pharaoh's Armies; third-highest ranking beneath Master of Pharaoh's Horses and the general
3. Coregent – ruler, second to Pharaoh
4. Deben – weight of measure equal to about 91 grams
5. Dynasties – Lines of familial rulers in the Old Kingdom, then Middle Kingdom, then New Kingdom (where this story takes place, specifically the 18th Dynasty)
6. Eagle-Omens – ancient belief that an eagle either represented in dreams or spotted in real life can signify importance in dream-interpretation and prophecy
7. General – highest ranking position of Pharaoh's Armies

8. "Gone to Re" – a form of the traditional phrase used to speak about someone's death
9. Great royal wife – chief royal wife of the Pharaoh before
10. Hedjet – white crown worn by Egyptian regents of the 18th dynasty
11. Ka – spirit
12. Master of Pharaoh's Horses – highest ranking position of Pharaoh's Chariotry; second-in-command to the general
13. Modius – the crown for a Queen
14. Pharaoh – the modern day term for the ruler or King of Ancient Egypt
15. Pshent – the great double crown of Pharaoh
16. Sed Festival – celebration of Pharaoh's thirty-year reign, and then every 3–4 years
17. Shendyt – a pleated royal apron or skirt lined with gold; royal shendyt worn by Pharaoh
18. Sidelock – a long lock of hair above the ear, kept despite a shaved head, to signify childhood; is usually braided
19. Sistrum – a musical instrument of the percussion family, chiefly associated with ancient Iraq and Egypt
20. Vizier – chief royal advisor to Pharaoh

GODS

1. Amun – premier god of Egypt in the Middle Kingdom
2. Amun-Re – a name given to show the duality of Amun and Re (the hidden god and the sun) to appease both priesthoods during the early part of the New Kingdom

3. Aten – the sun-disc god of Egypt (referred to as "The Aten"); a minor aspect of the sun god, Re
4. Bes – god of childbirth
5. Ptah – god of creation, art, and fertility
6. Re – premier god of Egypt in the Old Kingdom; the sun god
7. Tawaret – goddess of childbirth

PLACES

1. Aketaten – city of modern-day area of Amarna
2. Akhe-Aten – necropolis for the city of Aketaten
3. Ipet-isut – modern-day Karnak of Thebes, "The Most Selected of Places"
4. Malkata – palace of Pharaoh Amenhotep III
5. Men-nefer – city of modern-day Memphis
6. Saqqara – necropolis for the city of Men-nefer
7. Waset – city of modern-day Luxor

PEOPLE

1. Aburiash ("Burnaburiash") – King of Babylon
2. Ainamun – steward of Kiya
3. Aitye – steward of Nefertiti
4. Alashiya – King of Cyprus
5. Amenhotep III – Pharaoh; father of Amenhotep IV and Thutmose
6. Amenhotep IV / Akhenaten – second son of Amenhotep III and Tiye
7. Anen – Second Prophet of Amun; brother to Tiye and Ay
8. Ankhesenpaaten – daughter of Amenhotep IV / Akhenaten
9. Ay – Nefertiti's father; brother to Tiye and Anen

PROLOGUE

PHARAOH HOREMHEB OBSERVED THE FIVE PROPHETS' PALE faces: lips, trembling with victory; eyes, tinged with triumph. Their wicked deeds would soon be erased once he signed the edict laid before him. The reed brush drizzled ink into a slosh on the table as he held it, re-reading the papyrus scroll for the fifth time. His stomach turned over on itself and heaviness pressed into his chest.

It will be better for Pharaoh and for Egypt if future generations did not remember the heretic line of Pharaohs before and the wickedness of the priesthood, he reminded himself. The sharp intake of breath behind him made him grip the reed brush harder. His wife and queen, Mut, stood there. He felt her tears as his own, but he was in the wolves' den and so hardened his will. In his hand, he held the legacy of those who came before him. Pushing the chair back, he stood up with a graceful grandeur and placed the reed brush in its well.

The five prophets of Amun leaned forward in their seats, gnashed their teeth, ready to pounce, but Pharaoh Horemheb raised his hand to silence them. His guards stood at either side, spears in hand and swords sheathed.

"You said you would sign," one of the pale faces said in the silent moments after. "For the greater of E—"

"There are none greater than Pharaoh." His stare cut through the tension in the room, centering on the one who had spoken; the man drew his jaw in and forced his lips closed. "Before we sentence the past to death, you"—he raised his finger to all five prophets in the room—"*you* will remember."

Wennefer, the First Prophet of Amun, narrowed his eyes at Pharaoh. "But we all know the past. It is for the future generations to not know about the weakness of Akhenaten or the transgressions of those who opposed him. It is for Egypt."

"You will hold your tongue, First Prophet." Pharaoh's glare met Wennefer's equal. The two most powerful men of Egypt stood, seeing who would break their stare first. Finally, Pharaoh struck him down. "I, Pharaoh, the sole divine ruler of all of Egypt, appointed you, Wennefer, as First Prophet of Amun, and I can remove you."

Wennefer's upper lip twitched, but he slowly bowed to Pharaoh and then took his seat. "As Pharaoh says."

The other four prophets' faces became paler. *This* Pharaoh would keep his reclaimed power over their leader.

"By signing this edict . . ." Pharaoh Horemheb's finger jammed again and again into the papyrus on the table. "By signing this, Pharaoh is condemning the memory of those now gone to eternal erasure, condemning their memories to the bottom of the Nile, never to be seen again."

"Yes, Pharaoh," the prophets muttered. A few eyes began to roll and a few heads began to shake, but at the hot glare of Pharaoh, all movement ceased.

I just threatened their leader; they so easily forget, Pharaoh Horemheb thought.

"We discussed this edict. It is what is needed," Wennefer

said to Pharaoh as the other prophets nodded and murmured in agreement.

"And yet you feel no remorse." Pharaoh's eyes were centered on Wennefer, but his words were to all. "I, Pharaoh, have seen your drooling, your dancing feet, your hunger for this everlasting punishment to be pronounced. You, oh great, wise prophets of Amun—*you* desire this . . . but you are no better than those we are about to erase. You do not deserve to be remembered. Your wickedness lives on, but your deeds will be covered."

Pharaoh Horemheb's voice was no more than a whisper, yet strong enough to move mountains, causing Wennefer to shake at the knees and sit back down. They all muttered indecipherable words to explain away their demeanor.

Once again Pharaoh silenced them. "Only because this history undermines the power of Pharaoh—not just in the eyes of our own but also those of our foreign allies and enemies—will I, Pharaoh, sign it."

Queen Mut let out a despairing breath behind him. He forced himself to ignore her.

"But first," he continued, "we will remember those to be denied a place in history. We will know the truth, and we will acknowledge they lived and breathed. They are worthy of much more than this pitiful end. You will remember, and their lives will stay with you until the day you die. They will weigh heavy on your hearts, and they will haunt your minds even as you journey to the afterlife."

A silence settled in the room, inching its way further inside the bones of those attending there.

"As . . . Pharaoh . . . says." Wennefer clenched his jaw and crossed his arms over his chest. Leaning back, he nodded his head. "Where shall we begin with this . . . chronicling?"

Looking to the statue of Amun standing behind the prophets, Pharaoh drew in a deep breath. Amun had granted him his victory. "We shall begin with Pharaoh Akhenaten and the birth of his beloved . . . Queen Nefertiti," Pharaoh said as he rested back into his throne.

Queen Mut's hand came to his shoulder, as if to thank him for starting with her half-sister.

CHAPTER 1
THE TIME OF AMUN-RE

O<small>UTSIDE, THE ROCK'S ASHES BLEW UNDER THE SUN SPELLS</small> of the earth. The fiery winds whistled, carrying the cries of a newborn babe. Death crept and life blossomed. A mother whispered, "Her name shall mean 'The beautiful one is come.'"

Stroking the baby's buttery soft cheeks, the nurse Tey cradled the little girl, letting the mother hold the baby's tiny hand. With a soft whisper, Tey crooned, "Your name shall be Nefertiti . . . the Beautiful One . . . a name worthy of your mother's legacy."

Temehu smiled in the last moment of her life. A midwife placed aside the statues of Bes and Tawaret and closed Temehu's eyes, telling her to dream of life with Amun-Re.

Nefertiti let go of her mother's hand, and it fell with a thud. As if sensing her mother's passing, Nefertiti's little brow furrowed, and cries came forth.

Tey hummed an enchanting melody, forcing a smile even as the midwives and servant girls in the room wailed in mourning. She carried Nefertiti from that room filled with death and with life, toward the master's bedchambers; it was time for her to be blessed by her father, Ay, brother of the Queen of Egypt. She slowed to a stop as Nefertiti fell asleep in her arms.

As she looked at the closed door to the bedchambers, that morning's breakfast grumbled in her stomach and bile rose in her throat.

Temehu, her master . . . so kind and loving . . . was gone to Re. Death had taken her.

Tey had now inherited the duty to tell Temehu's husband that he would never see his wife again.

The servant boy opened the door for her. She swallowed and walked inside Ay's bedchambers.

"Ay," Tey murmured as her tears finally fell.

Ay turned to scold her for not using his official title, but at the sight of her watery eyes he held his breath, fearing the worst. "Temehu . . . or the child?" Ay asked, leaning the full weight of his body onto the table. His eyes scanned the baby bundle she held with sudden dread.

"Scribe of Pharaoh, Overseer of Pharaoh's Horses . . . your chief wife," Tey said as Ay closed his eyes, hating himself for wishing Tey's next words regarded the baby instead. "Your Thousand Splendid Suns, your Temehu, has passed from this life."

Ay clenched his fists and blew out the air he held captive in his chest. Sliding his fist to his forehead to shield his tears' escape, his strong shoulders slumped. His heart fell into his stomach as if someone had dealt a blow to the core of his soul. He had but one wife, Temehu; he longed for no other woman. The other men of his stature could have had several wives with one chief wife, but he had only Temehu . . . his one, his cherished, his beloved.

Wanting no witnesses to his pain—his weakness—he

bellowed, "LEAVE!" The blast of his yell defeated the candlelight on the table, and his servants scurried out of his bedchambers.

Tey made a bold decision and remained. The door closed behind her.

Ay pulled off his wig and fell to his knees. He let out a guttural moan and slammed his hands onto the table, not noticing Tey still stood at his door. He examined his wig's intricate human hair braids interwoven with golden beads as the sweet smell of susinum perfume reached his nostrils. His hand grazed his bald head as he threw the wig off to his side. Years of working to obtain an official's wig meant nothing now.

"Scribe of Pha—"

"I said *leave!*" he spat through his teeth as he spun to face her. The moonlight glistened on his tear-stained face. The shadows in the room hid the smudged kohl surrounding his eyes, but as he spoke, the same kohl revealed itself as it began to streak down his cheeks.

Tey could understand his anger at the life he had been handed. She wanted to collapse to the floor as if it were her own; instead she stood strong for her master's husband and walked toward him.

"*Leave*, I said!" Ay entreated her once more.

Nefertiti awoke to her father's yells. Tey held up the baby girl for Ay to see, hoping her small cries would cast light into his heavy heart. "Temehu brought forth this new life before she left us," Tey said.

"Tey, why do you cause me so much inner turmoil?" Ay asked. "First news of Temehu's journey to Re . . . and now of my newborn daughter?" He reached up to hold the baby's fingers.

"To lessen your sorrow," Tey answered, her eyes downcast.

"It is great still," he said as he pulled back from the child and climbed to his feet. *I cannot accept this child, not now. I need to see Temehu to know it's true,* he thought. "Take me to Temehu."

AY STEPPED INTO THE ROOM WHERE HIS WIFE'S BODY LAY. The midwife and servants dabbed the sweat from her face and bosom with reverence. Their tears dampened their work.

"My dear Temehu," Ay whispered to his wife's lifeless body as he knelt beside her.

The maidservants heard the mournful whisper and stepped back, bowing their heads. Ay caressed his wife's cheek. Wanting to melt into her and wail at his great loss, he only kissed her face and then her forehead. He examined her beauty, even in death, holding back his every cry, every tear, every tormenting ache.

Finally he said, "Prepare the burial. We will send the best we have with her in the afterlife." He wished the servants would leave so he could be with her alone.

As if reading his mind, Tey motioned for the others to leave. She placed a hand on Ay's shoulder and whispered, "I will make the arrangements."

She followed the servant boy out as he closed the door behind them. At its close, Tey could sense Ay's pain through the walls. She held Nefertiti close to her heart and buried her head into the child's wriggling warmth. With tears streaming down her face, she whispered, "Your mother was loved . . . and so you will be, the daughter of Ay."

IN THE COMING MONTHS, AY BURIED HIS WIFE WITH

honor and dignity. Because he blamed his newborn daughter for taking away his precious Temehu, he had only seen her the one time, not even looking at her since Tey first brought her to him. He didn't even know her name.

Instead, he spent his days in his chair by the window, meditating on the past. His favorite recollection always came to mind: the lotus garden in the courtyard . . . Temehu, bent over with a sly smirk on her face . . . him, trying to balance himself on the balls of his feet but falling backward into the dirt. Her subsequent joyous, hearty laugh rang throughout his memory.

He and Temehu had tried for so long to have a child, and the one child they had together took her life away. *And was the child worth it?* he thought wishing the child had died instead.

Queen Tiye, Ay's older sister, always looked out for him, knowing when and how to comfort him in his days of sorrow. She had sent her regards to his now seemingly small household and had even come herself on the morning of Temehu's send-off into the afterlife. Ay faintly smiled at that memory.

Tey interrupted his thoughts as she came and stood at a respectable distance from him. In her arms she held the cause of Temehu's demise.

Ay sighed and turned his head away from her. "Leave me, Tey."

"Scribe of Pharaoh," Tey said, "your daughter needs you . . . just as you need her."

Ay stood and pointed at the bundle Tey held. "I need Temehu! Not that girl!"

Tey persisted. "And Temehu is gone. Your daughter remains. Temehu died for this child. She wanted this child. Will you let her death be in vain?"

Her heart pulsed in her voice and behind her eyes. He

9

clearly was not the only one hurting. Ay went to slap her, but refrained and dropped his hand as she didn't flinch or bat an eye. She knew she was right, and now she knew he did too.

They stood almost toe to toe, and finally, Ay dropped his guard and found the strength to look upon his daughter for the second time in her short life.

"What is her name?" he asked.

"Temehu named her Nefertiti. *The beautiful one is come*," Tey whispered, glancing down at the baby. "Her last moments were smiling because she recognized this child would be her legacy. She loved your child and had only met her for such a short time. Will you love her as Temehu would have wanted?"

As Tey spoke and Nefertiti cooed, Ay's hatred for the girl melted. He reached out his hand and his daughter wrapped her small hand around his finger. Large, dark almond eyes beamed up at him. A perfect nose wrinkled in a small laughter at his touch. Tiny, cherry-rose lips parted into an open smile.

"It seems I was blind to what Temehu saw," he said and smiled at this lovely creature, the last living memory of his chief wife. "*The beautiful one is come* . . . my Nefertiti."

Tey brought the child closer to her father, and he took her in his arms. At that moment, she captured his aching heart. "Oh Nefertiti," he whispered. "My heart floated adrift when Temehu died, but now you have found it and stolen it back. You will honor your mother with elegance and charm, and you will dignify her death in the woman you will become."

Tey smiled at the gentleness of Ay's voice. Tey could tell Ay loved the women in his life more than others. She placed her hand on his forearm and said, "She will do much more than that."

Ay smiled at his young daughter as he pondered those words. He appreciated the kind touch of his new daughter's wet nurse. Not rebuking her for touching him, he instead looked to her with a warm smile on his face. Although he held back his words of gratitude for bridging his hate and love for Nefertiti, Ay realized it was the greatest joy he had felt since Temehu's passing.

"She will do so much more," Tey repeated in a whisper.

CHAPTER 2
THE TIME OF REBIRTH

THE SUN ROSE AND SET BEYOND THE GREAT HORIZON, AND Nefertiti grew with each passing day. Ay grew alongside his child: his shoulders gradually became upright once again, the dark circles under his eyes diminished, and the restless nights faded. His heart's wounds began to heal. Although Temehu always occupied his heart and always would, he found comfort in Tey's encouraging words, and her plainly attractive appearance and loving embrace for his daughter.

Some days would dawn and set without a single thought of Temehu. When he remembered as he lay down next to the empty headrest, he would hate himself, and the pain of losing her would come rushing back.

But Tey was always there to help him back to his feet. She grew increasingly more bold with him until one evening, when she was reporting on Nefertiti's day, he leaned in and kissed her. She had just finished a funny story of Nefertiti playing in the dirt, and her small chuckles had put light in his soul. He surprised himself with the kiss and sharply stood back, but Tey, now more comfortable and even more emboldened, naturally took his hand and leaned in for another kiss.

Four years after Temehu's passing and Nefertiti's birth, Ay married Tey and made her his chief and only wife. With Tey, he fathered two more children, and his heart finally felt full once more.

NEFERTITI REMINDED AY MORE OF TEMEHU IN FACE AND mind as she aged into a young woman of thirteen. Her laugh was deep and hearty, like that of her mother. When she was especially confident, the back of her hand rested somewhat under her chin and a sly smile crept on her face.

The only child of Ay's who followed him everywhere he went and where she was allowed to go, Nefertiti found special favor with her father. She fixated on reading her father's plans and documents for managing the chariotry horses and scribes of Pharaoh. Every night as she fell asleep, she told Ay she wanted to be just like him tomorrow.

Ay would laugh, rub her half-bald head, watch her sidelock braid shake about, kiss her cheek, and whisper, "I know you will, my Nefertiti."

Her half-sisters perfumed their bodies and had their servant girls paint their faces, but Nefertiti did not need to paint her face to receive favorable glances. Her cheekbones rose as high as the great tombs built by Pharaohs Khufu and Khafre; her eyes were so big and dark, some would say even the sunlight got lost in them. Unbeknownst to all, she savored her one little secret of biting her lips to give them their full illustrious cherry red glow to continue to amaze her admirers.

QUEEN TIYE NOTICED NEFERTITI'S BEAUTY EVERY TIME SHE visited her brother or when Ay brought Nefertiti to see her children at the palace.

"Your daughter," she said to Ay at her last visit, "Nefertiti, would make a lovely statue for all of Egypt—and the world after—to see. Her beauty, captured alongside my son, the Crown Prince Thutmose, forever and always, would bring admiration to his reign."

"I am honored," Ay said with a humble bow of his head. "I will give to you my first daughter, my beautiful one, Nefertiti, in marriage to the Crown Prince."

"As well as be a symbol of dignity when it comes to . . ." She trailed off, ending the royal formality of her words. "Before you agree, my brother, she will need to be strong."

"Tiye, what do mean?" Ay asked. "She is of strong mind and body, and will be able to bear children."

"No, Ay . . ." Queen Tiye looked around to make sure there were no eavesdroppers, and with a low whisper, continued, "The Amun-Re priesthood has grown very powerful. The priesthood holds more power and influence than Pharaoh himself."

"More power than Pharaoh?" Ay asked, not wanting to insult his sister with his doubt but incredulous all the same.

"Yes," Queen Tiye said. "Nefertiti will need to sway the people to Pharaoh, away from the priesthood. If the First Prophet of Amun dies when Pharaoh Amenhotep III still reigns, he and I will begin the transition of power, but as Meryptah lives, the principal power remains with him. He may outlive us, and so we need Nefertiti and Thutmose to be prepared to take the burden. Our royal court knows it, but I only tell you this because if what you tell me of Nefertiti is true, Egypt will need her as its next Queen."

"Nefertiti is all that I have spoken. Such aptitude for

learning . . . Her mind bears no equal, and she would willingly die for Egypt. Her loyalty knows no bounds."

"Then will you still hand her over, brother? It may be dangerous. She may die by revolt of the people."

"If she dies by the revolt of the people, then Egypt is no longer the home I want." Ay bit down hard on his bottom teeth. "When the land resorts to violence to rid itself of its divine ruler, the country is already gone."

"Good. They will marry when Thutmose is named Coregent." Queen Tiye smiled, but her eyes were dim. Her brother spoke the truth; she hoped Egypt, with all its wealth and riches, could survive this transition of power.

Their older brother, Anen, suddenly came into Ay's home. His calf-length pleated shendyt tied with a blue ornate sash that hung off of his right side swished as he stepped inside. At the sight of the Queen, he bowed to pay his respects. The leopard-skin imitation that hung across the left side of his body stretched from the weight of the plaster leopard head swinging forward just below his waist. His bald head shimmered with fresh perfumed oil as he returned from his bow. "Ah, is it not my noble brother and my Queenly sister!"

"Anen, Second Prophet of Amun, what brings you to my home?" Ay said with a slight nod of respect, but a harrowing weight set upon his brow. Anen had never come to Ay's home before, and it looked like he had just freshly shaved his body to present himself to the Queen. *It could just be it is his month in the four phyles to serve in the temples,* Ay thought. *Perhaps that is why he is not wearing his headdress.*

With a smile as wide as the Nile, Anen bowed once more to his sister. "What reason need there be? I wish to see my family, and I heard the Queen was in company."

"Please, come, sit with us." Queen Tiye offered a nearby chair.

He obliged, and his eyes shot daggers at his younger brother. "Now, pardon my discourtesy, but I overheard talk of marriage?"

Queen Tiye and Ay exchanged glances. What all did he hear? Queen Tiye feared he would take such eavesdropping back to his priesthood of Amun; the lives of the royal family may be in danger.

In Queen Tiye's silence, Ay responded, "Yes indeed, brother."

Tiye added with a curt nod, "Nefertiti will marry the next Pharaoh."

"Ah, I see. In that case, may I be so bold as to suggest one of my four daughters for marriage to the Crown Prince?" Anen said this as he sat flipping a coin through his fingers. "They rival the grace of Nefertiti in both face and body."

"But do they have her mind?" Ay asked. Blood raised to his cheeks. *How dare he take this from my Nefertiti! The Queen has already decided.*

"I am the oldest brother of our family. One of my daughters should be given the privilege—nay, the *right*—to marry the Crown Prince," Anen said with an increasing audaciousness. "In addition, I serve the god Amun. The Crown Prince would do well if he aligned himself with the priesthood."

"I serve the Pharaoh of Egypt," Ay said, "the divinely appointed one to lead us into greatness. The Crown Prince would do well if he aligned himself—"

"Enough, brothers," Queen Tiye said, quieting the room without raising a finger. "Brother Anen, your daughters are all very beautiful in both face and body, but even in sum they cannot rival the natural beauty of Nefertiti. Her mind is as equal as her image, and your daughters, do what they may, will never rival her privilege, her right, to marry my son, the

Crown Prince, the next Pharaoh of Egypt. She will forever sit by his side with her beauty immortalized in stone." Queen Tiye spoke with such a sharpness of tongue, Ay thought his brother would fall over dead from the strike.

Anen silenced for a moment as he pulled his body tight and straightened his back. "Sister, come now. The priesthood of Amun is powerful. I would hate to find the heir to the throne at such a disadvantage of having spat in the face of Amun's Second Prophet."

The snake's threat lingered in the air as Queen Tiye slowly breathed in its venom.

"Brother, there should be no disrespect to our great priesthood of Amun-Re, and relations should remain the same. I only try to persuade you due to my son's great admiration of Nefertiti and his wish to make her his chief wife." The half-truth easily slid from her lips. "The Crown Prince has a right to choose his wife, and he has chosen Nefertiti because of her unsurpassable beauty."

Anen slowly stood and with a tight jaw whispered, "As the Crown Prince wishes, my Queen." He bowed to his sister a third time and nodded to his brother. "Forgive the brevity of my stay. I have remembered there are other matters that need tending." He slowly bowed a fourth time to his sister and left Ay's home.

As he left, a deep pain descended into the depths of Anen's soul. *I am the elder sibling. Tiye has brought a slap to my face and insult to my family,* he thought. He mounted his litter and left toward the Nile with his company.

I will seek counsel with Pawah. At least one of my four daughters will be Queen of Egypt.

"WE ARE SETTLED THEN," QUEEN TIYE SAID AFTER ANEN'S departure. "Nefertiti will marry the Crown Prince Thutmose when he is named Coregent at the Pharaoh's third upcoming sed festival," Queen Tiye commanded.

"Yes, my Queen," Ay said with a deep bow.

"And remember, brother Ay: Nefertiti needs to know the burden she will face, but in due time. You may make her aware, but she is to discuss this with no one. When she is ready, Pharaoh and I will advise her and Thutmose."

"Yes, my Queen," Ay said again, nodding his head.

The deal in hand, Queen Tiye left with her servants and guards toward her barge, the Aten-tjehen, to the city of Men-nefer to tell her eldest son the good news.

NEFERTITI WATCHED FROM THE WINDOW AS HER AUNT stepped into the sunlight, a slave girl on either side shading Queen Tiye with a palm branch. Walking down the stairs to her father's office, Nefertiti thought to herself, *She is so regal. I wish to be like her someday.*

"Father?" she asked, knocking on his half-open door.

"Yes, my lotus blossom?"

Nefertiti sauntered into his library. She sat and gently placed the back of her hand under her chin and looked up at her father with her big almond eyes. "My aunt and uncle did not stay long. What did they have to say?"

He looked at her for a moment, reminding himself Temehu was not with him anymore. Busying himself with the scrolls on his table, he said, "Why are you interested in the events of your elders?"

"Because one day *I* will be an elder," Nefertiti said with her half smile. Her head tilted off-center.

Ay's conversations with his sister jumped to the forefront

of his mind. *Tiye was right . . . her unsurpassable beauty will be the most perfect image carved into Pharaoh's palace.*

Ay could never be upset with his firstborn daughter even when her curiosity got the best of her, hard though he tried. He always welcomed Nefertiti, whatever she asked of him. Her swanlike neck, her striking face, and her laugh—especially her laugh—he would always say reminded him of her mother.

"Yes, Nefertiti, one day you will be an elder. A very important elder." He paused, unsure how to tell her of her upcoming marriage and the burden she would soon carry. The sun caught him in the eye as he turned to glance out the courtyard window. He filled his lungs with the blossoms' scents. "Come, Nefertiti. Walk with me in the garden."

"Yes, Father!" Nefertiti exclaimed. It was a rare occasion she was invited to walk alone with her father in the garden. It most certainly meant he had something important to tell her, and he usually let her hold his hand while they walked.

"My lotus blossom," Ay said. She grabbed his hand as they stepped into the sun. "The Crown Prince Thutmose has chosen you to be his chief wife. Queen Tiye came here to tell me of the marriage."

Nefertiti smiled brightly. "Oh, that is wonderful, Father!"

She had expected such news to come sooner rather than later. Thutmose had held a special place in her heart since they were children. She had feigned interest in her father's work at the palace only to meet with her cousin. Whispering in the hallways about their dreams and plans for the future, they recognized they were meant for each other. Thutmose regarded her for more than just her pretty face—he appreciated her for who she was.

Happiness overjoyed her soul at their future, and she looked forward to standing by him as his chief royal wife. Pharaoh adored Thutmose, and she perceived she would be favored in his sight since she was now to wed his heir. She dropped Ay's hand and practiced walking down the throne room there in the garden. "I can't wait! I will be the best Queen and the best wife for Thutmose."

"Nefertiti . . ." Ay said, not wanting to dispel his daughter's excitement.

"Yes, Father?" The sparkle left her eyes at the sound of his voice.

Ay paused. Thoughts raced over each other in his head, but only one phrase escaped his lips. "You will be a great Queen, Nefertiti. Learn from Queen Tiye, as she is also a great Queen."

"I will! I will, Father, oh, I will!" Nefertiti said, the sparkle returned. She grabbed his hand and wrapped him in a tight embrace.

"I love you, my little lotus blossom," Ay said, struggling to take another breath.

Nefertiti let a bellied laugh escape her lips and strengthened her embrace.

"Are you trying to squeeze me as tight as you can?" A warm smile covered his face. Her laugh always produced that memory of Temehu in the garden; it was almost as if she were there with him in that moment.

"No, I am trying to squeeze the laughter out," she said and giggled, hugging him even tighter.

Ay escaped her squeeze, spun her around, and wrapped his arms around her entire body, trapping her arms against her sides. "We will see who squeezes the laughter out of whom!"

Nefertiti squealed with laughter.

Temehu, Ay thought, his heart growing warmer with the memories, *I am thankful for Tey bringing me our daughter and making me understand what you saw that day.*

He spun Nefertiti back around to face him. "I wish you

knew your mother," he said. "She would have been proud of you today."

"I know her because of you and Tey," Nefertiti said.

A tear almost welled in his eye, but he blinked it back. "Your mother saw the greatness in you when you were born. I only saw you as the bringer of her death . . ."

Nefertiti's smile vanished.

"But," he rushed on, "Tey showed me what you were: a baby girl destined for greatness; a baby girl worth my love in spite of my wife's passing. And now . . . now, my only wish is for your mother to see what I see at this moment."

"What do you see, Father?" Nefertiti placed her hands over his.

"A young woman not only destined for greatness, but deserving of it."

Nefertiti smiled her famous half smile, and Ay talked of her future life in the palace and the responsibilities she would have to Egypt and its people. She took in every word.

As Tey tended to Temehu's flower garden, she heard Ay's laughter and doting language in the corner of the courtyard.

Tey knew her husband loved Nefertiti more than their children, even as a child grew within her belly, but she loved Nefertiti too. She raised her and gave all she could to her, just as Nefertiti's own mother would have done.

"It has been a long time, nearly thirteen years since you left us," Tey whispered to the ka, the spirit, of Temehu as she cradled a blue lotus in her hand. "I am proud of the young woman she has become . . . I only hope and wish you are proud as well."

The winds responded with a sudden gust which whipped

through Tey's wig. She smiled, watching as Nefertiti stood conversing with her father about the grand, stable state of Egypt and how she would forever be remembered during this peaceful time in Egypt's history.

The peace, however, did not last.

CHAPTER 3
THE TIME OF UNREST

A RUCKUS IN THE STREETS OF WASET SENT CHILLS DOWN Nefertiti's spine, despite the warm morning air. "Father!" she yelled out, afraid of the chorus of wails lifting to her bedroom window.

"I am here, Nefertiti." He stood there with an unfocused stare into the streets. He tied his gold-embroidered blue sash to his pleated white shendyt, making sure the knot was in line with his sternum. "The Pharaoh has called a meeting of council."

Tey, hearing the noise, rushed out of their bedroom.

Spotting her, Ay said with a grim twist of his mouth, "Tey, wait for my return. Be sure the servants see to it the children are dressed and fed."

"Yes, Ay," Tey said, and she went to carry out her husband's orders.

"Father, may I come?" Nefertiti asked as she finished wrapping her sidelock of hair up into a high braid. The ends of her hair fell with a natural curl interwoven with pieces of gold jewelry.

"Nefertiti . . . " Ay refused to look at her, knowing the pleading in her eyes would get the best of him.

"Please, Father," she begged. Her words were perhaps even more effective than her eyes.

"Nefertiti . . . you may come. But you are to be silent," he said finally and left, striding from their home and into the street. Nefertiti followed close behind him. Guards were there to escort the Overseer of Pharaoh's Horses and his daughter to Malkata—the palace of Pharaoh Amenhotep III.

"SCRIBE OF PHARAOH, OVERSEER OF PHARAOH'S HORSES, Ay," Pharaoh repeated after the royal announcer, his voice carrying a solemnity that could crush a child's laughter. He faced the statues of himself, his wife, and his four daughters and two sons.

Ay was the first to arrive; even vizier Ramose was not yet present, despite living in one of the many wings of the palace.

"Yes, my Pharaoh, King of the Upper and the Lower?" Ay said with half a bow.

There had been rumors when the call for council came, ranging from the passing of a sister to the passing of his Queen. Ay silently pleaded with Amun-Re that death had not taken Queen Tiye, not Pharaoh's chief royal wife.

Not my sister.

Ay subconsciously halted his breath as the pain of that dark day, of Temehu's death, rushed back to him.

He looked to Nefertiti. *At least she lives in you, my daughter.*

No word came from Pharaoh, who stood with his hands clasped behind his back, stubbornly straight despite the pull of his shoulders. Silent, until his head dropped almost violently.

"Again, Amun-Re taketh away Egypt's firstborn."

Nefertiti looked to her father to understand what Pharaoh was saying, but at the shock on her father's face, she looked to the ground.

"Pharaoh . . ." Ay whispered.

"Crown Prince Thutmose is dead," Pharaoh announced, and then, having uttered the words, the great man's spine curled forward.

His words reverberated off of the stone walls and pounded in Nefertiti's head. Her jaw hung ajar and her mind raced. *Thutmose?* she thought. *Dead? No . . . no, it can't be. Not my friend, not my future husband.* Dryness invaded her mouth and numbness trickled down her limbs.

Another thought came to her: *My promised future now stands in limbo.*

After a short moment of silence in respect for the Pharaoh's son, Ay said, "Regrets of my family are with Pharaoh and his."

"Please . . . make way for Pharaoh to be in Men-nefer with the Queen, Overseer of Pharaoh's Horses." Pharaoh spoke softly as he caressed the stone cheek of his son's statue.

"It will be done, my Pharaoh."

Ay left with Nefertiti close behind, tears streaming.

AS THE SUN DESCENDED BEHIND THE SANDY MOUNTAINS, a loud mourning swept the city of Waset. News traveled from Men-nefer that the Crown Prince Thutmose had perished shortly after a sudden onset of illness, only a few months before his father's sed festival during which he would be named Coregent. Unfortunately, the tomb being built for his eventual journey to Re as Pharaoh in the Valley of the Kings was not yet complete; instead, Thutmose would begin his journey to the afterlife in the priest's tomb at Saqqara, necropolis of Men-nefer.

Tey gathered the children and followed Ay in his noble's barge down the Nile to the grand city of Men-nefer, where the Crown Prince Thutmose had been serving as a High Priest for Ptah—the god of creation, art, and fertility.

After the seventy days required for the royal burial preparation and grieving, all the imperial family came to travel the long road to the Tomb of Saqqara from Men-nefer. The Pharaoh wore the Nemes headdress used only to represent the Royal Ka, the royal spirit. Those who carried him in front of the procession dared not to look at him.

The long gold and blue stripes fell down the sides of Pharaoh's face and gathered in the back, yet such a royal presentation could not mask the sadness in his eyes. Their redness opposed the gold and the blue, defied them. His chin trembled; his bottom lip, chapped from biting, pressed firmly into the upper. His furrowed brow etched itself into the lingering grimace upon his face, having aged even more so since his son's sudden passing.

The same questions plagued his mind over and over again: *Why? Why Thutmose? So sudden for him to die . . . Why him?*

Queen Tiye had taken over rule while Pharaoh wrestled with his inner turmoil. His royal wife and daughter, Sitamun, walked like her sisters: eyes dry, her jaw tightly wound with each dip in the road.

The people of Egypt followed behind them as they came to the edge of the valley. The family continued on by themselves until they came upon the great pillars signaling the foremost entrance to the tomb.

Only Pharaoh Amenhotep III, Queen Tiye, and their children descended into the tomb with the servants carrying Crown Prince's sarcophagus and the high priests of Amun-Re.

Prince Amenhotep IV, the last remaining royal son,

glanced quickly at Nefertiti. After his sisters Sitamun, Iset, Henuttaneb, and Nebetah, he was the last of the family to descend into the tomb. He was the last of the family to do anything. *Would Father be this sad if I had been the one to die?* he asked himself. *No . . . they would have lived life as if I had never existed, just as they always have. Yet here I am, suddenly destined to be Pharaoh . . . having to marry Nefertiti . . .*

He swallowed. *My father's nightmare: his second son actually amounting to something.*

Nefertiti had often wondered why Amenhotep never joined in their games, why he sat by himself in the sun, labeled as "weird" and "unnatural" amongst his siblings, his father never mentioning him by name, his parents always calling him "the other son" . . .

Now he is the only son, Nefertiti thought.

Amenhotep looked at Nefertiti. *She is quite beautiful,* he thought, *but Kasmut has always been there for me.* His mother had told him the crown would now be his, and his dead brother's bride would become his chief royal wife. In defiance, he demanded that Kasmut, the daughter of Anen, to be his chief royal wife instead. His mother had forbade it, told him that if the question ever came up he was to state that he wanted Nefertiti as his wife.

"No!" he had yelled at his mother. "I don't want her as my chief wife. Kasmut and I are in love!"

Unbeknownst to him, his father had just walked into the room. Pharaoh grabbed his son by the arm and shook him, hard enough for a bruise to form, scolding him for yelling at his mother. He'd then yelled rhetorical questions—questions such as "Why can't you be like Thutmose?!" and "Why can't you be a son of whom I can be proud?!"

. . . and "Why can't you be the son I've always wanted?!"

His words still stung. He hadn't even been able to meet his father's eyes as he yelled at him for what seemed an eternity. Amenhotep's head had drooped lower and lower until he realized his chin was resting on his chest and his cheeks burned with shame. After his tirade, his father had taken a deep breath and calmly walked back whence he came, asking why Amun-Re cursed him with a perfect son, now dead, and an imperfect son, still alive.

His mother had then gently stroked the newly formed bruise on his arm. "Amenhotep, you will do great things. Your father will see in time . . . but first you must make Nefertiti your chief wife. And everyone, including Kasmut, must believe you chose Nefertiti to be your chief royal wife. You must never marry Kasmut."

"Why?" he had begged to know.

"I love you, Amenhotep. You must trust that you will know after you are crowned Coregent."

His mother and Kasmut were the only ones who had ever told him they loved him. Two women: his mother, always there for him when he did not live up to the image his father made for him; and Kasmut, always there for him when his brother dishonored him.

To which woman was he to give his loyalty?

After a long moment with hot tears welling in his eyes, he'd agreed to do what his mother asked and let Kasmut go.

As the sand now swirled around his feet at the entrance of the tomb, his mind raced to Kasmut, who stood only steps away with her father Anen and her family. He locked his trance on Nefertiti, daring himself not to look at Kasmut. He could not bear it.

Kasmut stood nearby, trying to trace his gaze. *Who is he staring at?* she thought to herself. She looked up to her father, whose mouth twisted into a half scowl and half grin.

Amenhotep's face was longer than most of the royal family, and he was taller and thinner than his older brother, sicker and weaker too. His bed became the friend his aching body longed for, until he found that the sun's rays gave him energy and relief from his daily aches. Grateful to the sundisc, the Aten, as he ruled high in the sky, casting his full rays upon his skin, Amenhotep dreaded the long descent into the darkened tomb. His long fingers reached for his sidelock of hair, but it had recently been removed to signify, at fourteen years of age, that he was no longer a boy. He was a man now. Embarrassed at reaching for the air that surrounded his head, he dropped his hand to his side, hoping no one saw his error.

Queen Tiye motioned for him to follow them, which he obeyed, but his eyes held with Nefertiti's until he disappeared into the tomb. Nefertiti sized him up in her mind. She too had lost her sidelock just two weeks ago when she turned thirteen—the age of marriage for a woman—but her father's gift, an elaborate wig with many jewels, sat upon her head and made her remember her childhood was over.

Nefertiti then watched Kiya, the Mitanni Princess sent to marry King Amenhotep III for political relations only a few months before, follow behind Amenhotep with the rest of Pharaoh's wives.

Kiya is young, around my age, Nefertiti thought as she watched the pitiful-looking girl descend into the tomb. Her thin hips were not good for bearing children and her unbalanced descent into the tomb showed her weakness. Ay had told Nefertiti that Kiya would most likely be passed on to the next King to keep the Mitanni in good favor with Egypt.

I hope Prince Amenhotep will still name me chief royal wife, Nefertiti thought as she bit her bottom lip—but she wished in her heart that she could still marry Prince Thutmose instead. The arid air soaked up her tears.

Anen likewise looked at Nefertiti. Brushing off the death of his nephew, his thoughts turned to his daughters. *The Pharaoh and Tiye do not value Amenhotep greater than Thutmose;*

they will not give his betrothed to Amenhotep. Thus one of my daughters will be his Queen—most likely Kasmut, since they have spent much time together. A slight smile crossed his lips. *All should be as it was: one of my daughters as the chosen Queen. The deed executed, the payment transacted. Thutmose—and his desire for Nefertiti—dead.*

The wails of his sister, Queen Tiye, traveled up from the tomb and broke Anen's thoughts. A slight tinge of guilt pressed in close . . . but her cutting words about his daughters drowned the feeling.

THE NIGHT WANED, AND THE COMPANY RESTED IN MEN-nefer. In the morning, they would travel back to Waset.

"Father?" Nefertiti asked as they looked at the starry reflections on the Nile.

"Yes?" he responded. He was remembering back to the burial of Temehu. It had nothing of the grandeur of a Crown Prince. *I will change this for Tey,* he thought. *She will have a burial deserving of her, not like the unbefitting burial of Temehu.*

"When I am Queen," Nefertiti asked, "will you still be an official of Egypt?"

"If the new Pharaoh wills it," Ay responded.

"If I am his chief wife, I will make him will it," Nefertiti said as she placed her arm through her father's. A sad smile crossed her lips, and her gaze lingered on the Nile. She longed for Thutmose.

Ay looked around to make sure no one stood eavesdropping nearby, for he knew the next words he said could be interpreted as heresy. "Nefertiti, you might be willing him to do many things," he said as a short whisper, his head bent down to his daughter. "You must be and do whatever it takes to gain his trust and keep in good close relation with Pharaoh and Queen Tiye."

Nefertiti's large eyes opened wider. "What are you saying, Father?"

"My daughter, the priesthood of Amun-Re holds more power than Pharaoh. He and Queen Tiye know this to be true. This is why they appointed young Crown Prince Thutmose as Head Priest of Ptah. They wanted him to take power away from the priesthood when he became Pharaoh . . . but it was all in vain, as he has already met his fate."

Ay saw a slight tinge of darkness creep into the sparkle of Nefertiti's eye, but he continued. He knew her pain even more so. "Queen Tiye worries Prince Amenhotep IV is not ready to handle such a feat as taking power from the most powerful priesthood in existence."

Her father's words stung her ears. "And now?"

"And now, the priesthood of Amun-Re has become more powerful than Pharaoh. Now, with the Crown Prince dead, they worry about Amenhotep IV taking Pharaoh's place."

"Queen Tiye is not sure if Prince Amenhotep can rule the nation on his own?" Nefertiti asked, uncertain of what her father was trying to tell her.

"In part. She will need you to stay on her side when it comes time to break away from the priesthood. I assume, since Prince Amenhotep adores his mother, he will follow her advice. But because of your beauty, I believe he will adore you as much, if not more, and will be more willing to follow your advice than his mother's. This is why Queen Tiye wants a member of her family with no association to the priesthood to be her son's chief royal wife . . . so she and the new Queen can present a united front when advising the new Regent."

Nefertiti felt her heart drop into her stomach. Was this also why Thutmose had chosen her, or had it been his mother's choosing? *Not as if it matters now,* she chided herself. "Is this the reason she chose me over Anen's daughters?"

"Yes, my lotus blossom."

"Do you suppose she will choose me again for Prince Amenhotep? Do you think Prince Amenhotep will choose me as well?"

"I would bet my life she will still choose you," he said. "They need you. I am not sure of the plan they will execute, but I know you will play an integral role in it. Pharaoh and his Queen will disclose the matter to you and the Crown Prince when the time comes. For now, you are not to discuss it with anyone, including Amenhotep."

Nefertiti bit her lip and cocked her head to the side as she gazed into the night stars. She finally asked, "In this plan . . . are they wanting me to help overthrow the priesthood of Amun-Re?"

"Not overthrow," Ay whispered, pushing his hand toward the ground as a signal for her to lower her voice. "Regain stolen power."

"But the only way to take their power would be to deny the power of Amun-Re," Nefertiti whispered, "and say it belongs to another god?"

"Yes, my daughter," Ay said. "You speak my thoughts. But—"

"But that is blasphemy." Nefertiti shook her head, not wanting to be a part of it. She wrinkled her nose and gulped down the hard lump forming in her throat.

"Pharaoh believes the state of Egypt will not continue in prosperity if the priesthood of Amun-Re usurps all Pharaoh's power. In three weeks' time, Prince Amenhotep will be named Coregent at the King's sed festival. Your marriage to the Prince will take place then, and you will honor the wishes of Pharaoh and Queen Tiye."

"But Father, to deny the power of Amun-Re?" Nefertiti threw her hands in the air.

"Do not question me, Nefertiti," Ay said with a firmness Nefertiti had not heard in a long time. She stepped back, looking to him as he let out a deep breath and slightly nodded his head. "You will do what is best for Egypt's prosperity. But remember, I do not know what they have planned. We are only assuming. Assumption is the worst tactic of a leader."

A moment of silence passed as Nefertiti weighed the decision to serve Egypt and become a heretic. "Yes, Father," she finally replied. She could not refuse his wishes. She longed to run away; instead, she forced a frigid smile.

"My Nefertiti . . . I promise you I will let no harm come to you." Ay drew his daughter into his embrace as the cool night air whipped around them. "As soon as the priesthood of Amun-Re dissolves and the new Pharaoh can regain the lost power, all will return to as it was."

Nefertiti only nodded, unmoving and expressionless, and repeated, "Yes, Father."

CHAPTER 4
THE TIME OF A NEW CROWNING

THEY WERE IN THE PALACE AT MALKATA. PHARAOH AND his Queen watched from their royal thrones as the dancers danced along the throne room and the servants served the best food and wine to the distinguished guests. The village people of Waset had traveled up the Nile to pay homage to the Magnificent King, Pharaoh Amenhotep III of Egypt, stopping just outside his palace and bowing low to his stone image, acknowledging his strength and divine appointment.

Nefertiti stood with her shoulders back, her chin lifted toward the firelight from the large alabaster oil lamps that lit the room. Vizier Ramose's gold collar glimmered as he walked forward, stopping before the Pharaoh and his Queen. The priests of Amun-Re preceded him, holding the Pshent, the great double-crown. In the adjacent room, Prince Amenhotep watched Nefertiti and admired the shadow line her body made against the light.

Kasmut made her way to him as she observed him staring at his soon-to-be new wife, clenching her teeth as tight as her fists. Clearing her throat, she broke him from his gaze.

"Kasmut!" he half whispered. "What are you doing here?" His eyes darted around; he did not want his mother to see him with her.

"After all this time . . ." she began, not sure whether to cry or yell as the silence grew between them.

Amenhotep closed his eyes, wishing she would not ask him the question he knew she was about to ask.

"Why did you not choose me as your chief wife?" she asked him. Her voice mirrored the shattered pieces of her heart.

Amenhotep averted his eyes and rubbed his arm. "Kasmut . . ." he began. He didn't know what to say. He wanted to wrap her in his arms and tell her he wanted her more than she could ever know, but his mother had made him promise to choose Nefertiti.

At his muteness, Kasmut pleaded again: "Why, Amenhotep?"

His mother's words echoed back to him: *All, including Kasmut, must believe you chose Nefertiti to be your chief wife.*

"Because . . ." he started as he took his time to think. "I am the Crown Prince, and . . . and I don't need a reason." The heaviness in his stomach came out in his shaky voice.

Kasmut's cheeks burned and her ears were set aflame. Taking shallow breaths, she tried to keep her composure. "Well then, Crown Prince—"

Amenhotep grimaced at her formality.

"If that is the best answer you can give me, I fear for the future of Egypt."

Amenhotep crossed his arms, and his stomach sunk lower. "Kasmut, I—"

She held up her hand. "If it is because she is more favorable to glance upon than me, tell me. If it is because she ignored you all through our childhood and now you need her attention, tell me. If it is because she thinks of you less than I do and so you need her approval, tell me. If it is because—"

Amenhotep interjected. "Kasmut. Silence."

She closed her mouth.

Words eluded him, but he didn't want her to think such thoughts. Her view of him was too important. "Kasmut, I . . ." he began again, and again trailed off.

How to make her believe I chose Nefertiti and not hurt her? he thought desperately.

That question had haunted him since his mother had made him promise, and now he was as clueless as ever. Praying to the Aten, the sun-disc, an aspect of the god Re, he asked for strength.

Suddenly, words parted his lips: "I will cherish you for the rest of my days, Kasmut, and the times we spent together I will always hold close to my heart. But our days of childhood are gone. I must think like a Pharaoh now. Nefertiti is the wisest choice as my chief royal wife. Her skills, skills she learned from her father, will be most valuable to me, and to Egypt."

The angry flame in Kasmut's eyes vanished. "Amenhotep, you will be Pharaoh. You say Nefertiti is the wise choice. Why can you not also marry for love? Can you not marry me as well? Keep Nefertiti as your chief royal wife and advisor . . . but marry me and love me all the days of your life."

Her question went unanswered as General Paaten stepped into the light. Long was he a loyal friend to the family of Queen Tiye. "Kasmut," he said, eyeing her, "your father taught you well to pay your respects to the son of Pharaoh."

"General Paaten!" Kasmut stepped back, startled by his sudden shadow and voice.

"The Queen saw you and the Crown Prince conversing and requested I see what it was you needed, Kasmut."

General Paaten peered down at her from his menacing height.

"I was just wishing the Crown Prince my best in his new marriage," she said through pursed lips.

"I see. Well, the Crown Prince needs to be preparing for his speech. Congratulations can wait till after the ceremony. Please leave the Crown Prince to his own for now," he ordered.

"Yes, General," she said. She bowed to Amenhotep and rose with a tear in her eye.

Amenhotep could not look at her. He had tried his best not to hurt her, but her question lingered in his mind. Why couldn't he marry Kasmut as well?

He would tell his mother he planned to marry Kasmut.

She and General Paaten left him as he attempted to return his mind to the oath he would recite later on in the evening.

Nefertiti caught his eye again as she stood elegantly with a wandering gaze embracing the grandeur of the evening. The light graced the contours of her face and body. It had been years since he'd spoken to Nefertiti. She along with the rest of his siblings and cousins—besides Kasmut, of course— usually ignored him and left him to play in the sun by himself. Now they were grown: he at fourteen and she at thirteen. He needed to take his own advice—leave their childhood in the past.

After all, she would soon be his wife.

"NEFERTITI," A VOICE WHISPERED BEHIND HER.

She jumped at the unexpected utterance of her name and peered over her shoulder to see who had said it.

The new Crown Prince emerged from the shadow.

"Nefertiti?" he said, more as a question than a salutation. Her dark eyes either made his stomach double over or his lungs shrink, he couldn't quite tell.

She views me as some incompetent boy who Pharaoh himself considers a failure, he thought. *Just as everyone else does.*

His lips moved, but nothing came out. *Why did I come over to her?* he asked himself. *Why can't I speak? Aten, please help me. She already assumes I am a fool. And now the future Pharaoh can't speak. Aten, why did you take my brother? Thutmose wanted to be Pharaoh, and I wanted Kasmut . . .*

She did a slow bow to show her respect. "Yes, Crown Prince of all of Egypt?" Nefertiti said, matching the tone with which he'd said her name.

He didn't realize he had been holding his breath until he tried to speak. "I . . . came . . . to tell you . . ."

What did I come to tell her? He mentally shook himself. *ATEN! You, heal my pains and give me visions. Hear me in your slumber,* he thought.

"Yes, Crown Prince? What did you come to tell me?"

His eyes hadn't left hers, yet tiny beads of sweat formed on his bald head as he thought of what to say. "I came to tell you how . . . splendid you look this evening," he said with a shrug of his shoulder to hide the blush of his cheeks.

"Thank you, Crown Prince," Nefertiti said.

He swung his arms ever so slightly and nodded his head.

"You look exquisite as well," she said at the awkward silence.

"You may . . . call me 'Amenhotep' in moments like these," he said, referring to the privacy of their conversation.

That was bold. *She isn't even your wife yet!* he scolded himself.

She smiled—and with it she found Prince Amenhotep's heart in her hands.

Maybe she ignored me because I never talked to her, he

thought. *Maybe it will be easier than I thought to have her as my chief royal wife.* His thoughts drifted back to Kasmut, whom he could see sitting by her father watching their conversation.

"As you wish, Amenhotep," Nefertiti whispered, making his pulse quicken.

His face beamed. *Maybe Kasmut is not the only one for me.*

"They will present me soon, and then they will present you," he said looking at her cherry full lips. *You fool, she already knows what will happen. Quit looking at her lips. Look at her eyes!*

"Yes, Amenhotep," she said back, realizing the power she would hold over this young man—just as her father had predicted.

He played with his father's ring upon his finger. "I will confess my fear to you . . ." he began. He looked up.

Nefertiti nodded, her lips pursed in concern, giving him the courage to continue.

"I will confess, since you will be my wife after tonight," he said as his painted eyebrows hung low over his eyes. "I know this is our first time speaking in this respect, but I feel you . . . you should know this."

"What is it, Amenhotep?" She tested her limits by reaching out one perfumed hand and placed it over his.

Instead of pulling back, he sighed. He decided to not tell her about Kasmut, but her dark, almond eyes searched his soul and drew out his hidden fears.

"I was never meant to be Pharaoh—" He shook his head, not accepting that this woman just pulled up his inner most fears, but he continued. "I have doubts . . ."

He did not finish his thought. A trail of silence followed. Then: "You would have been better to marry my brother. He was a strong leader."

"Amenhotep, you too will be a strong leader. I have no doubts," Nefertiti whispered to him as they found each other's eyes. He couldn't tell if the flicker in her eyes was from the firelight or from her dishonesty.

"The most beautiful woman in all the world tells me she has no doubts. Shall I believe her?" Amenhotep whispered back.

"You shall," she responded with a smile.

The music had stopped, and Amenhotep looked to his father. "We must go," he said to Nefertiti. *I cannot disappoint my father again,* he thought. *Aten, please come forth from your nightly shadow, so I am not late!*

They ran to the throne room behind the regal tapestries where the priests were waiting. His father was speaking about the greatness of Egypt, its might and power, the divinity of its reign and its ruler, and so on and so on. His voice droned on into the background as Amenhotep closed his eyes.

Shall I believe her? he thought.

NEFERTITI STOOD A STEP BEHIND AMENHOTEP ON HIS right side. She shifted her weight as she swallowed her lie. *I have doubts, but I cannot tear him down. As my father said, I need to gain his trust. I can't think of him as my "weird" cousin anymore. Poor thing—he seems so fragile . . . but at least he has a kind heart. With it, he can be great,* she reassured herself.

She had seen him talking with Kasmut before he approached her. They had spent a lot of time together in their childhood. *Perhaps he loves Kasmut? But Kasmut is the daughter of a prophet of Amun. If Father told me the truth, he cannot marry her if he is to move away from the priesthood,* she thought as she pieced the idea together.

MOMENTS LATER, THE WORDS TO START THE REST OF HIS life sunk into his soul as his father bellowed: "The Crown Prince Amenhotep IV and his betrothed, Nefertiti, daughter of Overseer of Pharaoh's Horses, Ay!"

Servants swung the curtains back, leaving Amenhotep and Nefertiti looking out to the nobles and officials of the court. The audience stood and cheered with the level of elegance required at such a regal event.

They walked down the throne room toward Pharaoh on the throne, his arms still outstretched. Nefertiti walked behind Amenhotep, arms at her sides, hips gracefully swinging, shoulders and chin high, just as instructed in the rehearsals.

The highest ranking priest, the First Prophet of Amun, Meryptah, waited at the second step of the throne. Hands clasped over his belly, he stood with the Second and Third Prophets, Anen and Maya, holding the ceremonial Pshent crown for Amenhotep and the Modius crown for Nefertiti.

When they mounted the steps, Nefertiti stopped halfway up and Amenhotep continued upward.

Meryptah took the great crown made of red copper and white papyrus from Anen, the Second Prophet of Amun, while another lower priest of Amun, Pawah, recited the language of the gods, granting the crowning of a divine king.

Amenhotep could not look at Anen, Kasmut's father. Instead, Amenhotep kept his focus on Meryptah as Anen's narrowed eyes fell upon him.

Meryptah lifted the crown in the air and began to lower it on the Pharaoh Coregent. The crown fit perfectly upon Amenhotep's head—they had fitted him for it the day before. He slowly turned around to face the hall, careful the double crown did not topple and mar his reign forever.

Remember the lines. You memorized them, Amenhotep. Remember what you are supposed to say, he thought as the little beads of sweat that had formed earlier trickled into the leather binding of the crown.

"I swear by Amun-Re to fulfill my divine purpose to lead the Upper and the Lower of Egypt boldly into prosperity," he uttered with a strength that caught him by surprise.

"People of Egypt," his father bellowed, "I present to you Pharaoh Coregent, having divine selection to lead the unified nation, both the Upper and the Lower, to a more prosperous future!"

The people cheered for their new leader. Nefertiti looked up to him and she saw the fear in his eyes, just barely hidden behind a pursed face exuding confidence.

Kasmut tried to find Amenhotep's eyes but failed. She wondered if Nefertiti had bewitched him already; the Amenhotep she knew would have tried to find her in the crowd. Yet to her dismay, his eyes remained steadfast.

The people cheered again.

Pharaoh bellowed once more: "Now shall be named chief royal wife of Pharaoh Coregent, Nefertiti, to stand with Pharaoh!"

Meryptah took the blue and gold Modius crown from Third Prophet of Amun, Maya. Nefertiti walked up to the step beneath him and he placed it upon her head.

Kasmut's stomach churned. She refused to watch their marriage ceremony take place. She slumped in her chair. She held on to hope, however, that one day, even if she couldn't be his chief royal wife, she could at least still be his wife.

THE FEAST CONTINUED INTO THE NIGHT AND THE NEXT. Anen refrained from drink because he was representing Amun; he instead sat in the corner of the throne room. Staring at the fine gold overlain in even the crevices of the room's walls, he wished he could numb his sorrow in the strong drink of the evening.

His pride fell to pieces on the floor; talk in the streets concerning his daughters had already reached his ears: Why were one of them not chosen as Queen? Why did Queen Tiye place Ay's daughter above his own? Was not he the eldest and a high ranking prophet of Amun?

After this Appearance of the King ceremony, it would be performed again in Upper and Lower Egypt. *I will relive the shame twice more,* Anen thought, not knowing how he would bear the questions that would arise. What would he say? *Ah, because Nefertiti is more beautiful than the sum of my daughters,* he thought bitterly, recalling the exact words his sister had used to describe them.

The urge to vomit increased, even though he hadn't eaten in days. His throat was thick and dry and his heartbeat elevated while he constantly replayed the events of that day in his mind.

Pawah said he would kill all of Ay's daughters if only I said the word . . . why did I not pay him to do so? Why did I only agree to get rid of Thutmose? I thought one death was enough to turn events in my favor. I was so sure Amenhotep would pick Kasmut . . .

The next day Anen prayed to Amun in his temple— silently for fear the other priests would hear him. He tried to sulk into the background. *Amun, hear my prayer. I pray Thutmose is safe as he journeys in the afterlife. I wronged him.* The knots in his belly twisted and turned as a deep-set weight came over his lungs and shoulders. *His death is on my hands. My fear of humiliation led me down this path, and even now, as extreme as my actions were, I still suffer humiliation. Perhaps this is my punishment for paying to take the life of the Crown Prince.*

After his prayer, he found Pawah there in the temple of Amun. Pulling him aside, he whispered, "I cannot live with knowing the blood on my hands."

Pawah stood up straight and crossed his arms slightly in front of his chest. "You must. I will not be executed because you cannot deal with your guilt."

"You killed him because I asked you to," Anen said.

"No . . . no, I did not." Pawah chuckled as he looked around to make sure no one was listening. "We all know the priesthood of Amun is more powerful than Pharaoh. I did it for more than just your money, you fool. If the new Crown Prince did marry your daughter, it would have sealed the priesthood's position as the sole ruler of Egypt. One day I will become First Prophet of Amun and I will see its power fulfilled. Amenhotep's marriage to Nefertiti is just a setback. Have no fear, brother," he said. "I am working on someone who will connect the priesthood to the royal family. All is not lost."

"We *killed* someone! Don't you see that?" Anen yelled. Pawah threw his hand over Anen's mouth and pushed him into the wall.

"Brother, you will keep your mouth shut, or I will shut it for you," Pawah said, towering over Anen. "Go home and do not speak another word."

As the days turned into months, Anen grew increasingly ill. He barely slept or ate. He would pass by the palace and just stare at the statue of Thutmose for hours at a time. His increasingly scrawny body coveted strong drink so he could at least find solace in sleep.

Kasmut often awoke to her father crying out in the middle of the night. He refused to eat and be with his family. Worried for her father, she knew she had to talk to Amenhotep again, somehow; but there was always an excuse, given by General Paaten or vizier Ramose or vizier Huy or Queen Tiye or whoever, as to why she could never see him. She looked to the papyrus on her desk and knew her letters to him probably never made it either. She sat on her bed and hugged her knees.

She told herself it was so she could speak to him about her father's pains; but secretly, she knew she wanted to see if Amenhotep was regretting choosing Nefertiti over her.

CHAPTER 5
THE TIME OF REUNITING

THE NIGHT COVERED THEIR WHISPERINGS, AS IT DID EVERY night since they were crowned Coregent and Queen. Every night since, they'd told each other more about themselves. Their night talks grew in depth until they began to share with each other the deepest and most remote reaches of their souls.

But every night, at the last moment before sleep overtook their eyes, Amenhotep would turn away from Nefertiti. He would compare their time with the time he spent with Kasmut before they were married, speculating. What if he had gone against his mother and married Kasmut instead? His secret rendezvous with Kasmut had diminished entirely; he supposed his mother had commanded General Paaten to keep her from him.

One night, as sleep almost overtook them and Amenhotep began his rollover, Nefertiti spoke again, causing his thoughts to drift from Kasmut to Nefertiti.

"My mother died during childbirth. I am the reason she is gone," Nefertiti said as she lay on her side in their royal bed. "Tey is only my step-mother. I still love her . . . but I wish I knew my real mother. My father tells me I resemble her likeness."

Amenhotep caught the glisten in her eyes from the moonlight as she continued.

"Sometimes, when I was younger, he gathered flowers from my mother's garden and laid them by my head so I would awake to their aroma and smell of her. He still misses her even after all these years."

"I did not know Tey was not your mother," Amenhotep replied. "My mother did not speak about such things. My mother . . ." His voice trailed off.

"What do you wish to say?" Her eyes could grasp any secret held deep within him and pull it right off his tongue, just as they did the day they wed.

"My mother and father loved Thutmose more than me. I have also known my father never had great expectations of the man I would become. I am always getting sick or feel pain in my muscles, bones, and back. Only the Aten's rays can heal me. My father sees me as . . . weak." He stopped, lest the last phrase overtake him.

Pushing the thought from his mind for fear of crying in front of his wife, he changed the subject to his mother. "I have worked every day to gain the love of my mother. She has given it once or twice, but I make a habit of disappointing her." He tried to blink back tears. "I will continue to my dying day to gain their love and approval."

That is why I married you and not Kasmut. Mother told me I could never marry Kasmut, even after I requested to make her my royal wife instead of chief royal wife. These thoughts he still kept to himself.

"I am . . . sorry." Nefertiti for once had no words. For the first time, she noticed her heart feel empathy for her husband. *I am more than a prize, a puppet in this scheme,* she thought. *I am here because he is my husband, and I need to love him as my father loved my mother. I now seek not to gain his trust because of some hidden agenda, but because I love him and he is my husband.*

Amenhotep whispered, "My mother wanted you for Thutmose, as did my father. As did Thutmose. My mother did not even seek a wife for me, but now, I'm all she has left."

"She is lucky to have you, just as I am," Nefertiti said. She rubbed his cheek to wipe away a tear as it fell.

"No, the luck is on my side."

She lifted her hand from his head as he turned his back to her, just as he did every night.

"See you tomorrow when the Aten shows his face."

"Amenhotep . . . ?" Nefertiti pulled his shoulder back toward her. "Do you love me?"

He couldn't respond. Maybe what he felt for her was love. He loved Kasmut, that he knew. Kasmut wouldn't have had to ask if he loved her. Guilt for his new feelings of appreciation for Nefertiti overwhelmed him. He couldn't say the words yet, but he had to keep her happy if she were to be his chief wife forever and always. "Yes . . . you have stood by me every step of this journey—even down the throne room when they crowned me Coregent."

He chuckled to hide his tears.

"Why must you ask, Nefertiti?" He stood up and went to the window to find the night's breeze. He knew why she asked. The moon outlined his slumped spine as he toyed with a small expired candle on the window sill.

"The moon has been full almost four times since I became your wife, Amenhotep . . . and you have yet to touch more than my hand," Nefertiti said, sitting up in bed.

"Nefertiti, I must confess yet another failure." He did not want to discuss it but knew he had to tell her eventually. Talking with her had become much easier with every night talk, but touching such a woman was still too daunting a task —and he thought for the most part his loyalty still remained with Kasmut. She was on his mind as he fell asleep every night. Well . . . Kasmut *and* Nefertiti, if he were honest with himself.

"Amenhotep, when will you learn? The mountain of failures you think you have, they are but the tiniest of mounds!"

A relief rolled through him as he realized he didn't have to say what his failure was. He focused on rebuking her argument instead.

"Yet they are still failures, mounds though they be," he responded as he continued to stare out the window.

"Look at me, Amenhotep." She got out of bed and stood behind him. "I say *look* at me! I am your wife. You shall not turn away from me!"

"I am Pharaoh!" he said with a snap of his head over his shoulder. He turned back to the window.

Nefertiti's mouth fell open. His outburst shocked both of them.

"You may be Pharaoh, but you are also my husband," she said in a softer tone.

Aten, I wish you could give me words to speak. I need your rays. You heal me, he prayed as he looked to the moon and wished for it to be day. The silence lingered, then his spine slumped further as she spoke again.

"Yes, you are right. You are a pharaoh . . . a pharaoh who refuses his wife—a woman whom you have said is the most beautiful of all the great and mighty Egypt!" She left his bedchambers with her wig and a hard throw of the heavy door behind her.

He watched her go, stuck in place with what little pride he had left, and then slammed his fist hard into the window sill. Stinging pain coursed its way up his arm, but he only shook it away.

"Why am I such a failure, not only as King, but as a

husband too?" he whispered to the sky. "Aten, though it be night, help me be a strong leader and man, for I still lack confidence. Please do not take my father now . . . nor ever. I cannot lead. The thought of leading a country makes my knees week. Wearing a crown and sitting on the throne gives tremble to my chin. The touch of Nefertiti sends spine-shattering shame throughout my soul. She is so beautiful—who am I to touch her? I am not good enough for her. Why can Nefertiti not realize I am not good enough? Everyone else sees. She was meant for my brother, who deserved her. Even my parents knew I would fail.

"I only want to live a life of insignificance with Kasmut."

NEFERTITI STOOD IN THE HALLWAY AND CLASPED HER ARMS over her stomach. She wanted to scream out as she bent over, but she bit her tongue and stood up to regain her royal composure: back straight, shoulders rolled backward, neck high. She began to walk the long hallways of the palace to ease her mind.

Whispers carried from around the stone hallway.

"I heard that she is not with child," one voice said.

"*I* heard she will not let him touch her," said another voice.

"Haughty princess—she would let no man touch her," the first voice responded.

Nefertiti held her breath to keep the tears from coming. Bracing herself against the wall with her hand, she bowed her head. The voices were nearing too quickly for her to hide.

Two servant maids rounded the corner and saw Nefertiti. Dread crept over their faces as they hoped she did not hear them.

Nefertiti lifted her head, and her tears obeyed gravity.

"My Queen," they both intoned, bowing as they passed by.

The one who had called her a *haughty princess* noticed the smudged kohl beneath the Queen's eyes. "May we be of service?"

"Yes, you may. Keep your words about the Pharaoh Coregent and his *Queen* silent or you shall have your tongue removed," Nefertiti said, looking past them. Even as a noble woman, a daughter of an official, she could never have made a threat like that. She puffed out her chest and lengthened her neck. The tone had to be set for her queenship. She was not a princess. She was a Queen Coregent. Queen Tiye would never have allowed such talk, but a warning for now would suffice.

Their eyes grew big. "Yes, my Queen," they said in unison as they hurried away, mute and silently thanking Amun for the Queen's warning and not her punishment.

"Nefertiti?" a familiar voice whispered behind her. Two hands grasped her shoulders.

A sad smile grew on her face.

Ay turned his daughter to face him. "What are you doing up this hour of the night?"

"Oh, Father!" She buried her face in his chest. After a few sobs, something occurred to her. "Why are you at the palace?"

Ay rubbed his daughter's back. "Pharaoh called me to the council on the items that he is to be buried with once he passes from this life. We discussed it for a long time." Ay gave a weary yawn. "Now—who or what causes my daughter to cry?"

"Father . . . am I not beautiful? Why will he not even kiss me? I have been encouraging, and we speak every night, growing closer to each other, but still he turns away from me. I hear the servants whisper, and"—she glared past him at where the two servants had disappeared—"just tonight they

LAUREN LEE MEREWETHER

were whispering. I should be with child now. I am so embarrassed!"

She cried some more. He half grimaced at the thought of Amenhotep causing his daughter to shed tears instead of brim with laughter and happiness at this early stage of their marriage.

Ay calmed his daughter by wrapping his arms around her and stroking her back. She was now about the same height as Temehu, and at the thought of her he wished that Temehu could be here for Nefertiti. She'd always had a way with words.

Nevertheless, he mustered what advice he could. "Nefertiti, the loveliest star of the night, dry your tears," he said as he wiped the smudges from her face. "He does not mean to embarrass you."

"Then why does he turn his back on me?" Nefertiti whispered.

"Trust and truth are united in marriage, my daughter. I have seen the way he looks at you, much how I looked at your mother in the beginning. He does care for you." He did indeed see Amenhotep's lingering stare at her during his time at the palace, so he hoped what he said was not all a lie.

"But you loved my mother so much . . . He cannot even say 'I love you' to me!"

"A love like the one I had for your mother comes after a long time of trust and truth," he said. "Remember in the days following your marriage you confided in me, thinking perhaps he wanted to marry another, but that with the situation he is in he could not? Think about how you would feel if Thutmose were still alive, yet you were forced to marry another."

Nefertiti swallowed hard. *Thutmose.* It had been a while since his face had flashed in her mind. She had been so focused on being a good wife and princess. More tears came as the suddenness of his name being spoken aloud brought up the buried pain at hearing he was dead . . . and the guilt of forgetting to think about him.

"There, there, my lotus blossom," Ay said. "In time, you and Coregent Amenhotep will come to love one another, and the others will fade as cherished memories. They will always have a special place in our hearts, but time makes us busy and we move on. The wound will never heal, but Amun-Re provides for us an escape from the pain with other people such as Tey—and you, my last remnant of Temehu."

Ay's eyes glistened as the heartache rushed to the forefront of his memory.

"And so it will be for you and the Coregent." Ay pulled Nefertiti's chin up to see her face to face.

"I do not understand why the wound never heals, Father. Will it always be a rift between us?"

The candlelit hallway cast a shadow upon her father's face.

"No, it will not always be that way. See my marriage with Tey. There is no rift there. Nefertiti, you will understand in time. That is my promise."

"But Father, the servants—"

"They are but servants. You are the future chief royal wife, sole Queen of Egypt." He ran his finger off her chin and touched her nose. "Go back to him now, and if he turns his back another night, you touch his shoulder and you whisper 'I love you.' Then you sleep and wake in the morning."

"But Father . . ."

"Trust me, Nefertiti. I am going to retire the night with Tey now, but I shall be seeing you over the next few days. Pharaoh desires to speak with his council again until every item is accounted for."

"As you wish, Father. Thank you," she whispered, and she

gave him one more hug. She knew when he was done speaking.

They smiled at each other, and he continued walking down the hall.

"Father!" she called after him.

He turned.

"I love you."

"I love you too, Nefertiti," he said. *I love you too, Temehu. Be with our daughter. Teach her to wait in grace.*

Nefertiti watched her father's shadow until it disappeared from the stone floor, then she made her way back to her bedchambers.

THE DOOR REMAINED AJAR, AND AMENHOTEP STILL STOOD looking out the window. The last candle burned out; the moonlight fell into the room.

He heard her light steps as she walked in and closed the door. She walked up behind him as he hung his head, still looking to the moon. Placing her hand between his shoulder blades on her way to the bed, she whispered, "I love you, Amenhotep. You have already given me your heart in the words you speak to me at night, and this is enough for me."

She is too good for me. Even now, as I refuse her, she still loves me. Would Kasmut? he thought. *I cannot keep pushing her away. I cannot condemn her to a life of loneliness . . . but will she be happy with me?* He felt her hand rub his back, and for once it cleared his mind of worry.

She dropped her hand as she continued to the bed, but suddenly, he grabbed her wrist. He slowly looked back up to the moon. "Come watch the night with me," he asked more than commanded, and he led her to his side.

The stars twinkled, and the moonlight filled the room.

"I have had time to think," he said. "I am sorry I yelled at you, Nefertiti. You deserve much more than that. You took my silence as me not loving you, but . . . I am *afraid* of you. I am afraid of you seeing me for what I truly am." In his head he added, *And afraid of what you would think if you found out that I still love Kasmut.* "I am afraid you will think you could have had a better life with my brother. He would have known what to do, and I don't. I never know what to do." *Especially now.*

Nefertiti listened, and after a short silence between them, she said, "I knew your brother well . . . but now I also know you, as we have shared our secrets every night since we were wed. You and your brother are not the same person, and so why should I compare the life I would have had with him when I am beginning my life with you?"

The question hit him at his core. Was that not exactly what he was doing with Kasmut?

She continued. "You are my confidant now. You have become my true friend, and if I can live the rest of my life with my true friend, then I will have had the greatest life I could ever have imagined." She placed her hand on his.

"I love you, Nefertiti," Amenhotep said as he rubbed her hand between his fingers and looked her in the eyes.

Had those words just escaped his lips? *No, I love Kasmut!* he thought to himself. *Or . . . maybe I love both Kasmut and Nefertiti.*

"I love you too." Happiness blushed her cheeks. She waited for him to embrace her or kiss her or something, but all he did was break their trance and look to the sky.

"The moon is very beautiful. I did not see before, but the moon gives great light. We try to hide the light of the moon with candles, but if we could just see the moonlight, it would be sufficient."

"Amenhotep, you are always the moonlight to me. No

candles are needed." Nefertiti surprised herself by meaning every word she said.

He slowly looked back to her, and as if touching an ancient statue of glass, he placed his finger on her forehead and traced the outline of her high cheekbone down to her chin.

She closed her eyes, cherishing the very first moment he touched more than her hand.

He didn't know what to do, but her lips had tempted him since the day he spoke to her. Still, Kasmut lingered in the back of his mind. When Nefertiti opened her eyes, he cradled her face in his hands and placed his forehead on hers.

I am not married to Kasmut, he told himself. *I am married to Nefertiti. This is my life right now, and my wife is stunning.*

The moonlight fell on her face, and their shadows allured him to step closer so their toes touched. She could feel her heartbeat pump feverishly in her chest, and all at once breathing became a chore. He lost himself in the abyss of her black eyes, and he pulled her close enough to taste her lips. He tasted them again, tasting the salt from her tears, and relishing in her soft sigh.

CHAPTER 6
THE TIME OF GUILT

"Pharaoh and his Queen," the messenger said with a deep bow, "and Pharaoh Coregent and his Queen. More ill news I must bear."

Queen Tiye held her breath. Pharaoh's chin fell only slightly as the messenger read aloud from his papyrus scroll.

"The brother of Pharaoh's Queen, Anen, Second Prophet of Amun, Divine Father, Chancellor of the King of Upper and Lower Egypt, has gone to Re."

"Anen . . . ?" Queen Tiye forgot her demeanor as tears welled in her eyes.

Nefertiti gasped, but immediately realized her display of emotion and held her stare on the great pillar of the hall.

"How did this happen?" Queen Tiye asked.

The messenger froze in fear, praying to Amun-Re not to have Pharaoh end his life with the words that were about to escape his lips. "He refused to eat and left this life due to a heavy heart."

Pharaoh's chest rose sharply and the air came out softly.

"A heavy heart?" Queen Tiye shook her head. "No, it cannot be."

The slaves who stood nearby fanning the royal family looked to one another in awkward silence, and the guards pretended to be interested in the hieroglyphs on the hall pillars.

Sensing Tiye's emotional distress, Pharaoh quickly responded so as not to have her embarrass herself further. "Prepare the burial. We shall send the Second Prophet of Amun, brother of the Queen, Anen, with only the best on his journey to the afterlife. Thus Pharaoh says." Pharaoh Amenhotep III spoke with a weaker voice than had accompanied his sed festival.

The four of them sat looking out to the throne room for a while. The slaves continued to fan them. The burst of air became a blessing upon Nefertiti's face. The heat began to make her eyelids heavy.

"Pharaoh commands all in the throne room to leave at once."

The doors to the throne room closed with a loudness that shook Nefertiti's eardrums.

"Anen, why did you have a heavy heart?" Queen Tiye said as she clenched her fist and brought it to her lower lip. A tinge of guilt crept over her chest. She knew why. She had thought his stature as the Second Prophet would be enough for him to duck his head and continue with life quietly, but she had clearly misjudged her older brother.

Coregent Amenhotep sat next to his father; Nefertiti sat next to her aunt. He glanced to his new wife with her white-cap crown: her jaw held tight, her shoulders shielding her neck. *Aten, oh great sun-disc, god of creation, take away the pain of my Nefertiti, just as my pain is taken away by your shining rays,* Amenhotep thought.

"I cannot bear this, my Pharaoh," Queen Tiye whispered to her husband. "The gods will not accept a heavy heart into the afterlife. My brother is condemned to this earth. His pride, his heavy heart . . . I saw it the day I went to the house of Ay. I should have said something else."

"My Queen, the past is past. We had to do what we had to do. If Anen could not bear it, then it was a sacrifice we agreed to make. Let us go forward. We will still send the very best we have with Anen, and we can pray to Amun-Re that he be merciful to his second prophet."

"I caused his death," Queen Tiye said to herself, not allowing Pharaoh's words comfort her.

Nefertiti felt the pain of her aunt transfer to her own heart. She had gone along with the plan, and so believed she had a small hand in his death as well. She had already lost her meal that morning, but the same wave of troubled stomach came to her again. *This time probably not for the same reason,* she thought, her hand moving to her lower belly.

"The gods have said it was his time," Pharaoh stated. "Just as they proclaimed with our son." He sighed and shook his head to remove the grief that still lingered. He wished almost at once that he could take back his words.

Queen Tiye stood up. "You promised me we would never speak of Thutmose."

"The Queen shall address Pharaoh as *Pharaoh*," he said with no inflection in his voice, yet his eyes betrayed his annoyance that she would be so informal with him in front of Amenhotep and Nefertiti.

Her eyes cut him to the quick. "Pharaoh promised his Queen to never speak of the Crown Prince." After a moment, Queen Tiye said through clenched teeth, "For the pain is too great to bear."

Nefertiti looked to her husband. *The dead can wait,* she thought, ignoring her own feelings for Thutmose. She saw the shame float across Amenhotep's face as his parents spoke of his dead brother. Her eyes spoke to him. *I have no doubts,* they said.

His eyebrow twitched as his father droned on about how great Thutmose would have been as Pharaoh if the gods had not decided otherwise. He looked to the floor and Nefertiti knew he was thinking that he did not want this—did not want her. He was thinking of what was lost. Thinking of Kasmut.

Nefertiti cleared her throat, blinking.

The royal couple stopped immediately and looked to her.

"What does the Queen Coregent wish to say?" Pharaoh said.

"The Queen Coregent wishes to say nothing," Nefertiti replied and looked to Queen Tiye, then to Amenhotep.

Realizing the words they had been speaking, and seeing the fallen back of their son, Queen Tiye looked away.

Pharaoh let out a sigh. "Pharaoh Coregent will fill his brother's place. The gods have granted us a spare son. Hopefully he will please Pharaoh as Crown Prince Thutmose would have."

"I . . . Pharaoh Coregent will please Pharaoh," Amenhotep stuttered.

"Of course he will," Queen Tiye said, giving him a warm glance.

"We shall see," Pharaoh muttered, losing some of his formality in his expression of doubt. Pharaoh motioned for Queen Tiye to return to her throne, and with an emotionless voice he said, choosing his words carefully, "With Anen now passed, the priesthood has a momentary lapse in power."

He took a deep breath and slowly let it out, again regretting his words. *Perhaps this is not the time,* he thought. "Pharaoh and the Queen have nothing more to say," Pharaoh said.

But Tiye thought otherwise. "The Queen wishes to discuss the matter more," she said at him.

Wide-eyed, Pharaoh almost cursed her for going against

his word, but Queen Tiye continued before he could. "Without the formality."

She stared him down until he agreed. "Son, daughter, we will be regaining stolen power from the Amun-Re priesthood," he told them in a single breath and without hesitation.

"Nefertiti knew of this," Queen Tiye told Amenhotep as his mouth hung open. "That is why we wanted her for you."

Pharaoh placed his finger on her lips to silence her as he continued. "They have become more powerful than the throne of Pharaoh. What the priesthood writes into law overrides that of what Pharaoh declares. The actions of the priesthood gather action from the people. The actions of Pharaoh gather cheer, but not action. The council of Pharaoh has created a plan to remove the power of the priesthood. They did not allow me to appoint the prophets of Amun, as Pharaoh's authority dictates, but rather took my appointments as 'suggestions,' choosing to make their own ruling. They will do it again, too."

Nefertiti sat on the edge of her seat, tapping her thumb against her thigh as she listened. It had been almost a year since her father told her about the power of the priesthood, but never the plan.

"We will worship the Aten, the sun-disc, once the First Prophet journeys to the afterlife," Pharaoh said. "I was not expecting the passing of Anen, but now there is a gap in their hierarchy—we may be able to move quicker than expected. We have seen Aten's power in healing Amenhotep's aches and pain, and we will use this to sway the people. When Aten begins to perform for them, they will drift away from the priesthood. When we declare a new priesthood, the people will follow. We will give back the worship to Amun-Re once the throne is reestablished as the sole divine authority of all under the sun."

"Will we not be labeled as heretics if the priesthood is more powerful than we?" Nefertiti asked as her assumptions of the plan were confirmed.

"Daughter, we must act quickly before the priesthood can respond," he responded. "And it must be the new Pharaoh's decree—I have my legacy. This will be the legacy of my son, the next sole Pharaoh. As soon as the First Prophet dies, Amenhotep will instigate the change either as Coregent or Pharaoh if I have already gone. I have already elevated Aten to my personal god, but as much, it has not been effective at removing the threat of the Amun priesthood. This is why we must take drastic action to remove the cult of Amun."

Amenhotep looked into his father's eyes. Was that pride he saw? He couldn't be sure.

Suddenly, a thought hit him like a blow to the stomach. "Kasmut is the daughter of Anen, the Second Prophet of Amun," Amenhotep said aloud.

The three of them stared blankly at him. His statement was obvious.

"You didn't want me to marry Kasmut because of political power?" Amenhotep jerked up out of his seat, his hands in fists. "You made me marry her"—pointing to Nefertiti —"instead of Kasmut because of some power struggle? You forbade me to ever marry Kasmut because you can't lead your own people!"

"Amenhotep!" Pharaoh stood and smacked his son hard on the cheek. "Remember your place! You disgust me, child," he growled as he took his seat again.

Amenhotep looked to his mother, but she averted her eyes and said softly, "Marrying Kasmut would undermine the entire plan of stripping the power of the priesthood."

Pharaoh continued when Queen Tiye could not finish her thoughts. "Your marriage to her would only strengthen the priesthood, you fool. Instead, you will marry your sisters,

Nebetah and Henuttaneb, to strengthen your claim to the throne, and my wife, Kiya, to further strengthen your relationship with the Mitanni. Should you have daughters, you will need to marry them as well as I have with your sisters, Sitamun and Iset. Women of royal blood in ceremonial marriage validate legitimacy of your divine appointment as Pharaoh."

"But I loved Kasmut. I only wanted to marry Kasmut," Amenhotep said ignoring a majority of what his father said.

The words rang through the throne room and reverberated in Nefertiti's chest.

"You are Pharaoh," his father said without hesitation. "Pharaoh does not enjoy the luxury of marrying for love. I was one of the few lucky ones," he said as looked to Queen Tiye, his chief royal wife. She smiled back at him.

"It's not fair," Amenhotep whimpered, not realizing the extent of the heartache he was causing his own chief royal wife. "I wish Nefertiti could have married Thutmose." He rubbed his cheek, almost certain it would be a mark of shame upon his face.

I do too, Nefertiti thought.

"Amenhotep, it would do you well to never think of Kasmut again," his father said with a shake of his head. He yanked Amenhotep's hand from his face. "We all wish Thutmose was here, but he is not here. He is dead. You are my only other son." He paused and shook his head. "You must take his place. The gods have spoken. They wanted you instead—for some reason we do not know—to lead the revolution."

At his son's silence, he pointed to Nefertiti and said, "Look! Son, you have Nefertiti, the most exquisite wife a man could ever hope to have—especially you. The people are entranced by her beauty, and they would expect no one else to be their future Queen. She is also quick and clever, having learned from her father skills you will need in a Queen to regain power. I would also advise you to take her father, Ay, into your council, for he is an asset to have by your side."

Amenhotep swayed where he stood, his head to the ground.

His father, sensing the weakness in his second son, decided to further insult him—perhaps that way he could push Amenhotep into being what he wanted him to be. "I assume Kasmut is the reason Nefertiti is not yet with child?"

Amenhotep was silent.

"There shall be none of that. She will need to be with child by the next full moon. She needs to validate her claim to the throne as chief royal wife. You are denying her what is needed to regain power."

"But Father—" Amenhotep began.

"Enough! Do you not think Nefertiti is beautiful and intelligent? Do you not trust her? Will she not make a good Queen? Can you not see her as the mother of the future royal bloodline?"

After a few moments, Amenhotep whispered, "I do."

"Then very well," Pharaoh said. "No more talk of Kasmut. Pharaoh commands her name to never be spoken by Pharaoh Coregent, forever and always."

It's not that easy! Amenhotep wanted to yell. *How do you just turn off feeling for someone? How do you stop thinking about someone?* He held his lips shut as he attempted but failed to keep the hot tears from streaking down his face.

His father refused to look at him, afraid of what he, Pharaoh of Egypt, would do to a crying man whom he had to call his son.

"Amenhotep," Queen Tiye said, "if you let yourself fall in love with Nefertiti, I assure you, you will not remember former infatuations."

Amenhotep wiped his arm across his face to rid himself of

the tears. At once, his gaze went to Nefertiti, and she took his breath away. The sting of tears in her eyes made him shut his mouth.

She held her hand to her belly. *He doesn't know,* she thought. *I wanted to surprise him . . . but would he be happy, knowing it isn't Kasmut's child? Did he mean it when he said he loved me? Or was he just using me since he couldn't have Kasmut?*

Minutes of silence passed. As Nefertiti turned away from the other three, Amenhotep finally broke the silence.

"Father, I know I was not the firstborn. I know I was not meant to lead Egypt. I know I was not in your confidence to take this legacy. I know you and Mother have so much doubt, just as I have doubt in my own ability. But Nefertiti tells me she has no doubts. I trust and confide in her, and I know that with her help I will be able to accomplish what you have asked. I also know marrying Nefertiti is what a good Pharaoh would have done, and so I am proud to have married her."

Amenhotep hoped Nefertiti would turn around to show him she had heard his words. She did not.

"Son, I do have doubts in your abilities—your speech, your stature, your quickness of mind—but Amun-Re and Nefertiti will be with you, and through them I have no doubts in you. You will be a great legacy."

His father's words smeared his self-image. He was nothing in his father's eyes without Amun-Re, without Nefertiti. He was nothing in his own eyes. Only the Aten viewed him as worthy. His mighty rays gave him strength.

"Amenhotep, listen to my voice," Queen Tiye said as she reached out to touch his chin. "You will be a great leader, just as your father. He had to learn how to be Pharaoh, just as you will. I have no doubts, just as Nefertiti."

Amenhotep smiled at his mother. He wanted to throw his arms around her neck and be safe in her warm embrace just as he did when he was a child—but he knew his father sat there watching for him to make another mistake.

He wiped the smile from his face. "I will make you proud, Father," he said.

"We shall see," Pharaoh replied.

Another moment of silence.

"Amenhotep, when you take away the power of the Amun-Re priesthood," his father warned, "remember to put your power to the betterment of Egypt. Those fools know nothing of politics and our foreign allies and enemies. They will run this great nation into the ground. You must be of sound mind to keep Egypt from falling . . . else all be in vain."

"Yes, Father," Amenhotep said, but he had not heard Pharaoh's words. Instead he thought, *I will build the greatest city the world has ever known, and I will be the most important Pharaoh to ever have existed. I will make such a lasting legacy on the people of Egypt that my father will look back on his journey to the afterlife and see my greatness.*

Nefertiti was not listening either. She had stopped listening when she realized her husband had been lying to her. His heart was not with her at all. Instead, she focused her thoughts on becoming a heretic . . . and, what would surely come next, the people rising up and killing them. The thought made her shudder, but the extra energy she expended to shudder suddenly reminded her of the immense heat in the air. Looking at the palm branch that had been left on the step below her, she longed for the burst of air on her face and hoped the Aten and his mighty sun rays of heat would be graceful to her as a child grew inside her womb.

CHAPTER 7
THE TIME OF GROWTH

THE DAY OF ADMINISTERING THEIR ROYAL DUTIES CAME TO an end. Two nights came and went without distinction. Nefertiti and Amenhotep had not spoken to each other since they had heard the news of Anen's passing. Each night they slept in the same bed, and each night Nefertiti turned her back to him.

Her silence somehow made him love her more. It confirmed that he meant something to her; she wasn't just a puppet from his mother. Each night he would try to find something to say to her but couldn't find the words, and eventually he would give up and turn his back on her own.

On the third night, as they were getting into bed, Amenhotep broke the silence.

"Nefertiti . . . ?"

She stopped what she was doing and looked to him, not responding.

"Nefertiti, I was mad that day. I said things I wish I could take back."

Nefertiti said nothing, so he continued.

LAUREN LEE MEREWETHER

"I am sorry I am also in love with . . ." He held her name back, following his father's command.

Nefertiti, however, filled in the blank rather curtly. "Kasmut?"

"Yes," he said, regretting his decision to break the silence.

She sat up. "I know, Amenhotep. I assumed as much when you did not touch more than my hand for the first four months of our marriage. It hurt when you confirmed those assumptions, but I knew it. What I didn't know and what hurt even more was when, even after you told me you loved me, you fought for her and not for your wife. It hurt me the worst to know I have no place in your heart, and you have just used me in bed—whether to satisfy your own desire or to tame my anger at your rejection, I'm not sure."

"Nefertiti, I have not simply used you!" he said. His heartbeat grew loud in his ears.

"It seemed so, the way you spoke of me and Kasmut!" she yelled back, her cheeks flushed with anger.

"And you think it's not the same way when you see me and Thutmose?"

Amenhotep! he chided himself. *What evil spirit possessed me to say such a thing?*

Her slow headshake and menacing grimace said everything, her anger rendering her mute. *After I accepted my situation and made the best of it,* it seemed to say, *you dare to say that to me?!*

"My words came out wrong, Nefertiti," he said, wishing he could stuff the words back into his mind.

She ignored him and finished getting into bed. With her back firmly turned to him, she closed her eyes.

"Nefertiti, please. At first, yes, I did not want to be with you because I loved only Kasmut. But how could I not? You'd always ignored me in the past, leaving me to believe you didn't think of me as Kasmut did. You were forced to marry me just as I was forced to marry you. My mother told me I could never marry Kasmut, but I kept thinking one day I would. Then I realized General Paaten was keeping me from seeing her. She would get word to me to meet, but she would never show. I would come back with a heavy heart, but I grew to see that you were always there with your kind words and gentle voice. Every night you would share a secret with me, and I with you. Every night I gave a little piece of myself to you."

He stopped. She remained still. She hadn't even flinched a muscle during his entire confession.

"Nefertiti, I love you. Hearing what my mother and father said, that only brought up old memories of the deep love I had for Kasmut. I assume eventually Kasmut will be but a memory. My mother has made her to me like Thutmose is to you. She might as well be dead to me, for I will never see her again."

"I'm glad I'm an acceptable replacement," Nefertiti muttered. But his words had indeed struck something inside her. Some nights she thought of Thutmose but forced herself to think of Amenhotep instead.

He climbed into bed, touched her shoulder, gently pulled her over to face him. "Nefertiti, I never used you. I do love you. Please know I do."

Nefertiti's eyes went to the bruise on his cheek, reminding her of his outburst at having to marry her instead of Kasmut. Another potential love of his fluttered in her mind: Kiya. Unlike Kasmut, he would be forced to marry her —but she seemed to be content in her own chambers painting. Kiya's face was dull and too brown to ever rival the bright and creamy tan of her own face, but she could tell in passing that Kiya's smile lit up Amenhotep's eyes . . . just as they were now lit up with the thought of Kasmut.

"Do you wish our children could be Kasmut's?"

The question caught him off guard. He knew he couldn't answer "Yes," but he also knew "No" would betray his heart.

"Your silence is well enough an answer," Nefertiti said.

She tried to roll back onto her side, but Amenhotep kept her pinned down on her back.

"Nefertiti . . ." he started, and then by the grace of Aten, words came to him. "A wise woman once said, 'I knew your brother well, but I also know you. You and your brother are not the same person, and so why should I compare the life I would have had with him when I am beginning my life with you?' "

The sparkle returned to Nefertiti's dark eyes, like the stars in the night sky. Slowly, ever so slowly, a budding grin appeared beneath those eyes, and she whispered, "So if I told you we were going to have a child, what would you say?"

"I would say the gods have blessed us," Amenhotep said with a mighty voice, thrusting his hand upward toward the heavens.

Nefertiti chuckled at his silly dramatics. "Then I would like to tell you," she said. "You are going to be a father."

The silliness stopped suddenly, and Amenhotep's hand slowly graced her belly. He studied her face in the moonlight —a face he truly had come to love. Gently, he bent down and kissed her belly and came back to kiss her rosy red lips.

"My Lady of Grace," he said. "I am honored that you, my chief royal wife, Queen Nefertiti, will grant me my firstborn."

Bright-eyed and smiling ear to ear, she wrapped her arms around his neck and pulled him in for another kiss. Running his hand from her belly up across her chest and around to her back, he pulled her into his own chest as he kissed her deeper, both of them loving the electrifying sensation of their touching bodies.

He forgot about Kasmut.

LATER THAT YEAR, JUST AS NEFERTITI BORE A DAUGHTER, Amenhotep's father, Pharaoh fell ill, leaving all of Egypt in Amenhotep's hands.

"Barely completing my first year as Coregent, and my beloved wife grants me a daughter!" Amenhotep exclaimed at the news as he stood up in his throne. "Take me to her at once!" he ordered a nearby servant.

The messenger, who had been reading aloud the day's news, stood mid-sentence. "Pharaoh Coregent, will you not have me read the remaining—"

"Nonsense! My Queen gives me a child, how can I—" Amenhotep started, but his mother stood up suddenly.

"Pharaoh Coregent is still learning the customs of Pharaoh," she said. Her voice was stern, but inside she was glowing. *He gave up Kasmut. If he is this excited to go see a daughter from Nefertiti's womb, I should let him go.* "However, in such a joyous occasion as this . . . servant, take Pharaoh Coregent to see his child. The Queen, chief royal wife of Pharaoh Amenhotep III, will receive the remaining news."

Amenhotep wanted to throw his arms around his mother, just as he had done as a child, but decided against it—she would expect him to show his capacity as Pharaoh Coregent in at least some respects.

The servant paused for a second at the Queen's unusual command, but immediately bowed and took the Pharaoh Coregent to see Nefertiti and their daughter.

The messenger continued the news from where he'd last left off reading aloud to Queen Tiye, who remained in the throne room: "Third Prophet Maya was chosen to take the position of the Second Prophet of Amun, and . . ."

As Amenhotep walked farther through the corridor, proudly marching behind the uneasy servant with a happy whistled tune on his lips, the messenger's words faded from his attention.

I like this feeling of freedom from the absence of my father, he thought. *I know I can be a great ruler without him telling me he doubts my ability. I feel empowered to make decisions. When Father passes, my first order of business will be to decrease the level of formality the royal family is currently forced to endure. There will be no restraint of emotion, so I do not have to be embarrassed if I say "me" instead of "Pharaoh." If I feel like yelling, I will yell. If I feel like crying, I will cry.*

The great wooden doors opened before him, and there was his wife—covered in sweat, breathing heavily, and smiling at him. The midwives were busy wiping the afterbirth from the baby's body and cleaning Nefertiti and her delivery seat. The hot water's trailing whisps of steam slowly vanished as the air was allowed to escape through the opened doors.

Nefertiti tried to stand for her husband, but the servant girls pushed her back to bed. Amenhotep instead knelt beside her and kissed her forehead. Taking the cool towel from the water pot, he dabbed her forehead. Together they smiled at the sounds of their baby crying.

"You have given me a child," he whispered to her. "How do I repay your generosity?"

She smiled all the more. "The pain was great—almost more than I could bear—but I ask nothing from you in repayment. Our child brings me joy as well."

He kissed her lips as the servant girls tried to stay busy ignoring such an uncommon display of affection from Pharaoh.

"Bring my child," Amenhotep commanded.

Aitye, one of Nefertiti's attendants, brought the baby girl to him. He immediately saw that she was smaller than usual, but this was to be expected, as she was three weeks early. But all was well; the doctors had said she was expected to live a normal life.

He took her in his arms as he sat next to Nefertiti. "She has your beauty, and, thankfully, none of my features," he said to his wife.

"She has your cheeks," she said, noting the babe's long face.

"Poor girl."

"No. She will know she comes from her father," Nefertiti stammered, trying to slow her breathing.

Amenhotep laughed. "I assume she will."

"What shall we name her?" she asked as she placed her hand on his forearm.

"The one Aten loves," Amenhotep responded.

"She who is beloved of Amun?" Nefertiti asked. "Meritamen."

"Meritaten," Amenhotep said as the child wrapped her fingers around one of his own.

"Amenhotep, we should name her for Amun-Re," Nefertiti whispered.

"She was born at midday, when Aten is full and round in the sky," Amenhotep said. "We will name her for the Aten."

The servants looked to him, confused.

"The Aten is a part of Amun-Re, and we shall name her for the Aten," he said, staring adamantly around until the servants looked away, accepting the reasoning.

"As you wish," Nefertiti said, and added in a whispered, "Meritaten." The fear rose up in her stomach again of what the future would bring. She wasn't quite sure how regaining the power of the priesthood would come about, but she guessed naming the firstborn of Pharaoh Coregent for the Aten was a good place to start. Pushing those thoughts from her mind, she focused on her new baby girl's coos.

"Announce to all of Egypt that my beautiful Nefertiti, the

Lady of all Women, She who is Great of Praises, the Great King's Wife, His Beloved, has borne unto me, Pharaoh Coregent, a daughter. Let a temple be built in dedication to the Aten at the forefront of the Temple of Amun at Ipet-isut."

A messenger ran to tell the Royal Scribe the Pharaoh Coregent's command.

Amenhotep took Nefertiti's hand and kissed it.

I am a father to the most beautiful child with the most beautiful woman to call his wife, he thought. *I could dance on the clouds of the Aten's rays.*

He paused. *It is a shame that I will not have the luxury as Pharaoh Coregent to show all of Egypt my happiness once Father regains his health.*

"WORD HAS COME THAT MAYA HAS TAKEN ANEN'S PLACE," Queen Tiye told her husband Pharaoh Amenhotep III as he lay in bed.

"Less prominence with Maya. All of Egypt knows he bought his place as Third Prophet. He is not fooling anyone into believing he has the tenure with Amun to intercede for the people," Pharaoh Amenhotep huffed. "At least it means less power for the cult of Amun."

"Anen should have taken Meryptah's place as the First Prophet, but with Maya in his place there is less respect for his position and for whomever succeeds Meryptah," Tiye said. "This could be good for Pharaoh."

"Now we just need Meryptah to die," Pharaoh said.

"He is ancient. We could start the transition, help Amenhotep and Nefertiti, if he would just pass from this life." Tiye placed her wig on its stand. She disliked the word *die*; to her it meant an ending, not the chance for a new beginning. The talk of death brought back tiniest tinges of guilt for Anen and sadness for her son, but she quickly gathered her thoughts to her husband.

"Amun gives him long life as his first prophet," Pharaoh murmured.

"Could we cut it short?" Tiye slipped in beside Pharaoh with a half laugh.

"We could . . . but if anyone found out, it would undermine the whole plan," Pharaoh said, turning to look at her. The pain in his arms, legs, knees, shoulders, feet, back, fingers, and toes wrapped around his soul and squeezed it. The light in his eyes dimmed, but brightened ever so slightly at the sight of Tiye, the love of his life.

"I'm only jesting, Pharaoh," Tiye said as she gently laid her head on his shoulder as to not cause more pain.

"If it were meant to be, the gods would take him as they did with Anen and Th—"

Pharaoh sucked in his breath, but it was too late. Tiye knew what he was going to say. She blinked several times and slowly pressed her lips together. "I miss him, Amenhotep. I miss our son. I miss the sound of his voice."

She rubbed her head into the side of her husband's chest. His hand swept in around her shoulder. Barely able to breathe now, she whispered, "I miss him so much."

"I miss him too," he said as he placed his other hand on her head, now shaking from her sobs.

"Why did I make you promise to never say his name again?" she asked.

"I am Pharaoh, my love. You cannot make me do anything," he half chuckled, then lifted her chin so he could look into her eyes.

"Then why did you agree to it?" Tiye whimpered.

"Because I love you, Tiye. I would do anything for you.

You were in pain, and saying his name only intensified your tears. I would never do anything to hurt you."

"I love you too, Amenhotep." She kissed him. "I ask you not to agree to it anymore."

"As you wish, my Queen," he said, and kissed her again.

She placed her head on his chest and he brought his lips to her head, saying with a kiss, "Thutmose was blessed by the gods to have you as a mother."

Tiye smiled brightly. She remembered watching Thutmose play on her barge with a frog that had jumped aboard. Her wet nurse held his brother, Amenhotep, in her arms as Thutmose played.

Thutmose was such a handsome, obedient child and Amenhotep was not. Amenhotep was born sickly, the doctor proclaiming him most likely to die, yet somehow he survived. She had often wondered why her husband treated Amenhotep so harshly while choosing to dote upon Thutmose. She'd once tried to talk to him about this, but he had threatened to pull her status of chief royal wife if she ever were to question him again or undermine his authority. Even though she was his chief royal wife and therefore considered Pharaoh's equal, his one power over her was to strip away her title and thus her authority. With such a title, however, she could be of more help to her sons than if she went against the wishes of Pharaoh and was demoted to simply *wife* or, even worse, exiled with nothing.

Over the years, Tiye had tried to understand what caused such a rejection of his second son to the point of not including him in their family monuments, choosing not to have him remembered in Pharaoh's familial stone image. Why had he *hated* Amenhotep so much?

She was afraid to ask, but she simply couldn't accept the only reason she had gathered: Pharaoh's vanity. Thutmose had taken his image upon birth, a mirror image of his father and his grandfather, athletic, strong, mighty, eloquent, a good leader; Amenhotep, although kind, was sickly, weak, and uncoordinated, the opposite of what Pharaoh thought of himself and therefore undeserving to bear his name. But custom ruled that the firstborn son was to be named after the Pharaoh before and the secondborn after the Pharaoh himself. Sadly, she wondered if he would have been treated differently had he been the third or fourth son with no namesake. Her husband refused to associate with someone who could bring question to him and his given title of *The Magnificent King*; and so her son, Amenhotep, endured his entire life thus far as an outcast.

Tears slid down her face, not for Thutmose, but for her living son, Amenhotep, whom she could only silently adore from afar.

"There, there, my Queen," Pharaoh whispered, misinterpreting his wife's melancholy. "Thutmose is on the journey to the afterlife. We will see him again one day."

"Yes, my Pharaoh," Tiye said. *Amun-Re,* she prayed, *please be with my son, Amenhotep. Please let his father see the greatness that he will become before he passes. Let Amenhotep know his father does love him—or if he doesn't, let him at least think he does before his time comes.*

CHAPTER 8
THE TIME OF EXILE

"How *dare* she?!"

Pharaoh's lips curled and his nostrils flared. He shot out of his throne with so much force his crown nearly toppled off his head. He slammed his fist into his leg, losing the control required of the position of Pharaoh.

"Bring Nebetah and Pawah to me! At *once*!" he raged to a few of the many royal guards that filled the throne room.

Attempting to regain some level of dignity for the position of Pharaoh, he yelled to the messenger, "Leave Pharaoh's hall now!"

The messenger hopped backward, bowed, and scurried out, as did the guards who received the order, eyes wide at Pharaoh's outburst and somewhat afraid for what he would do to the Princess.

Pharaoh paced in front of his throne, cracking his knuckles. Queen Tiye, Amenhotep, and Nefertiti sat still, afraid to utter a word lest they draw Pharaoh's wrath upon themselves. Nefertiti wanted to wrap her arms around her again-pregnant belly to shield the child from his anger, but instead tried to keep her queenly stance: upright, head forward, hands on her knees.

What will I do with her? Pharaoh asked himself, barely able to contain the thoughts from his lips. *How will I punish them? Nebetah, why must you disobey me? Why do you make me punish you? I cannot show weakness, not at a time like this. Curse you, Nebetah, for forcing my hand, so that I must deal with you as any other who chooses to disobey me.*

The guards escorted Princess Nebetah and her new husband Pawah, the Fifth Prophet of Amun, to the throne room.

General Paaten, standing at the door to the throne room, motioned for all to leave save two of his guards; the man could tell that his Pharaoh was not himself today, and no one needed to see his emotions or his lack of formality.

"You have disobeyed Pharaoh's direct command, Nebetah!" Pharaoh bellowed. "You will have your marriage to Pawah annulled immediately, or you will be exiled from the great Egypt."

"But Father, I love him!" she exclaimed, forgetting her place. Her long, black braided wig, interwoven with bits of gold, hung over her shoulder. Her dark brown eyes were not filled with tears but rather lit with rage and rebellion.

Pawah's mouth hung ajar at his wife's lack of restraint, but he soon regained his stately composure.

"You will do as your father, Pharaoh, commands, just as your older sisters have done and what your younger sister will do," Queen Tiye said. "We all abide under the rule of Pharaoh. Do not disobey his command."

"Mother, please. I love him," Nebetah said. At the Queen's silence, Nebetah's eyes narrowed and darkened, and her mouth became as stone. Since Nefertiti had been named chief royal wife to her brother, it seemed Pawah appeared to her from a dream and as an escape from having to one day marry her brother as well. She found comfort in Pawah: his handsome face, wise words, and strong arms. She would not let her mother or her father take him from her. Not like this.

Pharaoh shot a menacing glare at Amenhotep. *Where have I heard that before?* he thought. *This is your fault,* his eyes told his son.

Amenhotep cowered in his seat, slightly shaking. Before he could regain his composure, his father turned his glare back to Nebetah.

"Annulment or exile . . . thus Pharaoh says!" he bellowed.

"I will not annul! I will not marry *him*," she said, thrusting a finger to her brother.

"If Pharaoh wills it . . ." Pawah whispered to Nebetah.

Nebetah sunk back at Pawah's weakness. She'd thought her husband would always fight for her, for them.

Her father smiled at Pawah's respect for his command and was even a little surprised it came from him, a member of the Amun priesthood, and not from his own flesh and blood.

As if reading Amenhotep III's thoughts, Pawah then spoke directly to Pharaoh in his usual silky smooth voice: "However, if Amun wills us wed, it shall be. As the Fifth Prophet of Amun, I have already prayed to our great Amun-Re . . . and I am here to inform the great Pharaoh of Egypt that Amun blesses the union." Pawah ended this proclamation with a slight bow.

Amenhotep saw the vein on his father's temple bulge, saw his fists tighten into hard balls.

"And I am Pharaoh, the divine embodiment of Amun-Re, having been appointed by him to lead this great Egypt—and *Pharaoh* says *annulment* or *exile*!" As the echoes of his roars died down, he whispered, "Choose carefully, for it is your future."

Pawah's face drained of color. Their plan had backfired. He would have to go see Maya to figure out a solution. He glanced at his wife, then returned a steady gaze to Pharaoh and said calmly, "We choose exile."

Pharaoh ordered General Paaten to have his men escort them to the border. With that, he turned with Nebetah to leave the throne room. She glared at her family seated on their thrones. *They will pay for this—my father's and brother's lineage will pay for this,* she thought.

Nebetah stopped in her tracks, an idea to stay in Egypt suddenly occurring to her. "Pharaoh," she said as she turned around. "May I at least say goodbye to my sisters?"

Her father's face burned, but he replied, "You may . . . but you are to be out of Waset by nightfall."

"Thus Pharaoh says," she said under her breath, and she and Pawah turned to leave.

SHE FIRST REQUESTED TO GO TO SITAMUN, WHO HAD JUST borne a child, a few months before Princess Meritaten was born. Rumors had circulated that it was Pharaoh's baby, or some servant's child, and that was why Pharaoh had put her away.

Nebetah had her own theory, and she wanted to test it.

"Hello, sister!" Sitamun said. She waved Nebetah and Pawah into the small inner chamber of the palace. Her stewards were cooking and cleaning. Sitamun had called this wing of the palace "home" for the past eighteen months; it was small, but big enough for her, her son, and their servants, with three rooms including a dining area and a small courtyard. Sitamun's wet nurse held her son, Smenkare.

"Hello, sister Sitamun," Nebetah said as they embraced. "I've come to ask a favor of you."

"Oh? And what favor?"

Sitamun sat at her table and motioned for them to join

her. The stewards went to bring some wine for her and her guests.

Nebetah took a deep breath. "I suppose you have heard that Pawah and I were married against the wishes of Pharaoh."

Sitamun gave a slight nod, smiling.

"He wanted me to marry Amenhotep," Nebetah said.

"I had heard," Sitamun said. "You are either brave or stupid, I'm not sure which."

Nebetah shook off her sister's insult. "He gave us the choice to choose annulment or exile, and we chose exile. I came here to ask a favor—or, better, to ask for your help. But first, I must know . . ." Nebetah glanced back to Smenkare.

"You wish to claim sanctuary here?" Sitamun asked.

"Yes," Nebetah said.

The truth was there in her sisters' eyes as they locked gazes, but Sitamun only averted her own and looked to Pawah. "You will never be able to leave my wing of the palace. You know this." Her eyes narrowed at this man who had bewitched her sister into a life of exile, whether it be here with her or outside of Egypt.

"We understand, royal wife Sitamun," Pawah said.

She looked back at her sister. "I will send word to our father that you and Fifth Prophet of Amun, Pawah, will remain here until he acknowledges your marriage and removes his condition."

"Royal wife Sitamun, please do not put yourself and your new child's life and wellbeing in danger. Pharaoh could very well exile you as well," Pawah said, but there was only a glimmer of truth and sincerity in his words. The priesthood's plan to infiltrate the royal family had failed in a major way. First Prophet of Amun, Meryptah, would not accept him back into the priesthood after this disaster; perhaps, at the very least, if he and his new bride stayed in Egypt, a chance to further the power of Amun's prophets would present itself—and now, with her father's betrayal, he thought it should not be too hard to convince Nebetah of his plans to seal the priesthood's ultimate power in Egypt. He saw the darkness and rage in her eyes as Pharaoh pronounced their sentence.

"It is doubtful, Pawah, Fifth Prophet of Amun." Sitamun tried to think of a good explanation so as not to give away the true reason why Pharaoh would never send her into exile as well. "My father would never send us into exile because I am his royal wife, his eldest child, and his oldest daughter. I have stood by his side for many years."

"We thank you for taking this risk," Pawah said. "But please only do so if you are sure he will not exile you as well."

"I am sure of it." She walked to and opened the door to the guards who had escorted them there. "Tell Pharaoh that his royal wife Sitamun and her son, Prince Smenkare, are granting asylum to Princess Nebetah and the Fifth Prophet of Amun, Pawah."

She closed the door.

AS SITAMUN CLOSED THE DOOR BEHIND HER, THE GUARDS looked to one another questioningly. They decided a few would stay in case the princess and her husband were trying to sneak away; one guard would go back to Pharaoh and relay the message.

They drew sticks to see who would go. The one who drew the short stick reluctantly made his way back to the throne room.

As the guard had feared, upon hearing the message Pharaoh again lost his composure and thrust his head into his hand. His thumb and forefinger circling his temples, he sighed and whispered under his breath, "Cursed child."

Clearing his throat, he placed his hand back on the throne's arm rest where it was supposed to be. He leaned his head back and sat up straight.

The guard tried not to cower as he watched Pharaoh hitch his shoulders up, afraid at the outburst that would follow this morning's display.

But Pharaoh said nothing for a long time.

Finally, with a deep breath, Pharaoh said, "If the Princess Nebetah or the Fifth Prophet of Amun, Pawah, so much as step their toes out of the quarters of Pharaoh's royal wife, Sitamun, they are to be immediately escorted to Egypt's border. Thus Pharaoh says."

The guard let out a breath, thankful he would not be punished for bearing the bad news, and covered his audible exhale with a bow. "As Pharaoh says," he echoed, and turned to carry the message back.

Amenhotep looked to Nefertiti, meeting her gaze.

Why give up now? Amenhotep mouthed to her.

Nefertiti mouthed back, *Royal wife?*

Amenhotep shrugged in response.

No one noticed Queen Tiye look off into the distance, trying to hide a grimace.

AMENHOTEP SPENT MORE OF HIS DAYS OUT IN THE SUN, letting the rays of the Aten take away his physical ailments. The courtyard of Malkata became the place he dwelt most often. The more the Aten answered him, the less he prayed to Amun-Re, forsaking his divine appointment from Amun, the premier god of Egypt.

"Father," Amenhotep asked Pharaoh as he lay in bed.

"Yes, son." Pharaoh's hand took to his jaw, and he drew a

deep breath to release the pain. His body was pale and the beads of sweat around his face looked like little raindrops.

Amenhotep leaned forward with his elbows on his knees. "I would like to take down the roof of the throne room."

Pharaoh responded immediately: "No."

"Father, the Aten heals me and makes me stronger. When I am in his rays, I feel like the son you wanted," Amenhotep said, emphasizing these last words.

"Do not touch my palace," Pharaoh said.

Amenhotep lowered his eyes.

Pharaoh continued, "You are free to live here until you have your own palace, but this one is mine. You will not remove the roof of the throne room."

"But Father—"

"No. Thus Pharaoh says." He grabbed his throat; the voice that came out sounded like a sandstorm had blown over his vocal chords.

Amenhotep opened his mouth to speak, but said nothing for fear of what might happen if he were to speak against Pharaoh's command. As an indirect way around the request and final edict, Amenhotep said, "If we are to go to the Aten, should we not be making strides to turn the people?"

"We are. I have made the Aten my personal god, just as you have and will do once I am gone," Pharaoh said, wincing every time his jaw came together.

"Do you believe it is enough?"

"Yes, for now. When Meryptah dies, you will give the order to turn to the Aten. The people should follow you."

"If they do not?"

Pharaoh glanced over to his son, sitting there bent over. Pitiful. *Yes, son, I know what you are doing,* he thought. "If they do not, then you have failed them as a leader."

Amenhotep looked up, fire suddenly in his eyes. "Me?

Why me? Would it not have been you? *You* are the one who has led them for over thirty-five years!"

"No, son," Pharaoh said, too exhausted to become upset at the backlash.

Amenhotep's eyes burned a hole through the hot, dry air toward his father.

"You will need to inspire them to make the change," Pharaoh said. "Make them want to worship the Aten."

"How?" Amenhotep asked. "How do I make them want to worship another premier god besides Amun-Re?"

"This is why I wanted Thutmose on the throne. He could answer these questions for himself. As for you . . . Tiye and Nefertiti will help you."

Amenhotep felt slapped in the face. "Thutmose is dead, Father," he said. "I am what you have left."

"Yes, and I have asked Amun-Re, why take Thutmose, every day since his passing." Pharaoh closed his eyes.

"And he did not answer, did he?" Amenhotep said. "You should have prayed to the Aten."

"Amun-Re answers in his own way," Pharaoh replied.

Before Amenhotep could respond, the door flung open.

"Pharaoh and Pharaoh Coregent." The messenger bowed. "I bear great news. Queen Nefertiti has sent me to declare she has borne another child of Pharaoh Coregent."

At once Amenhotep's face rang with excitement, only to hear his father's words creep to him from his bed.

"Hopefully a *son* . . . for an heir," Pharaoh said weakly. "And perhaps another to replace my own son, should he perish."

Amenhotep turned to his father, his face growing red. "And hopefully the replacement does not fall ill of expectations."

Amenhotep wanted to yell, *Why, Father?! What have I done? Was it because I cannot run? I cannot shoot the arrow? I don't like hunting? I don't like to throw the ball? Is it because I have a long face? Is it because my nose is not perfect like yours? Is it because I bear your name and look nothing like you? Why have I always fallen short of expectations?*

But the messenger was still there, and the door was open for all to hear.

This should be a happy time for Nefertiti and me, he thought. *I will not let this man ruin it.*

"Messenger," Amenhotep said, still looking at his father.

"Pharaoh Coregent," the messenger said as he took a step forward.

"Take *me* to Nefertiti," Amenhotep said—and watched with delight as his father winced at his use of *me* rather than *Pharaoh.*

The messenger bowed as Amenhotep stood to follow him out.

They made their way down the hall in silence. Amenhotep wondered why Nefertiti would have the messenger say "child" instead of "son" or "daughter." *It is most likely a girl,* he thought. *She knew I'd be with my father and knew he would probably berate me more if I had another daughter. I love her so.*

As the door was opened, he found Nefertiti laying in the cot, propped up and holding a tightly wrapped bundle. He came immediately to her and dropped to his knees. She beamed up at him, and he caressed the back of her head and kissed her on the lips.

"Would you like see your new daughter?" she asked him as she turned down the wrap. The newborn's tiny sleeping face rolled toward her mother's arm.

"She is the most perfect child," he said. "The Aten has formed her well." He ran his pinky across her brow and watched her tiny mouth open and a little breath come out.

"What shall we name her?" Nefertiti asked.

"I gave Meritaten her name," he said, asking with his eyes if she would like to name this daughter.

Nefertiti volleyed back with a playful smile, wanting to name her Meketamen but knowing full well her husband would not agree to a name honoring Amun.

"How about Meketaten: protected by the Aten," she said.

Amenhotep agreed and declared another temple to the Aten be built in Heliopolis in front of the temple of Amun.

CHAPTER 9
THE TIME OF DEATH

PHARAOH DIED, AND HIS WORDS DIED WITH HIM.

Amenhotep sat on the stone steps to the courtyard with his hands on either side of his head, his elbows resting on each knee. His shoulders absorbed the rays of the Aten upon his body.

The chill in his spine hurt as it thawed in the sunlight. He numbed his thoughts as he sat there for hours, unmoving, the pain in his tailbone unnoticed.

Kiya, walking by behind him, paused to sit down next to him and let out a deep breath. "I am sorry for your pain, Amenhotep."

His eyes focused on the stone floor before him.

"I remember the stories you told me about your father, before you were wed to Nefertiti." Her eyes drifted back to him to see if he would move. He did not even a blink. At his silence, she put her hand on his arm. "I am sorry he could never see you how I saw you."

Amenhotep's chest filled with air and then he released it, but no words followed.

"We have not talked much since you were married to

Nefertiti. I miss our long talks about our fathers." She chuckled, a tear escaping from her eye. "It made me feel not so alone."

His stare at the stone floor intensified.

"I know you hurt, Amenhotep. I will go find your wife . . . perhaps she will ease your pain," Kiya said, rubbing his back. She stood up and walked away, stopping at the end of the hallway to look back at his still unmoving form.

He had hurt her, too. When his brother was still alive, they had spent many an hour together. He loved Kasmut, but Kiya loved him. He never saw her in that light, and she accepted it just as she had accepted her father's rejection of her. It hurt more that he chose such a beautiful woman as Nefertiti to be his chief wife, one whom she could not compare.

Looking to the floor, she made her way to find Nefertiti and found her in the dining hall.

"Queen Nefertiti, Pharaoh Coregent sits in the courtyard of the northwest wing," Kiya said.

"Thank you, Kiya, royal wife of Pharaoh," Nefertiti said. She had been looking all over the palace for him; she should have known he would be in the courtyard, where the Aten's rays fell.

"Queen Nefertiti, he says nothing. His pain is great," Kiya warned. "But perhaps he will speak to his chief wife?"

Nefertiti nodded in thankfulness, and to her surprise, Kiya continued in a less formal speech: "I want to give you my best wishes at this time. Although I was married to Pharaoh, he never talked to me, and he went so far as to seclude me. He made sure I was taken care of, and I had anything I wanted, but I did not know him very well. From what I could see, however, he was a great man . . . one who loved his family very much."

Nefertiti let out her breath, relieved at Kiya's familiarity.

"Thank you, Kiya. He meant a great deal to me. There has always been . . . something . . . between Pharaoh and Amenhotep. I never knew what it was, but I believe that is what is keeping Amenhotep from speaking to anyone."

"He will speak to you. He loves you, and you live up to what everyone calls you." Kiya's smile wavered as she pulled at her ear. *He used to speak to me,* she thought.

"I am more than a pretty face," Nefertiti said.

"I assume so, just as I am more than a plain face," Kiya said.

Her response shocked Nefertiti. She had never considered the possibility that Kiya would be treated a certain way for her looks, just as Nefertiti was. "I would think so," Nefertiti said.

It was Kiya's turn to be shocked. *Who would think the most beautiful woman of all women would think I am more than my face?* she thought, slightly pleased with this new Queen.

A moment lingered between the two women: one thinking she was finally going to make a new friend in her new Egyptian home; one thinking the other was out to take over her marriage.

The latter, Nefertiti, broke the silence. "I will do everything in my power to stay chief wife—"

Kiya took a half step backward, and one eyebrow went up in confusion.

"—when you marry Amenhotep," Nefertiti finished.

"I don't want to be chief wife," Kiya confessed. "I've seen the toll it took on Queen Tiye. As long as I have my stewards and food, I will be fine. No one here has befriended me, though, and it is friendship that I need now."

"Well, don't look for it in Amenhotep," Nefertiti said and turned to go to the courtyard.

"He has made it clear he does not wish to talk to me anymore," Kiya called back. "I was hoping to be *your* friend."

This stopped Nefertiti in her tracks.

"Nefertiti, look at me."

Nefertiti turned to face Kiya once more.

"I have no grace of my face like you, Nefertiti. Even if I tried, do you really think Amenhotep would love me more than you? I don't want to be chief wife. I know I will have to marry him to keep Egypt in good relations with the Mitanni, and I have been writing to my father, the King of Mittani, of my happiness and how Pharaoh takes good care of me. I assume Amenhotep will do the same as his father, and my letters of happiness will continue. But I am lonely, just as anyone would be if they were far from their homeland, stuck in a world of strangers confined to a palace. If it means your friendship, I will turn him down even if he tries."

Nefertiti looked her over. "If you are lying to get close—"

"I am *not* lying!" Kiya's face contorted and her heart welled up within her chest.

Her outburst visibly shook Nefertiti—but what would she have done if someone had just accused *her* of lying? Probably the same thing. "Kiya, I believe you," she said. "Please eat with us in the throne room when the time of mourning has passed."

"Thank you, Nefertiti," Kiya said. "May Amen-Ro bless you."

"Amun-Re," Nefertiti corrected with a slight smile.

Kiya smiled back.

And the two young women went their separate ways: Kiya back to her chambers to paint, and Nefertiti to find her grief-stricken husband.

NEFERTITI CAME TO AMENHOTEP'S SIDE. STILL STANDING, she placed a warm hand on his shoulder.

"Amenhotep, I'm so sorry," she whispered.

"What are you sorry about?" he asked, not looking to her. He rolled his shoulder to shake off her hand.

She pulled her hand away, not sure what to say. She could only imagine how she would feel if she lost her own father. "I'm sorry about the Pharaoh's passing," she said.

"He died. We all die," he said, staring rigidly into the stone courtyard.

"Yes, we all die." Nefertiti clasped her hands to her chest, gazing down at him. No words volunteered themselves. She sat down next to him, instead, saying nothing.

The silence was eerie: no winds, no bustling from beyond the palace walls, no insects calling . . . nothing. As if all of Egypt, even the winds and the insects, mourned the greatest Pharaoh of Egyptian history thus far in utter silence.

Not even her husband's breathing could be heard, as if he had joined his father in death.

Finally, as the sun began to lower in the sky, Amenhotep spoke: "The Aten feels the day must come to an end, and so do I."

He went to stand, but Nefertiti grabbed his wrist. "Please stay, Amenhotep."

He willingly sat back down. She waited for him to speak again; his trembling lip and heavy shoulder gave away his desire to tell her something.

"Nefertiti, why . . . ?"

He drifted off, not knowing how to word the question he wished to ask. He wanted to ask why he had always been a failure in his father's eyes, but he didn't want to ask it in a way that would damage his wife's view of him.

She rubbed his back, as if coaxing out the question.

"Why . . . Nefertiti . . . why was I never included in games, in family outings, in anything to do with my father or brother?" he asked. "Why didn't my father love me?"

"I'm sure he did, Amenhotep."

Shaking his head, he rolled his eyes in disgust and covered his nose and mouth with his hand. "No, he did not."

"*I* love you," she said softly.

His back slumped. He wrapped his other arm around her, pulling her to his side. "I know," he whispered.

"Your two daughters love you," Nefertiti said.

He pulled his hand away from his face and looked at his wife. "I know," he said. He looked back to the courtyard and placed his chin on his fist. *It should be enough, but it isn't.*

"What could I have done differently to gain my father's love?" he asked.

"Nothing."

He snapped back to her. "Why do you say that?"

"You can't *gain* someone's love."

"I don't understand."

"Not everyone has the capability to give love, Amenhotep. In a good situation, the love you give will come back to you, such as that of you and me. But sometimes, the love you give does not come back, and the person receiving the love will take and take until there is nothing else to give or until you learn to only give what you can before losing yourself entirely."

Amenhotep kissed her forehead and then her lips. "How am I so lucky to have found not only the most beautiful wife, but also the most kind and wise?"

She kissed him again and laid her head on his shoulder. "You should thank your mother," she teased, and gently poked him in the ribs.

He chuckled. "I should." His mind briefly pictured Kasmut, but not with the love he felt for Nefertiti, only as a kindred memory. Then his thoughts shifted to his brother, for whom Nefertiti had originally been picked. *My brother . . . even in death, our father still loved him more.*

"What is it, Amenhotep?" Nefertiti asked, feeling him tense up.

He unclenched his jaw and said calmly, "You were meant for my brother. Perhaps I should thank him for dying."

"Amenhotep, what is really bothering you?"

"The last words my father gave me concerned my dead brother," Amenhotep said. He'd begun to notice how much his stone seat hurt, so he pulled from Nefertiti and stood up, pretending his lower back wasn't screaming.

Nefertiti stood as well. "Would you feel better if you told me about it?"

"Yes," Amenhotep whispered, and he began to recount the last moments of his father's life.

"I love you, Father," Amenhotep had whispered.

His father looked at him but said nothing.

Thinking he had not heard him, Amenhotep said it again a little louder.

No response came.

He began to say it a third time, but Pharaoh interrupted him. "I heard you, son." He looked at the ceiling, and there would his gaze be until he died. "As Pharaoh, you should never repeat yourself. You still have much to learn. Use your mother to help you and guide you. Remember, the Pharaoh rules by divine appointment. He is the embodiment of Amun himself."

"Then why, if Thutmose was to be Pharaoh, didn't Amun save him?"

"Because . . . well, I don't know. If I were Amun, I would have taken another child besides Thutmose," he said, his eyes rolling toward Amenhotep. "Thutmose would have kept the position of Pharaoh from falling into commonality while I was sick." Pharaoh gave a small cough.

"You wish me dead," Amenhotep said stonily. "Then why can't Smenkare be Pharaoh? He is Sitamun's son. Why do you never speak of him? Have you even seen him? She is your royal wife—is he not your son?"

His voice had slowly filled with a vengeance. His father now weak in his bed, Amenhotep found it easier to summon his years of abuse onto the old man.

"Yes, he is my son," Pharaoh said with a bitter cough.

Amenhotep nearly fell over at the confirmation of the rumors which had disgraced the throne room so long ago.

Pharaoh wanted to chastise Amenhotep for his newfound confidence in his accusations, but his chest heaved up and down. Laying his head down, still rattling from the jarring movement, he asked, "Do I want all of Egypt to know I took my daughter, your sister, to bed?"

He slightly shook his head, loathing his mistakes of taking his daughter and now confessing to his son. "There was already an heir to the throne, and so no need to take your sister—an action looked down upon by all unless an heir was needed."

His hand went up to tenderly touch his jaw. The pain shot through every tooth that remained and into his jaw and neck and temple. He was sure his cursed mouth was the cause of his failing health. To speak meant excruciating pain, but he had to let the next Pharaoh know.

"Marriage to Sitamun was ceremonial, nothing more. When I found out she was with child and she started to show, I put her in Malkata, not to be seen or heard until the child was born. Once he was born, she was not to tell anyone who the father was . . . but I suppose rumor has defeated me."

"Why did you do it?" Amenhotep asked. He longed to know his father's seemingly only weakness.

"I had taken to the wine all day and all night when the messenger came to me with the news Thutmose had died," he said as he leaned his head farther down into the bed. A tear slid from his right eye. "I was full of so much wine. Your mother had already gone to Men-nefer, but Sitamun remained to comfort me. I took her then."

Amenhotep sat back in his chair. His great father, the unbreakable one, the one who could do no wrong, the highest of high, the greatest of praises, the Pharaoh of all Egypt, the Great Amenhotep the Magnificent—he who had rejected his secondborn son because he was not as great as his brother—had forced himself onto his own flesh and blood. Sitamun, Amenhotep's oldest sister, had disappeared soon after Thutmose's burial because, Pharaoh had said, she was so heartbroken at the loss of her brother. But then the rumors came, most of which were denied or brushed aside. *But they were true.*

"He is only five years old, Amenhotep," Pharaoh said.

"Pharaohs have taken the throne at a young age in the past. He could still do it. You never thought highly of me, Father—especially not enough to be Pharaoh," Amenhotep said. "You never loved me," he said again, hoping his father would deny his statement. Even after hearing about his father's shameful act with his sister, he still needed this man's love.

"All of Egypt believes he is my grandson, and therefore, you are the next in line and are old enough to know what to do to restore Pharaoh to his rightful authority."

"Father, *do you love me?*" he asked, every aching fiber of his heart wishing and hoping for the answer he so desired to hear.

But no such answer came.

"As Pharaoh, you will need to make sure the matters of Egypt are properly cared for and the allies of Egypt remain allies. We are a great, if not the greatest, nation. It is now your responsibility to make it greater," Pharaoh said, his voice now almost a whisper.

"Father, have you *ever* loved me?" Amenhotep asked, one hand holding his father's hand and the other gripping his elbow.

"Amenhotep, listen to me," Pharaoh said, his breath hitching at every syllable.

Amenhotep sat on the edge of the chair, hoping, *needing* the answer to be *Yes, my son, I have always loved you.*

Instead, the old Pharaoh sputtered out, "Egypt needs her Pharaoh. Remember to bring her back to Amun-Re, or else the people will reject you." He closed his eyes.

Amenhotep's shoulders slumped as he watched his father's eyeballs roll underneath their lids. Pharaoh opened his eyes one last time. Hope crept inside his stomach. *Perhaps . . .* he thought.

"Amenhotep, be the Pharaoh I knew Thutmose could be," the old man said as his eyes closed for the final time. He took one more breath and then no more.

Amenhotep stared. His father's hand lay limp in his own. His head rolled slightly to its side.

All of a sudden, his father's last words crept into Amenhotep's mind, and his body became like a ton of stones stacked upon one other: his muscles rigid, coldness hitting him in his core. The tightness in his chest struck him still and mute.

"Father?" he asked, trying to keep his voice from screeching.

His father's jaw hung slightly ajar and his chest remained still.

"No!" Amenhotep yelled and stood up. "How dare you, Father! Your last words to me are to be like my dead brother!"

He hit his father's corpse in the face, brought his hand up

to slap him again . . . then bent over him, fell to his knees and cried into his chest.

"Father, I love you! Please, do not leave me with those words as your last."

Banging on his chest, he yelled into his face. "Father, do you hear me?! Hear me, Father! Don't leave me with those words! Curse you! Curse you now and forever. *Curse* you!"

Still more tears came. He shuddered and whispered, crying over and over again, "Please, Father, tell me you love me. Please . . . *please*, Father!"

CHAPTER 10
THE TIME OF RELINQUISHMENT

THE SUN BLISTERED ON THE DAY THEY FINALLY LAID THE great Pharaoh Amenhotep III to rest in the Valley of the Kings. As the new Pharaoh was carried in front of the procession, the former Pharaoh's viziers of the North and the South, Huy and Ramose, led the people to the West Bank of Waset, while the oxen pulled the sled with the body behind them. The High Priests of Amun-Re, with their shaved heads, walked solemnly beside the dead Pharaoh as the incense they held swirled about their waists. The Mourners, crying and wailing women who beat their chests and smeared dirt on their skin, followed them as lower priests mingled amongst the procession, and two women skilled in playing their brass sistrums danced between the Mourners. The skill of the musicians reached perfection as they shook the sistrums' wooden handles in their hands with ever so much force to slightly swing the thin metal rings around the moveable brass crossbars, producing the sounds of a breeze flowing through the papyrus reeds of the Nile.

Pharaoh Amenhotep IV, now twenty years old, stood with his shoulders squared as they reached the tomb's entrance.

The priests stood the coffin upright and performed the ritualistic opening of the mouth ceremony. Queen Nefertiti looked to her husband as he began walking with the priests and workers into the tomb to lay the Pharaoh to rest. She followed him, as did Queen Tiye.

Amenhotep had said nothing but a few words in the past seventy days since Nefertiti had learned of his last encounter with his father. Instead, he had turned his back to her almost every night since. Still, Nefertiti had followed her father's advice and placed her hand on his shoulder, whispering, "I love you." She'd tried to be comforting, holding his head against her bosom, yet he still showed no feeling, no sadness nor sorrow that his father was gone. In the absence of emotion, though, she knew, his father's death was more than he had ever borne before.

When it was time for the royal family to leave and attend the funerary meal, Pharaoh Amenhotep stayed. "Leave. When Pharaoh is ready for you to lay the stone and seal the tomb, he will emerge from this place," he commanded.

The workers and priests bowed and left, followed by the royal family—except Queen Nefertiti, who stayed in the shadows.

Thinking he was alone, Amenhotep placed his hand on his father's golden mask.

"Father," he finally whispered. "I am sorry I could never live up to your expectation of me, but one day I will be as great a man as you once were. Even though I could never earn your love, I gave you mine daily. Life without you will be difficult, but the Aten will help me. I promise you, Father . . . I will make you proud."

He sat down by the stone sarcophagus and leaned his back against it. The cool stone drained the sun's heat from his skin.

"Aten—" he began to pray, but, noticing his wife in the

LAUREN LEE MEREWETHER

shadows, he silenced himself. "Nefertiti? I thought I asked everyone to leave."

"Amenhotep, I will never leave you." Her voice flowed as smooth as the Nile river. Stepping forward, she took her place next to her husband. "You have already made your father proud by being the man you are today. He *loved* you, Amenhotep. He loved you in his own way, in the way he thought best to help you."

"All he ever gave me was doubt."

"So you could better yourself," she responded. "Every father wants his son to be the best they can be. And remember, I have no doubts—and I never will."

"My love," he said, placing his hand on hers. "I love you, my cherished one." He brought her hand to his lips and pressed them firmly to her skin. "Come, let us leave my father in peace. I have said my last to him. If you say he was proud and loved me, I will believe you. You have never led me astray."

———

THAT NIGHT BEFORE THE SUN WENT DOWN, AMENHOTEP said his nightly prayer to the Aten as he lifted his mighty crown and placed it on its stand. He climbed into bed next to Nefertiti as the servants left the room.

They lay in silence, staring up at the ceiling as the last of the candlelight flickered away. For four years, Nefertiti had wanted to ask her husband if he really believed the Aten was mightier than Amun-Re, but each time she discouraged herself from saying anything. Today, however, she had seen him begin to pray to the Aten in his privacy, and the urge to know boosted her courage.

"Why do you pray to the Aten and not Amun-Re?" she asked him, unsure if he would become angry.

But he responded immediately, no anger apparent in his voice. "I pray to the Aten because he hears me. He takes away my physical pain. It is why I spend hours of the day outside in his warm embrace. And if I am in his embrace long enough, he sometimes gives me visions of the future. He shows me the grand and great Egypt of tomorrow."

He turned to face his wife. "Amun-Re does not hear me. I prayed countless times as a child, and never did he take away my ailing. Nor has he shown me any visions."

"You will be labeled a tyrant if you absorb the priesthood, or you will be labeled a heretic if you turn Egypt to the Aten," Nefertiti said. Her voice shook as she breathed out a flimsy breath.

"I know, my love. But as my father said . . . it will be my legacy. The people will see that the Aten is greater, and when they realize Pharaoh has not led them astray, they will forever remember how I saved them from their ignorance."

"I fear for our family," Nefertiti confided as she rubbed her belly, remembering the two daughters she bore. "The priesthood of Amun-Re will not go away easily. Eventually we will have to turn Egypt back to Amun-Re."

"I am Pharaoh, and you are my Queen. My word is law," he said solemnly. "We are safe. It is worse than death to kill the Pharaoh, and it is worse still to endure his wrath."

"And turning back to Amun-Re?" she asked. "After we regain the authority for the throne?"

"Of course, my love . . . if Egypt wants it after they have seen the glory of the Aten."

After a few moments of silence, he began to shift to his side.

"Will you turn away from me again tonight?" she asked of him.

"I have much on which to think," he said.

He waited for her to touch his shoulder, but she only whispered, "You can think with me."

"I know you believe me to be a heretic," he said as he rolled over and placed his hand on her hip. "But I promise, no harm will come to our family."

"I do not believe you are a heretic—I believe you are confused. Amun-Re is the premier god of Egypt, Amenhotep. Once we regain the power from the priesthood . . . promise me you will return Egypt to Amun-Re," Nefertiti pleaded. "For your family."

"My beautiful one, I will promise you what you ask . . . but if you come to realize that the Aten blesses more than Amun-Re and so should be the premier god of Egypt, we will remain faithful to the Aten." He kissed her cheek. "I can never refuse the most beautiful woman in all the world."

Her high cheekbones, the sign of beauty, power, and elegance, shone brightly in the moonlight. "As I cannot doubt the man who loves me," she whispered back, and kissed him on his forehead.

"And as there is only one Aten for the god of Pharaoh . . . there shall be only one *lover* of Pharaoh." He smiled as he began to kiss her face and her neck.

She giggled and wrapped her arms around him. "And who shall that be?"

"Why, I have chosen my Queen Nefertiti."

WITH THE FORMER PHARAOH'S PASSING AND BURIAL, Amenhotep was crowned sole Regent, Pharaoh of both the Upper and the Lower; with his new title, he named the Aten as his personal god and, the same as his father, Ramose and Huy as his viziers. Over the years, Ay had shown himself invaluable to Amenhotep's father, and if this man raised such a woman as Nefertiti, then he wanted Ay as his advisor; Amenhotep gave him the title of Fan-Bearer on the Right Side of the King, a trusted position. He also raised him in rank to Master of Pharaoh's Horses, the highest rank of the elite chariot division, a position just underneath General Paaten. His mother, now widowed, became the great royal wife to signify her stature as the chief wife of the Pharaoh before.

In the beginning, Pharaoh mostly performed the daily duties and wrote letters encouraging foreign relations, but he began to spend many hours in the courtyard, standing with his arms up to the sun, whispering to himself.

A while after the news of the former Pharaoh's burial, a letter came from the King of Mitanni, asking what was to become of his daughter and hinting at the fact that if she were to be returned a widow, their friendship may incur irreversible damage. One night, as they lay in bed, Amenhotep recited this letter to Nefertiti, asking how he should respond. His mother had already drafted the letter, but he wanted to see what Nefertiti would say.

"Just as there is only one Pharaoh of Egypt, there is also only one god of the Pharaoh," she hummed as he held her that night.

"As there is only one woman fit for me," he finished her sentence, and locked his eyes with hers.

She just hoped his infatuation with the sun-disc Aten would somehow bind his loyalty to her. "Although it is customary for the Pharaohs and nobles to have many lovers, I cannot stand the thought of you being with anyone else other than me," she responded.

"I know," he said. "Nor can I."

"If you keep your promise to me that I will be your only love, Pharaoh must do what he needs to do for the state of

Egypt," she said, referring to his upcoming marriages to Kiya and his sister Henuttaneb.

"I will always keep my promise to you, Nefertiti," he said as he traced her face with his finger. "As there is only one god of Pharaoh."

The new Pharaoh of Egypt has to secure his throne with strategic marriage . . . but with marriage always comes the right to have another lover, Nefertiti thought as he kissed her. *As long as he believes the Aten is the sole god of Egypt, he will not touch another woman.*

CHAPTER 11
THE TIME OF PHARAOH

EGYPT FLOURISHED SHORTLY AFTER, AND ALL LOVED Pharaoh Amenhotep and Queen Nefertiti, as all love those who reign over them when the times are good. As the wealth of Egypt grew, however, people spent their extra prosperity at the temples of Amun instead of at the temples of the Pharaohs.

"My son, look at these," Tiye said.

Pharaoh had called together his council, consisting of his mother, his chief royal wife, General Paaten, Ay, his viziers, Ramose and Huy, and lastly, Satau, the royal treasurer. They pored over the treasury's spending reports.

"Almost seventy percent of Egypt's wealth is going to the Amun-Re priesthood," Ay said with a slight shake of his head.

"Seventy percent?" Amenhotep said. "What was it when I became Coregent?"

Queen Tiye shot him a look and let out a sigh.

Satau said, "Around fifty-five percent, I believe."

"It has increased that much in just five years?"

"It increased from forty percent since the first sed festival of your father's reign," Ramose said.

"What to do? Meryptah is still alive. We cannot turn Egypt to the Aten yet," Amenhotep said as he put his hand on the table.

"I'm not sure there is anything you *can* do," Tiye said.

They all looked blankly at the scroll on the table. Nefertiti held her finger up to speak and then as soon as she opened her mouth, she shut it and put her finger to her lips.

"At this rate, how much longer until the Amun priesthood surpasses Pharaoh's reserves?" Tiye asked.

Ramose ran his knuckles across the table knocked them against the wood. "Two years," he said.

"Two years!" Tiye and Amenhotep exclaimed together.

"Meryptah will barely be dead in two years—if he is dead at all," Amenhotep said.

His mother shuddered at the word *dead*. "Your father and I did think about having him . . ." She trailed off, her meaning implicit. "But we talked ourselves out such an idea."

"In two years, if the Pharaoh is overwhelmed by the priesthood, it may be worth it," Huy said.

"We are speaking of murdering a man," Ay interjected. "The Highest Priest, the First Prophet of Amun, the most sacred man other than Pharaoh himself. Amun-Re does not look kindly on those who murder such men."

"There are consequences for doing such a thing, I know," Tiye said with a heavy breath. "What do you suggest? I would rather not have blood on my hands, especially *his*."

"Nor would I," Amenhotep said.

Ay stared back at them blankly.

Nefertiti finally spoke up. "We could build a city dedicated to the Aten."

"A city? Or a temple, my lotus blossom," Ay said. His cheeks turned red, but the new Pharaoh did not seem to care that he was so informal with his daughter, the Queen of Egypt.

Tiye did look over to him, but said nothing at his sheepish grin.

"No, not a temple. A *city*," Nefertiti said, examining their confused expressions. "We collect a small tax from all the people of Egypt to build the city, but also have a small part of the tax go to Pharaoh's reserve. This way we can at least stay ahead for a little while longer until Meryptah passes."

"By building a temple, we would have to dip from Pharaoh's reserves . . . but this way, we can indirectly take money from the priesthood," Ay said to himself, and looked to his daughter with a full chest and beaming eyes.

"With the city dedicated to the Aten, the people's money will go there by order of Pharaoh," Ramose chimed in, nodding his head.

The treasurer agreed excitedly. "Instead of to the Amun priesthood, thereby decreasing the power of the priesthood . . . and also creating a safety net in case Meryptah lives."

"When Meryptah does pass, we already will have made a few steps in the direction of turning Egypt to the Aten," Nefertiti finished.

In front of them all, Amenhotep kissed her on her forehead and rubbed her arm. *I am so proud to have such a clever wife. At least my father was right about her helping me in this journey,* he thought.

"And so we turn to the Aten just long enough for the priesthood to crumble, and then we turn back to Amun-Re to not jeopardize our afterlife," Tiye said, nodding her head.

"The Aten did give me a vision of his sun-disc between the two northern mountains yesterday as he continued to heal my pains," Amenhotep said. "The Aten desires a city dedicated to him because he is my personal god and the personal god of my father."

"You must not say 'me' or 'my,' Amenhotep. Pharaoh is to be regarded as 'him,' 'his,' and 'Pharaoh's,' " Tiye gently reminded her son. But the truth showed in her voice: she didn't mind his lack of formality so much. Even she admitted the missteps of formality in the throne room made her feel as though it were easier to breathe and be herself, but she also knew his speech had to garner every respect due the position of Pharaoh.

"Pharaoh will not fail you," Amenhotep said.

She smiled, and her eyes said, *I know, son.*

He opened his mouth, thinking he would have to defend himself against some comment about him and Thutmose; but, instead, at his mother's response, his mouth, slightly ajar, turned into a grin.

LATER THAT DAY, AS PHARAOH SAT IN THE THRONE ROOM listening to the incoming messages of the day, one struck his fancy: the workers in the valley needed water from the heat of the Aten.

Here's my opportunity! he thought.

Tiye and Nefertiti smiled when he began to speak. They were thinking the same thing.

"Supply them water—as much as needed to prevent sickness and death. Pharaoh is at one with the Aten after a long familial line of Pharaohs dedicated to him. Because of Pharaoh's proven worthiness to the Aten, a vision was granted unto Pharaoh wherein he saw a sun-disc between two mountains. The Aten guided Pharaoh to make a change, and the Aten, as the sun-disc, the Light of Egypt, told Pharaoh to build a city between the two mountains. A city dedicated to the Aten shall be built where one can first see the Aten rise on the east bank of the Nile River between the two mountains. The Aten wants the royal family to reside there, and so the palace shall be built behind the city closest to the horizon," Pharaoh Amenhotep proclaimed. "Thus Pharaoh says."

So it was written, and the tax began to take effect the next day. Taxes paid the Egyptian engineers to find the exact spot where they would build the city. Huy met with a chief architect and Pharaoh, Queen Tiye, and Queen Nefertiti to outline what was to be built in this new city of the Aten.

———

IT CAME TIME TO CONFIRM AMENHOTEP'S RIGHT TO THE throne so that he might do his duty as Pharaoh of Egypt.

Kiya, dressed in a long tunic adorned with gold and silver, walked down the throne room toward Meryptah, the First Prophet of Amun; her maidservants followed close behind with symbols of the Mitanni treasures for her dowry. All eyes were on her—including Nefertiti's.

He has to marry her, Nefertiti thought. *He has to keep in good standing with Egypt's allies. She told me she did not want to be chief wife and she would rather have my friendship than a husband. Or . . . is that what she said? Why can't I remember?*

Nefertiti had recently watched him marry his sister Henuttaneb in the weeks previous, but he had not yet touched her, just as he had promised. *He comes to me every night and sleeps by my side,* she reassured herself once again.

"He loves me . . . and only me," she whispered. "I have no doubts."

Meryptah relayed the Pharaoh's wish to accept the Mitanni bride and her dowry, and with these words signaled the beginning of the marriage feast, setup in the courtyard overlooking the palace's manmade lake his father had built.

Nefertiti took her seat at the right hand of Pharaoh. Kiya

LAUREN LEE MEREWETHER

took her place next to Pharaoh's left hand. Henuttaneb sat next to Kiya, and Tiye next to Nefertiti.

Most of the night, Nefertiti noticed Amenhotep's head turned to the left and not the right. It was too loud to overhear their conversation. Queen Tiye sat and ate in silence. *No doubt missing her husband,* Nefertiti thought.

As the moon rose in the sky, the marriage feast ended and the strong drink vanished.

Nefertiti now lay in their chambers, wondering if he would come to her or go to Kiya. The demons of her thoughts almost had her plotting against her new sister-wife when Amenhotep entered and came to lie down.

He kissed Nefertiti on the forehead and then her lips. "My one and my only," he whispered.

Her mind cleared; she smiled.

"I was starting to have doubts, Amenhotep," Nefertiti said with a blush of her cheeks.

"And why should such doubts surface, my love?" Amenhotep asked her as he stroked the side of her face.

"You have always seemed to be charmed with Kiya, even before we were wed. She fancies your eye?"

"My Nefertiti, only *you* fancy my eye. Kiya was somewhat of a confidant of mine when my brother was alive—really her and Kasmut, mostly Kasmut. Kiya understood what it was like to not live up to the expectation set for her."

Nefertiti noticed his eyes didn't light up anymore when he said Kasmut's name, nor when he spoke of Kiya, making her heart feel light.

Amenhotep continued while Nefertiti studied his face, "Her father sent her here to marry my father as a last chance for her to prove herself . . ."

"What did you talk about?"

"About her paintings, her musings in the palace, my new

role as Pharaoh, our daughters . . . She has many paintings of them playing in the courtyard with us. She said you were her friend, and that I should be very lucky to have you as my wife," he added quickly.

She remembered back to her first conversation with her. *I need to invite Kiya to dinner. I must confirm what she said about wanting a friendship over a husband.*

Something of what Amenhotep just said suddenly struck Nefertiti. "Wait . . . she paints our family?" She thought it a little weird to be painting another person's family.

"Yes. I agree that it seems strange at first mention. I asked her why she paints our family, and she said it isn't as lonely when she can paint others who are so clearly in love with their children." He smiled down at Nefertiti.

"Do you think she wants children with you? Do *you* want children with her?" The words spewed uncontrollably from Nefertiti's mouth.

He laughed. "To answer both questions—no. She said she was happy here without anything more than friendship. And I only want to have children with you."

Nefertiti had no response. A part of her did not believe him, but another part of her wanted to believe him. *He has never given me reason to doubt before. I am being silly,* she thought.

"Do not have doubts, my Queen. You are the only one with whom I wish to love," Amenhotep explained.

"How will you prove your love to me?"

Nefertiti had asked this as a tease, but Amenhotep's face dropped in worry.

"Do I not every night by staying with you instead of my other wives? All of the Pharaohs of the past consummated many marriages. I have only consummated ours. You are my hope and my strength, Nefertiti. You are the most beautiful woman in all of Egypt—nay, all the *world*. I should think myself blessed by the Aten to have such a woman as you, and all you ask is that I have but one lover? It shall be done!"

At this, Nefertiti leaned forward and kissed Amenhotep. Pulling back so the flesh of their lips almost touched, she whispered, "I love you, Amenhotep, my Pharaoh and my King. I always will love you. Once more"—she bit the bottom of her lip and slowly blinked—"do you love me?"

He placed his hand on her back and pushed her onto his chest, and his heart melted into hers.

"Yes, my Queen Nefertiti."

THE NEXT DAY, NEFERTITI FOUND THE DOOR TO KIYA'S chambers open, and so she stepped inside. In order to keep to her word and befriend the new royal wife as long as Kiya would refuse Amenhotep, she decided to pay Kiya a visit to try and befriend the quiet girl.

Nefertiti was greeted by Ainamun, Kiya's head steward. "Chief royal wife Nefertiti, allow me to bring you to royal wife Kiya," she said with a bow, then led her to Kiya in her sitting room, where papyrus scrolls were strewn all around her. Kiya sat in a chair with papyrus out in front of her and colored inks by her side. Ainamun bowed, then pulled up a second chair and left the two women alone.

"Chief royal wife Nefertiti," Kiya said with a bow of her head. "May we leave formalities alone for the moment?"

Nefertiti sat in the second chair and nodded her head. She glanced at what Kiya was working on: an immaculate, hyper-realistic painting of Nefertiti's children, Meritaten and Meketaten, with their wet nurse, playing in the courtyard.

"Oh Kiya," Nefertiti said as she reached out as if to touch it. In awe, her mouth hung ajar. "They look as if they were right here in the room with us."

"I've had a long time to perfect the techniques of painting," Kiya said, blushing.

"I can see," Nefertiti said as her fingers debated on whether to touch it or not. "I want all of my children to be remembered like this."

"What do you mean?" Kiya said. "Meritaten and Meketaten *are* all of your children."

A sly smile slid across Nefertiti's face. "You clever girl. You made this painting just so I would forget my place," she said with a chuckle.

Kiya laughed. "I did not!"

Nefertiti's face glowed. "I am with child, Kiya!"

Kiya's laughter dried up. "I'm so happy for you." Kiya put her reed brush down and forced a smile. "Do you know if it is a son or daughter?"

"The doctors had me perform the seed test," she said, referring to the Egyptian custom in which the woman relieves herself over wheat and barley seeds to confirm pregnancy. "The barley seed sprouted quickly, which the doctors assure me means it will be a son." Nefertiti's hands came together in front of her chest. "Praise be to Amun-Re," she whispered.

"Secretly . . ." she told Kiya, and Kiya leaned in. "I have been praying I could provide the heir to the throne soon to make Amenho . . . Pharaoh happy."

She'd almost uttered Amenhotep's name out of habit. *I have to remember his name is Pharaoh when there are others around,* she chided herself.

"I am sure Pharaoh will be happy whether it is a son or daughter," Kiya said as she picked her reed brush back up and resumed painting. "He will love them the same."

"I know he will. It's just . . . I know he also wants an heir," Nefertiti said as she unconsciously rubbed her belly.

"You are both young. You will have an heir in time," Kiya reassured her as she fixed the sunlight on Meketaten's nose.

"Thank you, Kiya. Pharaoh was right about you."

"What do you mean? What did he say about me?" Kiya asked with a fluttering chest.

"He said you were a good person to talk to when his father made him feel unloved."

Kiya smiled at the memory. "He was my only friend. But then, he and Kasmut . . ." Her voice trailed off, and then she stated, "He made me feel less lonely."

"I do not wish for you to be lonely." Nefertiti realized this girl truly was telling the truth to her that day in the palace halls. All she wanted was someone to talk to. "Especially when you have this gift to share!" Nefertiti gestured to the artful masterpiece of Meritaten and Meketaten.

"I don't know if Pharaoh told you this, but my father forbade me to paint," she said as she lowered the tip of her reed brush, remembering her father's words. "It is . . . not becoming of a princess."

"Why? This painting is unlike anything I have ever seen," Nefertiti said.

"Painting is a servant's trade," Kiya said. Her shoulders slumped and her eyes dropped to the floor.

"In Egypt, we have famous artists," Nefertiti said, trying to raise her spirits.

"Yes, but none of them are royal, are they?"

"Well, no, but if you love to do it and you are painting in a way that has not been done before . . ." Nefertiti stood up. "I want my family to be remembered like this!" she exclaimed, pointing to the painting of her girls. Kiya tried to get in a word, but Nefertiti exclaimed again, "I must bring this to Amenhotep!"

She grabbed the painting off of the easel, but Kiya grabbed her wrists. "It's wet!"

"Oh!" Nefertiti dropped the painting and stepped backward.

Kiya caught the corner and placed it back on the easel.

"What about the others? May I take one of them?" Nefertiti asked as she wiped her hand on the cloth lying on the back of Kiya's chair.

Kiya handed her one of the rolls on the floor. "Here is one of Meritaten."

Nefertiti unrolled it and let out an appreciative sigh. "This is wonderful, Kiya! I will show Amenho . . . Pharaoh, and let him know my request to have our images in stone represent us more like this!"

Kiya beamed at the chance she could finally mean something to someone, to succeed instead of fail. As Nefertiti turned to leave, Kiya grabbed her wrist for a second time. "Wait!"

"What is it, Kiya?"

Kiya had no response. Even though jealousy overtook her mind at times, she was thankful Nefertiti had kept her word and made her feel wanted. So instead of a reply, she jumped into an embrace with her newfound friend

Nefertiti's arms froze straight down at her sides and her shoulders raised past her neck. "What are you doing?" she whispered.

Kiya pulled back with watery eyes and said, "Thank you for believing in my paintings."

Nefertiti nodded and patted her cheek like she would do with her younger sisters when she lived at home. "You have done a job worthy of presentation to Amun-Re's appointed," she said, and watched the light grow even brighter in Kiya's eyes. With that, she turned to leave and show Amenhotep.

WHEN AMENHOTEP SAW THE PAINTING, HE FELL IN LOVE with it as well. He summoned his royal scribe, along with

Kiya. When they both had arrived in the throne room, Amenhotep declared, "Pharaoh and his royal family shall be captured in stone like this realistic painting. Thus Pharaoh says."

CHAPTER 12
THE TIME OF THE ATEN

Watching his wife regain her breath, Amenhotep sat back while the servants removed the stick from her mouth and wiped the sweat from her brow. He wondered at how Nefertiti seemed to grow in beauty each day when other women waned. He could not resist reaching out and cupping her face in his hands. He gazed into her eyes, then gently placed his lips on hers.

The baby's soft cries rose in the cool morning air as the midwives prayed to the two small statues of the god Bes and goddess Tawaret beside Nefertiti to vanquish any evil waiting to overtake the baby and new mother.

Nefertiti smiled, closing her eyes, and leaned back into her maidservants' arms as they lowered her to the cot next to the birthing chair.

Kiya was there to take her hand, beaming at her friend, the Queen, for allowing her to watch the birth of the princess.

Pharaoh Amenhotep knelt and clasped Nefertiti's other hand. "Bring my child," he ordered one of Nefertiti's nearby servants.

Aitye, having wiped the babe with a cloth, held the new child up for Pharaoh to see. "Pharaoh's daughter," she said with a bow, the baby outstretched in her arms.

Nefertiti's eyes watered at that word—daughter—but she forced a smile and a heavy, breathless laugh. *I was so sure Amun-Re would grant us a boy,* she thought. *The seed test proved it would be a boy!*

At Aitye's pronouncement, Amenhotep's face fell slack, but only for a moment, before he exclaimed to all, "My third daughter is a blessing from the Aten!"

He will still love this daughter the same as the others, she thought, again forcing a smile. *Just as Kiya said.* She opened her eyes to look upon her new child. "What will we name her?"

"It is morning now, and not only morning, but the first morning of the new year. She has the whole of the day and the whole of the year to grow and to live. We shall name her Ankhesenpaaten: 'She who lives through the Aten,' " he said as he grabbed the baby from Aitye's arms. Holding the new baby girl, one hand cupped behind her back and head and one under her rear, he declared to her, "Ankhesenpaaten, you will be a great woman in your day."

The little baby's cries became louder. Aitye motioned for him to hand her back. She wrapped Ankhesenpaaten tightly in the cloth, and her soft cries turned into soft snores.

Nefertiti motioned that she be allowed to hold her baby, and Aitye brought the child to her. Amenhotep helped Nefertiti sit up as the maidservants propped her up with blankets. Holding her baby girl, Nefertiti traced the outline of her forehead down to the tip of her nose.

"She is perfect," she whispered.

"As is her mother," Amenhotep whispered in Nefertiti's ear, bringing forth a bigger smile. He kissed the top of her bald head and kissed Ankhesenpaaten's forehead.

Kiya, smiling at the two, went out of the room to leave them to their new daughter.

After a few moments of adoration, Amenhotep murmured to Nefertiti, "When your body heals and you are ready, I would like to try again for a boy."

"I know," she whispered back. "I can understand your disappointment with another daughter . . ."

"I am not disappointed," Amenhotep said, almost believing his lie. "Ankhesenpaaten is a beautiful reincarnation of her mother, as are her two elder sisters. How can I be disappointed with all of the beauty that surrounds me?"

"I can see it in your face, my love," Nefertiti said. "Just remember, your mother and father had three daughters before they had your brother and you."

At this, he laughed. "This is true, my love. Perhaps we shall be as lucky!"

BEFORE THE YEAR ENDED, MERYPTAH, FIRST PROPHET OF Amun, succumbed to his failing health. Sadness swept the city of Waset, closely followed by panic: the link between the people of Egypt and Amun-Re had been severed. Anen was supposed to take his place, but he too had also passed. Now only Maya remained as Second Prophet. He was the only logical choice to become First Prophet—but without his tenure in Amun-Re's presence, the people feared he would not be an effective high priest. The people had forgotten Pharaoh as the highest priest of Amun, his divinely appointed.

Queen Tiye said to her son, before they entered the throne room to be seen by the people, "Amenhotep, remember: formality for the position of Pharaoh gives dignity and authority to his word. You have been slack in your words and actions. Make sure the people know you are Pharaoh, and Pharaoh will correct this crisis." She touched his cheek and smiled.

Amenhotep smiled back, but his eyes faded at the remembrance of his father, the Magnificent King. "Mother, do you still believe Thutmose would have been a greater Pharaoh than me, as Father did?"

Nefertiti, who stood next to him, immediately averted her eyes at the potential awkwardness the response to his question would bring.

Queen Tiye's jaw slightly dropped at the question, but she simply responded, "We prepared Thutmose much more than you, so yes, I do believe he would have been a better Pharaoh. Does that mean I think you will never reach the same height as he would have or as your father did? No. I believe you will do great and wondrous things that perhaps Thutmose could not have done."

She adjusted the white Hedjet crown on his head to where it sat perfectly in line with his long face.

"I know your father compared you and Thutmose all of your life, Amenhotep," she said, unusually struggling to find her next words before finally spitting out, "He . . . he could never accept you as you were. Son, please, as your mother and as the great royal wife, my only request is this . . . if Nefertiti ever comes to you with a concern about you and one of your children, you do not threaten to strip her title should she ever dare to bring it up again."

Amenhotep's eyes fully opened, and finally, after all this time, he could see his true mother standing in front of him. His heart beat so fast that he felt weak, and at last, when no words could come to his tongue, he threw his arms around her and buried his head into her shoulder. To his surprise, instead of scolding him for his affection, she enclosed him in her arms. She let out a heavy sigh of relief as the tension she had held in her shoulders for almost two decades melted away.

Nefertiti shrugged her shoulders and wrapped her arms as far as they would go around the both of them. She was a part of this family now.

Amenhotep took one arm and enclosed Nefertiti into the circle. He lifted his head and looked first to his mother and then to Nefertiti. His smile, full of content, told them what he thought. Nefertiti laughed and rubbed his shoulder as he released his embrace.

Queen Tiye adjusted his Hedjet again since it had fallen slightly to the side when he hugged her. "Shall we?" she asked, motioning for Amenhotep to lead them into the throne room.

"Pharaoh shall," he said with a grin as he led them into the throne room. Queen Tiye followed as her title of great royal wife bore a higher rank than that of Nefertiti.

Amenhotep sat on his golden throne of splendor and Tiye and Nefertiti took their respective seats on his right and on his left.

The messenger spoke: "Great Pharaoh of Egypt, the people suffer now as Meryptah, First Prophet of Amun, has passed from this life."

"Pharaoh does not wish the people of Egypt to suffer," Amenhotep said. "As Egypt goes into the next year, let it be known Pharaoh will provide for his people when the priesthood of Amun left them without a link to Amun-Re."

Amenhotep paused for dramatic effect, thinking to himself, *Father, these next moments are for you. I will make you proud of me. Thutmose could not have done what I am about to do because he wouldn't have believed in the Aten. I believe in the Aten, and he will see me through. Turning Egypt to the Aten will be my legacy.*

"Because the priesthood of Amun-Re cannot recover

from the loss of Anen, the Second Prophet of Amun, and Meryptah, the First Prophet of Amun, the Great Pharaoh of Mighty Egypt will intervene," Amenhotep bellowed.

The mass that had gathered to hear what the Pharaoh would say silenced every breath, whisper, and movement.

"The time of Amun-Re has passed, and it is now the time of the Aten," Amenhotep said, surveying the wide eyes that returned his stare. He continued unwaveringly, "The premier god of Egypt shall now be the Aten, the sun-disc, the Light of Egypt. The Aten has long been Pharaoh's personal god as well as the Pharaoh before. Because of this, all Pharaohs now passed are embodied in the Aten. Therefore, Pharaoh, the son of the Pharaoh before, is now the son of the Aten, thus Pharaoh will now be the sole link between the people and the Aten."

As his words sank in with his subjects, he slowly but forcefully stated, "Thus Pharaoh says."

CHAPTER 13
THE TIME OF REBELLION

As word of Pharaoh's edict spread, the people of Egypt arose and protested in the streets. Amun-Re, their King of Gods, their God of Gods, now usurped by his own appointed, the Pharaoh of Egypt, and replaced by the Aten, a small aspect of Re, not a god by their perspective, but only the sun-disc in the sky? Pharaoh, in one swift command, had overturned centuries of their traditional faith, and the greater of Egypt would not have it!

Nefertiti's fears of the people rising up against them were coming true. She looked out of their window as the sun waned on the horizon and the torchlights came out to surround the palace at Malkata. Thus the new year began in conflict.

Nefertiti stared out at the growing torchlights as the Aten disappeared for the night beyond the far palace's wall. "I am afraid, Amenhotep. What if the royal guard turns against us? What if they can't keep the mobs at bay?"

Amenhotep came and wrapped his arms around her chest. "We haven't much to fear, my love. My father's incessant expansions of Malkata will keep the people at bay." The undertone in his voice juggled between hate and admiration of his father's accomplishments.

Nefertiti only closed her eyes, wishing her husband was right.

At her silence, he continued, "The royal guard has sworn their life to Pharaoh, and if they go against their own word, Anubis will deny them entrance to eternal life. They will die keeping us safe. So far, there has been no bloodshed, just angry Egyptians, and I pray to the Aten the peace will continue. Now let us sleep. Huy has assured me he would wake me if the situation outside the palace turns violent."

"I can see Pharaoh's power is not what it should be," Nefertiti said. "If power remained with Pharaoh, there would be no protest."

"Yes . . . the priesthood is revolting, and the people follow the priesthood. Perhaps we were too late." Amenhotep pulled his wife away from the window.

"Perhaps," Nefertiti said.

"I know so. Huy made me aware that my sister Nebetah and her husband Pawah are leading the protests most likely at the order of First Prophet of Amun, Maya, but he could not be sure about the priesthood's involvement. I should have Nebetah and Pawah exiled for leaving the sanctuary of Sitamun as my father ordered, but I am afraid it would make matters worse," Amenhotep said. "At least Sitamun and Iset remain neutral."

"The great nation of Egypt is split in two: those who follow the Pharaoh and those who follow Amun," Nefertiti said as he pulled her into bed. "Rumor has it that whoever wins this conflict—Pharaoh or the people—will determine which god shall be the premier god."

"Yes, and we will prevail. But my love, let us think about this tomorrow," he said, tracing his finger to smooth the worry lines in her brow. "Tomorrow is another day. Let us sleep and not worry tonight, for it may be the last good night's sleep we get for some time."

She agreed, and they tried to sleep amid the noise and clatter outside the palace walls, but it was to no avail—someone knocked hard and fast on their door.

———

AMENHOTEP SHOT UP IN BED, JUST AS SERVANTS POURED into their room, startling his Queen to full alertness. The messenger quickly spoke as the servants dressed them for battle. The people had beat back the royal guard, the messenger explained; they had broken down the door to the throne room and ensued into the palace; Huy had already been killed.

Ramose suddenly appeared in the doorway, shouting, "A message has been received from Commander Horemheb stating he shall come to Pharaoh's aid with two legions from Middle Egypt."

Amenhotep quickly kissed Nefertiti as they wrapped his sword belt around his waist. "Keep safe," he said. "I will be back."

Nefertiti, now dressed, only whispered, "Our children." She took her maidservants with her behind Amenhotep, but instead of following him to the throne room she turned and went to their nurseries to see that they were safe. Opening the door, she almost collided with the blunt end of a lampstand. Merytre held it high above her head, and nearly collapsed at the sight of Nefertiti.

"My . . . Queen!" she said with short spurts of breath as she lowered the lampstand. "I didn't mean to hit you. I was trying to protect the children. I could not make it to your chambers in time, so I came here instead."

A maidservant pointed down the hall, her face white with terror.

Nefertiti pushed past her and gathered her frightened daughters in her arms. "Get inside and barricade the door," she commanded.

Twenty of her servants made it inside the room and began placing furniture, decor, anything they could find in the girls' bedchambers against the door as Nefertiti wiped her daughters' tears.

"Momma!" they cried and wrapped their tiny fingers around anything they could get ahold of.

Maidservants rushed to the back of the room to get more furniture, but all of a sudden loud bangs came on the door and men yelled behind it, their voices filled with the demons of the afterlife. The servants used their bodies to push against the barricade as a mob tried to make their way inside.

"Make it stop!" Meketaten yelled, pressing her hands to her ears.

Nefertiti wrapped her hand around Meketaten's head and ear and kissed her shaven crown. "It will be all right, everything with be all right," she kept repeating, hoping, if anything, the rebels would at the very least spare her children. She had dreamt about this night for the past seven years, and now, right here, it was coming true.

Will we all die tonight? she asked herself, and prayed to Amun-Re to spare them. *We are doing this to restore Pharaoh's authority,* she pleaded. *Your divine embodiment, your appointed one, please do not let the rebels kill us! Keep Amenhotep safe!*

A spearhead burst through the top of the door, bringing her prayer to an end as her maidservants and her children screamed.

Aitye rushed to Nefertiti. "My Queen, let us hide the children."

She motioned them away from the door as a makeshift

sword penetrated its wooden frame. Aitye grabbed Meritaten and Meketaten, one in each arm, as Nefertiti held Ankhesenpaaten and they went farther back in the room. Aitye pushed a small table back with her foot and placed Meritaten and Meketaten behind it and squatted with them, hissing, "You must be quiet. You must not cry. You must not say a word. They will find you and kill you if you do. Do you understand? Not a word, not a tear, do you hear me?"

They nodded their heads and she wiped their last tears from their eyes.

Nefertiti handed Ankhesenpaaten to Aitye, who gently placed her in her sisters' arms. "Make sure she does not make noise, my children," she told the girls, and pushed the table back against the wall. She draped a sheet over it so no one could see them.

Aitye stood and looked around. There were no hiding places for a fully grown woman. Nefertiti had been looking around too when their eyes met. Aitye immediately dropped her head to the floor; she could not save her Queen. Nefertiti, scared and not wanting to die, tried to search quickly again, but then took in a deep breath and thought to herself, *A Queen wouldn't leave her people to die without her.*

Another makeshift sword—a kitchen knife tied to a longer piece of wood—burst through the door, this time nicking one of her servants on the arm. "Ah!" she cried out. The gap between the doorframe and the door grew and the maidservants ducked lower to avoid the blows through the door.

"Grab something to defend yourself," Nefertiti ordered as she grabbed a small tabletop stone statue of Ptah, praying to Ptah to forgive her for what she might do with it. Aitye grabbed a wooden toy. Others grabbed various items as makeshift weapons, and they all tensely waited until the mob broke into the room.

"Protect our Queen!" Aitye yelled as they burst in.

HER MAIDSERVANTS WERE NO MATCH FOR THE MEN WHO
came in.

A rebel found his way to Queen Nefertiti, knocked the
statue out of her hand, and raised his sword to strike. She
screamed in fright as her maidservants tried to protect her,
backing to the wall and grabbing desperately at a forgotten oil
stand to use in defense. The soldier raised his sword again
and brought it down, but his non-military-issued sword
caught between the bronze fork at the top and Nefertiti
twisted the oil lamp, spilling oil into his face and wrenching
the sword from his grasp.

Another rebel pushed against the crowd of scrambling
men and women, coming for Nefertiti, his eyes fixated on her.
Nefertiti heard her children whimpering, but knew they
would be safe if they would only be quiet. She scrambled to
find the statue that was knocked from her hand as the rebel
drew closer. Just as she found it, however, she was caught by
her waist and thrown to the ground.

"You pitiful pathetic waste of royalty!" the man screamed
at her.

He walked forward as she pulled herself backward, away
from him. Her hand gripped the statue harder, not knowing if
she should throw it or use it if he came closer. She noticed
the knife of his spear had been broken off—but a sharp,
broken piece of wood could still kill her.

"How dare you denounce Amun-Re!" he screamed. "You
will pay for your blasphemy!"

He aimed his stick at Nefertiti and tried to thrust it
toward her chest, but Aitye had thrown the wooden toy at his
head, knocking off his balance, and the wood stick barely

missed the Queen. Nefertiti grabbed the end of the stick, yanking it out of the rebel's hand, and beat him over the head with it fueled with the rage of knowing her children were scared and in danger.

When he was finally down, Nefertiti turned to see Aitye, forced to the ground with no weapon to defend herself, being choked and beaten by a rebel. Nefertiti took the stone statue and threw it at his head, and by the grace of Amun, hit him in his ear with enough force to knock him off of her.

Another rebel came up behind Nefertiti and was about to sink his sword into her back before General Paaten, seemingly appearing from nowhere, took him by the shoulder and spun him around.

"You would kill the Queen of Egypt?" General Paaten asked, punching him in the stomach and then the jaw. "There is no afterlife for those who kill the Pharaoh or his Queen!"

The soldier ripped a short dagger from his belt and swung it upward. The blade slid through the skin on General Paaten's shoulder and up to his lower jaw, past his cheek and up to his forehead. Seemingly unaffected by the flesh wound, General Paaten grabbed the soldier's wrist and broke it, sending the dagger to the ground. Twisting his arm, he forced the man to the floor, picked up the dagger, and in one fluid motion slit his throat.

Standing to face his queen with the soldier's blood on his hands, General Paaten slightly bowed in her presence.

"Thank you, General Paaten," Queen Nefertiti whispered to him. She gazed around: the Egyptian guards had taken over the room and pushed the enemy out into the hallway.

"My Queen, if I may be so bold to suggest that for your own safety, I transport you to a safe place," he quickly told her, yanking his sword free from where he had plunged its tip into another man's side.

"Yes, General," she told him, averting her eyes; her

adrenaline draining, she was suddenly afraid she may be overcome with sickness.

Merytre went to get the girls from their hiding place, tears streaming down their faces. Merytre told them, "Now, I want you to be good and close your eyes and do not open them until I tell you. Understood?"

Nefertiti stared at General Paaten and asked, "Where is Pharaoh? Is he safe?" She took Ankhesenpaaten in her arms, and with Merytre, who led Meritaten and Meketaten, followed him to the entrance of the room.

Aitye, lying on the floor, grabbed Nefertiti's foot. "Be safe, my Queen."

"Aitye," Queen Nefertiti whispered. "General Paaten, she is still alive. We must take her with us," she ordered, seeing the blood on her head.

"No, my Queen," Aitye whispered. "Leave me. Your life is more precious than mine."

Queen Nefertiti handed the baby to Merytre, stooped down, and wrapped one arm underneath Aitye's arm. "You gave yourself to save me. I will not leave you to be slaughtered."

General Paaten peered outside the room and told them, "The halls are empty. We must go now." He wrapped Aitye in one arm and led the company out into the hall.

A soldier came running up behind them. "General! General! Commander Horemheb sent his fastest soldiers here first, but the rest are swiftly coming. We have retaken the throne room. They are retreating!"

"That's great news!" Queen Nefertiti exclaimed.

"Soldier, take Queen Nefertiti and her maidservants to Pharaoh," General Paaten ordered. "Pharaoh fought bravely, my Queen, and was held for his safety in a back chamber. Please excuse me, my Queen, I must return to the battle." He bowed his head slightly to Queen Nefertiti.

"Go, great General Paaten, and win this for Am . . . for the Aten," she said, and bid him farewell. *I must remember the Aten is now the premier god—the Aten is where my supposed allegiance lies.*

She stared back at the bodies littering the floor in the room.

At least until the priesthood is destroyed, she thought.

***

THAT NIGHT, A SOLDIER, SENT FROM GENERAL PAATEN, came to Pharaoh in the back room, where he and his family were being held.

Out of breath, the soldier stammered out, "The enemy was pursued, slaughtered, and . . . and . . . now has . . . given up. Princess Nebetah and Fifth Prophet of Amun, Pawah, desire to . . . to come to . . . discuss a treaty." The soldier swallowed, finally regaining his breath. "I regret to also report that Ramose was killed in battle."

Pharaoh hung his head at the last message, but with a tight fist and a determination in his soul to not let Ramose and Huy die in vain, he said, "Let them come when the sun god Aten shows his face to us again. Tell Princess Nebetah and Fifth Prophet of Amun, Pawah, Pharaoh has only decided to discuss this treaty because Princess Nebetah is sister to Pharaoh and the daughter of the great royal wife, Queen Tiye. If it were any other, they would be brought in to be executed as traitors to Egypt."

"Tell them," Queen Nefertiti added, "that they must choose his words carefully."

As the messenger bowed to turn and go, he asked, "And what of those who surrendered?"

Pharaoh drew in a deep breath, but he knew he must uphold Egyptian law. "Allow them to commit suicide, as the law prescribes for those who take up arms against Pharaoh. But if they refuse . . . execute them."

Then Pharaoh sent the scrawny, breathless messenger away.

Queen Nefertiti made sure no one was looking before she touched his arm. *So much bloodshed,* she thought. *But he was right to uphold the law.*

Queen Tiye, sitting across from Nefertiti and Pharaoh, turned to Merytre, her own steward, Huya, and Kiya's steward, Ainamun, and said, "Restore Malkata. I want no sign of struggle inside of the palace by tomorrow. You have the authority to do whatever it takes." The stewards bowed and left to begin the repairs with an armed guard at their side.

Royal wife Kiya sat in the corner playing with Meritaten and Meketaten while Aitye, now bandaged but thankfully alive, held Ankhesenpaaten. There was no sign of Pharaoh's sister and royal wife Henuttaneb.

THE NEXT MORNING, PHARAOH AMENHOTEP, QUEEN Nefertiti, and Queen Tiye appeared in the throne room in all of their Egyptian glory: gold crowns, gold capes and robes and sashes, and gold-encrusted sandals. Fifty soldiers lined the throne room. General Paaten stood at the right hand of Queen Nefertiti. Master of Pharaoh's Horses, Ay, stood to the left hand of Queen Tiye.

Princess Nebetah and her husband, Fifth Prophet of Amun, Pawah, entered the throne room with pride, chins raised, giving an aura as tall as the columns holding the throne room up.

"You dare not bow before the great Pharaoh of Egypt and his Queen?" Commander Horemheb asked Princess Nebetah as they stood before the throne.

"No, we dare not," Princess Nebetah said through her teeth as she and Pawah kneeled before Pharaoh Amenhotep, Queen Tiye, and Queen Nefertiti.

Looking up to her brother, seated in all of his golden glory on the massive stone throne, she uttered a slow, reluctant string of words: "We, Princess Nebetah and Fifth Prophet of Amun, Pawah, come to ask for Pharaoh's mighty and life-giving forgiveness, and to respect the god of our father's beliefs. Allow us and those who wish to follow us, great King, to move North, and grant us lords there, so we may practice our worship of Amun-Re."

At this request, Queen Tiye's face grew red with embarrassment and anger for her daughter's words, and she almost spoke before Pharaoh. But when Pharaoh Amenhotep spoke, she held her tongue.

"Sister of Pharaoh . . . Pharaoh grants your pardon. But you ask for half the kingdom and to share Pharaoh's power as the sole ruler of the great nation of Egypt?"

Queen Tiye felt an immense expansion in her lungs and took a deep, satisfying breath at the way her son conducted himself on the throne.

He looked to his sister and her husband with narrowed eyes and wrinkled brow. "One could assume you ask for treason: a way to overtake Pharaoh's throne. Have not you already tried?"

"We did not try to overrule Pharaoh without the gods' blessings. We fought for the history of Egypt," Princess Nebetah defended. "We fought for Amun-Re."

"And clearly, Amun-Re was not with you. The link between the people and Amun-Re, the priesthood of Amun, died with the First Prophet of Amun, Meryptah, and the Second Prophet of Amun, Anen. The Aten was with Pharaoh and Pharaoh's order to name the Aten as the premier god of Egypt, for Pharaoh has put down your rebellion in one day!"

The echo of his voice resounded in the room.

"Therefore, the Aten has proven himself to be the premier god of Egypt, and Amun-Re has stepped down!"

"Amun-Re has *not*! He would not abandon us!"

Princess Nebetah stood up, annoyance at her big brother's words clear in her voice. General Paaten's men came toward her with their spears pointed down. She pretended not to see them.

"Declare the Aten as the premier god of Egypt, and Pharaoh will spare your lives," Pharaoh Amenhotep said.

Queen Nefertiti slightly jolted in her seat. *He wouldn't kill his own sister . . . ?* She strained to see his face in her peripheral vision but could not while she faced forward. *I can't turn to look or else I may undermine his authority,* she thought.

A long silence filled the space between Princess Nebetah's lips as she tried to read her brother's face to see if he was bluffing or not.

Pawah stood up next to her and bowed at the waist. "Great and mighty Pharaoh of Egypt, may you grant us an hour's time to make our decision?"

"Pharaoh grants your request—but you shall remain outside the throne room under supervision from the great Egyptian military," Pharaoh Amenhotep said.

"Thanks be to Pharaoh for his gracious patience," Pawah said with a bow, and he took Princess Nebetah, under escort by the Royal Guard and Commander Horemheb, out the doors.

Queen Tiye placed a warm hand on her son's arm. "You did a great job, my son. I could not have been more proud."

"Thank you, Mother. Your words mean more to me than you know." Amenhotep smiled, hesitant to ask a question that might break her pride for him, but he decided to ask anyway. *It is worth knowing,* he thought. "Mother, I have a question: why wasn't Nebetah told about our plan? All of this surely could have been avoided."

"She married Pawah, effectively making her a part of the Amun priesthood," Queen Tiye said as she sat back in her seat and shook her head. "As such, we couldn't tell her."

"Have you told the plan to reclaim the power of the Pharaoh to my sisters, Sitamun, Iset, and Henuttaneb?" he asked.

"Yes, and they did not like it, but said they would go along."

Pharaoh Amenhotep looked down and pressed his lips together. "Are we alone in this?"

"Not necessarily, but almost. Your father's council knows, including Commander Horemheb. General Paaten agrees to do whatever is best for Pharaoh and Egypt." She glanced at the General in the corner, and he nodded back. "We have his trust, and therefore the trust of the military."

"I assume we have your father's trust, as well?" Pharaoh Amenhotep asked, peering over to Nefertiti. She nodded, and he turned back to face his mother. "And Commander Horemheb?"

"He agreed . . . reluctantly," she said. "I believe we have his trust as an official of the Egyptian military, but we don't have his heart."

"I don't think we have anyone's heart," Nefertiti said. "When I was cornered yesterday, seeing the hate from the man who almost killed me . . ." She shook her head. "I don't want to die for something I don't believe in. I think we all have a reluctance about the entire plan."

"I am not reluctant. My heart is in my father's plan," Amenhotep said. *Because I believe in the Aten,* he thought, but instead he said, "I want power restored to Pharaoh. I will die for that."

"And your sister and her husband are willing to die to keep

137

Amun-Re as premier god," she retorted. "Will you put them to death if they don't declare the Aten as the premier god of Egypt?" Her heart raced in her chest as she waited for his answer.

"If they make me," Amenhotep said, his own heart racing.

"She is your sister!" Nefertiti said.

Queen Tiye put her hand up to silence both of them. "We have to make an example of them if they choose not to follow the Aten. We must show Pharaoh's power and might."

"If they die for Amun-Re, we will have made them martyrs for the people," Queen Nefertiti said.

"I say we have them executed as traitors. Martyrs they may be, but the people will be afraid nonetheless," Queen Tiye said.

"But she is your *daughter*," Nefertiti said, thinking of her own three precious girls.

"No daughter of mine would deny the command of her father, the Pharaoh of Egypt, be married in secret, refuse Pharaoh's resolution, accept judgment of exile, use Sitamun to safeguard her, and then bring bloodshed and death to the house of Pharaoh," Queen Tiye said. "She is an embarrassment and a shame to this family. I no longer call her my own."

Nefertiti saw that Queen Tiye's face was flushed and her ears burned red. "Queen Tiye . . . I mean no disrespect. But if we execute them, the people may be afraid, but it will only increase their motivation to rise up again. Will Commander Horemheb come as fast as he did last night to save us? Will General Paaten sustain more casualties for a cause he knows is not real?"

"It is real to some," Pharaoh Amenhotep said, hurt his wife would say such a thing when she knew how he felt about the Aten and Amun-Re.

General Paaten, who had approached them unexpectedly,

whispered, "Pharaoh, if I may be so bold to interrupt . . . the conversation being had is getting a little loud. Some may hear across the throne room." He nodded to several guards and servants who lined the opposite end.

"Thank you, General," Queen Tiye said with a most gracious nod of her head.

"General Paaten, what are your thoughts? Should we execute the princess and her husband?" Nefertiti asked, hoping his response and longstanding relationship with Queen Tiye would at least cause her to reconsider her stance.

"My Queen, it is not for me to decide. However, I may also present a reminder to Pharaoh that his father had exiled Princess Nebetah and her husband and was to enforce the exile should they ever leave the sanctuary of the chambers of Sitamun," he said with a bow.

I do remember that now, Amenhotep thought. It had slipped his mind. How could he forget? "Thank you, General, for your insight. Please leave Pharaoh to speak with the Queens."

"As Pharaoh wishes," the General said, and turned to go back to his corner.

"As great royal wife of the Pharaoh before"—Queen Tiye straightened her back to be slightly taller than Nefertiti—"I would advise we carry out the execution if they refuse the Aten."

"I agree," Pharaoh Amenhotep said.

Queen Nefertiti wanted to speak again, but it was already decided. There was nothing she could do.

Pharaoh Amenhotep looked to his wife and placed his hand on hers. "Do not worry. She will go with the Aten."

"And if she doesn't?" Queen Nefertiti said. "Are you ready to spill her blood?"

"If she wills me . . . yes," he said slowly. "I had to spill great a many man's blood yesterday when she and Pawah led their rebellion against the palace. Both of my viziers are dead. One more will not cause me to lose more sleep."

Queen Nefertiti nodded in response. "Pharaoh is right," she said, and sat back in her seat, her hands neatly placed on her knees, thinking, *I am not going to be a part of this execution if it does take place.*

Amenhotep could sense, from her sudden change to formality, that she did not agree, but it was what his mother wanted him to do. His years of working to obtain his mother's approval would not be in vain. He winced, thinking back to his father's final rejection of him. No, he would do whatever his mother asked of him.

"It is time," Pharaoh Amenhotep said, and the guards opened the door for Princess Nebetah and Fifth Prophet of Amun, Pawah, to be escorted back inside the throne room.

The guards threw them to their knees before Pharaoh and drew their spears, ready to take them to their execution.

Pharaoh Amenhotep held his hand up and spoke: "Princess Nebetah and Fifth Prophet of Amun, Pawah. You have committed a great crime against Pharaoh, and, thus, against Egypt. Only because of your relationship to Pharaoh have you been granted this single time of pardon; otherwise you would join the others in execution. They were allowed to commit suicide, but you, in your leadership of the rebellion, your confession of this great crime, will die by impalement in front of the temple of the Aten for all to see—unless you declare the Aten as the premier god of Egypt and swear to live the rest of your lives under his rays."

A smirk came across Nebetah's face, but Pawah held his grimace.

Nefertiti thought, *Impalement is on their minds—a very rare execution, mostly due to the fact that no one is brave enough to risk taking up arms against the state. Pawah doesn't want to die . . . but why is Nebetah smiling?*

A silence came over them, and Queen Tiye narrowed her eyes.

A haughty tone came out with Nebetah's first word: "Pharaoh." She gave a slight chuckle and a shake of her head.

Pawah put a hand over hers, breaking off what she was going to say momentarily.

She thinks Pharaoh is bluffing, Nefertiti realized. *He is not bluffing. How do I make her see that her life hangs in the balance?* She opened her mouth and said, "Choose your next words carefully, Princess Nebetah, for they might be your last."

Another long silence filled the room. Queen Nefertiti's words made Princess Nebetah question herself. They had never witnessed impalement, but that was the law. To sit a live criminal at the top of a sharp spike out in front of the temple of choice and add weights to the baskets tied to their hands and feet while they slowing sank down on the pole until it pierced their brain, only dying after hours of agony and blood loss. Usually, depending on the severity of their crime, their body would not be given a proper burial—and without their body, they could not have the option of entering eternal life.

My father sent us to exile in Nubia and was going to carry it out, Princess Nebetah thought. *Perhaps his son would carry out his threat, but this time, I cannot hide behind my eldest sister Sitamun.*

Pawah held two fears in his eyes—one to die and the possibility of not having eternal life, and the other to deny Amun-Re as the premier god of Egypt—but he nodded to her. He would die with her or live in blasphemy with her, whichever she chose.

As much bloodshed as she and her husband caused, I don't wish eternal punishment on them, Nefertiti thought.

Finally, Princess Nebetah spoke: "My brother, Pharaoh Amenhotep." Her tone was now much more respectful. "We will declare Aten as the premier god of Egypt. Please also pardon those who have not yet been forced to suicide for fighting against the order of Pharaoh, and let us go in peace."

A sad smile crept along Pharaoh Amenhotep's face. "Pharaoh will pardon you . . . but those who have fought alongside you must die. As a part of your punishment, their blood will be on your hands."

Princess Nebetah glared at her brother on his throne. "You would slaughter your own people?"

"Pharaoh carries out the law when certain people of Egypt commit crimes against Pharaoh and the state," Pharaoh Amenhotep replied to her question. "*You* led them. *You* incited them to action. *You* equipped them. *You* gave them orders to take up arms against Pharaoh!" Trying to maintain a cool head, he took a moment to pause. "You brought them to their deaths."

Princess Nebetah's and Pawah's nostrils flared as their jaws tightened.

" 'Tis your burden to bear. Take your husband. Pharaoh has spared him," Pharaoh said.

They only stayed kneeling and curled their hands into balls of fury at his words.

"You, Pharaoh's sister, and your prince, may go in peace," Pharaoh said at their silence. *Not even a thank-you,* he thought, and decided that perhaps General Paaten was right about enforcing his father's ruling.

Princess Nebetah and Fifth Prophet of Amun, Pawah, stood and began to turn and walk out of the throne room.

Pharaoh found General Paaten's eyes and nodded slightly. He motioned to his soldiers, and they surrounded Nebetah and Pawah.

Princess Nebetah turned back to him. "What does Pharaoh wish now?"

"The Pharaoh before sentenced you both to exile for

refusing to obey his command. You have stepped away from your place of sanctuary," Pharaoh Amenhotep said.

"Brother, you wouldn't!" Princess Nebetah screamed.

Disgusted at the lack of respect, Queen Tiye slowly stood up and took a step to stand beside her son to show her utter disownment of Princess Nebetah.

"Because you, Princess Nebetah, and you, Fifth Prophet of Amun, Pawah, have violated the terms of your sanctuary, Pharaoh now enforces the punishment of the Pharaoh before to be carried out. You are hereby exiled to Nubia," Pharaoh Amenhotep said. "Thus Pharaoh says."

Princess Nebetah yelled and thrashed about when the soldiers grabbed them to take them to Nubia. "Brother!" she said, and pointed at him, eyes red and angry.

Queen Tiye spoke sharply, before she could say any more, "Pharaoh's grace will not be extended a second time."

Princess Nebetah yanked her hand back to her side and stormed out of the throne room, her husband following her. She glanced behind her shoulder, and her glare pierced through the throne room to her brother, Pharaoh Amenhotep. She would take everything most valuable to him if it was the last thing she did.

CHAPTER 14
THE TIME OF AKETATEN

"Pharaoh, I come with great news. The city for the Aten has been completed, as well as the palace for the royal family," the messenger said after he had paid respects to the ruler of Egypt. "The chief architect and engineers perfected every corner of the city."

I will finally get my own throne room with an open roof, Father, Amenhotep thought. "As Pharaoh has built this city for the Aten to rise above Egypt, the name of the new city will be Aketaten: 'the horizon of the Aten.' Prepare to move the royal family to the new city of Aten."

That night, Queen Nefertiti and Pharaoh Amenhotep lay by each other's sides, circling their fingers over each other's bare chests. "We will be in a new home soon," she said.

"*Our* new home," he responded, losing himself in her newly bathed scent of lotus blossom. "Our home . . . without a roof on the throne room, and many courtyards and open temples to praise the Aten."

"The Aten . . ." Nefertiti hummed. She closed her eyes, not wanting Amenhotep to see her inner turmoil raging inside of her mind. *Amenhotep's belief in the Aten,* she thought, *outweighs his belief in Amun-Re, but even though it is heresy, his belief keeps him loyal to me. One day, we will have to go back to Amun-Re as his father planned, and on that day, I may lose him to Kiya or another wife he brings into our marriage bed.*

His warm hand on her pregnant belly and his breath on her chest made her smile. She was his and his alone. He was hers and hers alone . . . for now. She knew in his mind, he needed his marriage to be this way, as the Aten was the one true god. She often wondered how far he would go, pushing the Aten on his people. *Perhaps Thutmose would have been a better Pharaoh for this task. In some ways, handing the throne to Amenhotep and telling him to turn Egypt to the Aten for a time is like handing a thief a temporary free pardon to steal whatever he wants. Will he turn in his temporary pardon when it comes due?* she asked herself as she half noticed Amenhotep whispering to their child.

"You will be a great child of mine, a great testament to your mother and me. I have prayed to the Aten that you are a boy, a son of whom I will be proud, no matter your skill or ability. I will be proud of my sons—*all* of the sons I will have —just as I love all of my daughters, your sisters: Meritaten, Meketaten, and Ankhesenpaaten, and all of the daughters I will have," Amenhotep said, and kissed the side of her belly, then came back to kiss the full lips of his wife.

"Will you still love me, only me, if we have another baby girl?" Nefertiti asked.

"Yes, my love, I will. Our daughters only surround me with more beauty than I could ever imagine—all blessings from the great Aten," he said as his fingers outlined her high cheekbones. "I will only ever love you."

"As there is only one premier god of Pharaoh," she said.

"There will only be one lover of him as well," he finished her sentence, and Nefertiti's mind rested for the evening.

———

THAT YEAR, THEY MOVED TO AKETATEN, THE CITY OF Aten, and with their move, the capital of Egypt also moved. Pharaoh declared no other temples to any other gods were to be built in the Aten's city, as he increasingly sat and stood and prayed in the open-roofed temples and courtyards of his new home. He continuously gathered new visions from the Aten, and all seemed well in the affairs of the state.

But one day, his newly appointed vizier of Egypt, Nakht, came bearing bad news.

"Pharaoh," he said with a bow; he held a scroll in his hand as he walked into the council room, built according to Pharaoh Amenhotep's demands. A few rays of Aten flowed into the room from the sky, and they surrounded Pharaoh's chair.

Ay followed Nakht, as well as General Paaten. "Sister, great royal wife Tiye," Ay said with a slight bow in her direction. "Daughter, chief royal wife Nefertiti," he said with a smile and another bow.

Nefertiti responded with a slight chuckle. *My father bowing to me . . . I will never get used to it,* she thought.

Nakht sat at the table with them and rolled out the scroll.

"Good news?" Tiye asked.

Nakht did not say anything at first, only shook his head, and Nefertiti's heart dropped into her stomach. *Oh no,* she thought. "What is wrong?" she asked.

"Even with the declaration of the Aten as the premier god

of Egypt and the completion of Aketaten, Satau reports the priesthood of Amun still collects sixty-eight percent of Egypt's gold in this past year." Nakht shook his head as he double-tapped the last figure of Satau's calculations on the papyrus.

"Well, at least it is decreasing," General Paaten said with a half grin.

"Not by enough." Queen Tiye closed her eyes and brought her forefinger and thumb to her forehead. Her eyes popped open as Nakht began to speak.

"The Amun priesthood, even with the proceeds from the tax for Akhenaten and the rate of decrease in their share, will overtake Pharaoh in just three years."

"So we must do more to remove the amount people give to the priesthood?" Amenhotep asked for clarification as he sat on the edge of his seat.

Ay nodded his head. "Yes. We must also increase the power of the state as well."

General Paaten sighed at Amenhotep's confused stare. "What Ay means by that, my Pharaoh, is our military has become lax after the rebellion. Many feel it was unnecessary bloodshed, and therefore they do their duty but they do not do it with passion."

"If I changed my name to honor the Aten instead of Amun, would it persuade the people to the Aten and put the passion back into our armed forces?" Pharaoh asked with a hunger in his eyes.

"It may, depending on the current state of Pharaoh's power against the priesthood," Ay said. "But then again, the priesthood of Amun garnered a rebellion against Pharaoh last year as well."

Nakht put his elbows on the table. "I did not want to bring this up now, but the two percent decrease was to fund the rebellion. Per Satau, they hid the expense in their records as 'benevolence to Amun's followers.' The people have not stopped giving to the temples of Amun."

"The priesthood of Amun funded the rebellion? They should all be allowed to commit suicide, then, just as the men who raised arms against Pharaoh!" Amenhotep stood and hit the table with a clenched fist.

"I agree, but they hid the expense well, and they will be able to justify the expenditure, as the expedient construction to Aketaten left many builders who refused to travel out of a job," Nakht said. "I have already spoken with First Prophet of Amun, Maya, and Second Prophet of Amun, Sitmun, who both swear on their lives the money went to help Amun's followers in their time of need."

General Paaten snorted and shook his head. "Their time of need," he muttered under his breath.

"They persuade people with money," Queen Tiye said, and shook her head, whispering, "the hypocrites." Priests were to keep only what was needed and give the rest to Amun-Re or back to the followers as a form of blessings, but there had not been a "benevolence" record in ages, and the priests lived mightily well.

"We have not changed anything," Nefertiti whispered. "Has this all been in vain?"

"No, daughter," Ay said. "We need to restore the power of Pharaoh," Ay said.

Nakht felt the eyes turn to him, and he let out the breath he was holding. "I cannot advise on further actions. Pharaoh must inspire the people to lessen or stop their contributions to Amun, and currently, based on these records, it has not happened."

"I will outlaw the worship of Amun-Re," Pharaoh Amenhotep said. "Our problem will be solved."

"We may incite another rebellion," Nefertiti said as she looked to General Paaten in the corner. His unsightly scar from his chest to his eyebrow made her close her eyes and secretly thank Amun-Re the scar was not her own. The memories of almost having a spear through her heart made her shudder, and the baby kicked inside her womb. Swallowing the lump in her throat, she realized all were staring at her.

"Are you well, child?" Queen Tiye asked her. "Your brow is beaded with sweat. It came about so suddenly."

"Yes, I . . . I am fine. Just reminding myself of the last time we . . ." she said, trailing off, and thought, *the last time we were heretics.*

"It will not happen again," Pharaoh Amenhotep said, and looked to General Paaten, who nodded in return. "The Egyptian army will remain by our side. Nakht, how much time will we need, if we outlaw the worship of Amun-Re, to deplete the priesthood's treasury?"

The vizier scribbled some notes and looked up. "Pharaoh, I am not the treasurer, but according to my calculations, to completely dissolve their treasury . . . and if they receive nothing more today forward . . . their treasury will be depleted in thirteen years. But we do not need to completely deplete their treasury—it is still the priesthood of our true premier god, Amun-Re, lest we forget. We only need to dissolve it enough so that Pharaoh's treasury is much greater, to show the people of Egypt that Pharaoh has more authority than the priesthood."

"And what better way to make Pharaoh forever and always more powerful than to deplete the priesthood's treasury? And then give them a portion of the state's treasury to regain their standing in the people's eyes?" The Aten's rays surrounded Pharaoh Amenhotep as he spoke. "If they accept the state's gift, it will be ultimate humiliation in the eyes of the people, and Pharaoh will then have proved his power over the priesthood."

Father would be proud of me for thinking of this plan, he thought as he looked to the semi-open ceiling of the room, soaking in the rays of the Aten. Despite his initial desires, Ay had talked him into only a partial opening in the council room, so the rays only shone on his seat, to portray his divine link to the Aten, but with the partially closed roof, passersby in the hallway would have a harder time hearing their conversations.

"Yes, son, but thirteen years? By then, the people may grow to hate you," Queen Tiye said, clasping her hands together.

"They may hate me, but they will also fear me for my power," Pharaoh Amenhotep said.

He could feel the rays of the Aten intensify upon his skin, as if guiding him to know this was what he was to do. He could barely make out the others in the room from the sun's rays falling through his eyelashes and reflecting from his nose and cheeks. At his mother's silence, he spoke as he stood and widened his arms upward towards the Aten.

"Is this not what you wanted, Mother? Is this not what Father wanted? The father who thought his son who bore his name could not do? And yet, even in his death, foretold me I would not be the Pharaoh my brother would have been? Yet it is still for me to wonder, would Thutmose have lived up to the expectations of our father? For the people of Egypt to know the power of Pharaoh? To prove the power of Pharaoh over all, including the priesthood of Amun-Re? Have I not done this by declaring the Aten as the premier god of Egypt, by committing to execution those who took up arms against Pharaoh's house, and exiling your own daughter and her husband? Have I not?"

His hands dropped to his sides.

"And yet, the priesthood still *gains*! The priesthood will

continue to gain . . . unless we bring them to the brink of death and then resurrect what is left."

The Aten had given him the words. The Aten had given him the strength. He felt at one with the Aten, drenched in his rays, sweat streaming down his back as if the Aten poured his blessings upon him. The Aten, the sum of all the Pharaohs before, was proud of him, and yet he still fell short of expectation, just as he had always fell short of expectation. He would please his father, and his fathers before him. He would please the Aten and finally prove to his father that he was worthy to be called Pharaoh's son, a son of the Aten.

Nefertiti's body clung to her chair. Never had she witnessed such a presentation of strength and eloquence of speech from Amenhotep. In some ways it made her desire him, yet in others it made her fear him.

Queen Tiye's mouth hung ajar. She had seen it with her own eyes: her son's transformation under the Aten. Now she believed it was complete, and she said a prayer to the Aten, thanking him for healing her son.

Ay and General Paaten said nothing—as who is to argue with the Pharaoh?

At the room's silence, Amenhotep said, in the voice given to him by the Aten, "Thus it be: tomorrow when the Aten is at the top of the sky, Pharaoh will declare that the name Amenhotep, 'Amun is satisfied,' is no more . . . only Pharaoh Akhenaten—'the living spirt of Aten'—remains.

"Pharaoh's Queen Nefertiti will no longer exist . . . only Pharaoh's Queen Neferneferuaten-Nefertiti—'perfect are the perfections of Aten.'

"We alone will mediate between the people of Egypt and the Aten. Worship of any god except the Aten will be punishable by one hundred lashes and a fine to Pharaoh. We will restore power to the throne of Pharaoh. We will give Egypt to the greatness the Aten has declared for her!"

CHAPTER 15
THE TIME OF CHANGE

"It's a baby girl, my Queen," Aitye told Nefertiti as she pulled the wooden stick from her Queen's mouth.

Nefertiti could feel the despair of that word—*girl*—deep within her aching belly and tired back.

Aitye brought the water to her forehead and gently wiped the sweat from her brow. "Another beautiful baby girl," Aitye said as she admired the crying baby in the arms of the midwife.

Nefertiti wanted to slap Aitye in her face, but the strength to do so escaped her. Instead she muttered, "That makes four daughters, but no sons for Amenhotep." She shook her head in bitter denial.

"Pharaoh Akhenaten, my Queen," Aitye whispered, ducking her head so no one else would hear.

The desire to slap her again washed over Nefertiti, but she felt herself lose balance squatted above the birthing pot. A myriad of arms caught her as she fell, and she gave into their embrace. The messenger went to tell the Pharaoh of his daughter, but Nefertiti stopped him. "Do not tell Pharaoh he has a daughter. Tell him he has a child," she said.

"As you wish"—he inhaled to say her new long royal name in one breath—"Queen Neferneferuaten-Nefertiti."

Nefertiti rolled her eyes at her new bestowed name from her husband, but bit her lip and turned away from the messenger turning to leave. "Aitye, come near me," she said, taking many breaths as they continued to prop her up on her cot.

"Yes, my Queen?"

"Bring my daughter here."

Aitye went to the baby girl, who was being cleaned by the wet nurse, wrapped her tightly, and handed the bundle to Nefertiti, smiling. "She is a beautiful one. She looks like you, my Queen."

Nefertiti looked at her new daughter and began to cry. She missed Waset, Malkata, her father, her husband, and the name her mother gave her. Now, she held another daughter.

"What is wrong, my Queen?" Aitye asked.

She slapped her away as the messenger re-entered. Nefertiti was hoping to hear Amenhotep's voice, but only the messenger's came: "Pharaoh Akhenaten will come see his daughter after he has finished worshiping. Pharaoh says the Aten is giving him a vision."

"Cursed! Did I not tell you to say 'child,' not 'daughter'?" Nefertiti yelled at the poor man.

"My Queen," he said with a bow. "I did say 'child.' Pharaoh said the Aten gave him the knowledge to know he would have a daughter."

At this, she cried even harder. The Aten gave him a vision! Of course! Even the gods knew she was cursed to only have daughters. Aitye tried to comfort her, but Nefertiti just held the baby close to her heart and pushed Aitye away. "Leave! Leave me!" she cried, and all left except Aitye, who knelt next to her where her husband should have been.

The greater of the day passed, and Nefertiti refused to let

the wet nurse take the child. The baby's cries were incessant, and the wet nurse finally coached Nefertiti how to feed her own child. Nefertiti sucked in a quick breath, and a spontaneous laugh thrust from her lungs. The closeness, the connection to her daughter, caused her heart to race.

"Why?" she asked the wet nurse. "Why did you not do this for me with my other daughters? This feeling," she said as she watched her baby girl drink her milk, "is like one I have never felt before."

"The breasts get sore, my Queen, and sometimes the nipple splits, causing much pain. It is a diligent labor, unbefitting work of a queen or noblewoman. But whatever my Queen wishes, so it will be done."

And so Nefertiti wished for the baby to remain with her for the night and dismissed the wet nurse. She lay in bed holding her daughter, now sleeping. Lost in her thoughts, tears welling in her eyes, Nefertiti summoned her head steward.

"Merytre, I request royal wife Kiya's presence," she said, and Merytre left to carry the request.

As Kiya entered the room and Ainamun closed the door behind her, leaving the two royal women of Egypt and the new princess alone, she smiled.

"Kiya!" Nefertiti whispered with a deep breath. She needed to talk to someone. Her father was not in Aketaten but rather in Saqqara, attending the burial of a priest of Ptah, and so she needed her friend. "Kiya," Nefertiti said again and extended her hand.

Kiya grabbed it and sat beside her on the bed. "May I?" she asked, and Nefertiti extended the baby girl to her. "She is beautiful," she said, admiring the girl's soft lips and cheeks.

"He still hasn't come to see her," Nefertiti said, more tears welling in her eyes.

"Who?" Kiya said, preoccupied with the baby's face.

"Pharaoh Amenhotep . . . Akhenaten." She sighed. *Why can't I just stay Nefertiti and he just stay Amenhotep—at least in the palace or when we are alone?* she wondered. It would make no difference there.

Kiya looked up at her with a gaping mouth. "He has not come? Why?"

"Before we moved here, he promised me he would love me and only me, even if I had another daughter," Nefertiti began. "But once we moved here . . . I'm just not sure anymore. He is different. He won't even let me call him Amenhotep anymore—everything must be addressed to Pharaoh Akhenaten. This place . . . it has a hold over him."

"I don't understand, Neferneferuaten-Nefertiti," Kiya said.

"Oh Kiya! Don't call me that name. Please call me Nefertiti." The Queen slapped the bed. "I hate that name," she said under her breath.

Kiya nodded in return, feeling her friend's frustration.

Shaking her head and looking to the ceiling, Nefertiti clenched her jaw. "He believes in the Aten, you know. He believes the Aten is the only god of Egypt."

"Yes, it looks that way by the recent commands he has given," Kiya said, shrugging her shoulders. "So what if he believes it? Is it a crime?"

"Egypt has many gods, and Amun-Re is the premier god," Nefertiti said. "But he is the only one who believes otherwise. This place . . . he has spent nearly every hour of daylight in the sun, under the Aten. He claims the Aten gives him visions. He had a vision of this place. He had a vision of his daughter. He had a vision for Egypt. He had a vision for his future son . . . he has a vision for everything. He isn't the same person I married, Kiya. He is different. He speaks differently. He feels empowered by the sun, by the Aten. He has been by my side for every birth except this one, and why?

Because he was praying to the Aten. He has been praying to the Aten all day. It is night now, but I'm sure he is out praying to the Aten to show his face again, like he has been doing the past weeks—nay, *months*. I don't feel as important to him as I did once," she confessed. "He has found another love . . . the Aten . . . and soon, it will spread to you and Henuttaneb and other wives he'll take."

Kiya placed a hand on her thigh as she shifted the newborn into one arm. "No. If it is with the Aten, he won't want Henuttaneb or myself. How can we compare with a god?" Kiya smiled, nodding at the Queen, trying to be reassuring.

Nefertiti only shook her head. "Because, now, with another daughter, I'm afraid the Aten will give him a vision to be with *you* so you can give him a son. Amenhotep . . . I mean, Akhenaten, thinks he is one with the Aten, and it gives him a new courage to go beyond what he thought he was capable of."

"He will not go beyond you, Nefertiti. And as I promised you—if he tries, I will say no."

"You would go against Pharaoh, who may exile you for refusing his command?" Nefertiti asked with a raised eyebrow. *She* wouldn't risk a life of destitution to go against Pharaoh; how could Kiya?

"For you, I would," Kiya said.

Her words caused Nefertiti's cheeks to blush at her own selfishness.

"I made you a promise, and I intend to keep it. You are the chief royal wife, and you should bear the next heir to Egypt—not me, a rejected princess from Mitanni."

"You are truly a woman of nobility." Nefertiti smiled. "And I thank you."

"Nefertiti, it may be out of line for me to speak what I am about to say, but I have some advice that may help."

"Kiya, you will never be out of line with me. You are my friend."

Kiya smiled and continued. "If Pharaoh Akhenaten is not the man you married, and you are afraid of losing him, maybe it would be best to start being with him. If he is out praying to the Aten to show his face again at night, then join him. Not now, of course, but once you heal."

"I know you don't understand the intricacies of Egypt's religion, Kiya, but if I am seen worshiping the Aten after Pharaoh's decrees, the world will assume I also believe it." Nefertiti's chin dropped. "I won't do it."

Kiya's eyes opened wide. "Don't you *want* the world to believe it? If not, are you not undermining Pharaoh's power to make decrees?"

Nefertiti opened her mouth, but her mind could not formulate a response. *Of course, she is right . . . but I don't want to.*

"When he is out worshiping the Aten, join him. Take your children with you to show him you and your children are just as important to him as the Aten. I will sit at the edge of the temple or the courtyard and paint the picture for the sculptures and records keepers to chisel into the rock so the world may forever know the love you had for each other."

"Or forever know we were heretics," Nefertiti said, crossing her arms.

Kiya placed the baby in Nefertiti's arms. She scooted next to Nefertiti's side, both of their backs against the headboard. "No . . . I think the world will see the love, my Queen. In a time where Pharaohs and men of noble stature have many wives, and many children from those wives, and he, Pharaoh Akhenaten—or if he goes back to Amenhotep one day—only loved one wife and only had children with one wife, especially after four daughters . . . I think the world will see how much you and your daughters mean to him."

"Thank you, Kiya," Nefertiti said, tears falling from her eyes.

Kiya gave her a much-needed hug and kissed her forehead.

A servant opened the bedchambers door and escorted the Pharaoh inside.

"Ah! The Aten has blessed Pharaoh with three lovely women in his bed! The Great of Praises, Neferneferuaten-Nefertiti, the Beloved of the King, Kiya, and my newest daughter, Princess of Egypt!"

"Pharaoh Akhenaten," Kiya said as she stood up and bowed. She turned to look at Nefertiti and bowed to her as well. "It is late, and I shall retire for the evening. Bless the night to you both." She turned and left with the servant.

"My beautiful Queen!" Pharaoh said, and walked to her with his arms raised. "And my stunning new daughter!" He lifted the baby girl from her mother, high into the air and back into his arms again. "She looks entirely as her mother does." He buried his head into the baby's chest. "Your sisters will be jealous," he whispered, "for they take some after me."

"I missed you this morning," Nefertiti said. "You are usually by my side when our children are born . . . or you have come right away in times past."

"My love," he said, turning to face her, and shrugged his shoulders. "I was with the Aten! He has given me a vision that one day I will have a son."

"We will have a son?" Nefertiti asked, hoping she was in the vision, yet still wondering if he saw another woman as the mother of his son.

"Who else would it be but you, my love?" He bent to kiss her, but also to hide his expression as he thought, *I do not want to admit I did not see who the mother was in the vision. It was only of my son and me.*

But Nefertiti took what she wanted to hear and peace grew in her heart. "Amenhotep," she said softly.

"My name is now Akhenaten," he said in a firm voice. "You will call me Akhenaten."

Nefertiti shook her head and let out a huff. "I thought your re-naming conventions were to show the people of Egypt we belong to the Aten. Are we changing our names in moments like these as well?"

"Thus Pharaoh says."

His back was to her, so she lifted her head and hands in prayer to Amun-Re to give her patience. She folded her hands in her lap, deciding to give Kiya's suggestion a try. Perhaps she could coax him back to her by indulging in his obsessions for a while. "Well, then, Akhenaten, when I have my strength back, I would like to join you in the temple if you would have me."

"You want to join me in the temple and worship the Aten?" he repeated, spinning around and almost dropping the baby in his haste.

Nefertiti lunged forward to catch her daughter, but he held on to her and pressed her close to his neck. She looked up and said, "Yes, if you will have me."

"Praise the Aten! I have prayed for this day to come! My beautiful wife to join me in my daily worship!" He grabbed her hand and kissed it all the way up her arm and to her lips. The baby girl's face contorted in screaming silence.

Giggling, Nefertiti wrapped her arms around his neck and slowly kissed him back. *Maybe Kiya was right,* she thought. *Just for a time. I will still worship Amun-Re, though—in my mind, since he has outlawed all other gods but the Aten.* She stroked her baby's head until the wrinkles disappeared and peace rested on her face.

He raised their daughter between them and asked, "Have you decided on a name?"

"I was waiting for you to come to see her."

"The Aten did not give me a vision for the name of the child. However, as I see that she looks like you in every way, we should name her . . . Neferneferuaten Tasherit—your younger, your junior."

"You would name a child after me?" Nefertiti asked, honored and touched, her hand to her heart—even though *Nefertiti* Tasherit would have been just fine with her.

"Why would I not? When this daughter of mine possesses all of the beauty of my wife!"

"I love you, Am . . . Akhenaten," she whispered. "Whatever your name, I will always love you."

The wet nurse had brought in a small bed for the newborn, since Nefertiti had wanted her through the night, and Akhenaten placed Neferneferuaten Tasherit, now asleep, in the bed. He came to his wife.

"You were brave today without me there with you," he said as he rubbed her shoulders. "I wanted to be there with you, but the Aten was gracing me with his presence."

"I know, my love," she said, and kissed his hand.

He brushed his leg against hers and pulled her backward into bed. Holding her waist as they lay on their sides facing each other, he said, "I love you, my Queen Neferneferuaten-Nefertiti."

Perhaps in his own way, he does love me. Her eyes closed, and after a long day, she fell asleep.

CHAPTER 16
THE TIME OF DECLINE

"Pharaoh Akhenaten."

The messenger bowed before the straight-backed Pharaoh seated in all of his golden glory, shimmering underneath the rays of the Aten. Most could not look at him because the glory that surrounded him shone so brightly, and the messenger kept his eyes closed as he looked to the Pharaoh. It had been a year since Neferneferuaten Tasherit was born, and, much to Nefertiti's despair, Pharaoh's delusions had only become more intense.

"Speak, messenger," he commanded.

"Word has been sent from Master of Pharaoh's Horses, Ay, in Waset, and from vizier Nakht, in Men-nefer. The lashes are numbering close to a million and each city has collected two years worth of taxes in these fines alone since the Pharaoh's edict was carried out: worship of any god except the Aten shall be punished by one hundred lashes and a fine to the Aten."

Two years means we can turn Egypt back to Amun-Re more quickly now, Nefertiti thought—but Pharaoh focused on the first part of the message.

"One million lashes in the past year." Pharaoh pressed his lips together. He lifted his face toward the sky in his roofless throne room and began to pray to the Aten as his great heat fell upon his face. "Oh great sun-disc in the sky, the great and all-seeing Aten . . . the people continue to worship Amun-Re. How shall you wish, O great Aten, for Pharaoh to proceed?" He forced his eyes to remain open to receive the Aten's visions as he stared into the blinding sunlight.

The reflection from his golden collar reflected the light back underneath his jaw, and Pharaoh Akhenaten imagined what he looked like to those in the throne room and knew they believed he was the Aten's chosen link to the people.

Closing his eyes and dropping his head just as a cloud passed by overhead, he announced, "The great and glorious Aten has given me a vision." Opening his eyes, he could see nothing but blurry objects, and the vision came to him in that blur. With a long face, he stayed quiet until the rays of the Aten were on his shoulders once again. "Thus was the vision from the Aten: General Paaten, Master of Pharaoh's Horses, Ay, and Commander Horemheb will send the military through the streets of Waset and Men-nefer to destroy the statues of Amun and overturn the worship sites. The people will not find a place to worship Amun in all of Egypt to spare their lashes."

The people will love me now that I have removed their temptation, he thought.

Queen Nefertiti and Queen Tiye sat silent, theirs jaws tightening and their shoulders rising to their necks.

"Thus Pharaoh says," he ended, and stood with his arms outstretched. "Thus the *Aten* says."

Queen Nefertiti tried to garner a look from Queen Tiye as shallow breaths made their way out of her nostrils. *What is he doing?* she thought. *We will now more than ever have another rebellion, if not an assassination. What of our children? Is he thinking about our children? Why won't Queen Tiye say anything, do anything?*

Her unborn baby kicked her hard and she bent forward from the pain. *Not you too,* she thought as she regained her breath. *You are to worship Amun-Re with the rest of Egypt.* Her mind drifted to her four daughters who had been worshiping with their father in the temples to the Aten. She had tried to teach them about Amun-Re, but Akhenaten had found her one day and threatened to give her one hundred lashes as well. Her poor children were growing up in the world of the Aten, and it frightened her for their afterlives. She could only hope and pray to Amun-Re that one day she could turn her husband's mind around; she feared all the more, however, that his mind was too far gone.

Another messenger came from Waset and was next in line to speak. Pharaoh took his seat, not noticing the tension held in his wife's and mother's stature.

"Pharaoh Akhenaten, I come with a message from Treasurer of Egypt, Satau, and Master of Pharaoh's Horses, Ay," the messenger said.

"Messenger, speak the message," Pharaoh Akhenaten said.

"There are significant gaps in the fines given and the monies received throughout the territories. They believe the officials are taking a share of the fines."

"Pharaoh believes he should ask the Aten to know if this is true." And so saying, he raised his face to the Aten and prayed, "O great Aten, what shall you wish Pharaoh to do with those who take from you?" Dizzy from the sun, he rolled his head around on his shoulders and dropped his chin to his chest, the gold still reflected in his eyes. "Even though Pharaoh does not look into your face, O great Aten, you give another vision still! Pharaoh is grateful for your presence!"

He looked at the messenger and said, "The Aten does not wish for Pharaoh to do anything, for the officials are carrying out his deeds, and so they shall be allowed to take what they need."

The messenger bowed and bravely said, "Master of Pharaoh's Horses, Ay, believes there is corruption in the ranks of the officials."

"No, the Aten would not allow corruption. The officials are taking what they need—thus said the Aten! Do you dare call the Aten a liar?!" he bellowed.

"No, Pharaoh," the messenger trembled.

"Thus Pharaoh says," Pharaoh Akhenaten said. "Thus the Aten says."

The messenger stayed bowed, beads of sweat falling down his face. The sun shone brightly in the throne room. "Pharaoh Akhenaten . . . one more message from the Master of Pharaoh's Horses, Ay."

"Speak the message."

"Since the close of the temples of Amun-Re and the outlaw of worship of any god except the Aten, the Egyptian people go hungry, as a significant number of jobs were lost with the edict. Ay requests Pharaoh and his council to meet to determine how to provide surrogate jobs for the many artisans, priests, traders, and other professions who can no longer provide food for their families."

"They shall work for the Aten," Pharaoh said with a chuckle, not sure why Ay wanted a meeting to discuss a very simple solution. "The artisans who sculpted for Ptah, Amun-Re, Bes, Isis, and the others will now sculpt for the Aten. The priests shall now be the local priests for the Aten, and they must come to Pharaoh to understand and interpret the gifts of Aten, for Pharaoh alone is the divine one of the Aten. However, the priests for Amun-Re shall never be priests for the Aten unless they declare the Aten the premier god of Egypt and come to Pharaoh and ask for their due."

Pharaoh Akhenaten smiled. *My father would be so proud of*

the Pharaoh I have become. I have kept the position of Pharaoh with its formality, and I have made the priesthood of Amun-Re nothing. You hear, Father? I alone have done this with the Aten, not Amun-Re! Thutmose could not have done this! I did this, not you!

Still smiling, he said, "Thus Pharaoh says. Thus the Aten says. Tell Master of Pharaoh's Horses, Ay, that no meeting of council will be needed."

The intense pain in Nefertiti's abdomen came again, and she leaned forward suddenly. "Pharaoh," she said, wincing, and began to suck in breaths.

"Yes, Queen Neferneferuaten-Nefertiti?" He turned to look at her. A wave of familiarity crossed his face and for a slight moment, Nefertiti thought she saw Amenhotep behind all of the golden splendor—but then it was gone as he commanded a maidservant to assist her to her chambers. He stayed on his throne and looked forward, not watching his nine-month-pregnant wife leave to give birth to his child.

Nefertiti held back her tears until she reached the midwives, and then the intense pains came back and she nearly toppled over. A watery substance ran down her leg and they began the preparations. Her mind reeled, not focused on the intense pain but rather thinking, *Amenhotep would have come with me . . . but Akhenaten sits on his throne ignoring the people's pleas for faith and food.*

NEFERTITI FELL BACK INTO THE ARMS OF HER MAIDSERVANTS and they laid her on the cot next to the birthing pot. The maidservants loudly prayed to the Aten to protect the new child and the Queen from the evil spirits.

Aitye, kneeling beside Nefertiti, dabbed the sweat from her master's brow, afraid to tell her the sex of the child.

Nefertiti moaned: her energy drained, her mouth dry and pasty, her head throbbing. "Aitye," she whispered.

"Yes, my Queen," Aitye said, taking her hand.

"Do I have a son?"

"My Queen needs to regain her strength," Aitye said, and had another maidservant begin to fan the Queen as she dipped her rag into the water again and dab around her neck and chest. "Rest for now."

"No, Aitye. *Do I have a son?*" Nefertiti asked with a more rigor.

"My Queen has given birth to a beautiful baby girl."

Nefertiti only stared back at her servant and then looked to the ceiling as Aitye continued to dab water on her neck. The slight breeze from the servant girl's fan cooled the warm water on her body. She closed her eyes and clenched her teeth. The cool water felt good after so much sun. *Yes, the water is so refreshing,* she thought as the breeze cooled the water droplets on her forehead. *Amenhotep said he would love all of his daughters, but Akhenaten had a vision of a son. I will have a son, he saw the vision of me with his son. I should not worry about this daughter.*

She opened her eyes as her maidservants propped her up. "Aitye, bring my daughter."

"Yes, my Queen," Aitye said, and brought the newborn to her.

"Again," Nefertiti whispered, "a beautiful baby girl."

The messenger asked her, "Queen Neferneferuaten-Nefertiti, what message should I bring to Pharaoh?"

"Tell Pharaoh he now has five daughters."

There is no use in hiding the fact she is another daughter. He pledged his love to her and promised there would only be one lover of Pharaoh, just as the Aten is the one god of Egypt. I have nothing to worry about, she thought, but in the back of her mind, she was afraid of this new Akhenaten and what visions he might receive from the Aten.

The messenger bowed and left. He swiftly returned and said, "Pharaoh worships the Aten with royal wife Kiya and his daughters. He will see his new daughter when they have completed their praises."

"Why is royal wife Kiya with him?" Nefertiti asked.

"She worships the Aten with Pharaoh, per Pharaoh's command."

"Pharaoh commanded she worship the Aten with him? In my place? With my daughters?"

The messenger was silent. He felt pity for his Queen—so many daughters and no sons, and now perhaps being replaced with another wife by the slightly unstable Pharaoh. He had prayed to Amun-Re that she would have a son. *Perhaps,* he thought, *Amun-Re knows Pharaoh's son would only allow the heresy to continue. Perhaps it is best he not have a son just yet; however, for my Queen's sake, I wish she could have a son.*

Nefertiti looked to the messenger, knowing he couldn't answer for Pharaoh, and dropped her face to her baby girl's forehead. "Remember Amun-Re," she whispered. "Surely he punishes me for not teaching my children about him."

Aitye's gaze dropped to the floor as her maidservants came near to their Queen and said a quiet prayer to Bes and Tawaret to keep the evil spirits from her and the new baby girl, despite the decree to not worship any gods except for the Aten. But they all knew the Queen would want the prayer to go to Bes and Tawaret and not the Aten, and because she fought alongside them when the rebels came, they would do whatever she truly desired and face whatever lashes they would receive if caught.

Nefertiti closed her eyes and let their prayers cover her. The messenger, who was loyal to his Queen as well, stood by the door guarding it from anyone who might hear the prayers.

That night, Pharaoh did not come to their chambers. Nefertiti sent the messenger to see if he would name the child, and to also tell her where he was staying the night.

"My Queen," the messenger said with a bow as he returned. "Pharaoh stays in the temple of the Aten tonight."

A flame lit in Nefertiti's heart. He hadn't abandoned her yet for Kiya or Henuttaneb, even after the fifth daughter.

The messenger continued. "He commanded you name the child, as the Aten has given him no visions on the child's name."

Nefertiti had given her name a lot of thought—there had been little else to do that day. She wanted to somehow bring glory to Amun-Re, but under the guise of the Aten, and in that moment, Amun-Re gave her a name.

"Declare unto Pharaoh that his child's name shall be . . . Nefernefereure: 'perfect are the perfections of Re.' "

The messenger's eyes grew wide. "My Queen . . . may I speak?"

"You may," she said, ready to defend her decision.

"Pharaoh may not accept that name, as it does not give glory to the Aten."

"But it does," she said, smiling coyly. "The Aten is a part of Re. Even Pharaoh himself cannot deny this."

The messenger smiled too. "You are wise, Queen. May you live forever." He bowed and went to tell Pharaoh his child's name.

"I will live forever in the stones of this throne room . . . as a *heretic*," she said to herself as she looked out the window toward the valley of the two mountains. Although she was weak, she had garnered enough strength to walk to the window, and now she found Pharaoh's shadow cast by the flame in one of many temples of the Aten. "He may never turn Egypt back to Amun-Re," she whispered, letting the realization of her statement sink into the depths of her soul.

What am I going to do? she thought, and sunk her head into her hands on the window sill. A tinge of guilt spread through her soul. Perhaps, if she had not encouraged his belief to keep his loyalty to her in the beginning of their marriage, this whole ordeal may have ended by now.

Again, she repeated to herself: *What am I to do?*

CHAPTER 17
THE TIME OF DIVISION

PHARAOH STAYED IN THE TEMPLE, AND HE DID NOT COME out even to the throne room. Messengers lined the doors, only to be told to retire and that Pharaoh would perhaps see them the next day. But the next day came and went, as did the next, and then the next. Messengers began to plead to see Pharaoh. Pharaoh told them he could not be bothered in his worship to the Aten, and so his chief royal wife would rule in his place until his worship satisfied the Aten.

Looking about the throne room, Queen Nefertiti, although sore and in pain, assumed her place on her throne. She'd had the servants move her throne to be in line with Pharaoh's, now that she was to rule in Pharaoh's place.

Almost as soon as she had taken her seat, a messenger came forth quickly to her and said, "Queen Tiye is not feeling well and will not join you, my Queen."

She nodded, and he ran away. She took a moment to breathe while the Aten beat upon her brow and the golden collar reflected the Aten's rays into her eyes. *No wonder he has so many visions,* she thought, trying to make out the people in the throne room through the blinding light.

"In Pharaoh's place, Queen Neferneferuaten-Nefertiti will hear Egypt and its allies," she said as the first messenger came forth.

"My Queen," the messenger said. "The vassal state, Byblos, was lost to Egypt."

"Lost?" Nefertiti wanted to sink back into her throne. *What a great start to my coregency.*

"We came months ago with the message that Byblos was under attack, my Queen. Pharaoh sent no armed guard, however, declaring the Egyptian military's divine duty was to protect Pharaoh and his Queen, as they alone are the mediators between the Aten and the people of Egypt." There was a slight hint of annoyance in the messenger's voice, much as he tried to hide it.

"Is there any chance of restoration?" Nefertiti asked.

"No, my Queen."

Nefertiti closed her eyes. *When did they come? What was I doing at the time? In bed with my pregnancy? Oh, how Amenhotep has let Egypt fall so much . . . this loss will ruin Egypt's reputation as a military power,* she thought.

She opened her eyes. "Are the other vassal states in need?"

"There have been many letters from vassal states in Syria and Palestine requesting for reinforcements, food, and money."

"Has Pharaoh responded?"

"Yes, but he sends very little, which in return prompts more letters requesting assistance—"

"Send Commander Horemheb to Syria and Palestine to resolve the matters there."

"There are not enough soldiers, my Queen. And what of food and money?"

"Find the unemployed, draft them into the military," she said, "and pay them a fair wage."

We need the money from the state to outlive the Amun-Re

priesthood, she thought—but right now she could not have Egypt lose another vassal state.

"Discuss what money is needed with vizier of Egypt, Nakht," she said, "and make it so the vassal states have what they need. For food, take from the royal grain houses."

"Pharaoh has a most wise and kind Queen," the messenger said, and bowed.

As he left, another messenger took his place.

"Pharaoh's chief royal wife, Queen of Egypt, I come with a message from the King of Babylon, King Aburiash. He again sends a letter asking why Egypt does not punish those who murdered and robbed his caravan in Caanan, a land owned by Egypt. He again asks why Egypt does not return gifts for the gifts he has sent. He wishes relations well with Egypt, but there is no avenger for the blood of his people and no gold in his mines."

"How many letters have been received from King Aburiash?" Nefertiti asked.

"This is the second letter."

She took in a deep breath and slowly exhaled. *Amenhotep would not be this neglectful,* she thought, *but Akhenaten . . . Pharaoh Akhenaten is obsessed with the Aten. He will not know what I do as ruler in his place. He did grant me the right to rule in his place—and rule I shall.*

"Guard, bring in the other messengers," she commanded.

Six hundred and thirty-seven messengers filled the throne room.

As the room grew quiet, Nefertiti stood up. "If your message deals with vassal states or foreign allies, please go with General Paaten into the courtyard. Give your message to him, and he will give them to me." Flames raced down her back as she watched a third of the messengers leave with General Paaten. "Delay the order!" she yelled, believing there were too many messengers to have only waited a few days.

They all turned to look at her.

"How long have the remaining messengers been at Aketaten?" she asked, not wanting to hear the response, but they rushed at her faster than she could hear, and she was only able to pick out some voices:

"One month!" came a shout.

"Eleven months!" came another.

"Seventeen months!" Another.

She wanted to put her hand up to shield her face from the overflow of responses.

"Queen of Egypt, I have been here three years, including a few months at Malkata in Waset," one said once the others had settled down.

Speechless, she sat down on her throne with the grace of a swan. "To the messenger who has waited three years: have you presented your message, or are you only waiting for a response?"

"Pharaoh has heard my message," he said, stepping forward. "However, Pharaoh issued a new decree that he would only see three messengers at a time, and those messages dealing with Egypt's state of affairs would go first. My message is from the King of Cyprus. A fellow Cyprian has since come this past month with another message from our King."

Amun-Re, please be with Egypt, Nefertiti prayed.

"If your message has not received a response since two years, stay, and any fellow messengers from the same sender, stay as well. If your message is regarding vassal states or foreign allies and is less than two years old, see General Paaten in the courtyard," she said.

Her subjects did as they were told.

"If your message deals with affairs of the state, such as unemployment, food, or money, go with the chief royal guard,

Jabari, to the dining hall. Give your message to him and he will give them to me," she said.

About a hundred messengers remained.

"Speak your message," she said, and pointed to one of them.

"Princess Nebetah and Fifth Prophet of Amun, Pawah, have requested re-entry into Egypt. They have agreed to change their names to Princess Beketaten and Prophet of the Aten, Pawah, to show they have turned from Amun-Re to the Aten."

Knowing full well they had not had a change of heart, but rather a drastic change of living conditions in exile, Nefertiti said, "They may come to Aketaten with Pharaoh or to Malkata with great wives Sitamun and Iset."

She would want the same pardon had she fought for her beliefs in Amun-Re. *If I had fought* . . . The thought remained with her.

"Yes, my Queen," the messenger said, and bowed and left.

"Speak your message," she said, pointing to the man who said he had waited for a response for three years.

"King Alashiya of Cyprus has sent copper and lumber to Egypt and has received nothing in return. He asks for silver to build his army to retake his lands and avenge his murdered copper workers from Negral, the Babylonian warlord."

His fellow Cyprian spoke as soon as he ended. "Now he sends again more copper in return for sweet oil and a specialist in eagle-omens to help rebuild their food supply and learn the outcome of the constant warring between Cyprus and Negral."

Nefertiti nodded. "Send one thousand talents of silver to King Alashiya of Cyprus, along with two containers of sweet oil and Studier of Eagles, Neterheb. Return to your King with Egypt's friendship."

They both nodded in appreciation and the scribe wrote ferociously as she spoke again: "Speak your message."

She pointed to the next set of messengers.

A LONG DAY CAME AND WENT, AND FINALLY GENERAL Paaten and Jabari came back to the throne room.

As soon as General Paaten saw Nefertiti, he ordered, "All remaining messengers come back when the Aten shows his face again, and we will respond to your messages then."

The guards escorted the messengers from the throne room. The messengers grumbled as they left, proud of the accomplishments from the day but angry that they stood all day with their message still unheard.

"Send a message to the vizier of Egypt, Nakht, and Master of Pharaoh Horses, Ay, to come to Aketaten immediately," Nefertiti called out, and a messenger ran off.

"Queen Neferneferuaten-Nefertiti," General Paaten said with a bow, and Jabari did the same.

"General Paaten, when did Pharaoh make such a decree to only see three messengers a day?" she asked as she sunk back into her throne, her back tired from sitting straight-backed all day.

"After the birth of Princess Meketaten. He declared he wanted to spend more time with the Aten, and with his daughters."

Her heart sank a little. *He put our family above the welfare of Egypt . . . and now Egypt's prestige and reputation may be scarred,* she thought.

"What of your messages of the vassal cities?" she asked him.

"They are mostly needing soldiers, food, and equipment," he said. "They are under attack from territorial ravagers and warlords. They are surviving but will soon be overtaken—if they have not been overtaken already."

"And of the foreign allies?"

"They wonder where Egypt is, when they have sent such precious gifts from their home world but the gold that is like dust in Egypt . . . stays in Egypt."

She shook her head. "Our gold, we need," she said. "But at what cost?"

The three of them looked to each other until Nefertiti spoke. "Send Commander Horemheb to the vassal cities, leaving men, one hundred debens of gold, and two containers of grain at each, until he gets to the northernmost city. There he shall send a messenger here to give us the state of each vassal city on his journey home."

"Most wise, my Queen," Paaten said. "And for the foreign allies?"

"I have already committed so much of Egypt's resources in today's responses," she whispered dizzily. "Scribe of Pharaoh, how much has the Queen committed today?"

He looked to her of the odd request, as he was only the scribe. He scrambled back through his scrolls, trying to quickly tick and tie what was sent.

"What of the affairs of the people of Egypt?" she asked Jabari, while the scribe calculated.

"The people go hungry, as they cannot find work. Many of Egypt's people were put out of work when Pharaoh declared all temples closed and banned all worship of gods other than the Aten. Because there are now so many priests of the Aten, the people's money can only go so far for the priesthood of the Aten. And because Pharaoh and his Queen are the only mediators between the people and the Aten, they do not give as much to the priesthood or the temples, as the priests cannot take their requests to the Aten. Also, because Pharaoh only hears three messengers a day, many of the people's requests have gone unanswered, as Pharaoh has not yet heard their requests to give to the Aten."

The scribe interrupted, announcing, "Queen Neferneferuaten-Nefertiti has committed half of the Egyptian army, four hundred containers of grain, six thousand talents of silver, four thousand debens of gold, one hundred fifty containers of sweet oil, two artisans, one engineer, and one eagle-omen specialist."

"We will need to wait for the treasurer's calculations as well." Nefertiti grimaced, not knowing how much of the treasury she just depleted and how much longer now they would need to collect to outrank the Amun-Re priesthood. Her mind drifted back to the fines for worshiping other gods. *At least we have some income.*

"There are many prayers and pleas, my Queen," Jabari said. "Mostly for work, for food."

"We have a need for soldiers," she said, raising her voice, "as I have just committed half of the army to help our vassal states and allies! There is work."

"Yes, but the treasury will only go so far to support all of Egypt as soldiers, my Queen." He bowed in respect.

The thought of taking over the Amun-Re priesthood's funds entered her mind, but she quickly dismissed it. *To steal from Amun-Re would be unforgivable,* she thought.

She kept her hands on her knees in her royal position and straightened her back yet again. Her breasts ached, and her bottom felt like it was splitting open. Pains shot through her pelvic bones all the way up her back and into her head, but all she could do was close her eyes and bite the inside of her cheek.

Merytre, who had stood by her side all day, could see now that her Queen needed her. She took a step forward and bowed to the General and the chief royal guard. "Queen Neferneferuaten-Nefertiti has given birth not even a month ago, and yet she sits all day in Pharaoh's place. Perhaps the messages can wait for her majesty tomorrow?"

Nefertiti looked with love at Merytre. "Perhaps," she said.

General Paaten could see the pain in her crumpled shoulders and in her undercurled toes, and agreed that tomorrow would be best. They would come back in the morning—and hopefully her father Ay and vizier Nakht would have made a safe journey by nightfall tomorrow, as well, to discuss the state of the treasury.

The General and the chief royal guard left the throne room and Merytre helped Nefertiti from her throne in privacy. Bent over and walking down the steps, holding on to Merytre for fear of falling, Nefertiti made her way to her chambers.

"Perhaps a warm bath, my Queen?" Merytre asked.

"Yes, Merytre, yes."

PHARAOH WAS NOT SEEN OR HEARD FOR DAYS, WHICH turned into weeks.

Those weeks were filled with responding to years-old messages. News spread that Queen Neferneferuaten-Nefertiti was hearing and responding to messages, and more neglected messengers poured into the throne room. She and Queen Tiye were baffled at the Pharaoh's lack of involvement in these affairs, but they sifted through each one as they came. Satau sat at a desk next to the throne, ticking and tying each commitment against the state.

Each evening, Nefertiti would find her husband naked in the temples of Aten. She would worship with him a little while and try to talk to him about the state of Egypt, but he refused to listen, saying the Aten would take care of all. She learned to sleep by herself again, as he stayed out in the temples praying and begging the Aten to come again.

The eighth week came and went and Nefertiti again sent a messenger to Pharaoh urging him to come to his council room. Hours passed, and finally Pharaoh Akhenaten appeared, eyes bloodshot and body drenched in sweat.

"Pharaoh has had a vision from the great Aten!"

"Pharaoh, the state of Egypt is poor," Nefertiti began, brushing off his announcement.

"*Silence*, woman!" he bellowed, and all eyes in the council room went wide at the tone he struck with his wife, the supposed love of his life. "All shall hear the vision: behold, a boy in pain and suffering, but the Aten lifts him up to Pharaoh and he rules Egypt," he said, clueless to everyone in the room. "This boy is my *son*," he said, "as I was son to my father, who is now the Aten!"

I pray to Amun-Re I can have this son the Aten keeps showing him, Nefertiti thought, rolling her eyes. She did not understand her desire to still keep him loyal to her. He had not *even* been to see how she fared after giving birth to their fifth daughter. He had not *once* been to see his child and did not respond to the name she'd given her. Now, he called Nefertiti "woman" in front of everyone, including her father and Queen Tiye.

"Son, sit down," Queen Tiye said. Her paling skin and sunken shoulders indicated the long years of queenship heavy upon her shoulders. Medical specialists had come from across Egypt to look at her, but Nefertiti noticed even in her sickness, she still stood strong.

Akhenaten took his seat underneath the Aten's diminishing rays as they fell across his shoulders and the back of his head.

"Son," she said. "Egypt needs its Pharaoh."

"Pharaoh is here," he said. "Pharaoh has always been

here." He stood up and walked around the room, as if to demonstrate his presence.

"Pharaoh has not been here," she said. "Queen Neferneferuaten-Nefertiti has been here, serving in your place while you worship the Aten naked and drunk!"

He raised his hand to his mother but restrained himself at her unflinching eye. "Pharaoh was not drunk . . . but yes, Pharaoh was increasing his dedication to the Aten by praising and worshiping him in purity. And Egypt is the greater for it."

"How?" Queen Tiye shook her head at his ignorance of affairs.

"Because I have prayed for Egypt. The Aten has promised to give me visions of what needs to be done."

"Pharaoh, almost half of the state's treasury has been depleted in resolving disputes with vassal states, foreign allies, and job creation for the Egyptian people," Nakht blurted out, his fists hitting the table in punctuation.

"Who did this?" Pharaoh spun around. Rage in his eyes and a snarl on his lips, he demanded to know. "Who did this?!"

"*I* did," Nefertiti said, and stood up quickly, immediately regretting the decision as her hand shot to her pained back.

"You? You are not Pharaoh!" He rushed to her with a wagging finger and a solid gait.

"You said for me to serve in Pharaoh's place!" she yelled back. "And believe me, I served."

Those in the room shifted uncomfortably in their seats as they sat slightly baffled at the loss of control, the lack of respect, and the utter unusualness of the situation.

"You serve the Amun-Re priesthood!" Pharaoh bellowed. "This explains why you deplete our treasury when we are trying to overcome them. We have a *traitor* in our midst!"

She gasped. *"What?!"*

Those in the room looked to the floor.

"You deplete my treasury so that the priesthood may grow again and overthrow the Aten!"

"Never! I depleted the treasury to clean up your neglect!"

"*MY* neglect?!" he asked. "*Your* neglect!"

"How is this *my* neglect?" Nefertiti yelled back.

"You have not given me a son!" Pharaoh shouted.

Nefertiti's legs went weak, but she stood strong. Her eyes ate at him, and the servants walking outside the council room stopped in their tracks to hear the yelling through the half-open roof and see what Queen Neferneferuaten-Nefertiti would toss back his way.

"*YOU!*" Nefertiti yelled, and opened her mouth to continue.

"Enough!" Queen Tiye shouted, and touched Nefertiti's shoulder, gently pressing her into her seat. "Sit *down*, son."

He obeyed his mother.

"What has been done is done, and we need to move forward."

"Agreed," Ay said along with Nakht, Paaten, and Satau, who were also in the room.

"The Aten has granted me one last vision for the day," Pharaoh said as everyone closed their eyes for a short moment. "The Aten says to take the Amun-Re priesthood's treasury and use it as Egypt's own. The Aten says to take from all the gods' priesthoods and use them as Egypt's own."

Ay looked to Nakht, who looked to Paaten, who looked to Satau, who looked to Nefertiti, who looked to Queen Tiye, who looked to Pharaoh.

"Thus Pharaoh says," he said with a chuckle as the scribe of Pharaoh wrote his words with a shaky hand. "The problem seems solved to Pharaoh. Thank you, O great Aten in the sky!" He raised his hands, smiling at Nefertiti. "The Aten is not mad at Neferneferuaten-Nefertiti. He has provided a remedy for her actions."

"Am I no longer your Queen?" she asked, raising her eyebrow at her lack of title in his address to her.

"You are my Queen, my chief royal wife," he said. "As there is one god of Egypt."

Those words, though technically what she wanted to hear, were said with a distain, and their distaste crept onto Nefertiti's face.

Nakht stood up and said through his teeth, "I will notify the state officials to carry out your order." He bowed and then, as he straightened, said, "Pharaoh, if I may, this action may cause another rebellion."

"The Aten has not given me any such vision. Be on your way."

Nakht nodded and left for Waset.

General Paaten stood behind Queen Tiye and watched Nakht leave the room. He closed his eyes, knowing the vizier had spoken the truth.

Before anyone else could garner the courage to speak, Pharaoh said, "Pharaoh is tired and will retire for the evening. You all shall do the same," and left the room.

Nefertiti felt pity in her heart for the man. He was clearly not himself. She wished they had never moved here. The sun —the Aten—was taking away the man she loved, Amenhotep, the man she married and to whom she gave four daughters. The fifth one, however, was born to Akhenaten, a father who couldn't even turn out to see his new child.

Nefertiti stood up slowly, trying not to revisit the shockwave through her back, and left the room with the others in silence, her face flushed with embarrassment for both herself and her husband. She wanted to cry, but she willed her tears to stay welled inside her eyes.

AITYE STOOD BY THE COUNCIL ROOM, WAITING FOR THE Queen to come out. When Nefertiti appeared, she and another servant helped their Queen to her chambers to draw her another warm bath.

"The water is ready, my Queen," Aitye said as she finished placing the last lotus blossom in the water. The maidservants helped her undress and Aitye helped lower her into the stone pit.

Akhenaten has still not come to our bed, Nefertiti thought. *I wonder if he went to praise the Aten on his way.*

Her thoughts didn't have to wander for too long, however, as he swung open the door and asked for all to leave.

Nefertiti, soaking in her bath, commanded Aitye to stay.

"Pharaoh said to leave," Aitye whispered, shrinking back.

"Pharaoh, I need one servant to stay and help me with my bath," Nefertiti said.

"Only one may stay," he said, and Nefertiti looked to Aitye and nodded.

Aitye smiled hesitantly and knelt down again to rub the Queen's back.

Pharaoh walked around the dividing wall and looked at his wife in the bath. "Such a beauty," he said. "I received word we had another daughter."

"Yes . . . a while ago. I named her Nefernefereure."

"Very well," he said, and shrugged his shoulders. "A fitting name."

"Do you want to see her?" Nefertiti wondered why he did not care to refute the name.

"I already have. She was brought to the temple with me. Royal wife Kiya painted me holding her. I liked her painting so much I gave it to the stone sculptor."

"Isn't she a beautiful daughter?" Nefertiti wanted to know why Kiya had failed to mention this to her. Did he order her to silence? *Why am I still jealous over this stranger who has done*

183

nothing but make life miserable for me? Because . . . he is Amenhotep underneath it all.

"Yes! I now have five beautiful daughters . . . but no son."

"We will have a son," Nefertiti said, wondering where the strange man before her would go with this conversation. "I will bear you a son."

"After five daughters, one begins to doubt your ability to produce an heir." He walked around the tub, glaring at her. "Pharaoh is considering consummating his marriage with royal wives Kiya and Henuttaneb."

His words stabbed her in the heart. Amenhotep would have never made her feel this way. She hardly knew this man anymore.

"After all we have been through?" she asked, almost a whisper.

She leaned forward into the bathwater, sitting up straight, and wished her back was new again. Aitye sensed the pain and rushed to massage her lower back.

Pharaoh turned away from his wife and rubbed his hand on the smooth stone wall. "I need a son . . . and the Aten has shown me a son."

"I can have your son," she said. "You gave me your word."

"I do not remember saying such a thing," he said, his hands now firmly folded behind his back; he still refused to make eye contact with her.

"My love . . . since you believe Aten is Egypt's only god, don't you think I, Queen Neferneferuaten-Nefertiti, should be Pharaoh's only wife?" One last attempt to keep him loyal to her by appealing to his deeply held belief. As the words flowed from her mouth, a heaviness crept into her stomach.

Pharaoh Akhenaten hesitantly replied, "The Pharaoh of Egypt does not limit himself to one woman. But have I not told you I have chosen you as my chief wife, my only love?"

"Then the Pharaoh lies," Queen Nefertiti whispered, trying to pull the guilt from the depths of her soul.

He snapped, spinning to face her. "The Queen shall silence her tongue!"

But Nefertiti went on, her eyes dancing in fury. "When we built this great city of Aketaten, the Pharaoh Amenhotep told his beloved Queen, his chief royal wife, that because Egypt has now only the Aten as its premier god, then Pharaoh shall only have one woman as his lover."

"Pharaoh Amenhotep is *dead*!"

Nefertiti sucked in her breath and bit her lip.

He continued. "And so as it is, Pharaoh Akhenaten is a god divinely appointed by the Aten. He shall have whatever he wants!"

"Even a foreign wife? What good will a foreigner do? If she ever bears you a son, he will be a half blood, not fit to rule the great Egypt. Are not I the most beautiful Queen in all of the lands?"

"My Queen, you *are* the most beautiful Queen in all of the lands . . . your brown and godly eyes, your cheeks that raise to the sky, your lips as soft as silk from the foreign lands, your skin as smooth as the waters of the Nile, and your hips as graceful as the rising of the sun. Yes, my Queen, you are the most beautiful in all of the lands." Pharaoh Akhenaten still averted his gaze.

Queen Nefertiti smiled and stood up, masking the pain under a seductive glare. "Then why must you share our bed with another?"

Her nakedness caught the corner of his eye, and he couldn't help but feel a longing for the wet skin of her body.

"All of the great Kings of Egypt had more than just one wife, my Queen . . . but you, my captivating Queen, will always be the Queen of Egypt," he said as he came to her and smoothed the back of his hand over her brown cheek.

"Is this not a new Egypt? An Egypt where there is only one god and so one lover of Pharaoh?" Queen Nefertiti asked again. She felt Amun-Re leave her as she turned from him once again to fulfill her selfish desires.

Akhenaten stepped into the bathwater with her and shooed Aitye away.

"Yes, it is," he said. "But what about a son?"

"Meritaten can marry Smenkare," Nefertiti said. "They can provide the next heir. It will still be through your bloodline."

"I suppose . . ."

"And in the meantime, let me have another child. Perhaps the Aten will grant me with a son?" She drew her arms around his neck.

Forgive me, Amun-Re, for denying you, she screamed in her mind, pleading with him to not turn from her. *I do so only to keep his love for me. Please let me have a son!* she prayed. *Please do not let him take another lover.*

"Yes, my Queen Neferneferuaten-Nefertiti." He kissed her. "As you wish."

CHAPTER 18
THE TIME OF QUARREL

"PHARAOH OF EGYPT." THE MESSENGER BOWED.

"Speak your message," Pharaoh Akhenaten responded with a wave of his hand. Even though his mother told him he could not be in the temple today, he was glad to at least have his open-roofed throne room where the Aten's rays could still touch him.

"Princess Beketaten has come to Aketaten to request a short stay with her sister, royal wife Henuttaneb," the messenger said with another bow.

"Princess Beketaten?" Pharaoh asked, glancing around and raising a hand for an answer. "Who?"

"Princess Beketaten is the former Princess Nebetah," the messenger said. His shoulders immediately shrank away from the Pharaoh's flaring nostrils.

"Under what trickery has she been allowed back into Egypt? Under a false pretense of loyalty to the Aten?!" Pharaoh stood, slamming his fist into the arm of his throne. "Has she not disobeyed a direct command of Pharaoh? Send her to the temple of the Aten in Waset to face her punishment of impalement!"

"Pharaoh . . . Princess Beketaten comes under pardon from Queen Neferneferuaten-Nefertiti, from when Pharaoh gave his ruling authority to her during his time in the temple," the messenger said, and after the words came out he hoped he hadn't condemned his Queen to Pharaoh's wrath.

"What?!" Pharaoh yelled. "Guard, bring Queen Neferneferuaten-Nefertiti to me! *Now!*"

A member of the royal guard bowed and rushed out to find his Queen.

QUEEN NEFERNEFERUATEN-NEFERTITI SAT IN THE courtyard as royal wife Kiya instructed her how to paint her children as they played before them. The wet nurse held Princess Nefernefereure, off in the shade.

The guard stood in the doorway leading to the courtyard and took a deep breath before walking up to his beloved Queen. "Royal wife Kiya," he said with a bow to her and then a bow to Nefertiti. "Queen Neferneferuaten-Nefertiti, Pharaoh wishes to see you in his throne room. I'm afraid that it is not under the best pretense," he added.

"Under what pretense does he wish to see me?" Nefertiti asked as she dipped her reed brush in the ink to make a stroke.

"He is angry for the pardon bestowed to Princess Beketaten, formerly Princess Nebetah."

"The pardon I bestowed in his place," she said as she looked at her unfinished painting.

Kiya looked to Nefertiti and whispered, "I thought he would be happy his sister came to the Aten."

"As did I," Nefertiti said. "The one thing he wants for Egypt, and now he can't accept when his sister comes to the

Aten." She knew Nebetah's switched allegiance probably wasn't real, but Pharaoh wouldn't know that.

"May the Queen please come with me?" the messenger asked.

Nefertiti put her reed brush down and asked Kiya to finish the painting for her, for she did not believe this would be a short visit. Kiya squeezed her hand as if to wish her luck and watched as they left the courtyard. Listening to the children's laughter in the background, Kiya closed her eyes and wished for her friend to return to them soon.

———

THEY PASSED PRINCESS BEKETATEN ON THE WAY TO THE throne room. She looked to Nefertiti with a bittersweet glance: a friendly smile perched on her lips, but a cold darkness lingered in her eyes.

Nefertiti smiled back and said, "The Queen says to make yourself welcome in Aketaten."

Princess Beketaten nodded. "Thank you, most gracious Queen Neferneferuaten-Nefertiti." With a knowing sneer, she left at once to find her sister Henuttaneb.

"My apologies, my Queen," the guard muttered under his breath before they entered the throne room.

"I have nothing against you, whatever the outcome," Nefertiti said.

He bowed his head as she walked inside.

"*There* is my wife, who stabs me in the back!" Pharaoh bellowed.

Nefertiti said nothing until she was seated next to Pharaoh—her throne, now next to his, was on an even ground. She turned to look at her husband, who was practically fuming from the ears. "For what does Pharaoh wish to see his Queen?"

He stood up and planted himself before her. "You," he said with his finger in her face. "You!"

"I . . . what?" she asked, gazing up at him, the picture of patience and innocence.

"You undermined my authority as Pharaoh! You pardoned Nebetah! Why would you do that? My father before me gave word for her to be exiled—*I* gave word for her to be exiled— and then you go and devalue both Pharaohs' word?!" He threw his hands in the air out of exasperation. "What is wrong with you? Are you ill in the head?"

"What is wrong with *me*?" Nefertiti asked, one eyebrow shooting toward the sky, and partially laughed at his comment, thinking, *I'm not the one prancing around naked singing praises to the sun!*

"Yes, you!"

Nefertiti grinned and shook her head. "Perhaps if Pharaoh performed the function of Pharaoh and sat upon his throne and ruled Egypt, he would not have had to name his Queen—who, might I add, had just given birth to his fifth exquisite daughter, whom he refused to see—to rule in his place."

"You!" he yelled again, but Nefertiti cut him off.

"Perhaps if Pharaoh had not neglected four years worth of messengers, the state of Egypt would not be this dire. Our foreign allies think we have abandoned them. They have sent no more gifts. We are losing vassal states. We had to seize the treasury of Amun-Re to make up for *Pharaoh's* neglect. Egypt's prestige is damaged, and all you care about is a little pardon for your exiled sister? Your sister, who came back and even changed her name to honor the Aten?"

He fumed for a moment in silence then lashed out. "Be gone, Nefertiti!" He threw himself back onto his throne. "Be gone," he said again in a low grumble. "Pharaoh says leave Aketaten!"

Nefertiti stayed, wanting to say more, but he was still Pharaoh. Given his mental state, she decided to leave. Standing up, she turned to him one last time and said, "The Queen is sorry if she offended Pharaoh through a quick decision that had to be made." She took the first step down and added over her shoulder, "It was not the Queen's intent to undermine the word of Pharaoh. I do love you, Pharaoh Akhenaten."

He averted his eyes and sulked. She continued down the steps out the throne room and back to the courtyard. She willed the tears in the backs of her eyes to stay put as she came upon Kiya finishing up her painting. "It's beautiful, Kiya," she said, and bent to kiss her cheek.

"The painting evoked a kiss from the Queen?" Kiya said.

"It did. You took my worthless scratchings and made it worthy to be looked upon for all of time."

"What did Pharaoh wish to say to you?"

"Pharaoh has ordered me to leave the city."

"Oh, Nefertiti! Forever?"

"I hope not . . . but if that is the case, will you join me in my father's house in Waset? Or, perhaps we could go live with Sitamun and Iset in Malkata." She laughed to keep from crying.

"Of course! You know I will follow my best friend," Kiya said.

"As will I," Nefertiti said, and gave her a long embrace. When they finally pulled apart, Nefertiti's eyes had glistened over.

"Nefertiti, everything will be as it should," Kiya reassured her. "Pharaoh is simply angry. He will realize when you are gone that he needs you by his side."

Nefertiti just shook her head and bit her lip, debating to tell Kiya the whole truth or not. Finally, as a rogue tear slipped down her face, she whispered, "A few nights ago, he

LAUREN LEE MEREWETHER

said he wanted to consummate his marriage with you and Henuttaneb because I was not giving him any sons."

"I will say no," Kiya said as she put her hands over Nefertiti's. "I made you a promise long ago."

"If Pharaoh commands, no one can say no."

"*I* will say no," Kiya said. "I don't believe in your afterlife, anyway, and I'm not afraid to die. I will miss these precious girls and watching them grow up, but I will not go back on my word. If he sentences me to die for not following his command, then so be it."

Nefertiti all of a sudden became sick to her stomach as heat tingled in her face. "I can't ask you to die for this, Kiya. If he commands it, then *he* will have been the one to go back on his word, not you."

"*I will say no,*" Kiya said again with fervor.

Nefertiti embraced her again and kissed her cheek once more.

"I will leave and take all of my daughters with me. We will see if he even notices." Nefertiti chuckled, masking the pain of what her husband had put her through this past year and pushing the thought of Kiya and him together out of her mind.

"He will notice," Kiya said. "I promise. You are not entirely gone from his heart, Nefertiti."

———

"SISTER!" HENUTTANEB SQUEALED, THROWING HER ARMS around Beketaten's neck. "I am so happy you have returned!"

"I can't breathe, Henuttaneb," Beketaten gasped.

Henuttaneb let go of her neck and wrapped her arms around her body instead. "I thought I would never see you again," she said.

"Silly! Of course you would see me again."

"But you were exiled."

Beketaten closed the door and peered out the window to make sure no one was listening. In a low voice, she said, "So, sister . . . what do you think of our brother's rule?"

"All the Aten orders?" Henuttaneb let out a heavy sigh. "I know why he is doing it, but I think he has taken it too far. Mother didn't tell you because you married Pawah."

Beketaten shook her head. "Sitamun told me after we had rebelled, but this has gone on long enough. He seized the treasury of Amun-Re. Unforgivable!"

"What are you going to do about it? Get more people killed? I was lucky you told me to take a trip with Iset and Sitamun to Men-nefer. I might have died. Why didn't you warn Mother?"

"Because at the time I thought Mother was encouraging the turn to the Aten, and Nefertiti too," she said. "Now I know they are in just as much trouble as I am, with Pharaoh running around like some zealot and them not having a way to stop it. But they did let my mad brother exile me. They knew who I fought for, and yet they did nothing. They are nothing to me, and I will work every day to see that all three of them pay for what they did to Pawah and their own people . . . and me."

"So what are you going to do?" Henuttaneb asked, stepping away from the intense venom of her words.

"The only way for a Pharaoh to stop reigning is through his own passing," Beketaten said. "Otherwise, this madness will continue."

"You want to *kill* our brother?" Henuttaneb whispered.

"Yes. Not *me*, but someone else could certainly do it," she hissed back.

"Is that wise? He has no heir to the throne."

"So?"

"Without an heir, the throne is up for the strongest and

most influential person to take it—usually by force," Henuttaneb said. "We could be in civil war . . . and with the state of Egypt as it is, we will never recover."

"You make a good point." Beketaten said, placing her hands on her sister's shoulders. "Little Henuttaneb can *think* now, I see. Could Nefertiti be pregnant again? She didn't look it when I saw her this afternoon."

"She just had Nefernefereure a few months ago, and Pharaoh has spent many hours in the temple of Aten. I am not sure. Perhaps we can afford to wait a while."

"Perhaps," Beketaten said, scratching her cheek absentmindedly as she stared out the window, trying to think. Suddenly, she noticed Nefertiti and her five daughters and some servants with many bags as they boarded a barge on the Nile. "Where is she going?"

"I don't know . . . let me find out."

Henuttaneb left to find a messenger. A while passed before she came back, white-faced. "Pharaoh told her to leave Aketaten . . . for pardoning you."

Beketaten threw her hands in the air. "No son from Nefertiti, though that little wretch is getting just what she deserves. How does it feel, Nefertiti? To be sent away from your home for doing what you think is right?"

Henuttaneb shrugged off her sister's comments and instead worried about the future of their country. "With Nefertiti gone now, how will he have a son?"

"You are his wife, aren't you? And Kiya, too? His mind is half gone now, and I'm sure we could make a compelling argument to consummate his marriages. One of you is bound to have a son—and at least for you we will time it just right."

"Kiya will not," Henuttaneb said. "She has made a promise to Nefertiti."

"We will persuade our brother to command her into his

bed," Beketaten said, and cracked her fingers. *Payback is gold,* she thought, remembering her time spent in exile.

"For Egypt?" Henuttaneb asked, reluctant to agree to that plan.

"Yes, for Egypt. For Amun-Re. For *me,*" she said. For how could she say no to her older sister?

"LOTUS BLOSSOM!" AY SAID WHEN HIS DAUGHTER GRACED the entry to his home.

"Oh, Father!" Nefertiti said, and fell into his arms.

"To what do I owe this surprise?" Ay said as he wrapped his arms around her. Looking up, he saw the maidservants bringing along the children. "And my granddaughters!"

"Father, there is so much that has happened," Nefertiti said, tears welling in her eyes. "May we stay here?"

"Of course, my daughter," he said, stroking her cheek. *Akhenaten, you had better not be the cause of my daughter's tears again.*

He hugged each of his five granddaughters, and Tey came to greet her step-daughter and grandchildren as well. Nefertiti kissed Tey's cheek. "Hello, Mother," she said, then rubbed her belly. "Hello, future brother or sister."

Tey opened her mouth to respond, but the wet nurse entered with Nefernefereure. She let out an audible gasp and went straight to hold her newest granddaughter.

Nefertiti laughed. Ay was relieved to hear her laugh. He had not heard it in such a long time, and with it came memories of Temehu.

"She is beautiful, just as *you*"—Tey pointed to Meritaten, and then to each of her other granddaughters in turn—"and *you* and *you* and *you.*"

"Come, Nefertiti," Ay whispered, and pulled her into the garden.

"I see Tey has kept up my mother's lotus garden," Nefertiti said, smiling around her as the beautiful blossoms burst forth in the high sun.

"She has," Ay said.

A moment passed as they walked through the garden.

"What brings you here, my daughter? Why are there not guards with you?"

"He sent me away." She looked away toward the lotus blossoms.

"Why?"

"He thought I undermined his authority when I gave a pardon to Princess Nebetah, who had changed her name to Beketaten and had turned to the Aten just as Pharaoh had asked. I told him that if he wanted to rule Egypt, he needed to sit on his throne and rule Egypt."

Ay nodded, then shook his head. *Nefertiti,* he thought. *Always right, but always speaking her mind when she should not.*

"He couldn't refute anything I said, and so, like a child, he told me to leave Aketaten."

After her father did not respond, she stopped and stooped down to dip her hand in the water of the garden and drizzle the drops over one of the pink lotus blossoms. She shook her hand off and looked up to Ay.

"I don't think he loves me anymore, Father."

"Nonsense! He is only angry, and he has been acting . . . strange these past few years. Give him time, and he will miss you and his daughters and ask you return to him."

"Kiya told me the same," she said, looking back to the flower. "He wanted to consummate his marriage with her and Henuttaneb because I could not provide him a son."

Ay stooped down and plucked one of the smaller

blossoms. "In his mind, he may choose to do so, now that he has banished you from the capitol."

Nefertiti closed her eyes as tears she had willed to stay broke through.

"But make no mistake, my daughter. He does love you. I think we all know he is sick in the mind. His obsession with this plan to restore the power of Pharaoh by turning to the Aten . . ." Ay filled his lungs and sighed. "He has done it, however. The people fear his position, and after the short rebellion, the people and officials do what they are told. He has restored the power to Pharaoh—so much so, he was able to overtake the treasury for Amun-Re just as he planned."

"But he stays with the Aten," Nefertiti said. "If he could just let the people go back to Amun-Re, everything should be as his father planned, but I'm afraid he will exhaust his power as Pharaoh and the wealth of Egypt will be expended. It will never be as it should."

"The Aten has some sort of hold over him . . . but 'never' is an absolute."

"I feel so guilty, Father. I was so afraid he would bring Henuttaneb and Kiya into his bed . . . but he promised me that so long as the Aten was the only god of Egypt, there would be only one lover of Pharaoh. I have kept reminding him of that promise even as he debates consummating his other marriages. I am partly to blame." Tears ran down her face. "I have disappointed you, and more so, I have disappointed Amun-Re. It is no wonder he no longer hears my prayers."

Ay sat down and pulled Nefertiti beside him. As she cried on his shoulder, he held the small pink lotus flower in his hand. "Nefertiti," he whispered. "Do you know why the lotus blossom was your mother's favorite flower?"

"No," she whispered back.

"The lotus closes up at night, retreats back into the water, and then blooms again in the day. It does this every single day. Your mother . . ." He laughed, remembering her face, her eyes —not as clear as they had been, but still he remembered. "Your mother always told me, 'Ay, every day is a new day. It doesn't matter what you do, you can always wash yourself clean and start anew.' "

Nefertiti smiled at her father's memory. "I wish I could have known my mother. She seemed like a very wise woman."

"She was the wisest. She was my only love. Amun-Re blessed me with Tey, but Temehu will never leave my heart." Ay stared at the lotus garden, wishing to hear her laughter. A grimace covered his face. If only he could lift away the pain his daughter felt!

"If he asks for me to return, what shall I do, Father?" Nefertiti whispered.

"Wash yourself clean and start anew," he said, and kissed her forehead. He lifted up the flower and weaved it into her wig. "Go back to him, Nefertiti. Your heart is with him—I can see it. He is in a confusing place, one from which few return. Trust and truth are what makes a marriage. You must be the mind for both him and yourself. You must be the support on which he can lean, and maybe you will be to lead him out of his place of madness. You are a great woman, my lotus blossom. You are strong and wise. Be the Queen that Egypt needs you to be. Amenhotep and Akhenaten—*both* need you and need your understanding. You cannot reason with him like you could before."

"I know, Father," Nefertiti said, and buried her head further into his shoulder. "I know."

CHAPTER 19
THE TIME OF WINE

A few weeks came and went until Henuttaneb was fertile, and Beketaten said it was time.

They found Akhenaten pacing back and forth in the courtyard. Beketaten leaned against the door, watching him pace. *He is much darker than I remembered,* she thought. *Must be his days spent in worship to the Aten. Pitiful fool.*

Henuttaneb joined her in the doorway and together they coyly sauntered up to Pharaoh.

"What troubles you, brother?" Beketaten asked him.

Ignoring her, he continued to pace back and forth, mumbling something about Aten and Nefertiti.

"Pharaoh, what troubles you?" Henuttaneb asked.

"I need the Aten," he said, paused his pacing to stretch his arms out to the great sun-disc in the sky. Then he continued walking back and forth.

Beketaten looked to Henuttaneb and slightly shook her head. "Where is your Queen?" she asked, leaning forward with her hands on her hips.

At this, he stopped in his tracks and jerked his head

toward her. He then threw his eyes to the ground. "She is with her father in Waset."

"Why did she leave?" Beketaten asked to goad him a little more. *No one exiles me,* she thought. *He will pay.*

"Because she pardoned you!" At her feigned surprise, he continued. "She undermined the authority of Pharaoh!"

"If I were Pharaoh, I would not have sent away my Queen, the most beautiful woman in the world, because of a . . . misunderstanding," Henuttaneb said, her arms loosely crossed in front of her chest.

"You are not Pharaoh. *I* am Pharaoh!"

"Yes, you are, brother." Beketaten put her hand up to silence Henuttaneb, then added, "You are Pharaoh . . . and you have no son for an heir."

He continued to pace.

"Now you have no other way to have a son, since you have sent away Queen Neferneferuaten-Nefertiti."

"I have other wives," he spewed.

"Yes, you do . . . and they are most willing to bear the heir to the throne."

"But I made a—"

"You are Pharaoh, and you need a son," she said, her eyes ablaze.

Henuttaneb followed. "As the Aten has said—he has even given you a vision—and Queen Neferneferuaten-Nefertiti can only seem to give you daughters."

"Yes . . ."

"Here is royal wife Henuttaneb—*your* wife. Call your royal wife Kiya as well," Beketaten said, thrusting Henuttaneb forward into his arms.

"But—"

"Shall we not have an heir to the throne? What shall happen if you should perish with no heir? Do you wish Egypt to fall into civil war over who is to become the next mediator between the people and the Aten?" she asked, eyes narrowed.

"No," he said.

She had him right where she wanted him.

"Great. We shall celebrate your consummation!" she yelled, and snapped at the royal cupbearer whom she had already lined up with goblets of wine.

He ran over with three fairly large goblets of wine.

"Drink, brother. Drink, great Pharaoh of Egypt. For you shall have a son!" she said, and took a small sip.

He hesitated but then gulped down the entire goblet.

"Another for Pharaoh," she said.

He drank the next one quickly too.

"The Aten does not give me visions when I indulge myself," he said somberly at the third goblet.

"You don't need anymore visions. He has already given you the vision of your son," Beketaten said as they slowly made their way to his bedchambers. "Here—drink some more." She lifted the goblet to his mouth.

He swallowed and said to Henuttaneb, "I will be in my bedchambers. I will call should I decide to consummate."

Beketaten clenched her teeth. "You must! With your Queen and chief royal wife gone, you have no way to conceive a son without consummating your other marriages."

He put his finger up as he spun to face them. "But—"

"You told her to leave . . . to be gone—those were your exact words, were they not? Do you think she will ever come back to you willingly? Do you think she will ever let you touch her again? After how you have treated her? After the embarrassment you have put her through by commanding her absence? She is the most beautiful woman in the world, is she not? She has already given you five daughters. After what has happened, do you think she will ever give you any more children?"

Silence made his shoulders slump. "No."

"Then you have no choice," Beketaten said. "Here—drink some more and the Aten will give you a vision showing you what is right. Go to your window and drink in the light of the Aten."

"I will go to my window," he said, and he turned to leave for his bedchambers.

ONCE THERE, HE PULLED UP A CHAIR TO HIS WINDOW. THE wine burned down his throat, and the heat from the Aten made him dizzy. He was too dazed to notice that he had never called the royal cupbearer to his room with more wine, but when he came every so often Pharaoh took and drank it anyway.

After drinking all afternoon and into the evening, Pharaoh watched in a haze as the sun began to set on the horizon. Still no vision . . . he slammed his fist on the window sill.

"Aten!" he cried out, his words slurred, and almost lost his balance. "Please give me direction. Show me the mother of my son!"

He fell over and grazed his head on the chair. The sunlight came just over the sill, directly into his eyes—and there he saw Henuttaneb and Kiya as the mothers of his son.

Too drunk to rationalize why his one son had two mothers, he pushed himself up after the Aten had left him and finished off his goblet of wine and knew he had to consummate with both wives—because the Aten had showed him he must.

The royal cupbearer came in almost immediately with another goblet. Pharaoh grabbed it from the tray with so much force that wine was sent flying across the room.

"Call . . . Que-Quee . . . Henuttaneb . . . to my bed!" he ordered, and threw the wine down his throat. "And bring more wine!"

———

A messenger came to Henuttaneb's chambers. "Pharaoh wishes you to his bedchambers."

Beketaten, who had been pacing back and forth in front of the window, stopped and smiled at her sister. "Go and make a son," she said, and walked over to Henuttaneb, who was slowly standing up from her chair, looking at the messenger like a child looks to a menacing stranger. Wrapping her arms around her, Beketaten saw her reluctance and ordered, *"You will have a son."*

"Yes, sister," Henuttaneb said, averting her eyes.

"Make Egypt proud and produce an heir."

"I will."

"Make sure he calls Kiya as well," Beketaten ordered as Henuttaneb left the room.

———

Henuttaneb rolled out of Pharaoh's bed and wrapped her fine white linen dress about herself. "Pharaoh, call royal wife Kiya as well in case I do not have a son with you—for the Aten has told you in a vision."

"The Aten has showed me you and Kiya are the mothers," he said as he grabbed some more wine from the bedside table. *"Kiya!"*

Henuttaneb called the messenger to bring royal wife Kiya to Pharaoh's bedchambers. She scurried away, biting her lip and hoping her older sister would be proud of her. She felt only a desire to vomit.

KIYA SAT IN HER CHAMBERS WATCHING THE STARS BEGIN TO light up the night sky when the messenger came. "To his bedchambers?" Kiya asked. Her heart paused and goosebumps covered her skin. She had wanted to hear that call years ago, but not now . . . not after her promise to Nefertiti, and not after seeing the man he had become.

"Yes, my Queen," the messenger said with a slight bow.

"I . . . I refuse to go."

"My Queen." The messenger stood with his hands clasped in front of his stomach as he rocked back and forth on his heels. "Your refusal will be unwise. Pharaoh has had much to drink."

"I'm not going." Kiya turned back to the window.

"I will tell Pharaoh your response."

"WHAT?!"

Pharaoh threw the almost-empty goblet of wine against the back wall. "She dared to not do what I say?"

He stumbled out of bed, grabbing his shendyt from the bed and trying to wrap it around his waist as he yelled and stormed out of the door. Going from one side of the hallway to another, he finally made his way to royal wife Kiya's chambers, gulping down another large goblet of wine.

He threw open her doors. His face flustered red and his mouth turned up into a fit of rage.

"KIYA!"

"No!" She shrunk back from his bloodshot eyes and hot stare. He came closer to her. The stench coming from his body and breath were almost suffocating. "I will not!"

"I am Pharaoh!" he yelled. "Aten has showed me you!"

"The Aten is wrong!" she yelled back.

At this, he reached for her, ripping her dress as she pulled away, but he caught her by the arms, picked her up, and threw her on her bed. Stumbling forward from the sudden change in weight upon his feet, he fell on top of her.

She tried to get out from underneath him, but his weight was no match for her delicate painter's arms. "The Aten is right, all the time," he said, and exhaled a deep breath into her face.

She tried not to breathe, for the smell burned her nostrils. "Please . . . please don't do this."

He moaned, not hearing her, feeling something gurgling to the top of his throat, but then it slid back down. "Aten," he murmured as he kissed her on the mouth.

Squirming, she broke the kiss, banging her fists into his shoulders. "Amenhotep! Stop this now!"

He hit her hard in the face. The gold rings he wore etched their insignia into her cheek.

"I . . . *Akhenaten.*"

He came up onto his knees, straddling her, and looked at his hand, wondering why his gold rings now had blood on them.

The pain reverberated through her eye and the side of her head. Blinking several times, she had to gather her senses again. Looking at him still intently staring at his hand, she took the opportunity and tried to throw him off of her again, but he grabbed her by her neck and hit her twice in the same spot. She screamed for help, knowing it would not come—she was his wife, and there was no law forbidding him from her bedchambers. And he was Pharaoh—there was no law he could not break.

"I—Pharaoh!" he said. "Aten—!" He could barely form words.

Her eyesight blurred as she clawed him away. Finally, the

heel of her hand landed square in his forehead. He toppled backward as she slid off the bed and to the floor. Using her elbows, she moved to a nearby table and slowly raised her upper body. She turned to look back, only to find him there, looking right at her . . . cheeks flushed, eyes dark and empty, the tips of his ears red hot. Intent on her, he attempted to get off the bed. However, a surge of oozy wine vomit stopped him in his advance.

He fell backward onto the bed and lay there, unmoving.

Kiya pressed her forehead to the chair leg; the tenderness of her cheek made her wince. She lowered her face and cradled her head in her elbow, lying there on the floor. Her sobs only made her head and face hurt more, but she cried anyway.

NEFERTITI LAY IN HER CHILDHOOD BED WITH THREE OF HER daughters. She looked out the window as the soft breathing of her children comforted her.

She had found that she was with child the day prior and had debated sending word to Pharaoh, afraid it may be another daughter but hoping it would be a son. *A son,* she thought. *I have not heard word from anyone in the palace. I wonder if he has brought Henuttaneb and Kiya to our bed.*

She shook her head as a tear rolled down her cheek. "He wouldn't," she whispered to herself.

No, she thought. *Amenhotep would not, but Akhenaten . . . Akhenaten might if the Aten gave him such a vision.* She took a deep breath as her thoughts turned to Kiya. *I do not want him to execute her for refusing him, but I want him to be faithful to me,* she thought.

She quietly cried as she prayed to Amun-Re, hoping he

would take care of both Kiya and Akhenaten despite neither of them worshiping him.

"I will send word in the morning," she whispered.

If he knows I am with child, perhaps he will not seek out Henuttaneb and Kiya. Yes . . . that is what I will do.

She fell asleep shortly afterward as the stars twinkled in the night sky. Morning came all too quickly, and her three daughters poked and prodded her until she groggily opened her eyes. "Children of mine," she said as she forced herself awake. "Why must you get up at first light?"

"We're hungry," they whispered, their hot morning breath in her face.

I wish I was at the palace so Merytre could take care of this, she thought as she wrinkled her nose and pushed herself up in bed.

"Aitye," she whispered to the sleeping servant girl on her floor. "Aitye," she said again a little louder.

"Yes, my Queen," Aitye said with a start as she lifted her head and blinked.

"The princesses are hungry."

"Of course, my Queen." Aitye stood up and rubbed her eyes. "Come, children, I will make you breakfast."

Nefertiti called out to her as they left the room. "Aitye . . . also have word sent to Pharaoh that his Queen Neferneferuaten-Nefertiti is with his child."

"Yes, my Queen," Aitye said as she continued out the door, but as the words sank in, she whipped her head back around with bright eyes. "Yes, my Queen! I will!"

Nefertiti smiled at her and knew she was hoping for a son as well.

***

MORNING CAME, AND KIYA AWOKE STILL LYING ON THE

hard floor. She rolled to her back and tried to sit up, but immediately felt the need to lay back down; the room spun around her, and her head felt ten times heavier. She looked to her side and saw Pharaoh Akhenaten passed out beside her, belly down and completely naked. His shendyt lay dangling off of the side of her bed.

He must have awoken and tried to come near me during the night, she thought as she crawled to her window, keeping her head level with the floor. She curled up into a ball beneath the sill, where the floor still hid in the shadows, and began to cry again, not knowing what to do with this monster who slept in her room.

CHAPTER 20
THE TIME OF SILENCE

HIS EYES SLOWLY OPENED AND ROLLED BACKWARD AS THE sunlight hit them. He went to raise his head, but the spinning of the room sent him plummeting back to the floor. Moaning, he cradled his head in his hands, shielding the sunlight from his face, and massaged his throbbing temples. After a moment of quiet, he rolled to his back, attempting to make out his surroundings.

Turning away from the light, he murmured, "Aten," his tongue thick and dry in his mouth. "What have you done to me?" He took in a deep breath, only to gag from a horrid medley of smells. His sweat drenched the floor where he lay. More than anything, he just wanted to shut out the sun and go to sleep, but his stomach urged him otherwise. As he pulled himself to his side, what was left of his stomach contents spewed from his mouth.

Through her tears, Kiya watched him vomit all over her side table. Gritting her teeth, she crawled over to the bench at the end of her bed and grabbed her small stone statue of the Mitanni god, Adad. Forcing herself to stand despite the horrid condition of the left side of her face, she wrapped her fingers tightly around the statue's base and stumbled over to Akhenaten. Raising the statue high above her head, she thought, *It would be so easy . . .*

"Aten!" he yelled again. "Help me . . . someone, please."

Just hit him, Kiya. Hard in the head. I could say he fell. He was drunk—everyone saw. I could kill him and no one would know. Perhaps Egypt would be for the better.

Then he turned his head into the shadow her body cast onto his face. He dropped his head so it lay vulnerable on the floor.

She froze.

Do it, Kiya!

But her arms came down and she dropped the statue on the bed.

"Who is there?" he asked.

"It is I, your royal wife Kiya." Disgust filled her words. "Do you know what you did?"

"I don't remember why I was so mad," he said in a daze, trying to make out Kiya's face. "I don't remember how I got here. Am I in my chambers?"

"You are in *my* chambers," she said, solemnity oozing from her lips.

"Why am I in your chambers?"

"You ordered me to your bed, but I refused. And then you came to my bed and tried to take me here by force."

"I wouldn't do that," he said as he tried to sit up but fell back over.

She walked around to the other side of the table so he could see her face.

"You did. Against my will! You hit me!" She angled her face so that its wounds shone in the sunlight.

"I wouldn't do that!"

"You did! Look at me!"

He blinked a few times and shook his head in dismay.

Sleep called him. His body wanted to be still. His throat thirsted for water. His chest burned inside his ribcage. The room spun all around him unless he lay perfectly still, and even so, it still twirled.

"I don't remember," he finally said.

"*I* remember," she cried. "You were my friend once. Now you are dead to me!"

"Kiya!"

He sat up and tried to reach for her hand, but she tugged it away.

"You disgust me, Pharaoh Akhenaten."

Kiya went and opened the door and called Ainamun to dress her wounds and to call the servants to help Pharaoh to his chambers.

As the servants held Pharaoh by both arms and Ainamun charged the maidservants to clean the chambers, Akhenaten said to Kiya as he passed her out of her room, "Kiya, I don't remember . . . but I am sorry."

Kiya grimaced. Akhenaten scared her, yes, but this was clearly Amenhotep. Forgiveness came to the tip of her tongue, but the memory of him striking her because she called him Amenhotep came to the front of her mind. She kept her mouth shut, and he left. Ainamun took her back into her room and shut the door as the servants cleaned her bedchambers and tended the bruises and open gashes on her face.

———————

THE DAY WENT INTO THE BETTER PART OF THE AFTERNOON and Pharaoh laid in his bed, curtains drawn to keep the Aten from seeing his disgrace. Slowly, as the haze lifted, as he replenished his body with water, bread, and sleep, he felt the tinge of guilt creep inside his soul as the prior night with

Henuttaneb and Kiya slithered into his memory. He prayed to the Aten—in his mind, for his mouth was too tired to speak.

Hear me, O Aten, in my grief as I hide my face from you. Why would you give me such a vision? Why would you make me send away my Neferneferuaten-Nefertiti? Forgive me, O Aten, for the pain I have caused my royal wife Kiya, and grant my Neferneferuaten-Nefertiti the grace to forgive me as well. The wine made a mockery of me, and so I sing your praises to restore me to your divinely appointed.

Tears fell out of the corners of his eyes as his chest tightened. He would order silence, just as his father did with Sitamun, if it resulted in a child.

No one will know, he thought. *Aten, let me bear my burden alone. Heal my friend, my wife, Kiya. Heal my sister, my wife, Henuttaneb. Keep Nefertiti from this that I have done. Although many men hit their women, and I have not wronged another man by forcing myself on his wife, I cannot bear the thought of hurting the women in my life, O Aten. Please take their pain and place it on me and help me carry it.*

The day ended, and Akhenaten finally was able to stand up and walk to the window, where he drew the curtains back to look at the stars. His view of the sky darkened.

"Aten, please . . . no more visions—you are asleep and yet you still send me visions? I am too weak to go to the temple to understand them."

He could not make sense of these new visions. The Aten flooded his eyes with them even when he closed his eyes. Dark spots danced with one another; the harder he pressed his eyes together, the more they danced. He spent the majority of the past few years staring up at the great sun-disc receiving as many visions and healing power as his body could stand before he had to break the mediation between the people and the Aten. Now he wanted the visions to stop, but they continued all into the restless and sleepless night, looking like the haunting gashes on Kiya's face.

THE NEXT DAY CAME, AND FOR THE FIRST TIME HE DECIDED to not go to the temple of the Aten and instead go to his throne and receive messages. His head still reeling, Pharaoh felt his throne envelop his body as he sat with arms spread wide on the armrests of the throne, his legs pressed against the front.

A messenger entered and bowed.

"Speak your message," he said.

"Pharaoh of Egypt, I come with a letter from the King of Mitanni. He requests Egypt's help in fighting off the Hittites, who have come to take Mitanni's western border. He requests chariots and gold and has sent silver in return for the generosity of Pharaoh. He hopes Pharaoh Akhenaten sends gifts as his father once did."

Pharaoh's gaze had drifted up toward the morning sky. Pharaoh had only heard every other word or so; he was not paying attention to the message. The silence made Pharaoh realize the message was over and he said, "Oh . . . send ten debens of gold," he said, and shooed him away.

The messenger bowed and the scribe scribbled on his papyrus.

The next messenger came in.

"Speak your message," Pharaoh said, thinking only of Neferneferuaten-Nefertiti and wishing he had never sent her away.

"Pharaoh of Egypt, I come with an inquiry from the King of Babylon. He requests a response as to why his three convoys of precious Babylonian gifts have been unrequited with gifts of gold and silver. He also requests a response as to why Pharaoh has not sent his armed guards to the border to secure the convoys, as the last two he has sent have been attacked and robbed."

Pharaoh sighed. He looked up to the tiny amount of Aten's rays that barely graced the stone wall behind his head. *Aten,* he prayed. *Hear me, O Aten. Please . . . I need your visions now. I need to feel your rays upon my face and body. I cannot be Pharaoh without the strength you give me.*

The messenger cleared his throat and broke Pharaoh from his prayer. An awkward stare lingered between the two until the messenger squeaked out, "Does Pharaoh have a response for my King?"

"Send ten debens of gold to the King of Babylon. Pharaoh will send some of the Egyptian military to the border where the convoys usually cross and provide an armed escort."

The messenger bowed again as the scribe scribbled. He turned to leave, but then Pharaoh said quickly, "To confirm our friendship, Pharaoh will also include twenty debens of silver."

"The King is most gracious." The messenger bowed once more and left, muttering under his breath, "But not as gracious as the Queen or your father."

ANOTHER MESSENGER ENTERED, AND ANOTHER AND another, until Aten was high overhead.

Yet another messenger entered, and Pharaoh recognized him as Egyptian. He sat up a little straighter, hopeful this message would be easier to hear.

"Speak your message," Pharaoh said with a wave of invitation and a slight smile on his lips.

"Pharaoh of Egypt, I come with a message from Waset, the house of Master of Pharaoh's Horses, Ay. Queen

Neferneferuaten-Nefertiti wishes with gladness to declare she is with Pharaoh's child."

The smile suddenly grew, and his heart became light. But as soon as the happiness came, it sulked away. He stood up, smashing his fists into the arms of the throne. Pushing his hands onto his head, trying to squash the visions of his son's mothers out of his head, he let out a roar. He dropped to his knees and fell with his face to the ground.

"Why do you come now? Why not yesterday?!"

"I did, and the day before, but Pharaoh did not listen to messages then as he does today," the messenger said.

Pharaoh pounded the ground, seemingly trying to push his forehead through the cold stone.

"LEAVE ME!"

When he heard the throne-room doors close, his shoulders began to shake the tears from his eyes, and he screamed until his throat was raw.

"AHHHHHH!"

He lapsed into silence.

"What have I done?" he whispered to himself.

"What do you make me do?!" he yelled, and came up pointing to the sky. "You did this to me! You and your visions!"

The clouds covered the Aten, and he fell into shadow on the dais in front of his throne.

"ATEN! Help me! Do not hide your face from me, Aten! I know not what to do now!"

He looked up to the sky, hoping the Aten would reappear, but he stayed hidden behind the clouds.

"Aten . . ." he whispered as he dropped his chin to his chest and spread open his arms, leaning his back into the front of the throne. "Please tell me what to do."

The clouds moved on and the sun shone down onto his

shoulders. Pharaoh chuckled out of relief. Looking up, he slowly opened his eyes to receive the Aten's visions.

He finally knew what he needed to do.

He picked himself off the floor and settled back onto his throne.

"Messenger!"

One of Pharaoh's messengers standing in line outside the door rushed in. "What message does Pharaoh wish to send?" he said with a bow.

"Summon Pharaoh's royal wives, Henuttaneb and Kiya, to the throne room."

Pharaoh sat back against the cold stone plated in gold and drew in a deep breath, spending his time waiting for them to arrive worshiping the Aten from his throne.

THE THRONE-ROOM DOORS OPENED AND HENUTTANEB looked to Kiya with wide eyes, wondering what happened to her face. They both nodded to Pharaoh as they came up just before the first step.

"Royal wife Henuttaneb . . . royal wife Kiya," Pharaoh said. "Pharaoh listened to his sisters Princess Beketaten and royal wife Henuttaneb when they said Queen Neferneferuaten-Nefertiti could no longer give me a son if Pharaoh has banished her, nor would she come back after her banishment."

Kiya's eyes narrowed. *This was Henuttaneb's doing?* she thought. *Beketaten, how could you, after Nefertiti pardoned you? Ungrateful and meddling children!*

"But Pharaoh has received word that Queen Neferneferuaten-Nefertiti is with Pharaoh's child," he continued. "Pharaoh's dearly beloved will give him his son. The Aten must have changed his mind, and as such, the royal wives of Pharaoh shall not utter a word about their consummation of marriage with Pharaoh . . . or risk the consequence of death. When royal wife Kiya's wounds have healed, Pharaoh will request Queen Neferneferuaten-Nefertiti return to Aketaten. If royal wife Kiya or royal wife Henuttaneb are with child, they are not to reveal that Pharaoh is the father. Although Pharaoh has committed no legal crime, Pharaoh loves Queen Neferneferuaten-Nefertiti and promised her she would be the only lover of Pharaoh. Pharaoh does not wish his Queen to endure the truth."

"Pharaoh, could I, Princess Beketaten, be so bold as to speak?" a voice came from the shadows. Her long body sauntered out of the darkness.

Kiya turned to look at this monster. She wanted to stab a knife in her back for taking advantage of Akhenaten in his mental turmoil.

"What if Queen Neferneferuaten-Nefertiti gives birth to another daughter, and your royal wives Henuttaneb or Kiya give birth to a son? Is Pharaoh to deny his only son?"

The question caused Pharaoh's heart to race, and he became all too aware of the sweat on his brow. "If Pharaoh has a son," he said, lifting his face to the Aten for strength. "Pharaoh must acknowledge the truth of the first vision from the Aten, and Pharaoh shall call him his son."

"And what of the Queen?" Princess Beketaten asked, her voice a sly whisper.

"The Queen . . ." He squeezed his eyes shut and then opened them wide to receive the full force of the Aten. "The Queen will"—he gasped at his new vision—"have her revenge."

No, Beketaten thought. *I will have my revenge, you pathetic fool.*

CHAPTER 21
THE TIME OF SUSPICION

NEFERTITI COULD NOT SLEEP FOR DAYS AFTER SHE SENT HER message. There was no response. Ay and Tey tried to comfort her. Her children gave her hugs and kisses. She would politely smile and kiss them back, and they did bring her a certain amount of joy.

One night later on, when she had given up hope, Pharaoh requested her back to the palace. She looked at her five beautiful daughters as they slept.

Meritaten, now almost ten years of age, tried so much to be like her mother. Kiya had painted her several times sitting just as Nefertiti sat on the throne, or coordinating her sisters in bringing flowers to the Aten's temple just as she'd seen her mother do.

She will be a good Queen. I hope she is not turned too much to the Aten. The next Pharaoh and Queen will need to go back to Amun-Re, Nefertiti thought, but she often wondered if Pharaoh still intended Meritaten to marry Smenkare. *He could not turn his own back on his daughters he treasures so much,* she thought. She closed her eyes and shook her head. *Amenhotep would not . . . but Akhenaten might.*

Her gaze drifted to her second oldest.

Meketaten, my melodramatic one, she thought, and quietly chuckled while she kissed the young girl's forehead. *It is always something with Meketaten,* she thought. *But I wouldn't trade her for the world.*

"Ankhesenpaaten," she whispered.

The shy one, she thought. *Always the last to join in on conversation, the last to gain courage to play with her sisters. So much self-doubt—just like her father. Or rather, like her father once was. He now has no self-doubt—not with his obsession with the Aten.*

Nefertiti looked away and walked over to the window sill where she rested her elbows on the edge. The cool night air hit her face as if as a blessing from Amun-Re, and so she prayed.

"Amun-Re, I am not a high priest, but please hear me," she whispered. "Give Ankhesenpaaten the confidence of her father, but without the mental turmoil of such an obsession. I see so much of Amenhotep in her. Out of all of my daughters, she is the one I fear the most will grow to inherit her father's madness."

She heard a creak in the bed and turned to see if one of them had awakened. The little one, Neferneferuaten Tasherit, had turned onto her side. Nefertiti ended her prayer and went to the bed where she lay. She swept her hand over the little bald head. A doll hung tightly under her arm.

"My name's sake," Nefertiti whispered. "If I was truly as beautiful as you, I now know why everyone made a fuss over me."

She kissed her forehead and smiled, seeing her own curious personality starting to show in her daughter. She held no interest in make-up and perfume; she wanted to read.

"You will be my legacy," she whispered in her daughter's ear. "I will live on through you." She gave her another kiss on the cheek; the little girl squirmed into her blanket and took a deep breath, but did not wake.

Nefernefereure, almost a year old, was in another room with the wet nurse. Her personality had not yet come out, but Nefertiti loved her all the same.

And if this newest child, she thought as she touched her belly, *is another daughter, I will love her the same as Amenhotep would have.*

Having taken over one of her sister's vacant rooms, Nefertiti went and lay down in a bed all to herself. She didn't cry and felt stronger for it. He had hurt her enough.

I have to accept that he is not the same person and will probably never be the same person, she thought. *He will never remove my banishment. Is his pride worth his daughters as well? Is he content to never see them again, never worship with them again, never hold them again? It seems so. This is my life and I must accept that it will not change. I will make the best life for my daughters and myself— with or without Akhenaten.*

Heaviness came upon her eyes, and she finally fell into a long slumber, her body aching for the precious sleep which had eluded her for so many nights.

WEEKS CAME AND WENT AND STILL NO WORD FROM Pharaoh. Nefertiti and her older daughters worked alongside Tey in her mother's garden. One day, Tey gave birth to a girl whom they named "Mutnedjmet," or *Mut* for short. Nefertiti loved her new half-sister and spent time holding her almost as much time as she spent with her own children.

With the help of Aitye, Nefertiti learned to cook for her children. She upheld her knowledge of the state of foreign affairs via her nightly walks in the garden with her father.

Her father longed to hear her laugh again, to remind him of Temehu and to see her daughter's happiness.

But laughter had left her soul.

———————

ONE DAY, WHEN NEFERTITI'S BELLY BEGAN TO PROTRUDE, Pharaoh sent word back to her requesting that she come back to the palace with their children. She was overjoyed and yet found herself wishing she could stay. She did not realize how much she had missed Ay and Tey until she had spent this time with them.

Perhaps, she thought as her royal guard moved away from the home of her childhood, *Akhenaten's banishment was a blessing in disguise.*

———————

THE NEXT DAY, THEY ARRIVED IN AKETATEN ON A BARGE. Her daughters squealed as they saw their father waiting for them on the shoreline under the shade of a palm tree.

Kiya stood off behind him, ready to welcome her friend home. She worried Henuttaneb's small belly might be the topic of conversation among the servants; she hoped the child would be a daughter so that Nefertiti would never have to know about what went on while she was gone. Pressing her hands against her own slender waistline, she was at least relieved she had kept her promise to Nefertiti. Her face had healed nicely, too, as if nothing had ever happened.

———————

THAT NIGHT, NEFERTITI LAY IN BED BESIDE HER HUSBAND. The strange quietness prompted Nefertiti to clear her throat.

He offered her some water, and she sat up and drank. They both laid back down.

The wind raged outside, but Nefertiti hardly noticed. *Something seems different,* she thought, remembering back to her arrival on the barge, to Kiya's polite smile and unrequited embrace.

"May I ask you something, Pharaoh?" she asked.

He moaned a "Yes" as he rolled onto his side.

"Why did you keep me away so long? Even after I sent word to you that I was with child?"

"I . . . I was afraid you would not want to come back," he said, but this was only part of the truth.

"I will always come back. Do you remember what I would tell you during the first years of our marriage?" She took his hand. "I have no doubts."

"You have doubts now. It is why you never say 'I have no doubts' anymore." He pulled his hand away from hers and folded his arms over his chest. He wanted her to tell him he was wrong, that she still held no doubts, but at her silence, he felt the same wave of failure pass over him as when his father berated him.

Her mouth popped open slightly. How, in his state of delusion, could he have possibly observed her statements, or lack thereof?

"It is puzzling," he continued, "when your Queen clearly has doubts about your ability, but the Aten gives you many visions to rule the great Egypt and so you yourself have no doubts. So who is wrong? The Aten and Pharaoh, or the Queen?"

"Amen . . . Akhenaten—"

"Do not call me *Amenhotep*. I never want to be called Amenhotep again. I have changed my name."

"Akhenaten," she said again, scolding herself for letting his former name slip her lips. The past few months had seen her refer to him as Amenhotep in her thoughts, but now she was thrown back into his world. "Why? Why do you hate that name so much?"

He shook his head and bit his tongue.

"Do you remember how, when we first married, we would lay in bed telling each other our secrets? We never do that anymore. I slept alone many nights because the Aten needed your worship when he was gone from the sky. I will not lie to you . . . but I did resent you for leaving me. You were my true friend, but I feel as if you have abandoned that friendship and the life we had together."

"The Aten is our god, Neferneferuaten-Nefertiti, and I am the sole mediator between him and the people of Egypt—and you are the second! He must take precedence."

"At what cost?" She turned to her side to face him. "The cost of not answering a simple question about your former name to your wife whom is the supposed only love of Pharaoh? The cost of waiting months to see your newborn daughter? The cost of leaving your wife in bed alone almost every night? Forcing me away from you? Proposing to consummate your other marriages at the expense of your word to me? *At what cost?*"

He turned to face her, to scold her for questioning his loyalty to the Aten, but suddenly noticed how much she glowed in the moonlight. She was indeed stunning. His eyes grazed over her perfect face. He had missed her all of those nights. He had consummated one other marriage and had attempted to consummate the other. Guilt ate at him as he tried to formulate a response.

"Do you even love me anymore?" she asked, trying to reach the Amenhotep she knew still lingered inside Akhenaten.

His memory flooded back to the questioned he had posited to his father: *Father, do you love me?* He turned his face to the ceiling as tears trickled from his eyes and wet the linen sheet.

Nefertiti saw his tears. She had to be strong for him. He struggled with his inner turmoil, she knew. Even if he didn't love her anymore, she would always love him for the man he used to be and the man he struggled to be now.

"Amenhotep was my father's name," he whispered. "My father never thought I lived up to his expectation of his namesake. My former name was the greatest reminder of my most visible failure."

"Your former name was the man I married. The man I *miss*." She immediately regretted her words. *He told you his secret! Just let it be,* she thought to herself.

At this, his eyes closed and he felt the guilt of his broken promise overtake his soul. "I must go to the temple of the Aten. He must know I have not left him."

He began to sit up, but Nefertiti latched onto him, her arms wrapped around his shoulders.

"Please. Stay. Don't leave me again."

"You don't understand . . ." He tried to unhinge her hands.

"Please tell me," she said. "I will always be here for you. Whatever you need."

"I cannot. It was a vision. That is why. It was a vision."

"Please stay. Worship the Aten in the morning."

She got him to look her in her eyes. He lost his will there.

"I will . . . worship in the morning," he said with a sigh and laid back down, thinking perhaps he eluded her all these years because he knew she would take ahold of him and the people of Egypt would suffer without his dedication and his link to the Aten.

He rolled over to his side and faced the wall.

Nefertiti was going to speak but remembered her father's words from so long ago. So rather, she put her hand on his back and said, "I love you, Akhenaten."

He shut his eyes. He wanted to tell her he loved her and had missed her so, but the words would not come.

She waited for a few seconds, then removed her hand and lay back down to sleep.

He waited till he heard her rhythmic breathing, then rolled onto his back and gently grabbed her warm hand. "I love you too, my Queen. I promise to you now, again, that you shall be the only lover of Pharaoh."

Under the darkness of the night, Nefertiti smiled at those words.

I can do this, she thought. *We will be as we should. Everything will be as it should.*

MORNING CAME AND AKHENATEN WENT TO THE TEMPLE. Nefertiti came later with their daughters, bringing gifts of flowers to the Aten. He held her hand as their older children stood looking up into the sky, their eyes closed and lips smiling.

Meritaten tried to open her eyes—just like her father—to receive the Aten's visions, while Neferneferuaten Tasherit was more interested in the stone structure beneath their feet, tracing each line with her foot. Nefertiti recalled doing such an act herself when she was younger. It amazed her the stone could be cut so precisely and laid so well, not even a crumb of bread could fall between the joints.

After the morning worship, Pharaoh went to the throne room at his mother's urging, and Nefertiti and her maidservants took the girls to the courtyard where Kiya could usually be found painting. When they arrived, the girls went running about, but Nefertiti looked around, unable to find Kiya.

"Aitye," she said, motioning her close. "Please find Kiya

and ask her to come to the courtyard."

"Yes, my Queen." Aitye bowed and went off.

Nefertiti sat on the stones watching her girls play. She noticed Beketaten and Henuttaneb walking along the perimeter, peering in when they came to one of the entrances that surrounded the courtyard. Nefertiti had seen this behavior from them before. They would stop and point to Neferneferuaten Tasherit and whisper to each other and laugh.

Nefertiti stood up and walked around until she ran into them as if by accident.

"Oh, Queen Neferneferuaten-Nefertiti! We didn't realize you were walking," Beketaten said with a slight bow.

"Yes, I need to stay fit with my son coming soon," she said, pointedly rubbing the growing mound on her belly.

Beketaten's eyes narrowed. "You know, my Queen," she said with a flick of her wrist, "once one has five daughters, most would expect a sixth." A nasty smirk appeared on her face.

"I prayed to . . . the Aten that it would be a son," Nefertiti lied. "I believe it will be a son."

"And if it is not?" Beketaten said. "Will you still believe the Aten is the premier god, the only god of Egypt?"

"I believe what Pharaoh believes," she lied again.

"He believes he had a vision of a son," Henuttaneb chimed in.

"*My* son!" Nefertiti said back.

"He does have two other wives," Beketaten said as they began to walk around her, then added in a whisper, "And you were gone for a long time . . ."

Nefertiti had to regain composure and slow her breathing; she swallowed the lump in her throat.

He promised me, she thought. *He promised me.*

She looked out to her daughters playing, and Beketaten's

words haunted her: *Once one has five daughters, most would expect a sixth.* And what then? What would he do, indeed? Would he give her a seventh chance?

She stood tall. *Yes, he would, because he loves me,* she thought, trying to convince herself Beketaten was getting her back for not standing up for her when he banished her and Pawah. *I gave her Pharaoh's pardon. I was only sent away because I gave pardon to YOU!* She wanted to run over to them and yell these words in Beketaten's face, but the opportunity had passed.

"My Queen," a voice said behind her, knocking her from her thoughts.

She spun around to see Aitye.

"Royal wife Kiya is in her chambers. She does not wish to paint today."

"Why?"

"She did not say."

"Stay with the children. I will be back with royal wife Kiya."

She marched off to Kiya's chambers—but on her way there, she had to pass the sisters once more.

"What is wrong, Queen Neferneferuaten-Nefertiti? Does Kiya not want to face you after what happened?" Beketaten said, and Henuttaneb jabbed Nefertiti in the arm, which only produced a smile on Beketaten's face.

Nefertiti stopped. "Why? What happened?"

Beketaten looked down then back up at her and with a chuckle and a raised eyebrow said, "What do you *think* happened?"

Nefertiti shook her head. "I don't know what happened, of course. It was why I asked you the question." *Ah, my comeback. The time is optimal again,* she thought. "Might I suggest you remind yourself that you would not be here if I had not given Pharaoh's pardon to you. At this very moment you would still be wasting away outside of Egypt's borders."

Beketaten's face fell flat. "And you wouldn't have been absent when the Pharaoh had his vision," she said with cold, hard eyes. "However, I *am* most gracious for your pardon, Queen Neferneferuaten-Nefertiti."

Nefertiti bit the inside of her cheek.

Henuttaneb looked between Beketaten and Nefertiti, drawing back from the intensity of their stares.

Nefertiti turned and resumed her walk. When she had gone almost to the corridor, Beketaten whispered, loud enough for her to hear, "Go see how your best friend fared in your absence."

Nefertiti wanted to cut the tongue out of her evil face as she clenched her fists and walked to Kiya's chambers.

SHE KNOCKED ON THE DOOR BUT RECEIVED NO ANSWER. She banged. No response.

"Kiya!"

Finally, Ainamun opened the door. "Queen Neferneferuaten-Nefertiti, royal wife Kiya wishes to see no one at this time."

"Why?" Nefertiti asked with a glass-cutting voice. "Is she hiding something?"

"She feels ill," Ainamun said with a calmness in her voice.

Nefertiti glanced behind her and saw Kiya sitting on a chair next to her table. "She doesn't look ill," Nefertiti said as she pushed her way inside.

"My Queen!" Ainamun said with slight annoyance.

Ignoring her, Nefertiti went and sat across from Kiya, who tried not to look at her.

Kiya had stared at her bed all night every night since Akhenaten had been there. When she did fall asleep, it was in this chair.

Nefertiti studied her face. She had not realized it when she had met her on the shore the day prior, but now she saw clearly that there were dark circles under her eyes and her skin appeared to be dull and pale. *Perhaps she truly is sick,* Nefertiti thought.

Nefertiti took Kiya's hand across the table. "The Aten's ray will make you feel better," Nefertiti said as she found her eyes. "Come with me to the courtyard."

Kiya finally smiled with her lips, but not with her heart. "I want to stay inside."

"What happened while I was gone?" Nefertiti asked outright. "Beketaten seemed to insinuate something."

Kiya's lips pressed tightly together in response, and then she muttered under her breath, "Of course she did."

"Everyone wants to think I am ignorant, but I know Henuttaneb is with child, and there has been no word for the beating or execution of an adulterer . . ." Nefertiti trailed off, looking to the window.

There was a moment of silence between the two of them.

"If you are my friend, you will tell me. Kiya . . . is the child Akhenaten's?"

Kiya's brow began to bead with sweat. *Pharaoh ordered us to not tell her . . . Beketaten should not have hinted at the fact! If it is a son, though, Pharaoh would surely claim him. Do I lie to my friend? Do I tell her what he did to me?*

"Well?" Nefertiti asked, visibly shaking her from her thoughts. Nefertiti felt her heart sinking into her stomach; Kiya's silence could only mean one thing.

"We shall see," Kiya finally said.

"What is that to mean?"

"It means, *we shall see.*" Kiya stood up and leaned over with both palms flat against the wooden tabletop. She took a slow breath while straightening her back. "I am tired and ill, my Queen. Please . . ."

"Are you with his child as well?" Nefertiti stood too, her eyes shooting daggers at Kiya.

"No." It was the only firm answer she could give. *I know she is angry,* she thought. *I would be too. I wish I could tell you everything, Nefertiti.*

Nefertiti circled the table and stood with her nose almost touching Kiya's. "Are you sure?" she snapped through her teeth, thinking her friend had willingly betrayed her. After all, Kiya had said she was not afraid to die for refusing Pharaoh's bed, and yet here she stood, alive and well.

When Kiya did not speak, Nefertiti strode out of the room, and Ainamun closed the door behind her.

Kiya sat back in her chair and laid her head over her arms. "I did refuse," she whispered, and Ainamun came up behind her. "Now she thinks I have betrayed her."

Ainamun could not formulate any words to tell the young Queen, so instead she stroked her back as Kiya's tears fell.

NEFERTITI LINGERED AT THE CHAIR WHERE SHE USED TO SIT as Kiya would teach her how to paint. The papyrus was blank; Kiya's red and black ink wells had dried up. She pushed the chair over and threw the papyrus to the ground with a grunt.

How could she? She thought these words over and over as she kicked each reed container which held the dried paint at the walls of the courtyard.

Her girls stopped playing, startled by their mother's burst of anger. They began to crowd around Meritaten, pushing her in front of them. They had never seen their mother in such a destructive mood.

Nefertiti looked over, seeing Neferneferuaten Tasherit's little eyes fill with tears. Nefertiti stopped and took a deep breath, raising her face to the Aten.

It was Akhenaten who made the command, not Amenhotep . . . but she said she would refuse him, she thought. *And Henuttaneb? He probably commanded her as well. Her child is certainly his. He is not the man I married.*

She longed to be next to her father so she could let go of the hurt she held inside. *Wash yourself clean and start anew,* she remembered her father's words.

"It is so hard," she whispered to herself.

The night prior, she suddenly recalled, something had felt . . . wrong. It seemed that the day shed light on the deeds done in darkness.

Should I approach Akhenaten? How will he react? He obviously has scared Kiya into not saying anything to me—or she was too overwhelmed by guilt to speak.

As she mulled this over, her daughters' whimpers took her attention away. She looked to them and held out her arms and they ran up to her. She knelt to one knee and embraced all five daughters at once.

"What should I do, my beautiful children?" she whispered.

Meritaten stroked her mom's shoulder. "Do what you always do, Mother. You decide what is best for Egypt and then you act. One day I will do the same."

Nefertiti looked to her eldest daughter. "You are wise beyond your years. 'Beloved of the Aten' . . . my Meritaten."

At this Meritaten smiled and pushed her sisters in closer as Nefertiti tried to extend her arms wider.

Nefertiti then rose and let Aitye care for her children as she went to the throne room. She would accompany her partially deranged husband in ruling the lands. He would need her to perform the simplest of tasks, surely.

If he knew I was suspicious, he would not be able to deal, and would perhaps irrationally sentence everyone to exile—or death, she thought bitterly.

She took a deep breath before opening the doors to the throne room.

The past is the past . . . but Kiya knew better. She had her mind about her. She told me she would refuse him but did not—and so I will refuse her.

———

SHE TOOK HER PLACE NEXT TO PHARAOH AKHENATEN. Queen Tiye sat to the left side of her son a little way behind Nefertiti's and Akhenaten's thrones.

Nefertiti spoke only loudly enough for Pharaoh to hear as messengers approached, yet Pharaoh once again began to look to the Aten to give him visions. Fortunately, in his delusions, Nefertiti's words became the Aten's words, and so Nefertiti ruled Egypt through Akhenaten.

Queen Tiye realized what Nefertiti was doing and eventually—at Nefertiti's great relief—had her throne moved closer as well so she could help Nefertiti rule the country. She appreciated the older Queen's wisdom and years of experience.

Weeks passed and Nefertiti began using this newfound advantage to try and persuade Akhenaten through his visions that the other gods needed the people's praise as well, but Akhenaten refused those visions as false. Queen Tiye would only shake her head in disappointment at her son, but would try as well, only to fail.

Nefertiti had not spoken with Kiya except a polite "Hello" as they occasionally passed through the halls, and when they sat next to each other at Meritaten and Smenkare's wedding feast alongside Sitamun, Henuttaneb, Beketaten, and Iset. The sisters all talked amongst themselves and seemed to ignore Nefertiti and Kiya. Kiya tried several times to engage Nefertiti in conversation but was met with a cold shoulder.

After the subsequent wedding feast in Upper and Lower Egypt, Nefertiti noticed Kiya never came to the courtyard anymore and the servants made fewer trips to her chambers with painting supplies. She actually smiled grimly, hoping Kiya was in her bed crying for breaking her one promise to her—crying for how much pain she had brought to her friend.

Kiya spent her days in her chair or curled underneath her window. She still could not sleep in that bed. Ainamun had tried to have another bed made, but Kiya refused, saying it would only confirm Nefertiti's suspicions.

Little did she know that Nefertiti had already confirmed the suspicions in her own mind and was plotting to have Kiya removed permanently from the royal court. Most nights as she curled up and held his arm, she would whisper to Pharaoh Akhenaten, "The King of Mitanni wanted his daughter to have a child by now. If she is unable, or refuses, then perhaps you should send her back in shame." She loved Kiya enough to not whisper her sentence of a shameful return to Akhenaten while he was receiving a vision from the Aten— but still, she wanted her gone by Pharaoh's command.

He would often respond, "There is no need to bring her shame." He began to call Kiya the "Greatly Beloved of the King" and "Good Child of the Living Aten"—actions, Nefertiti knew, which stemmed from his own guilt.

Months passed as Nefertiti's stomach grew large, round, and healthy, as did Henuttaneb's. The servants whispered in the hallways, wondering if the son would be Henuttaneb's or Nefertiti's. Would it prove or disprove the vision of the Aten given to Pharaoh? Would it confirm or deny his belief that the Aten was the sole god of Egypt? And if his vision proved to be false, would Egypt rise up against their Pharaoh?

CHAPTER 22
THE TIME OF THE SON

HER TEETH SUNK INTO THE WOODEN STICK IN HER MOUTH as Nefertiti squatted over the birthing pot.

"Once more"—the midwife put her hand to the Queen's lips to silence her whimpers—"once more!"

Nefertiti regained her breath and took in a long inhale, then exhaled with every force of her being. She fell backward into her servants' hands and they took her up and laid her on the cot while the midwives tended to the birth.

"Aitye," she whispered, trying to regain her breath.

"Yes, my Queen?"

"Tell me I have a son."

Aitye did not respond, only smiled.

Nefertiti grabbed the back of Aitye's head and pulled her face close to hers.

"Tell me I have a *son*!"

Shocked at the Queen's actions, Aitye just cried, "I cannot."

After a moment of silence, she continued, "You . . . you have a precious daughter."

Nefertiti forgot to breathe. She let go of Aitye's head and shook her own, finally whimpering, "No . . . no."

The messenger looked to the ground, and the room was silent save for a crying female child.

"Next time, my Queen," Aitye stuttered.

"Aitye, I doubt there will be a next time," Nefertiti said quietly. Her spirit had given up, finally given up on the thought of having a son. "Send word to Pharaoh that he has a sixth daughter from his Queen Neferneferuaten-Nefertiti."

The messenger bowed and went out to give the message to Pharaoh.

"If Pharaoh does not show his face to me today," she told Aitye, "her name shall be Setepenre—'The Chosen of Re'— because although I prayed for a son, Re has chosen a daughter."

"Yes, my Queen," Aitye said.

The wet nurse tried to stifle a cough as Aitye took the baby from her and handed the new child to Nefertiti.

"Another exquisite daughter," Nefertiti said, her voice monotone. She remembered how she had cried when she held Neferneferuaten Tasherit for the first time. The feeling came over her again, but today was different; she felt such a finality about this child. Her heart knew this would be her last child with Akhenaten.

She would not bear the heir to the throne.

No tears came. Instead she smiled at her precious child. "I will love you, Setepenre," she said, knowing Akhenaten would not come to her side that day. "I will never leave you, my chosen of Re."

THE DAY PASSED AND PHARAOH STAYED IN HIS TEMPLE, worshiping the Aten, sending word to Henuttaneb that the

Aten had told him she would be the mother of his son, and that he would have to proclaim him as his child.

Beketaten heard the message as well.

"Henuttaneb, would you like to come with me to see how our sister-wife is doing?" she said with a sly smile.

"Neferneferuaten-Nefertiti is going to be angry," Henuttaneb said, knowing Beketaten's intentions were not of the friendly sort.

"It is even more fun when she can't do or say anything," Beketaten said.

"We don't even know if my child will be a boy or a girl." Henuttaneb still sat in her chair, unmoving. Her sister had dragged on her nerves the last few months she was there. The more she saw the callousness in how she spoke about their family, the uglier she became and the less of an idol she was for Henuttaneb.

"I can tell that it is a boy. Sitamun looked and carried the same as you when she was pregnant with Smenkare," Beketaten said, confirming Henuttaneb's suspicions about her sister's intentions.

Henuttaneb rolled her eyes and planted her arms firmly on the arm rests of her chair. "We are going to look foolish if I have a girl as well."

"Let us go congratulate the Queen on *another* daughter." Beketaten lingered at the door. "Come, Henuttaneb."

Beketaten was still the elder child, and perhaps for this reason Henuttaneb felt loyalty to her. She slowly picked herself up from her chair and waddled behind her sister.

"Besides, you need the exercise to make your first delivery go more smoothly," Beketaten said, eyeing her pitiful sister.

"You try carrying a child for almost eight months, and then I can be the one to criticize how you look!" Henuttaneb snapped.

"Oh, sister," Beketaten laughed, walking over to her and

draping her arms on Henuttaneb's shoulders. "I have much bigger plans for my life than having children for Pawah. He agrees our work matters more than reproducing offspring."

She pushed her to the door and out into the hallway toward the Queen's chambers.

"What is this work you have been referring to since you came here?" Henuttaneb finally asked. For months she had listened to Beketaten drone on and on about her work and watched her send messengers under the cover of darkness to Pawah.

Beketaten stopped in the hallway and grabbed both of Henuttaneb's shoulders. "Just think of it as a homecoming and say nothing more about it. Promise me!"

"Yes, sister." Henuttaneb loved her sister, and all the memories they had made when they were little, but there were times when she was frightened of her. The way her dark black eyes bore into hers, and the slight prick of her nails into Henuttaneb's skin as she held her shoulders was just enough to make Henuttaneb not want to cross her path.

"Good girl," Beketaten said and patted her shoulders. She whistled her way down the hallway.

They eventually ended up outside of Nefertiti's chambers, where they let themselves in.

Kiya had been walking behind them for several minutes, but the echoes of Beketaten's whistling masked her light footsteps. She wanted to see the new princess and wanted to try to make things right with her friend, but instead she saw the two women—the same two women who had manipulated her childhood friend, the Pharaoh, into forcing himself onto her—proceed uninvited into Nefertiti's chambers.

She held back and at the crack of the door just listened to the conversation.

"Leave now," Nefertiti ordered as soon as she saw them. She didn't have the patience to deal with them right then.

"Or what?" Beketaten said. "Are you going to reverse your reversal of Pharaoh's command? I'm sure he would love for you to do that. Henuttaneb might have three sons by the time you come back from your banishment next time."

Kiya gritted her teeth.

"I will have Pharaoh command you to be beaten," Nefertiti said. "Forty lashes each."

"And how are you going to do that?" Beketaten said. Henuttaneb chuckled. "It's not like Akhenaten has his head on straight to understand anything you say."

"Why are you so mean to me?" Nefertiti asked. "I have done nothing to—"

"Nothing? The Queen who does nothing when her husband exiles his sister from the great Egypt? The Queen who does nothing when her husband gives her the alternative to die by impalement? Yes . . . you *have* done nothing! You coward of a Queen!"

Kiya could hear Beketaten's spit hit the floor.

"I tried to talk your brother and your mother out of the impalement and the exile because you had not been told about the plan to restore power to the position of Pharaoh," Nefertiti whispered back in a semi-hushed voice.

"Ah . . . the plan. Do you see how it has turned out? The only time Egypt was doing better was when you ruled in Pharaoh's place. He doesn't deserve the throne and never did. Mother would make a better Pharaoh than him. He has let this country go to the wolves, tossed it out like it was yesterday's bread—and *you* let him do it!"

"Can't you see he is ill in his mind?!" Nefertiti yelled back. Pain tinged her words; she was still sore from childbirth.

"Of course I can," Beketaten said, smiling coyly.

"That is why we made him drunk that night," Henuttaneb said.

Beketaten jabbed her elbow into her ribs.

Nefertiti paused. "What did you say?" She yanked the blanket off of her legs and swung them to the ground, standing up to face them, shoulders squared. "*What* did you *say?!*"

Henuttaneb shrank back a little bit, but Beketaten stood where she was with both hands firmly placed on her hips.

Kiya's nails made her palms bleed as her anger crowded in her jaw. "They did this," Kiya whispered in response to Nefertiti's question.

"What did you say?" Nefertiti said again through her teeth, staring at Beketaten, matching the same dark cold gaze as hers.

"You heard her." Beketaten shifted her weight to her other hip and leaned forward as if inviting Nefertiti's vain anger. "We simply couldn't wait for a Queen who is a failure at having sons to bear a son."

"You don't even know what the child will be!" Nefertiti yelled in Beketaten's face.

"It will be a son," Beketaten said with a cool voice. "Just like the *vision* your beloved Akhenaten had." She raised her arms high above her head and looked to the sky in mockery.

Nefertiti raised her arm to backhand Beketaten's cheek, but then Henuttaneb screamed.

"Water is running down my leg!"

Nefertiti looked and saw blood instead. She dropped her arm and immediately called for her own midwife. "Hers is not clear like mine!" Nefertiti said, pointing to the blood that ran down Henuttaneb's leg when the servants arrived. "Help her!"

They immediately brought the birthing pot. She was going to have this child in Nefertiti's chambers. A midwife yanked out a small statue of Bes and Tawaret from her bag and said a quick prayer before she placed them back in her bag and attended Henuttaneb.

"Why is this happening so early?" Henuttaneb cried. "I am supposed to have another month."

The midwife put the wooden stick between her teeth so she could bite into it and pressed her finger to her lips. Servants held her arms and one held her back as Henuttaneb pushed.

Soon the sound of a crying baby burst into the air.

Nefertiti looked at the newborn and her heart sank deep into the pit of her stomach.

A baby boy who looked exactly like Pharaoh Akhenaten.

"A baby boy!" a servant said to Henuttaneb as she fell back, and they laid her on the stone floor, since Nefertiti's birthing cot had already been removed.

A messenger went off to tell Pharaoh that his royal wife bore him a son.

Blood slowly filled the floor as it flowed from Henuttaneb's bottom. Springing into action, the midwives scurried about, leaving one of the servants to hold the newborn, still covered in afterbirth and crying for his mother's warmth.

Henuttaneb kept calling for her mother, who by this time was surely on her way after receiving word from a messenger. By the time Queen Tiye made it to Nefertiti's quarters, goosebumps had fallen over Henuttaneb's body. She was slurring her words, beginning to drift into a daze.

The midwives did everything they could to stop the bleeding, but no matter what they put against her or inside her, they would remove it soaked in blood.

AITYE FINALLY TOOK THE CRYING BABY FROM THE SERVANT and cleaned him and tightly wrapped him. Queen Tiye and

Beketaten were now kneeling and holding Henuttaneb's hands as the midwives worked to try to stop the bleeding.

Queen Tiye placed her other hand on her forehead. "She is warm," she said, and bent her head, wishing she could be in the temple of Amun-Re to plead with the priests to save her daughter. But instead she could only hope Amun-Re would hear her silent prayer.

The baby's cries finally softened and quieted as the wet nurse slowly swayed with him back and forth.

Pharaoh Akhenaten appeared in the doorway with a smile on his face.

"The vision granted to me by the Aten has been fulfilled!" he bellowed as he took the baby away from the wet nurse and lifted the bundle up to the heavens, stepping beside Henuttaneb—not looking down, really not even noticing she was there.

"My son has been born!"

He gave thanks to the Aten and enveloped the baby in his arms as he looked upon his firstborn son.

Nefertiti stood across the way from him and watched as the same look of pride passed over his face as when he had first held Meritaten.

Queen Tiye looked up to Nefertiti and saw the corners of her mouth had slightly turned down, but her lips were pressed firmly together. Her eyes were glistening. Tiye took a breath and knew that as abundant as their lives were, everyone faced hardship in such a way that it hit them right in the core of their heart.

Turning to whisper to her daughter, who had become increasingly pale, Queen Tiye said, "My daughter, my precious daughter, you shall see this through."

"Mother," Henuttaneb said, and with a weak hand pulled her mother close to her face. "Tell Nefertiti . . . I am sorry."

She could not die with a heavy heart; she could not die knowing she stole her sister-wife's one love.

Tiye looked up to Nefertiti once more, but said nothing. *Now is not the time,* she thought as Aitye began to urge Nefertiti back to her bed, insisting that she rest herself.

Beketaten heard Henuttaneb's whispered words—*Tell Nefertiti I am sorry*—and her ears boiled. *She is sorry? Nefertiti should be the sorry one! If she had just had a son for once, my sister wouldn't be dying on this stone cold floor. We could have gotten rid of our mad Pharaoh and be on with the betterment of Egypt by now. No, Henuttaneb, Nefertiti is not sorry. She is only sorry when it benefits her. I will make her be the sorry one—for you, Henuttaneb.*

Beketaten kissed her sister's forehead and stroked the strands of her wig out of her face.

For you, she thought.

SOME HOURS PASSED, AND HENUTTANEB DIED THERE ON the floor of Nefertiti's chambers.

Pharaoh Akhenaten appeared to be so engrossed with his son over the window, letting the rays of the Aten fall upon his child, that he did not notice the room plunge into sudden silence.

Queen Tiye observed her daughter's face. It seemed so peaceful now.

Beketaten stood up and left the room with a strong back, her shoulders, neck, and head squarely erect, not a tear in sight. She stopped long enough at the door to glare at the chief royal wife laying there in her soft bed while her sister lay dead on the floor in a pool of her own blood.

Queen Tiye, with a soft voice, commanded the servants to send word to the priests of the Aten to ready the burial for the King's daughter, royal wife Henuttaneb, in Akhe-Aten.

She stroked her daughter's plump cheek once again and closed her eyes. Burying two children was almost more than she could bear.

Nefertiti lay in bed watching her husband hold his child from another woman—when he had promised her *she* would be the only one. Her heart felt as dead as Henuttaneb's. She might as well have been the one to die, for he would not even have noticed.

CHAPTER 23
THE TIME OF LIES

AFTER THE REQUIRED DAYS OF MOURNING, THEY MADE THE march to Akhe-Aten and back.

Pharaoh announced from his throne, "The name of Pharaoh's son will be Prince Tutankhaten—*living image of the Aten*—as his existence was given to Pharaoh in a vision long ago and now the vision has been fulfilled. May his name forever remind the people of Egypt that the Aten is the sole god of Egypt! His mother, royal wife Henuttaneb, is now beginning her journey to the afterlife. Therefore, his new mother will be Pharaoh's royal wife Kiya."

"Kiya?" Nefertiti looked to him, trying to keep her voice steady. She had thought she, as chief royal wife, would be named his new mother. "Why not me?"

Pharaoh kept his gaze forward. "Kiya has no children. Would you expect Pharaoh's beloved wife to be childless?"

Nefertiti said nothing and pushed her spine against her throne's back.

SHE SAT NEXT TO HIM FOR THE NEXT PASSING MONTHS, refusing to whisper into his ear any longer, as he had his visions. Relations with Egypt began to suffer once more. Queen Tiye was sick again and not able to come to the throne room. Her presence might have convinced Nefertiti to help Pharaoh for the greater of Egypt, but truth be told, she wanted him to suffer looking a fool.

Messenger after messenger asked Pharaoh for gold to buy medical supplies, to send the Egyptian doctors, as sickness had broken out in the North. The Egyptian military asked for relief because they too were now sick and dying. But Pharaoh's visions supposedly told him to keep the path and "the Aten would provide." He did send one container of gold to each ally, but soon after the gifts became less and less and began to stop coming at all.

Only letters and messengers graced the throne room by the end of the year.

NEFERTITI LEFT THE THRONE ROOM, UNABLE TO TAKE ANY more of his rantings, and went to the most peaceful place she had ever known in Aketaten. She had stopped trying to talk Akhenaten into sending Kiya back to the Mitanni after Henuttaneb had let slip they were the ones behind his commands. Still upset at her friend for not refusing him, she wasn't talking to Kiya, but there was no more maliciousness weighing her heart down. She smiled in the cool early evening breeze as the fiery red sun began to dip behind the courtyard wall.

Beketaten found Nefertiti alone in the courtyard. Sneaking up behind her, she caught her by surprise when she whispered in her ear, "It should have been you."

Startled, Nefertiti turned to face her. "Oh, it's you." Then she turned her face back toward the courtyard. "What do you want?"

"I want you to know that I wish you died instead of my sister."

"You know, if I didn't have my six lovely daughters, I would have wished it as well. But the Aten said I could live." Nefertiti pursed her lips, crossing her arms. *So Pharaoh says.*

Beketaten smirked. *She will live . . . but she will live in misery. I will take everything from her, just as she let me be stripped of everything I had,* she thought.

"So, my Queen," Beketaten began. "I want you to know what transpired during your lengthy stay in Waset."

"I don't want to know," Nefertiti said, putting her hand up, but Beketaten slapped it away.

"How dare—"

"I think you *do* want to know," Beketaten said. Using her height and weight, she cornered Nefertiti, stopping her from escaping. "My barge is ready, but I feel you must know before I leave Aketaten."

Nefertiti tried to put her hands over her ears, pleading, "I don't want to hear . . ."

But Beketaten grabbed both of her wrists and pinned them against her stomach and began her tale. No matter how much Nefertiti tried to struggle, Beketaten continued.

"Kiya, Henuttaneb, and myself discussed at length with Akhenaten how his poor wife Nefertiti would never be able to give him a son—but he had two other willing wives, did he not? The Aten had given him a vision showing either Henuttaneb or Kiya as his son's mother, but he must act on the vision for it to be fulfilled.

"He took some wine to think on it. Then he had the vision we told him about. Surprised? No, I didn't think so. To make him vulnerable, it was Kiya's idea to send the cupbearer to him, frequently, until he was drunk enough to call Henuttaneb and then Kiya into your bed."

Nefertiti whimpered.

"They both went like little lambs doing as they were told —Kiya especially. During our talks together, she told me how she was jealous of your relationship with Pharaoh. He was her friend first, but Queen Tiye took him away from her. She could have been the chief royal wife if it weren't for you, and then they wouldn't have had to sneak around without you noticing. Did you really believe your husband was out in the temple of the Aten all of those nights he left you alone in bed? No . . . he was warming Kiya's bed!"

"No!" Nefertiti slammed the back of her head against the stone of the pillar. "No, this is not real. You are lying. If they were doing that, she would have been with child. There is no way she could not have had at least one child by now!"

But Beketaten continued. "She was glad when you were banished, for they could have all the relations they wanted with you gone. She said her sterility was both a curse and a blessing. She could never have children, so there would never be a witness to their relationship. Don't you see, you stupid Queen? You have no one. Even your best friend betrays you, and you are stupid enough to believe her. I tell you the truth. Why would I lie? I have nothing left for me here. My sister is dead, my brother and mother dead to me the day they exiled me . . . I have nothing here except my own conscious telling me to tell you the truth. Why hide it now that Pharaoh has claimed my sister's son as his own?"

She let go of Nefertiti, who stood shocked, still for a moment before collapsing to her knees.

"Poor, dumb, stupid Queen, all alone." Beketaten clicked her tongue against her teeth, shaking her head in a façade of pity. "Now you know the truth, and I have overstayed my welcome."

Beketaten strode away to go to Waset to stay with her sisters, Sitamun and Iset, and carry out her work. *Live with that truth,* she thought as her lips curled into a grim smile.

Still on her knees, Nefertiti replayed all that Beketaten had told her. Was it real? Why would she lie? Was Kiya really in bed with her husband the entire time, playing her the fool? Did Pharaoh lie to her to keep her happy? In his mindset, maybe.

But Kiya . . . Kiya wouldn't do that to me. "She wouldn't," she whispered. "But she . . . she did not refuse him, either. Or so I think. Henuttaneb, definitely, and Kiya too, because she said she would die before betraying me. But she is alive. She keeps a secret from me, and now I know what it is."

Her eyes narrowed in hatred. She stood up, and like a lion chasing its prey, she stormed off to Kiya's bedchambers.

ON THE WAY, HOWEVER, SHE RAN INTO QUEEN TIYE, WHO was strolling, trying to keep herself mobile while her health failed her more with each passing day.

"Queen Neferneferuaten-Nefertiti, may we walk together?" she asked. "I must speak with you."

"Not now," Nefertiti curtly responded as she strode past her.

"It is important, and I fear I may not have much more time left."

Nefertiti stopped in her tracks, took a deep breath, softened her face, and turned around. She let Queen Tiye take her arm as they walked mostly in silence first, but then Queen Tiye stopped to gasp for air. Shaking her head, unable to make the journey, she turned around and began to walk arm in arm with Nefertiti back to her chambers.

"My daughter . . ." she began.

Nefertiti nearly tripped at the sound of Queen Tiye calling her *daughter*.

Queen Tiye coughed and held up her cloth to her mouth to catch whatever came up. Nothing this time. "Nefertiti . . ."

"Yes?" she responded as she put her other hand atop Queen Tiye's arm. "I'm here."

"I want you to know something."

They continued to walk.

"What is it?" Nefertiti asked.

Queen Tiye held up her hand to silence the conversation until they reached her chambers. When they arrived, Huya helped Queen Tiye into her bed and pulled up a chair for Nefertiti. Placing her hands on her thighs, she waited until Queen Tiye regained her breath.

Finally, she said, "I am dying, Nefertiti."

Nefertiti averted her eyes. She had known for a long time now that Tiye had been sick but did not want to accept that the only other sane person who had done her no wrong was actually dying.

"When Henuttaneb died, I saw something in you that I felt a long time ago," Queen Tiye said. "My husband had also promised me I would be his chief royal wife, and that as long as the Aten was his personal god he would only ever share my bed."

Nefertiti let out a deep exhale. *Yes, and he was faithful to his promise,* she thought. *Thutmose would have been faithful to his promise as well.* She shook her head. Why would she think of Thutmose at this time?

"He never admitted it, but Smenkare is his son," Queen Tiye said and tried to breathe again.

Nefertiti's eyes raised up to the old woman lying in her bed. "Smenkare is Sitamun's son," she said, trying to verify what she knew. *This can't be,* she thought.

"Yes, he is the father of his daughter's son," Queen Tiye

said, her eyes glistening. "It was why he let Nebetah stay with Sitamun after exiling her. He did not want the world to know he consummated a ceremonial marriage to his own daughter. It was why no man was ever punished with the taking of Pharaoh's wife and daughter, or why she and a lover were never punished as adulterers."

"I'm sorry," Nefertiti said finally, rethinking all that had happened to this great Queen.

"Egypt needs a ruler—"

She began coughing again. Huya brought her clean cloths and made her drink some wine. When her coughing died down again, she continued.

"It is a wonderful thing, to be the powerful Queen of Egypt, but it is a cursed thing. You thought the same when you came back from Waset—I could see it in your eyes. When my son made known what he had done, I saw your face mirror the emotions of my heart."

"Oh Queen Tiye." Nefertiti threw herself on her knees next to the bed. She grabbed the Queen's hand and began to cry. "How do you continue? How do you live each day?"

"Because"—more coughing—"Egypt is my love. I will do whatever is necessary for the good of Egypt. She needs a capable ruler whom the people fear and respect, not a priesthood of corrupt men feigning their dutifulness to Amun-Re. Remember, that is why we started this journey."

Nefertiti placed her forehead on Tiye's knuckles. "But how do you live each day knowing he has broken his promise to you? Akhenaten doesn't love me anymore. I have been betrayed by him and those I once called friends."

"My child, he loves you in his own way. His mind has been taken over by delusions which are his reality. I live each day because Egypt needs me to live, but I fear I am close to making the journey to the afterlife."

Her voice had turned raspy, and she raised her hand to lift Nefertiti's chin up.

Looking into her eyes, she said, "You are a powerful Queen, as am I. Powerful Queens cannot let their emotions get the best of them. They must do what is best for Egypt. They must not harbor hate—only wisdom, authority, and grace. You must take my place. You must now doubly persuade Akhenaten to return to Amun-Re. Continue to feed him visions to turn Egypt back to Amun-Re. Rule Egypt in his place, should he fail. You are an adept leader. Ay has said there is no more cult of Amun. Pharaoh controls the power now. Use it for Egypt."

Nefertiti closed her eyes and debated confessing her sins to Tiye.

After a moment, she opened her eyes and spoke. "Queen Tiye, it is my fault we are still with the Aten. He promised me that so long as there is one god of Egypt, there would only be one lover of Pharaoh. I did not do my part in trying to persuade him back to Amun-Re." Tears fell down her face. "And now Amun-Re punishes me with no son."

Queen Tiye closed her eyes and leaned her head back as she stifled a cough. "The past is in the past, and you have endured the punishment from the gods. My son did not keep his promise to you, and so you have nothing now to fear. You are the powerful Queen of Egypt, the chief royal wife of Pharaoh Akhenaten, the beloved Queen of the People. Persuade him back to Amun-Re . . . and if he doesn't, do what you must."

Her eyes held a secret as Nefertiti pondered her last words. She opened her mouth to speak, but Huya shooed her away to let the great royal chief wife get some much needed rest.

CHAPTER 24
THE TIME OF OBSESSION

Tiye—great royal wife of Pharaoh Amenhotep III and Queen of Egypt—passed in her slumber shortly after. The cries of Pharaoh Akhenaten swept through the entire city of Aketaten. Those who hated him for banning worship of their beloved gods felt only sorrow in their hearts for him as they each thought of their own mother, and still others hoped her death would help him realize the Aten was not the sole god of Egypt and turn back to the one true way of Egyptian theology.

Instead, Pharaoh Akhenaten withdrew in his grief. He locked himself in his chambers and refused to see messengers, food bearers, his children, and even his chief royal wife, though she tried to attend to him. He only allowed the royal cupbearer so he could drown his sorrow in the unforgiving strong drink.

Nefertiti took the throne in Pharaoh's absence while the ninety-day burial preparations took place. At her request, Master of Pharaoh's Horses, Ay—her father—came to her side to help her rule. She heard messages from the Mitanni, Cyprus, Babylon, and all the vassal states.

They were all failing.

The sickness, or "plague" as the messengers called it, had overtaken their armies, though it had also taken the Hittites, forcing them to stop their attacks. Nefertiti requested the return of the Egyptian troops as they could spare. Over three-fourths of their army was abroad. With the passing of Queen Tiye came a gap in perceived power; a strong home military presence could help remedy that perception.

Of course, with such an update, they always requested more and more gold. Nefertiti summoned vizier Nakht and treasurer Satau to help her with the requests. Cries of Egypt's abandonment arrived, guilting Nefertiti into giving more gold, but due to the lack of economy from the banned worship of the gods, the Egyptian treasury was slowly being depleted. No more work in the temples, no more artisans in the streets selling trinkets and statues for worship, no more donations with their tax being given to the priests, and only a minority worshiped the Aten and even less gave donation. The treasury was not replenishing.

Ay and Nefertiti paced back and forth in the council room. Pharaoh had refused to join. General Paaten was on his way from the North. He left his post with a granted request from Queen Neferneferuaten-Nefertiti to attend the funerary procession for Queen Tiye, as he had been close to her and her family for many years.

"Father, what do you suggest?" Nefertiti said.

"We must turn Egypt back to the old religious ways, my daughter."

Nakht crossed his arms. "The economy in the religious sector once made up almost half of the income. If we continue like this, and with the rate we give away gold to our allies, Satau tells me Egypt will be bankrupt in the next six years. We have already seized the stores from all of the priesthoods from the other gods. We must make a decree that allows worship of the other gods."

"Pharaoh would have me exiled or executed and then make another decree invalidating mine," Nefertiti said, throwing her hands in the air.

Ay nodded. "Yes, you are right." He paused his pacing and levied both hands on the table. "You must convince Pharaoh to turn back."

"How? He won't see me. I have tried to console him, but he refuses to even open the door. I know what I must do, but when will it be too late?"

"It might be already too late," Ay said with a sigh.

Just then General Paaten came into the council room. His cheeks flustered, he did a quick bow to Nefertiti and another bow to Nakht. "My Queen. Grand vizier of Egypt."

"General," Nefertiti said.

"My regrets, my Queen and Master of Pharaoh's Horses, on the passing of Queen Tiye. I have ill news at such a time, but I feel pressed to report. I come from Lower Egypt with rumors of another rebellion forming and spies being sent to Aketaten. I cannot fully confirm their validity, but I have reason to believe that there is truth in the rumors."

"The Queen has already requested the Egyptian military to be returned to Egypt from our allies," Nakht said.

"This is good. We will need Commander Horemheb back in Egypt to help us put down another rebellion."

Nefertiti sat down in defeat. "Father, this is worse than I imagined. People are going hungry in the streets and cannot find work. Our treasury will be depleted. We lost Queen Tiye and the power she held, and now Pharaoh Akhenaten has stonewalled himself in his chambers . . ."

Ay rubbed her back. He did not have the answer, and hatred burned in his heart toward Pharaoh for putting his beloved lotus blossom through so much.

"We must return to Amun-Re and the other gods," she said. "They punish Egypt for their lack of worship."

"It would seem so, my daughter."

"We must tell Pharaoh," Nefertiti said.

They all agreed that after the procession later in the day they would need to confront their disillusioned king. For the good of Egypt.

NEFERTITI MADE AN ATTEMPT THREE TIMES A DAY TO SEE her husband in the days, weeks, and months after the procession, but he refused to let anyone inside of his chambers and refused to leave the chambers himself. He had created a small temple to the Aten beside his window and worshiped the Aten all day and all night, sleeping where he prayed—if he slept at all.

She found herself alone every night, and morning came earlier and earlier as the pains crept into her legs and her arms. The days hit as if a thousand stones had been dashed upon her body in her sleep, but she eventually rolled over and placed her feet on the floor—Egypt needed a ruler.

Nefertiti welcomed the military home after long years away from Egypt with a grand feast after they were settled, hoping it would bring Pharaoh out. Instead it only caused more hatred toward their Pharaoh because he refused to see them; they were sick and injured—some missing limbs and digits, many still bandaged—but they came to the city of Aketaten for the feast, held in the largest courtyard situated in front of the palace.

Their grumbles rose in the night air, and Nefertiti stepped before the angry soldiers and gave her address from the front steps of the palace.

"Men of war, men of battle, honored men, Pharaoh knows

of the sacrifice you make for this great country and respects you and the fallen—he does."

She could tell they wanted to yell out against her but because of their respect for her, they silenced their tongues—save for the myriad of coughs and hacks which simply could not be helped.

"I, Queen Neferneferuaten-Nefertiti, have put forth this feast to honor you for your great contribution to this country and its allies."

Commander Horemheb, Ay, and General Paaten stood on the steps below their Queen, staring out into the room full of ranking men.

"Pharaoh must tend to other matters and has sent his beloved Queen, his lady of the Two Lands, his greatly beloved, to you to show he still stands behind you," she said, hoping they would believe in the boldness with which she spoke her lie.

A few moments passed and the men began to settle down. Once their reluctant contentment with her answer reached her senses, she ordered the feast to continue.

"Distract them with food and wine," she whispered to several nearby servants.

LATE INTO THE EARLY MORNING, DAY ONE OF THE FOUR-DAY feast finally ended, and her father, General Paaten, and Commander Horemheb escorted Nefertiti to Akhenaten's chambers at her request.

She knocked and a servant cracked the door open.

"Pharaoh wishes not—" he started, but Nefertiti, with Paaten's help, pushed the door open anyway. The servant tried to stop the Queen but found himself in the shadow of Commander Horemheb and subsequently backed away.

She looked around his greatly disheveled chambers, empty wine goblets all around, and finally spotted her husband—on his knees, facing the rising sun, naked and worshiping, arms spread wide, eyes closed, face toward the budding light.

Nefertiti walked to stand between him and the window.

As soon as he felt the light disappear from his eyes, Akhenaten spoke.

"Pharaoh wishes you to leave."

"Pharaoh Akhenaten, it is your wife, Queen Neferneferuaten-Nefertiti," she said. "There was a feast to honor the soldiers who have returned from our allies' battlefront. You have disrespected them by not showing your face." She wanted to slap him for the embarrassment he brought to the throne.

There was silence for a while as he sat unmoving. "As you have disrespected Pharaoh by entering his chambers uninvited," he said, opening his eyes.

His comments crashed against a calloused wall Nefertiti had long since built around her heart. She could smell the wine in his sweat.

"Your council, your country, your people, your wife, your children . . . we need you."

His blank stare in response sent her to rage.

"We *need* you! Do you not understand that you are neglecting everything you promised to protect and love and rule? Do you even remember your vow when you were crowned Pharaoh?"

General Paaten, Commander Horemheb, and the servant stood as still as the stone, not wanting to behold Pharaoh's wrath. Ay only looked at the Pharaoh with disgust.

Pharaoh remained silent until finally teetering to his knees. He spoke softly.

"Do you wish to be banished?"

"Do you wish this city to be overrun with rebels again? If

you do not find yourself on the throne, ruling Egypt and letting the people return to their worship of the gods, the people will rise up against you. When did you last attend a meeting with Nakht? He is your grand vizier, is he not? Egypt will go bankrupt . . . *bankrupt* . . . in six years! We are not bringing in the money we did when the economy flourished with religion. You have starved the people of their faith. You must return them to their old ways. The cult of Amun is *gone*. The priesthoods of all the gods except the Aten are *gone*. Your mother, Queen Tiye, told us that we have the power—but you, with your neglect, are destroying what we have gained. You must obey your father and your mother and finish their plan to restore power to the throne."

He remained silent. His hand dropped to the floor to find another wine goblet. He attempted to drink, but only a few drops fell onto his tongue.

Seeing his nonchalance, Nefertiti added, "Your father would be ashamed."

The fog in his eyes disappeared. "My father would be *proud*. He, as a part of the Aten shows me, is proud of me each and every day. *All* of the Pharaohs before are proud of what I have done! They are now being worshiped as the Aten, and I am a son of Pharaoh, a son of the Aten of whom they are most proud!"

Nefertiti wanted to shake the sense into him. "All of the dead Pharaohs are not in the Aten!"

He glared at his wife. "The Aten will remain the sole god of Egypt," he said, and closed his eyes again. "Now, wife of Pharaoh, remove yourself from my worship and never make mention of the man who called himself my father or of Queen Tiye ever again."

Nefertiti stood still. "If you will not rule, I will. Make me Pharaoh Coregent," she demanded.

"As you wish. But, Neferneferuaten-Nefertiti . . . if you declare the people may worship the other gods of Egypt or declare Amun-Re as the premier god, I will have you impaled outside the temple of the Aten at the foremost of the entrance of Aketaten."

His icy glare made her feet take a step backwards.

"If you refuse me to allow the religious backbone of the Egyptian economy to continue, what are we to do about Egypt's pending bankruptcy?"

"You are now Pharaoh Coregent, are you not? It is your job to find a solution. But mind my generous warning." He barked at the servant, "Queen Neferneferuaten-Nefertiti is now Pharaoh Coregent Neferneferuaten. Have grand vizier Nakht declare this to all of Egypt."

He put his hand to his head when the bellowing sound of his voice overtook his ears.

"The Pharaoh Coregent shall remove herself from Pharaoh's worship," he said, and shooed her with a few flicks of his hand. Nefertiti took a side step to allow the light to fall again on his face.

All of a sudden, a messenger burst through the doors.

"Pharaoh's daughter, Setepenre, has died, as did her wet nurse. Pharaoh's daughter, Nefernefereure, has fallen ill with the same sickness of coughing blood."

Nefertiti gasped. *"No!"* She began to run out the door toward her babies, but stopped at the entrance to Pharaoh's chambers, looking back to see if Akhenaten was following her —but he stayed where she left him, praying to the Aten.

"She's your *daughter!*" Nefertiti yelled, gasping from disbelief that her husband would sink to such depths.

"Pharaoh's son is the only one of importance now," he said.

Nefertiti's face contorted. She wanted to scream at him,

"You are the failure your father knew you would be!" but an overwhelming rage muted her tongue. Instead, she left to tend to her sick daughter.

CHAPTER 25
THE TIME OF PLAGUE

NEFERTITI RAN WITH GENERAL PAATEN TO THE NURSING chambers where her two youngest daughters were staying with their wet nurses. She threw open the doors and found one wet nurse crumpled on the floor, unmoving, the other standing in the corner of the room holding Neferneferure as the young girl coughed up blood. Setepenre lay still as stone in the royal crib.

Nefertiti looked first to her newborn and then to the one-year-old. She tried to go to the one-year-old, but Aitye was there by the door and blocked her path.

"No, my Queen!"

Nefertiti tried to knock her down, but General Paaten instinctually grabbed Nefertiti's shoulders, pulling her back.

"My children! My *daughters!*" Nefertiti yelled.

The wet nurse holding Neferneferure spoke, her voice calm. "My Queen, you must not. This child will die, and if you hold her, you will die as well. I have seen it spread, first from Mara"—she nodded to the dead wet nurse on the floor —"then to the little Princess." A single tear fell down her cheek as she nodded to Setepenre. "It is now spreading to Princess Neferneferure."

She patted her back as the little girl lay limp on her shoulder, struggling to breathe, blood spatter from her mouth staining the shoulder of the wet nurse's white gown.

"Leave us in these chambers and do not come back until we are dead," the wet nurse said, tears now streaming down her face. "Long live Pharaoh's chief royal wife," she whispered.

Nefertiti commanded her general and servant girl to unhand her, to let her go, but her words fell on stony expressions.

"Take the Queen from this room of death," the wet nurse said to General Paaten.

He nodded and pulled Nefertiti out of the room, accompanied by Aitye.

Hot tears raced down Nefertiti's face. Her body had forgotten how to breathe.

Aitye bit her lip, not wanting to add to the Queen's pain, but gathered the courage as she closed the doors to the nursing chambers. "My Queen . . . I asked Merytre to hold Princess Meketaten in her chambers as well, since she was with Neferneferure this morning."

Nefertiti finally took a shaky breath and stared at Aitye in disbelief.

This is not happening to me, she thought. *Amun-Re, why are you punishing me? Why? Have I not paid enough already?!*

"My Queen!"

A messenger came running up to her, but General Paaten put his hand up and said, "Pharaoh Coregent Neferneferuaten."

The messenger nodded. "Pharaoh Coregent, reports are coming in from the Northern border." He took a deep breath. "It is the plague."

Nefertiti hung her head. She longed to hold her babies, but General Paaten's hard grip on her arm made her mind silence her heart.

Egypt needs me now. I must put aside my daughters.

Tears welled in her eyes as she looked into the room where her sick and dead children lay. She would not be the one to hold them while they died.

"Pharaoh Coregent," the messenger said again. "Many messengers have come."

"Yes." Nefertiti stepped away from the nursery. Her heart cried out, *Children, forgive me!* but with the will of her mind, she kept her eyes dry and her mouth shut. "I shall hear the messengers."

Her heart sank deep within her chest, and some of her soul died along with her daughter, Setepenre. If Nefefneferure and Meketaten were to die as well, surely she would only be half alive.

As she sat in her throne, it became apparent that it was the return of the military abroad which had brought home the plague. She ordered all halt of the military and that the soldiers be confined and isolated.

As she closed her eyes and rested the back of her head against the cool stone of the throne, she thought, *I did this, I killed my own daughter. I ordered the military home from a diseased land. I am to blame.*

She forced her eyes to open, feeling the stares of all who stood in the throne room. Stares that begged the question, *What do we do?* She straightened her back and cleared her throat.

"Pharaoh Coregent wishes to send correspondence."

The scribe pulled out papyrus and readied the inkwell, nodding to Nefertiti when he was ready.

"The plague from our Northern allies descended upon Aketaten and all of Lower Egypt with great speed. It is a fast killing disease," she announced. "It has taken Pharaoh's youngest daughter already, within a fortnight of showing symptoms. Two more of Pharaoh's children are at risk of death as well. Take precautions and isolate anyone showing signs of the plague. Wishes be it takes as few as possible."

The scribe nodded that he had completed her letter.

"Make copies of this letter and send it to all of the officers of Upper Egypt. Have messengers send copies to our allies in the South."

The messengers bowed and left to complete their tasks.

MORE MESSENGERS POURED IN, ONE AFTER THE OTHER, from their northern allies, crying out to Nefertiti.

"Gold!"

"Help!"

"Disease!"

She looked up to the Aten, who shone high over her head, drenching her body in sunlight. The Aten calmed her for a brief second before sweat began to pour from her back. She took in a steadying breath.

I cannot send any more money to our allies, I must take care of Egypt first, she thought. *I cannot bankrupt this great nation's treasury for allies abroad when we, at home, are dying.*

Having made up her mind, she crafted answers to deny the pleas of aid and gold.

THE MITANNI KING SENT HIS OWN RESPONSE ONCE HE received Nefertiti's answer, but by then, Setepenre and Nefefneferure were both dead and buried. Meketaten, though having not fallen ill with her encounter with her sister that one dreadful morning, fell ill in the months afterward.

OH HER WAY BACK TO THE THRONE ROOM, NEFERTITI stopped in the courtyard and noticed the eerie silence. She wandered the palace looking for her children. Finding them in the temple of the Aten, her heart stopped. Meritaten and her husband Smenkare, Ankhesenpaaten, and Neferneferuaten Tasherit were all kneeling, facing the sun with their arms open wide. Their father prayed aloud to the Aten to heal their sister, Meketaten, with his rays of light.

She shrunk into the shadows of the corridor.

I have taught them to worship the Aten, she thought. *What have I done?*

A messenger was nearby, and she ordered him to go bring forth Smenkare and Meritaten.

They came out to meet her. "Pharaoh Coregent Neferneferuaten wishes to speak with us?" Smenkare asked.

"Prince Smenkare. Your mother, the royal wife of the Pharaoh before, Sitamun . . . did she not teach you about Amun-Re?" she asked him.

"Yes, she did, but having spent the past year with Meritaten as my wife in Aketaten, I have come to know that my mother spoke lies. The Aten is the sole god of Egypt," he responded with the sun in his eyes, and Nefertiti's daughter, Meritaten, held to his arm, gleaming with a proud smile.

Nefertiti took a slight step backward, her mouth ajar. *I have done this,* she thought again.

"Do you know who your father is?" she asked, hoping

Sitamun had told him so she could have something to regain his trust in the knowledge of his mother.

"Yes . . . my mother never told me, but when I moved here, Pharaoh Akhenaten revealed all. He said my mother has lied to me a great deal. As such, I am Pharaoh Akhenaten's brother and his firstborn daughter's husband, and therefore should be the next heir to the throne. My mother was to deny me my right to rule, and so I have disowned her."

"You disowned your mother?" Nefertiti asked. Akhenaten had caused all this trouble because he wanted a son; why would he let his half-brother know of his right to the throne?

"Yes, Pharaoh Coregent Neferneferuaten, of course. She wished me to live a life hidden under a stone. No mother of virtue would wish that upon her only child, especially one destined to be the great Pharaoh of Egypt."

"Have you told her you no longer worship Amun-Re? Have you told her of your disownment?"

"Why would I tell her such things? The worship of the false god Amun-Re is banned, and she is not worth the papyrus," he said with a look of disgust.

She could think of nothing more to say, only nod. Nothing came to mind of how to regain his trust. She had created a daughter who so longed to be like her mother and father worshiping the sole god of Egypt, the Aten; she had taught Meritaten disbelief in the other gods, in the true premier god of Amun-Re.

Thus, she thought, *my punishment truly begins. Perhaps Amun-Re was gracious to Setepenre and Neferneferure.*

She excused Prince Smenkare and Princess Meritaten and turned to walk to the throne room. With every step fear rose inside of her as she realized that she would never be able to turn Egypt back to the old ways. She would be killed and her children would be there to disown her, to literally cheer as she was hoisted up to be impaled.

Helplessness overcame her senses as she found a crevice in the wall and slid down into the darkness.

Amun-Re had abandoned her. Queen Tiye was dead. Her father stayed in Waset, away from sick people, at her order. She had sent the General and Commander to Lower Egypt to find out more about the rumors of rebellion. The only person left whom she could talk to was Kiya, but Kiya had betrayed her for a long time according to Beketaten. Her rage for her had diminished after talking to Queen Tiye, but her resentment had grown into something far uglier.

Desperation filled the sweat in her brow, however, and after much inner debate she forced herself up to go to the royal wife's chambers.

Nefertiti knocked on the door and was greeted by Ainamun.

"Royal wife Kiya is not feeling well at this moment," Ainamun said.

Nefertiti pushed past her anyway. She found Kiya sitting at the table, looking at the bed again. She took a seat opposite her.

"It has been a while since we were here last," Nefertiti finally said to break the silence.

"Yes, it has." Kiya found a small smile.

Nefertiti wanted to slap such a smile off of her face. Instead she averted her eyes and drew in a quick breath. Exhaling slowly, she looked back to Pharaoh's so-called "greatly beloved." No longer only pale, an ashen glow exuded from her face. The dark circles she had seen before had etched themselves deep into her eye sockets. The past two years had stolen Kiya's youth entirely.

"All of my children worship the Aten," Nefertiti said, turning to look out the window. "I did not teach them about the true premier god, Amun-Re."

"Worshiping and teaching about the other gods of Egypt

was outlawed, sister. You did the best you could do," Kiya said.

Nefertiti hung her head. Even after all this time, Kiya still stood by her side and called her "sister." In her own state of vulnerability, when Kiya could easily return her hatefulness, she instead came to her aid.

Still, the devil sitting on Nefertiti's shoulder began to whisper jealousies into her ear. *She is only edifying you because she knows she betrayed you. She feels guilty and is now trying to win your friendship back.* The devil got the best of her and her hard heart beat again.

"As did you," Nefertiti said.

"I don't understand . . ."

"You did the best you could as well . . . to sneak around with Akhenaten after promising you would refuse him."

Kiya opened her mouth to speak, but shock gripped her vocal cords.

"I know the truth. He came to you all those nights he was supposedly in the temple of the Aten," Nefertiti said with an icy glare. "Beketaten told me that you are sterile, and so never had to worry about discovery. You helped them plan Henuttaneb's pregnancy by getting him drunk with wine!"

"I did *not!*" Kiya finally croaked out. She got up and sputtered out some incomprehensible words as her thoughts amused themselves jumping back and forth between anger, guilt, depression, resent, and regret. *Why would Beketaten say lies about me? Hadn't she done enough already?* was the only clear thought in her mind.

She walked over to the bed behind Nefertiti and jabbed a finger at it. Her boiling anger at Beketaten muted her tongue, and she hated herself for not being able to speak the truth.

"*I did not!*" she screamed finally as she picked up the wrapped wool headrest from her bed and chucked it at the wall. It made a thud as it hit.

"Why would Beketaten lie to me?" Nefertiti shouted back, standing up to face her. "She has no reason to lie! You, on the other hand, have *every* reason!"

Two messengers arrived at Kiya's chambers and knocked at the open door. Kiya nodded to them while Nefertiti turned and shouted, "What is the message?"

They looked at each other, and the first one said, "Pharaoh Coregent, royal wife Kiya, I bring word from a messenger of the King of Mittani. It would be left in the throne room, but it also concerns royal wife Kiya, which is why I bring it to Pharaoh Coregent now." He bowed quickly and returned to standing.

"Speak your message," Nefertiti said.

"The King of Mitanni demands his daughter to be brought back to him, as Egypt failed to come to the Mitanni's aid against the plague and failed to respond with the might of Egypt against the Hittites. He accuses Pharaoh Akhenaten of creating a treaty with the Hittites and blames Egypt's collusion with their enemies for Egypt's weak response and delayed gifts and aid."

Part of Nefertiti jumped for joy—finally, she could get rid of the imposter she once thought a friend! But part of her cried because she would be left all alone once more.

Nefertiti's tongue tied itself until she could only spit out, "Next message."

"Pharaoh Coregent Neferneferuaten—" The messenger hesitated with a look to the ground, but then raised his head and spoke clearly: "Princess Meketaten is dead."

WITH SOLEMNITY AND HEAVY HEARTS, THEY BURIED THE second oldest child of Pharaoh in Akhe-Aten.

Nefertiti reached for Akhenaten's hand as they stood in

the burial chamber and watched Meketaten's sarcophagus lowered into its stone home. Her fingers graced his, but they hung unmoving. She closed her eyes. She tried once more to wrap her fingers around his. He let her, but did not return the embrace. He stood unmoving, staring into the light of the torch.

"The third child we have had to bury," she whispered. "Won't we be each other's comfort?" She longed for the warm embrace of his arms while she cried and let her heart ache. Her heart dropped some of its burden when he began to speak, but fell twice as fast when he completed his sentence.

"We will find comfort enough in the Aten."

A quiet cough from Kiya came behind them. After the announcement of Meketaten's passing, Nefertiti had neglected to respond to the Mitanni King, and so Kiya stayed in Aketaten. Another stifled cough echoed in the stone resting place.

IT SEEMED THAT AS SOON AS THEY SAW THE DAYLIGHT WHEN they came out of the tomb, a vision leapt upon Akhenaten.

"The Aten speaks!" he said.

His servants held his arms as he nearly toppled over from the impact of the vision.

"What does he say, Pharaoh?" Nefertiti asked him, hoping it was to stay with her tonight so they could grieve for their three daughters now on their journey to the afterlife.

"There is a . . . missing piece to Pharaoh's reign," he said as he stared into the sun. "I must return to the temple!"

He stayed there day and night, leaving Nefertiti alone, as he was brought his wine.

ON THE FOURTH DAY, HE EMERGED.

Ordering his servants and family with him to the throne room with haste, he claimed he needed to reveal what the Aten had shown him. As he sat in his throne, he ordered that he, as the high priest of the Aten, be married to his eight-year-old daughter Ankhesenpaaten, to further claim his right to the throne and establish his legitimacy in the absence of Queen Tiye.

Nefertiti closed her eyes and looked to the floor, wondering how she would get Egypt—and, more importantly, her children—back to Amun-Re, as he crowned his daughter his wife in ceremonial marriage.

His heretic prophesies spread through their family like a disease. The scribe scribbled the marriage into the records. There would be no feast or celebration in this time of death.

A loud thud sounded behind them. Turning, they saw Kiya had collapsed to the floor.

Nefertiti felt her foot take a step toward her, but she stopped when Pharaoh said, "The court shall hold a great feast honoring the ceremonial marriage between Pharaoh and his daughter!"

"Pharaoh, your royal wife Kiya has fallen to the ground," Nefertiti said.

How could his mind not grasp the severity of the plague around them? The same plague that had just claimed the lives of three of their children!

Nefertiti motioned to the stewards in the corner.

Ainamun came with several servants and helped to carry Kiya back to her chambers.

"She has fallen in favor for the marriage!" Pharaoh said, and stood up. "Let all of Egypt know the good news!"

Before he left, he turned back to the family standing behind him and smiled at Nefertiti.

"Pharaoh Coregent may now rule in Pharaoh's place."

And then he was gone with his new wife to the temple of the Aten.

WITH A HUFF, SHE SAT IN HER THRONE AND DISMISSED everyone from the throne room and called for Ainamun to give report on royal wife Kiya. Messengers were now a rarity at Aketaten, as was the staff, as most had already succumbed to the deadly disease. She hoped her family in Waset were safe; she had not heard from them in a while. Ay had come to the burial of his granddaughters but quickly left to not endanger himself and thus his family.

The sun shone overhead, beating upon Nefertiti's brow. Shaking her head, she remembered when Amenhotep had demanded an open-roofed throne room for his palace.

Amenhotep . . . she thought. *I miss you so much. I wish you would come back to me. I would do anything for you to come back to me.*

Finally, Ainamun entered the throne room. She bowed before Nefertiti and said, "Pharaoh Coregent, royal wife Kiya is not well and has not been well these past few days."

Nefertiti thought, *Even more so than when I saw her last? Two months can change so much.*

"Is it the plague?" she asked.

"She has not coughed up blood, but the swiftness of the disease tells me it may be."

She debated risking her own health to go see Kiya, but the desire burned within her to confront Kiya one last time, if indeed it was the plague, about her betrayal of their friendship.

"Take me to her," Nefertiti commanded as she stood up and began to walk to the door.

Ainamun's feet firmly stayed where they were.

"If it is the plague, Pharaoh Coregent, you will fall ill as well and possibly die with the others."

"I am aware of the potential consequences."

Ainamun bowed her head and obliged to her command, but wished Nefertiti would not go. If she were to die, they would be left with Pharaoh Akhenaten.

AINAMUN OPENED THE DOOR TO REVEAL KIYA LAYING IN her bed.

A servant approached them before they entered. "Royal wife Kiya has begun coughing up blood. It is taking her quickly."

"I must see her," Nefertiti said.

"Pharaoh Coregent will get the disease as well," the servant said, and stepped in front of her path to the bed.

"I will take that chance."

"At least put this around your head," the servant said, and draped a clean lightly woven linen over her crown and face.

Nefertiti obliged and went to Kiya's bedside.

When Kiya noticed Nefertiti's presence, she smiled faintly, knowing why she was there. Hope rose in her heart that Nefertiti was also there because she still cared for her.

"What is it? Why are you smiling?" Nefertiti asked.

"You were right, Nefertiti," she said, hiding a cough with the linen she grasped in her hand.

"Right about what?"

"I loved Amenhotep."

Nefertiti gritted her teeth, but her tears came almost to the point of pouring out.

Kiya continued. "He was my friend and confidant . . . but you were so happy."

"Did you go to him? Did you betray me?" Nefertiti did

not want to wait for the prologue. She did not want to know, but she needed know. She wanted the truth as a quick bite of the poisonous asp, not as the tiny pricks of a billion ants.

Images of that night raced through Kiya's mind: the violation and betrayal by her once-upon-a-time friend, Amenhotep, as she wept underneath the window that morning with her throbbing head and bloody nose and violated body.

"Tell me, Kiya . . ."

The urgency of her words brought Kiya back from her memories. Her eyes focused on Nefertiti. Apprehension cornered every detail of her face; her mouth trembled in fear, but her eyes searched for truth.

"I did not," she said in one breath.

Nefertiti dropped her head to her friend's chest. *Curse you, Beketaten! Curse you, Henuttaneb!* she thought, and clenched her teeth as she pulled Kiya's dress into her fists.

Kiya closed her eyes and thought about Akhenaten's attack as she felt the weight on her lungs burn inside her. *The dead and dying can bear this burden. The living should not dwell in the past,* she thought. *I cannot hurt Nefertiti more. Akhenaten won't remember—now, especially, as the Aten has his mind far removed from this reality.*

"I'm so sorry, Kiya, for the accusations I have made," Nefertiti moaned into her dress. "Please forgive me."

"Nothing to forgive," Kiya coughed pitifully. She closed her eyes for a minute. "Nefertiti, I lied to you."

"What? What . . . was your lie, Kiya?" Nefertiti's heart skipped and fell into her stomach again.

"I told you once that I would refuse Pharaoh should he command me," she said, and caught her breath to continue, "and that I was not afraid to die. But—"

She coughed violently until the rag teemed with blood.

The servants came to wipe her lips and handed her another cloth.

"But . . . I am afraid to die. I am afraid of what lies next. I am afraid of the darkness."

Her words took Nefertiti's breath away as the realization hit her hard in the face. Her accusations, her conniving ways to have her friend sent away, and her avoidance for the past two years because of her own jealousies all shook the very ground she knelt upon. She looked into her friend's eyes.

"Kiya, I don't want to lose you."

Those words, Kiya thought, *forgive all.*

"As long as you remember me, you will never lose me," she said as her chest struggled to rise. A few moments passed as Kiya coughed and coughed, trying to turn her face away from Nefertiti.

"Kiya, don't leave me. Please, I need you here. I never learned to paint." Nefertiti chuckled and saw Kiya smile.

"You will learn. Thank you," Kiya whispered with a shallow breath, "for being all I ever wanted."

"What is that?" Nefertiti took her hand.

"A friend."

Her face relaxed, her eyes dimmed, and she sank slowly into the linen wrapped wool bed. Her chest no longer struggled to rise and fall, but rested.

The pit of Nefertiti's stomach crawled to the top of her throat. Her body remembered how to breathe again and it took a sudden inhale. Her fingers shook as they went to cover Kiya's eyes and slide her eyelids down.

Standing up as tall as a tree next to the bed, Nefertiti said nothing, felt nothing as she held Kiya's hand. The Aten poured his rays into her room.

She remembered a silence like this when Pharaoh Amenhotep III died. No birds, no insects, no wind, nothing made a sound out of respect for the great man. Now a silence out of respect for a great friend, a most loyal friend, swept nature.

Nefertiti could only force the words from her lips: "Send her to her father for a Mitanni burial."

The servants slowly began making preparations as Nefertiti stood beside her friend—a friend whom she had treated so unkindly and took for granted.

"Send word to her father that he has lost a great daughter, a great royal wife, most beloved of Pharaoh. Beloved by me," she whispered, still looking down at the plain-looking girl who in death had become beautiful. A glow had erupted from her, it seemed, as if she had finally found peace. But then the moment was gone and all Nefertiti saw was her dead ashen-colored friend.

She let her hand drop, and she turned to walk out of the room and go somewhere, anywhere. She couldn't quite discern where she was going. Her feet seemed to know. They took her back to her chambers, and she quietly closed the door. No thoughts were in mind.

Then with the rage of a thousand horses rushing forth from her lungs, she let out a guttural scream which pulled her body in on itself. The reverberations beat back against her ears, as her fists sunk deep into her stomach and her knees bent low to the ground.

How did my life end up like this? she wanted to scream. She dug her nails into the side of her arm and she found the courage to breathe once more.

She let out a raspy yell and hurled a candle at the wall. *If I had only had a son! But no! Amun gave me six beautiful daughters!* The air escaped her lungs as she kicked over a nearby chair. *They all believe the Aten is the sole god of Egypt!*

"I am cursed!" she yelled as she sent the golden discs adorning their relief table across the room. "Egypt is in ruin!"

She knocked a small statue to the ground. *And I lost three of my precious daughters to the plague!* Her screams attacked the stone walls around her and raced back to her ears as she threw a lampstand to the ground.

And Kiya! "Kiya!"

She tore a curtain from the window, tears gushing from her eyes.

"Kiya . . ."

Her hands grabbed for anything they could touch and she ripped the sheets from the bed. *I accused her of betraying me when she had done nothing.* The tapestry hanging from the wall was no match against her rage.

"And my husband." Her breaths were shallow as she bent over, trying to catch her breath. "Pharaoh Akhenaten!" She screamed his name again and again, disgust filling her mouth.

I have let him go mad! I have done this!

She collapsed against the back wall.

She looked at the destruction of her bed chambers and fell to the floor, lying curled up underneath the window, weeping.

AITYE STOOD OUTSIDE NEFERTITI'S DOOR, VALIANTLY guarding it against anyone who dared question her beloved Queen's behavior.

NEFERTITI STAYED IN HER CHAMBERS, DESTROYING everything she could find, not eating, barely sleeping, for days on end.

Losing track of time, she awoke to Aitye holding a cool cloth to her face. Aitye had tiptoed over the mess to her as she lay there unresponsive, and helped her sit up. She had also brought her food and drawn her a bath. Nefertiti didn't ask how much time had passed.

When she emerged, she learned that Kiya's body had been sent back to Mitanni.

NEFERTITI RULED DURING THE DAY, DECLINING PLEAS FOR help and trying to stockpile treasury funds to last Egypt a little while longer in order to keep Egypt afloat. At night, Nefertiti would send word to Pharaoh Akhenaten, asking him if she could bring Egypt back to Amun-Re for the sake of the Egyptian treasury, and he would respond the same.

"The Aten will provide, as he has always done for me. If you betray the sole god, you will face impalement."

He could forget anything at will, but his threat to me he would always remember, she thought every time he sent the same message back.

Nefertiti slept in her torn and damaged chambers, which she ordered to not be touched; they reminded her of her failures as a mother, a Queen, and a friend. She came to love the darkness, where she could hide and sob away the time. Aitye drew her a bath every morning and night, and the warm water became her addiction.

CHAPTER 26
THE TIME OF TORTURE

SHE DEALT WITH ONE DAY AT A TIME UNTIL NUMBNESS guarded her soul.

Aitye left her soaking in the bath one morning when a messenger from General Paaten came and knocked on the door.

"I have a message for Pharaoh Coregent Neferneferuaten," he said, and pushed past Aitye, but Aitye held her ground.

"I will take the message to her," she said.

The messenger saw the destruction behind the cracked door and decided it was probably best to let someone else deliver the message. "General Paaten and Master of Pharaoh's Horses, Ay, have captured a spy from the growing rebellion against Pharaoh. General Paaten wishes to speak to Pharaoh Coregent in the council room, and there they will proceed to the throne room."

"I will tell Pharaoh Coregent," Aitye said.

The messenger left and Aitye returned filled with visible dread and grief.

Nefertiti sat in her tub with one elbow on a knee, staring

at the stone wall in front of her, expressionless, her mind as lukewarm as the water in which she sat.

"Pharaoh Coregent," Aitye said.

Nefertiti, without moving, responding, "What is it, Aitye?"

"The general has captured a spy. He requests your presence in the council room."

Nefertiti lay motionless in the tub. Everything hurt to move.

Aitye crouched eye-level with her. "My Queen."

Nefertiti looked to her.

"General Paaten has a spy. He requests your presence in the council room."

Nefertiti closed her eyes, then finally opened them with an audible exhale. Uncaring of the open door, she slowly stood up and allowed Aitye to dry her naked body. Her children were heretics, her friends dead, her husband mad, her country in shambles. Her face held no expression as monotony filled her words.

"What else do you have for me, Amun-Re? What more punishment do you give me? I will take it! There is nothing more you can do to me!"

She looked to Aitye. "There is nothing else I can lose." Queen Tiye's wisdom came to her: *Do what is best for Egypt; Egypt needs a strong Pharaoh, a Pharaoh who will defend them.*

Aitye cowered in fear. This new Queen, this new master, she did not like. Feeling her pain, though, she nodded her head in agreement and continued to dry Nefertiti's perfumed skin as she stepped from the tub.

After Aitye dressed her, Nefertiti marched to the council room. She would deal with this spy and let the rebellion know she was not to be trifled with. She would be a stone Queen for all to see, forever engraved in the walls. She would bring Egypt back to its former glory if it were the last thing she did.

"Pharaoh Coregent Neferneferuaten," General Paaten said with a bow as Nefertiti walked into the room.

"My daughter," Ay said with a warm smile.

She tilted her head but said nothing. At this, her father's smile vanished. She went and stood where Pharaoh usually sat and General Paaten stood across from her. Ay, wishing he'd been able to give his child a long embrace as she entered, left the entrance of the room and stood side by side with Paaten.

"A spy?" Nefertiti began. She couldn't look at her father. He had promised her that if she was loyal, if she was patient, if she was a good wife, it would all fall into place. Her lips pressed tightly together.

"We have found a spy in the midst of the palace: a man posing as a servant to Pharaoh. He refuses to speak, but we know he is from the growing rebellion of which I had heard rumors about before the plague struck," General Paaten said. "I also believe we may be losing Commander Horemheb to our plan. He sees no end in sight—and I agree with him—but I made Queen Tiye and Pharaoh Amenhotep III a promise that I intend to keep."

"The question is: How long will his loyalty to the royal family outweigh his loyalty to Amun?" Ay asked.

"It is the same question we all ask ourselves." General Paaten shook his head. "Beketaten married an Amun prophet and they tried to kill her own brother through a rebellion. They did not believe loyalty to family ever outweighed loyalty to Amun. I have no evidence whatsoever to tie them to this plot, but I would wager my firstborn son—if I had one—that they are behind it."

"They fight for Amun-Re. Can you blame them?" Nefertiti said as she sat down with a stiff and straight back.

"No, I cannot. Nevertheless, we are bound by our oaths to

protect Pharaoh and Egypt from any threat," General Paaten said. "The people know the consequences of raising arms or conspiring against Pharaoh no matter what decrees he makes. They will answer for their crimes."

"Yes, they will. They are breaking our law," she said, but in truth, she almost sympathized with them. She never would have thought about conspiring against or rebelling against Pharaoh if she had been a subject, but perhaps break the law in the privacy of her home by worshiping the way she knew to worship. Then again, madness had overcome her husband. "And what do we do when the threat to Egypt is Pharaoh himself?" Nefertiti asked, her eyes as cold as stone, cooling the red puffiness beneath them.

General Paaten put both hands wide on the table and hung his head. Lifting it slowly to look at her, he pursed his lips as no answer came to mind.

"Do we let them come?" Nefertiti asked him. "Let them kill him and our family?"

"Never!" Ay banged on the table with a hard fist.

"So that Egypt may return to Amun-Re and the other gods of Egypt who have been neglected?"

"No," General Paaten said. "If we do that, we let them take the power of Pharaoh. We let all of this that has happened be in vain. We must do everything we can to prevent the uprising."

"They will not stop with just Akhenaten. They will come for me as well, as I have feigned loyalty to the Aten all these years—so well, in fact, that my children only believe in the Aten," she hissed through her teeth. "It may be worth the sacrifice."

"Pharaoh Coregent," General Paaten said, walking over to her. Kneeling down, he whispered, "Your sacrifice has already been great. I will not allow you to sacrifice any more."

Ay stood and watched them as the general's words sank

into his soul. *No . . . I will not allow you, my precious lotus blossom, to suffer any longer either. I will protect you—like I should have done years ago when they first approached me.*

Her hand graced the scar on the general's face, and she kissed his forehead. "You saved my life when they rebelled the first time. Do not let me cause another scar to your body. I only ask, if they come and if the end is seemingly near, that you take my children and my servants, if you can get to them."

She paused wanting to say Kiya's name as well—but she was dead and no longer in need of saving, so she continued.

"Leave Egypt forever. Protect them from the people who want us all dead. Take what you need from the treasury—I give you an order to be prepared for when that day comes."

General Paaten, after a moment of silence, dropped his head in obedience. "Until that day, however, I will protect you with all whom I command," he said.

"My heart is with you, General Paaten."

She stood and looked to her father. Ay could not hide the shame blushing his cheeks.

General Paaten glanced between the two of them, lost in their own silent conversation, and after a few moments hid a cough and asked, "Now . . . what do we do about this spy?"

"We put the fear of Pharaoh Coregent in him. We make him tell us what he knows," Nefertiti said with black eyes.

Ay nodded, but his heart fell into his stomach. She had reached out for help so many times before, but he had only given her kind words of encouragement; he'd never taken the time to help his daughter when she was in need.

"I have nothing left to fear," she said.

Her words punched her father in the bowels of his stomach.

"So it shall be," General Paaten said.

Walking from the room, she first had her royal dress,

crown, and golden cape draped on her, then entered the throne room and took her place seated upon her throne to wait for the doors to open. General Paaten and Ay stood on either side of her.

"Bring the bone-breaker," she ordered a nearby soldier, knowing she had to put the fear of Pharaoh into the spy should he force her hand. She looked to General Paaten, who nodded in agreement.

Ay looked to the doors, awaiting their opening, not wishing to see his beloved lotus blossom shrivel and sink into darkness.

———

THE DOORS TO THE THRONE ROOM SWUNG OPEN WITH A loud whoosh. Two soldiers pushed the spy forward and goaded him by the sharp tips of their spears. He appeared before Nefertiti standing on the ground at the base of the steps to her throne.

General Paaten, who stood at the step below, crossed his arms at his silence. "You will bow to Pharaoh Coregent."

The spy stood and rocked on his heels, clasping his hands into a firm knot in front of his stomach. "I do not bow to heretics."

"I am Pharaoh Coregent Neferneferuaten!" she bellowed, and shot up from her throne. The echo resounded off the walls and attacked the corridors. Taking a few steps closer to the detainee, she said, "And you will obey Pharaoh!" as she swished the bottom of her golden cape behind her.

He spat on the stone floor. "I will never bow to you or your blasphemous husband."

Nefertiti strutted deliberately to the detainee. Her dress slithered on her body like a loose snakeskin as she walked to the first step. She let him take in the shimmering gold that lit up the room from the sun's rays. His jaw dropped just barely, but he shut it closed. Nefertiti, although hardened and calloused, still captivated every man to lay eyes on her.

She glared into his eyes. "You will bow to the Pharaoh Coregent of Egypt."

As she turned to walk back to her throne, she looked to General Paaten, and he gave a motion to the soldier who was sent to retrieve the bone-breaker. The soldier picked up the heavy bronze club and hoisted it over his head.

Nefertiti reached her throne and finally looked to her father. She saw sorrow behind his hardened gaze, but she ignored it; she needed to be the strength Egypt lacked now. Akhenaten would eventually die—either from madness, wine, or old age—and when that time came, she would be there to turn Egypt back. Until that time, Pharaoh could not risk another rebellion. She sat down with an elegant grace.

"If you will not bow by your own free will, then Pharaoh will make you bow."

He glowered at her in silence.

Nefertiti nodded to the solider, and with that, the solider swung the club.

A loud bone-breaking *CRACK!* filled the throne room, followed by an intense cry of agony.

The soldiers looked to Nefertiti to see if she would flinch at the sound, but she did not. She had felt more agony than this poor man would ever feel.

Another swing, another bone-breaking sound, another cry of agony followed.

The guards who held the detainee finally let him go, and he fell to the floor. His fists beat the stone, his forehead pressed to the ground, his eyes tightly squeezed shut, and his mouth moaned in pain.

"You choose to bow with your head to the floor . . ."

Nefertiti paused as she watched him writhe in pain. "Pharaoh Coregent is flattered. Take him away," she told the guards.

They picked him up, and all watched his legs dangle behind him as they dragged him away to the palace prison. They could still hear his cries as he disappeared down the corridor.

"Foolish pride," Nefertiti whispered under her breath. "Foolish, all of it, so foolish."

"Pharaoh Coregent, may I speak freely?" General Paaten asked his Queen, a little shocked by her iciness yet proud to have a ruler who could do what needed to be done.

"Yes, General Paaten, you may always speak freely. You have earned that right."

"He will answer our questions, but not without . . . extreme persuasion."

"Use whatever means you deem necessary, General Paaten. He is a criminal and must pay for his crime of conspiracy against Pharaoh."

He nodded. "Yes, Pharaoh Coregent."

"After we receive our answers from the spy," Nefertiti said, "should we publicly execute him to send a message to the others?"

Ay's eyes fell to the floor, and he bit his tongue.

"I think it may help lessen the speed of the attack, yes."

Ay looked back up. "He may also be made a martyr, and to silence a martyr would take an act of Amun-Re."

Nefertiti sighed. "Perhaps the best course of action is to keep him hidden in the prison, then."

"TAKE HIM TO THE BURIAL-PREPARATORY ROOM," GENERAL Paaten ordered the guards.

"General," Ay said, pausing while the guards did as they

were told. "The royal army will need to tighten its defenses. Let me see to it. Both of us do not need to be interrogators."

"Queasy stomach?" General Paaten chuckled and put his hand on Ay's shoulder.

Ay smiled with the right side of his face. "Yes," he lied.

"Very well, Ay. You, Master of Pharaoh's Horses, tend to the military, and I will begin the questioning. Should you find yourself with nothing to do, I may need a reprieve."

Ay nodded as a sign of respect and left.

Paaten journeyed to the burial-preparatory room. The guards had lain the spy on the stone table. "I want to see his face," he told the soldiers.

They strapped him down with ropes, face up. Beset, one of the priests of the Aten—formerly Anubis—who performed burial preparations, was summoned and came as commanded ready to begin the mummification process, but was surprised when he found a living subject. A soldier pulled him aside and filled him in. He nodded in agreement.

"Listen closely, spy," General Paaten said. "Since I do not know your name, I will refer to you as 'the intruder.' If you do not answer the questions I ask you correctly, I will not kill you, but I will order Beset, priest of the Aten, to slowly cut off and take out pieces of your body."

"You . . . you just said you wouldn't kill me," the man said. "How can I live without pieces of my body?"

"The body can adapt."

His eyes widened. "I will never tell you anything! Just kill me now! Your time spent torturing me will be a waste!"

"I remember you saying you would never bow to Pharaoh Coregent either," General Paaten said with a grin, and looked pointedly at the man's bloody, swollen knees.

His guards laughed beside him.

"Let's begin with our first question, shall we? Who sent you to spy on the great nation of Egypt?"

"This is not Egypt. This is some man's fantasy. Egypt is where my loyalties lie."

General Paaten took a flattened bronze stick and whacked the intruder's knees. He cried out in pain.

"Answer the question: Who sent you to spy on Pharaoh?"

The intruder glanced to Beset, situated in the corner mulling over his instruments, then looked steadily at the general. "Who do you think?"

General Paaten whacked his knees again. "Answer the question!" he bellowed. "Who sent you to spy on the Pharaoh of Egypt?"

The intruder moaned in pain. His body sunk beneath the ropes. He hung his head, whimpering. General Paaten raised the stick again.

"Wait! Wait . . . I'll tell you," the man whispered. "It was . . . the People's Restoration of Egypt."

"We can't hear you," General Paaten said.

"The People's Restoration of Egypt!"

"Good," General Paaten said, encouraging his good behavior by lowering the stick. "Question two: What are you here to do?"

"I don't know." He shrugged his shoulders and averted his eyes.

"Do you think us stupid? Every spy has a mission. What was it that you were sent here to do?" General Paaten bellowed, then raised the stick and sent it crunching into the intruder's knees.

Nothing but cries of agony answered him.

After a few moments in pain, the intruder replied, "I cannot tell you. Ask me another question . . . any question . . . but that one I cannot answer."

General Paaten observed his grimacing face. "Very well. We will come back to it. Are there other spies in Egypt?"

"I cannot answer because I do not know."

General Paaten nodded to Beset.

The priest went to the wall where an array of apparatus hung from hooks. He grabbed a sharp knife and handed it to General Paaten while the soldier went to a fire and came back with a hot bronze rod.

"If you do not answer us, we will cut off each of your fingers, starting with the tip of this one. Then we will sear the wound, so that you do not lose too much blood in the beginning. What is it that you were sent here to do?"

"I told you I cannot answer."

General Paaten handed the blade back to Beset. "Chop it off," he told him.

"No. Please. No!" the man yelled as Beset crouched lower.

"Answer the question."

"I cannot!"

Beset cut into the first joint of the intruder's pointer finger on his right hand. The intruder screamed. The finger's tip dropped to the floor and the soldier seared the wound with the hot bronze rod. The intruder yelled out again and again.

"If you do not answer our questions, you will see all of your fingers and toes lying about this floor," General Paaten told him.

"I cannot see," the man mumbled.

"Beset!" General Paaten ordered.

Beset mixed salt, cedar oil, and palm wine used to dry out corpses and whisked it in front of the man's nose. He began to gag.

"Please . . . just let me die . . ."

"Answer one of the two questions," the general said, "or next we will take your entire hand."

"No, please do not take my hand, please—"

"Then answer the question!"

At his silence, General Paaten pointed to the intruder's

left wrist and the soldier ran back to heat up the bronze rod again while another held down his hand.

"NO!" the intruder yelled, and squirmed, trying to get off the table to no avail. At the first prick on to his wrist, he screamed, *"I will answer!"*

General Paaten held his hand up to stop. He let the intruder catch his breath.

"There are other spies in Egypt," the man said. "There are many who oppose our Pharaoh . . . many who are willing to raise arms against him."

"How many?"

"Thousands."

"And what were you sent here to do?"

Silence.

General Paaten pointed at his wrist and nodded to Beset, who began to slice again despite the man's cries for mercy.

His legs twitched in pain. *"Pleeease,"* he cried as the knife tore through the tendon. "Stop! I will tell you!"

General Paaten held his hand up to stop the cutting.

"I was sent . . ."

The intruder's eyes rolled back into his head.

"Beset, the mixture."

After whiffing some of it, he came to again.

"You were sent to Aketaten to . . . ?" General Paaten said, jarring his memory.

"I was sent to report back on Pharaoh's habits."

"Why?"

"They plan to kill him."

"Who did you send your report to? Who is leading the rebellion, or rather the People's Restoration of Egypt?"

"I cannot answer . . . you will have to kill me."

"I cannot kill you. I can only continue cutting body parts off until you decide to speak or until you have no more unnecessary body parts left. Continue, Beset."

The man yelled out again and again. He passed out a few more times, unable to be woken with the mixture, but each time he came to they resumed cutting. He would only give up the name of his handler—one of the messengers, Henut—but would not give up the leader of the movement.

General Paaten left the room and told his soldiers to bandage his wounds and put him in the prison after they had finished cutting off his ears, his nose, all his toes, both feet, one hand, and all but one finger on the other hand.

As he walked the lone corridor back to the throne room to tell Nefertiti what information he had been gleaned, General Paaten whispered to himself, "He would have made a great soldier."

***

After hearing what he had to say, Nefertiti asked, "How much was he tortured?"

"He will most likely die from infection. If he does survive, he will never live a normal life again."

Nefertiti looked up to the Aten and shook her head. "Perhaps Henut will give us more information."

General Paaten nodded and sent word to have Henut arrested.

CHAPTER 27
THE TIME OF DESPERATION

Henut led to another who led to another and then another until seventeen men had been hacked apart, most of whom died later from blood loss or infection. General Paaten was no closer to finding the leader of the rebellion or washing out the plan to kill Pharaoh.

Because Egypt's allies no longer sent gifts or responded to her requests, and money no longer freely circulated Egypt due to the ban on worship, Nefertiti saw no other choice but to forge an alliance with the powerful and wealthy Hittites to keep Egypt afloat. Her ad hoc council now consisted of Nakht, her father, General Paaten, and Commander Horemheb. They agreed with her move to ally with the Hittites, albeit reluctantly, and so she sent a letter with gifts of medical supplies under Pharaoh Akhenaten's name.

While they waited for their response—should it come back at all—Nefertiti, on her own one night later, began drafting an edict that the ban on the worship of all gods other than the Aten would be henceforth removed. She would suffer whatever consequences her husband dealt her, but the economy of Egypt was now drained to the dregs, and it was very probable the Hittites would not be a reliable source of income.

AY, NOTICING THE CANDLELIGHT AT THE STRANGE HOUR, walked into the council room and found his daughter bent over the council room table writing laboriously on papyrus.

"My lotus blossom, what are you doing here so late?" he asked.

Nefertiti looked up and smiled. The burden in her shoulders fell some at the sight of her father, until she remembered his broken promises.

"Why have you not gone home to be with Tey?" she asked, her smile vanished.

"I was hoping to spend some more time with you, my daughter." He sat down next to her, like a mouse trying to sneak past the cat.

"Why? So you can fill me with empty words?"

Ay said nothing. Her tone cut him to his heart. He'd expected it the last time he saw her in the council room, but not tonight. Raising his eyebrows and blowing out his breath, he turned to face the candlelight.

"Father, I just feel so hopeless. I'm sorry. I did not mean to disrespect you," Nefertiti said. She tried to keep her chin up, but her head just kept falling as if wanting to shake her tears loose.

Seeing her despair, his fatherly instincts took over and he pulled her close to his chest. "My lotus blossom, I am the one who should be sorry. I saw Pharaoh's decline and yet I tried to uplift you when I should have protected you."

"It is more than just Akhenaten, Father. Setepenre, Neferneferure, Meketaten, Kiya, Tiye . . . I miss them so much." She closed her eyes to listen to her father's steady heartbeat. "I feel so lost without them. I have failed them all."

"Look at me, my daughter," Ay said, pushing her away and lifting her chin to bring her eyes level with his. "You have not failed anyone. You have done the very best you know how, and that is all anyone can ever ask of you."

She fell into his embrace and as his arms wrapped around her she mumbled, "I have you, and that's all I need."

"No, Nefertiti. You have yourself—and *that* is all you will ever need."

He looked over her shoulder, attempting to read what she had been working on when he came in. After a few moments, he summoned the courage to ask, "What is it you are writing?"

Nefertiti jumped from his arms and pulled the papyrus away before her father could see—but even at her age, under his firm glance, she relented and let him read it. His eyes peered over it.

"Nefertiti . . . you realize he will have you impaled? You said so yourself, it would be in vain to issue this type of decree because he would only reverse it the next day!"

"Yes, but perhaps Pharaoh, however feared he may be, would not be able to levy any sort of power over the people. I would be a martyr to them."

"Yes . . ." Ay stroked her back. "Daughter, we will eventually turn back to Amun-Re. But we will do it when it doesn't involve getting yourself killed."

"How, Father? We are losing supporters fast. Commander Horemheb is not going to support this much longer, despite his oath to the royal family. Pharaoh Amenhotep and Queen Tiye's plan is no longer working. We have a few more years left in the treasury, after we stopped giving to our foreign allies, but will it outlast Akhenaten? Who is to know?"

Nefertiti accepted the worst: she would have to lose him completely in death before the country could be restored.

"He has drunk much wine, Father, and he has become so obsessed with the Aten and his visions to eclipse all else. There is no reasoning with him—no way to reach him!"

A moment of silence passed between them.

Nefertiti whispered, "I have thought about . . ."

"Thought about what?"

"Taking his life. But I could never do it. I love him, Father."

Ay smiled grimly. She *had* thought about it.

"You love *Amenhotep*. This man is not him."

Nefertiti only looked into the candlelight and watched the fire's flame—this little flame, dancing happily away, not knowing it would soon suffocate and die.

"Rarely can a man come back from such a fallen state as his," Ay said, "much less for a few moments of clarity to be reasoned with. It would take an act so great—a fate worthy to his soul—to jar him from his madness, if only for a moment."

"I would cherish that moment with him, even one so brief." Nefertiti felt wetness on her cheeks and realized she could not remember the last time she cried.

"As I would your mother."

Ay wrapped his arms around his daughter. Her pain traveled into his heart, and he could no longer keep his own tears at bay.

"Wait a little longer, my lotus blossom, and all will be as it should. I give you my word."

"How can you be so sure?" she asked as she dried her tears.

He took the papyrus from the table and let it burn in the lampstand.

"Don't fathers always know?"

He looked to the door and whistled twice.

Nefertiti's eyebrow raised, wondering why he was whistling at this hour.

The answer to her question walked in the door.

BEKETATEN AND PAWAH SAUNTERED IN.

Nefertiti stood up. Her glare matched Beketaten's own.

"You coward," Nefertiti hissed.

Beketaten only smiled in response.

Pawah spoke, shaking his head in mock disapproval. "The Pharaoh Coregent should not treat her guests in this manner."

"I should never have pardoned you, you worthless—"

"Pharaoh Coregent." Commander Horemheb stepped inside the council room, leaving two guards outside. "These are the leaders of the People's Restoration of Egypt. They have come to you in hopes of striking a deal."

"You? *You* are behind the rebellion?" Nefertiti stood straight, pointing a finger at Beketaten.

"We wish no more bloodshed," Beketaten said, "but we know that as intelligent as you are, you see the decay this great nation is falling to. The people need a strong Pharaoh, not one hidden in his temple, threatening the very lives the gods have appointed him to oversee. You must see this, my Pharaoh Coregent."

Her lips spoke the truth Nefertiti had realized long ago, but her eyes mocked her.

I refuse to give her any satisfaction, Nefertiti thought.

At her silence, Pawah weighed in again. "We have already approached your own father, Master of Pharaoh's Horses, Ay. He sees the pain you bear for Pharaoh's actions and Pharaoh's ill will toward you. How long has it been since you have shared a bed?"

Nefertiti slammed her hand into the table, the candlelight reflecting the fire raging in her eyes. "You will not speak to Pharaoh Coregent about love or pain! You dare bring Pharaoh's bed into this audience?"

She turned sharply toward her traitorous father. "And you, Pharaoh Coregent's own father, conspiring with the enemy?"

"I did it for you, my lotus blossom," Ay whispered. "Would you rather have a thousand men die . . . or one?"

Nefertiti choked back her tongue and clenched her teeth as tight as she could.

"The people will rebel. They will come by force," he said as he grasped her shoulders.

Commander Horemheb stepped to the other side of Nefertiti. "Pharaoh's army will protect him, as we have given our oath, but the hearts of my men are far from him. They will fight, but I fear a weak fight they will give. If they lose, the power of Pharaoh is gone."

Shallow breaths. Her heart raced. Trapped, as the moonlight poured down on her.

"You need to finally listen to us," Beketaten said. "He even has an *heir* now."

Nefertiti's eyes narrowed. *You liar. I hate you.*

Pawah held up his hand to silence her and diffuse Nefertiti's outrage.

"Pharaoh Coregent, think about it in this way." He drew an arc on the table in front of him with his finger. "If you simply gave him poisoned wine to drink, he could fall asleep and die a painless death."

"You wish me to murder my own husband," Nefertiti said.

"It would be hemlock—a painless way to die. Just as if fatigue has overtaken the body until the body just . . . sleeps. Nothing that would raise concern, nothing to take away from the power of Pharaoh—and everything to gain."

"Hemlock leaves your brain awake. He wouldn't be in

sleep. He would know what I had done to him," Nefertiti said, blinking back tears. She wanted to scream at her father, *Is this what you wanted? For me to be a murderer? I would endure a thousand of these lifetimes before doing this!*

"You don't know me at all, Father," she said.

His eye twitched, but he grasped her hand. "He trusts you, Nefertiti. I did not know what they were planning. If we did not have to involve you, we wouldn't have."

A tear, despite all Nefertiti's might, escaped her eye. "Father . . . you, above all people, disappoint me."

Ay clenched his jaw. "I will have to live with your disappointment, Nefertiti. Egypt needs a Pharaoh. And did you not say to me the thought had crossed your mind?"

"A fleeting thought borne of desperation! You are quick to forget the rest of what I said. I am willing to see if the madness takes him or if old age does." She wiped her tear.

"We don't have that long," Commander Horemheb cut in. "The rebellion is ready to strike. If we don't go along with their plan, they will bring the rebellion *now*."

Nefertiti pointed at Beketaten and Pawah. "We have their leaders, do we not? Here in the core of the palace, surrounded by Pharaoh's guards!"

"They are not for Pharaoh." Horemheb's monotone voice gave her the answer she needed. Nefertiti shot a glance to her Commander. Was he not for Pharaoh either?

"You are outnumbered, Pharaoh Coregent," Beketaten said. "One way or another, the Pharaoh will die."

"Lotus blossom," Ay breathed, grasping her shoulders again and turning her to face him, "listen to me. Think of your daughters, think of your sister Mut, think of your grandchildren, think of Egypt and her future. I have tried my entire life to give you everything you needed and wanted. I tried desperately to be both your father and your mother. Temehu would be proud of you, and she would be ashamed of me. But even she would know that the life of one man is not worth tens of thousands, is not worth this nation's decay, is not worth the blasphemy he has set upon Egypt. She would know this. She would bring him the wine and while it took over his body she would lay his head in her lap and stroke his cheek and tell him how much she loved him. She would do this—and deep in your heart, you know you must too."

Tears streamed from Nefertiti's face. "But Father, I still love the man beneath the madness."

"I know, my lotus blossom." But Ay said no more.

Nefertiti had always hoped her father would help her turn Egypt back to Amun-Re when the time came, but not like this. She looked to the ground after he released her. She looked to Beketaten, whose upturned lips almost made her change her mind. But then she looked to Pawah, whose face hid in the shadows.

There was no way out.

Finally, she whispered, "I will be your executioner."

Commander Horemheb let out a sigh. Beketaten smiled fully just as the last of the candlelight flickered.

CHAPTER 28
THE TIME OF BETRAYAL

COMMANDER HOREMHEB ESCORTED HER TO HER HUSBAND'S chambers, where he waved off the guard, and the cupbearer came holding the wine goblet, careful not to spill.

"He has just demanded more wine," the cupbearer whispered. "Your timing is impeccable."

"Do you have it?" Commander Horemheb asked.

A small papyrus-rolled satchel of powder appeared in the cupbearer's hand.

"I have been waiting until instructed," he said.

"Now is the time," Commander Horemheb said, looking to Nefertiti. He placed his hand on her back as the cupbearer swirled the powder into the wine.

"It should only take a few sips," the man said.

Nefertiti nodded in response as he handed the goblet to her.

"We honor you, Pharaoh Coregent," he said with a bow. She bit her lip as he turned to walk away.

"By morning, we shall have you as Pharaoh," Horemheb said.

"By morning, the darkness will have covered our deeds,"

she whispered. "Is that why the Fifth Prophet of Amun and his wife came under the veil of darkness? They know the wickedness of what they ask, yet they shall not dirty their own hands."

Commander Horemheb held his tongue. Her boldness in stating the obvious caused him to shudder at his own denial of it. *This is wicked,* he thought.

"They choose to see murder and war as the same crime," she said as she began to walk toward the chambers door, "yet they want me to do their bidding"—she placed her knuckles to the door—"in the dark"—and she knocked. "Where no one will see."

"Enter," Akhenaten called from inside. She pushed open the door, never leaving Horemheb's eyes until she closed the door behind her.

Horemheb dropped his head. "What have we done?" he asked himself.

NEFERTITI TURNED AROUND AND SAW HER HUSBAND, AT least clothed in his royal shendyt, facing the moon and praying for the Aten to return. She held the goblet close to her chest as she walked toward him.

Am I to blame? she asked herself, feeling his death sentence in her hand. *If it weren't for me encouraging his belief in the Aten to keep me as his only lover, we might still be happy together. I might have borne his son. Egypt might not be in decay. Am I to blame?*

Her eyes glistened in the candlelight.

"Have you brought my wine?" he yelled out.

"Yes, my love."

He spun around and saw that it was his beautiful wife carrying his wine and not the cupbearer. "My

Neferneferuaten-Nefertiti!" His face beamed, his mouth a bright smile.

Her brow begin to bead with sweat.

He walked to her and placed his hands on either side of her face. "It feels as if ages have passed," he whispered, kissing her forehead. "And yet time does not grace your face, my beautiful one."

Temptation seeped into her soul, almost letting her fingers spill the wine to the floor. But her loyalty to Egypt kept the goblet firmly clasped in her hands.

"To what do I owe your presence?" he asked, pressing his lips to hers.

This was the man she loved; this was the man she was about to murder.

"I come to . . ."

Guilt strained her vocal cords, but she had to try one more time to save his life.

"Yes, my love, anything for you," he said.

She took her chance.

"I come to ask for the greater of Egypt . . . that you please allow the worship of other gods."

His smile vanished.

"I see," he said. "No. Only the Aten shall be worshiped in my Egypt."

Nefertiti continued to look him in the eyes. The gold-inlaid jewels of the goblet pressed into her palms.

"Egypt is in decay, my love. When we outlawed the worship of other gods, Egypt's economy went asunder. We are nearly bankrupt. We have lost our foreign allies. Egypt will not last much—"

"Silence!" He pressed his finger to her lips. "The Aten will provide for Egypt!"

"How?" she asked, pushing his finger away. "How will he

provide? He has not provided in years. Years! Akhenaten, listen to me. We must—"

Akhenaten hit his chest. "There is salvation in the Aten! Not the other false gods!"

"Because *you* say they are false?" Nefertiti brought the cup closer to her chest to protect its contents from his movements. "The sun gives no salvation to Egypt, Akhenaten!"

He turned to walk toward the window. "*My* salvation is there!"

"The rebellion grows! Most of the military and servants of the palace and the city take part! Your salvation will end with your slaughter and that of your family."

"The Aten will provide," he said.

"They will kill us, my love," she whispered.

"Let them come. The Aten protects his only prophet." He spread his arms wide, stepping toward the window.

"The Aten protects his son!"

"And when the Aten sleeps?"

"His shadow covers me. Have no fear, my beautiful one. Have no fear. The Aten does not like your doubt of his ability."

"The Aten is not the one I doubt," she said.

But he was already too engrossed in watching the stars and praying to the Aten to forgive his ignorant wife of her doubt, to understand what she meant.

"Please, Akhenaten . . . allow the worship of other gods . . ."

He closed his eyes, ignoring her as he resumed his worship of the Aten.

A tear slid out of her eye as she watched him.

They would come for him.

Doubt crept into her mind. Would her father,

Commander Horemheb, and General Paaten at least command their armies to protect her and her children?

She accidentally let some of the poisoned wine fall from its goblet onto the stone floor.

Would they protect her now?

The wine soaked into the floor, leaving a stain the color of blood.

Akhenaten had fallen to his knees at the window, praying loudly for his wife, his one true love—other than the Aten—to lose her doubt.

He still loved her.

I will deal with Beketaten and Pawah tomorrow, she thought as she placed the half-empty goblet on a nearby stand.

She bit her tongue and closed her eyes for a moment. *I can order the torture of seventeen spies, but I am too weak to poison the one threat against my country.*

"I will always love you, Amenhotep," she whispered. "I wish you a quick, painless death when the time comes."

When he drinks the poison, it would be as if the cupbearer gave it to him. She nodded at the small consolation she gave herself at her hand in her husband's murder. *Yes, perhaps I will think of it in this way.*

She opened the door and stepped out with nothing in hand. Closing it behind her, she wiped the tear from her eye as she straightened her back and looked straight ahead to face whatever lie there.

"Goodbye, my love."

EPILOGUE
THE TIME OF REMEMBERING

"QUEEN NEFERNEFERUATEN—OUR LONG-PAST QUEEN Nefertiti, the most upright of us all—chose not to be a part of their deeds of the dark," Pharaoh Horemheb announced to the five prophets of Amun. They had all leaned forward, eagerly listening to his recounting.

"*Your* deeds of the dark." Queen Mut pointed to the First Prophet Wennefer. Her eyes held a rage against the priesthood.

"Not mine," he said, his arms still crossed over his body as if to protect himself from his brothers' mistakes.

"*All* of your deeds are done in the dark," Queen Mut hissed, referring to the sins the priesthood had committed against her family. Her eyes turned to Horemheb, begging her husband to continue the recounting, to shed light on the priesthood's greatest transgression, before he cast it out to be forgotten by history and buried by the passage of time.

First Prophet Wennefer jabbed his finger in the air. "There is no proof!" He knew of which deed she spoke. Hatred lingered in the air between her majesty and the priesthood.

"No proof was needed," Queen Mut forced out between her teeth.

"We are a different hierarchy of prophets, my Queen. Placing the blame for past events on us is unwise, especially as we move forward to erase—"

"Silence!" Pharaoh Horemheb threw his hand in the air.

The sun sank lower. Servants dashed in to light the candles and lampstands.

Pharaoh Horemheb leaned back in his throne. His lips were parched, as he had been speaking for the greater of the day. For now, their memories were safe, but he had much left to tell before he signed the edict to erase them into oblivion.

They sat in silence until the sun left them for the night.

The First Prophet Wennefer stood. "We thank Pharaoh for his recounting. However, Pharaoh will now sign the edict."

"There are none greater than Pharaoh. You will not order him to take any action!" Pharaoh Horemheb said. "You are so quick to forget, First Prophet Wennefer. Perhaps Pharaoh should dismiss you and find a replacement, perhaps with someone who values the sanctity of the legacy of Pharaohs before and who knows there are none more powerful than Pharaoh."

"My apologies, my King of Egypt." First Prophet Wennefer bowed and took his seat.

Pharaoh Horemheb rubbed his bottom lip with his finger. *Yes . . . there is still much to tell.* "There shall be no signing of the edict tonight. We will retire for the night and meet again at the first morning light, for the complete legacy of the Pharaohs before still has yet to be told. Pharaoh will continue the recounting tomorrow."

He stood up, bringing his arms outspread as the prophets also rose.

"May Amun be with us all."

THE STORY CONTINUES
SECRETS IN THE SAND, BOOK II

Secrets in the Sand Book II

1335 B.C. Egypt is failing. Allies are leaving. War is inevitable.

The power struggle for the throne should have ended long ago, but yet it rages onward shrouded in conspiracy and murder.

307

Pharaoh Akhenaten's plan to regain power from the priesthood of Amun is done, but his religious zeal has stripped the economy and the people's morale.

Whisperings of rebellion fill the streets as enemies close in on Egypt's borders leaving Nefertiti to fend off political wolves as she attempts to stabilize the nation and keep her crown.

EXCERPT FROM CHAPTER ONE: THE TIME OF WAITING

The thud of Nefertiti's heart numbed her chest as a bitter taste settled on her tongue. Leaning back into the door of Pharaoh's bedchambers, she felt the numbness in her chest drop like a weight to her stomach.

Should I go back? Should I take the poisoned wine back?

Her breath hitched as her arms lay limp at her sides. The agony of the answer to her question attacked what was left of her dignity and seared its red stain upon her cheeks.

No . . . what is done is done, she thought, and lifted her head from the door and straightened her back, lifting her chin to the sky.

"Amun"—her thick whisper clogged her throat—"forgive me."

I leave the wine for you, Amun, and for Egypt. I leave it for the safety of my family and myself. Her hands balled into fists as she thought of Pawah and Beketaten's threat of rebellion, of her children's lives. *I leave the wine for him to drink, if the gods will him gone. When the time comes, I wish him a painless death.*

The numbness took her lungs as the tears she held behind her eyelids came to a stream down her cheeks. She wiped a tear from her eye as she stared into the hallway, her face lit only by the hall's torches.

"Goodbye, my love," she whispered, and began to walk down the hallway to face whatever may become of her, knowing she would have to deal with Pawah and Beketaten in the morning.

"Is it done?" Chief Royal Guard Jabari whispered, stepping from the shadows.

Nefertiti stopped in her gait and shuffled back a step as her red-rimmed, widening eyes found his. It took a moment for her to recognize him, and then her shoulders released their tension and her hands relaxed. *You too, my chief of guards? My father, my commander, my chief royal guard, all a part of this plan to kill my husband.* She pressed her lips into a grimace. *And now, I suppose, so am I.*

Her gaze dropped to the stone floor. "The morning sun shall uncover what is to be." Her words danced over to him and painted his expression with confusion. Not wanting to say more, Nefertiti continued her walk down the long corridor toward her bedchambers.

"When the gods want him gone, he will drink of the poisoned wine," she whispered to herself as she let her fingers slide across the cold stone of the wall. *I have said my goodbye.*

Jabari watched her go before hurrying to the council room to tell Beketaten, Pawah, and all those who awaited the news.

Beketaten pounded a fist into the table after she heard Jabari's incomplete report. "So? Did he drink?"

"At the morning's first light we shall see," Jabari said again.

Beketaten shot up. "Coward!"

Pawah took his wife's hand, calming her as he guided her

back in her seat. Turning to Jabari, he asked, "Did she at least leave the wine in his chambers?"

Jabari nodded. "She emerged with nothing in hand."

"Then it will only be a matter of time," Master of Pharaoh's Horses, Ay, said from the corner. "My daughter did well."

"We are short of *time*," Beketaten said through her teeth.

"Yes, but let the Coregent keep her dignity," Commander Horemheb said. "She is not a murderer. She knows Pharaoh must be dealt with in order for Egypt to survive, but . . ."

"But *what?*" Beketaten gripped the edge of the table. "We all do what we must do," she said as she leaned toward him. "And if she must give the Pharaoh poisoned wine to save herself, her children, and Egypt . . . what coward would not do it?"

"My daughter is no coward," Ay said, uncrossing his arms and putting his weight firmly planted on both feet.

In the back of the room, Jabari and his subordinates, Khabek, Ineni, and Hori, shuffled their feet, their eyes darting back and forth between the leaders of the People's Restoration of Egypt, Pawah and Beketaten, and the second- and third-highest ranking commanders of the Egyptian military, Ay and Horemheb. They looked to each other, wondering where the other would place his loyalty.

"Of course our Coregent Neferneferuaten-Nefertiti is no coward," Pawah said, sensing the tension in the room.

Beketaten's glare snapped to Pawah.

"As you said, my wife, one way or another, he must die. If he drinks the cup laid for him tonight or tomorrow or a month from now, he will die. The Coregent did what she said she would do—she brought him the poisoned wine." Pawah looked to Commander Horemheb, who had escorted her there and reported back that he had witnessed her pour the hemlock in the wine goblet she took to Pharaoh.

"Egypt will not suffer more if he is alive one day or seven days," Commander Horemheb said, nodding. "It would matter," he added, "if he were alive for *years* more."

"Yes," Pawah said, resting back in his chair. "And then more *drastic* measures would have to be taken."

"Should a rebellion come, you will spare my daughter and her children in your attack," Ay said. It was less a question than a commandment.

"It is hard to control an armed, angry riot," Pawah said, swirling his finger over an imaginary point on the table. "Sometimes, they just get . . . bloodthirsty." He pushed his finger into the table as his eyes lifted to meet Ay's, making his point.

Ay took a step and leaned forward on the table, both hands supporting his hearty frame. "You will control those who fight for you."

"Of course." Pawah slid his hand from the table as the shuffling of feet in the corner of the room slowed and stopped. "Just as I assume you would as well."

"My men follow my order," Ay said.

Pawah smirked, shaking his head. "Of course, Master of Pharaoh's Horses."

Ay stood up straight and peered down at this enemy he had to call an ally. *When this is all over, I will make you pay for forcing my hand and convincing my firstborn to murder her husband.* He gritted his teeth and put his hand on the top of the dagger's handle that hung from his belt. *You can threaten your rebellion—you can imply my men will betray me . . . and now, having no other option, I have gone along with your plan to return Egypt to its former glory. But, in the end, I may even kill you for what you have made me do to my Nefertiti, my precious lotus blossom.*

Pawah sneered, adding, "We will follow your wishes . . . for now."

WATCH FOR THE COMPLETE SERIES AND COLLECTIONS

THE LOST PHARAOH CHRONICLES

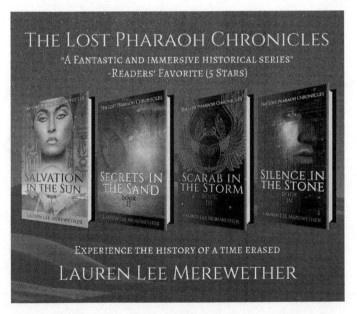

The Complete Quadrilogy

Be sure to check out the *The Lost Pharaoh Chronicles Prequel and Complement Collections*.

Go further into the past with the Prequel Collection and find out how Pawah rose from an impoverished state to priest in **The Fifth Prophet**, how Tey came to Ay's house in **The Valley Iris**, why Ay loved Temehu so much in **Wife of Ay**, General Paaten's struggle in the land of Hatti in **Paaten's War**, and the brotherhood between Thutmose and Amenhotep IV in **Egypt's Second Born**.

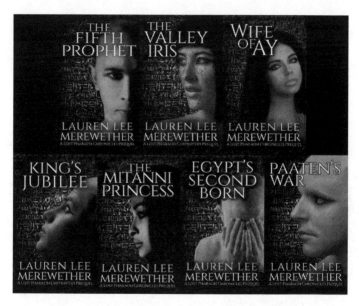

The Prequel Collection Releasing 2019-2021

Dive deeper into the story with the Complement Collection and find out exactly how Pawah transformed the naïve Nebetah into the conniving Beketaten in **Exiled**.

Please note the complement collection will contain spoilers if you have not read the series and relevant prequels first.

For *Exiled*, the reader should read this book one of the series, **Salvation in the Sun**, and the prequel, ***The Fifth Prophet***.

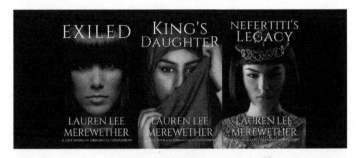

The Complement Collection Releasing 2021

Order each book on Amazon
or sign-up at www.laurenleemerewether.com to stay updated
on new releases!

A LOOK INTO THE PAST

As readers may have gleaned from this novel's prologue and epilogue, the account of Pharaoh Akhenaten was removed from history by a later Pharaoh. Only recently, archeologists have uncovered and are continuing to uncover bits and pieces of what happened during the Amarna period, the period of time this series covers. The author has taken liberties in *Salvation in the Sun*, book one of The Lost Pharaoh Chronicles, where there were uncertainties and unknowns in the facts.

The Amarna period is known for its deviation from traditional Ancient Egyptian art and theology.

Regarding art, it encompassed more realistic, intimate and stylized renderings both in relief and sculpture. Kiya's paintings in the novel were meant to provide the inspiration and explanation behind this period art.

Regarding theology, the religion of the ancient Egyptians swung from a polytheistic worship to a monotheistic worship as indicated in the novel. After dealing more with religious reforms and neglecting or dealing poorly with foreign relations, Pharaoh Akhenaten did not keep the nation at the height his father and mother had achieved for Egypt. It has been assumed he suffered from Temporal Lobe Epilepsy, Marfan's syndrome, Loeys-Dietz syndrome, or some other disorder, which looks to explain why he believed the sun made him feel better—perhaps due to a severe vitamin D deficiency. Visions were common in his family line and only intensified in each generation, most likely due to inbreeding. There are two main theories on why he led Egypt to monotheism: Akhenaten tried to take power from the cult priesthood of Amun, or he just simply had different beliefs for Egypt. It is accepted that he died in Year 17 of his reign.

In the historical record, Henuttaneb was a King's wife, but the name of which King has been erased. She is more commonly associated as a wife of her father, Pharaoh Amenhotep III, but there is little evidence confirming this theory. Because Akhenaten's reign was erased, unlike that of his father's, the author assumed it a better theory that she was in fact her brother's wife. A brother and sister relation was proven through DNA in the resulting offspring of Tutankhaten. Some say that when interbreeding occurs, first cousins such as Nefertiti and Akhenaten could show as brother and sister; however, no record has been uncovered depicting Nefertiti ever bearing a son. Despite the DNA results, Akhenaten has been accepted as Tutankhaten's father; thus, the author decided, since Akhenaten's other sister Nebetah was not named as King's wife, his mother then should be Akhenaten's sister, Henuttaneb.

Smenkare could have been another brother, half-brother, son, or lover of Akhenaten. There are a few who attribute Smenkare and Nefertiti as one and the same, only dressed like a man. Some DNA tests have shown that Smenkare could also be the father of Tutankhaten. Additionally, some believe Tut's nurse, Maia, is actually a reference to his true mother,

Meritaten. Tutankhaten's children's mother presumably was his chief royal wife, as well as a daughter of Akhenaten; however, the DNA of their mother shows no father-daughter relation to the mummy identified as Akhenaten. If the children's mother was not Akhenaten's daughter, then their mother is an unknown lesser wife of Tutankhaten; if the children's mother *is* Akhenaten's daughter, then Akhenaten's mummy is actually someone else (presumably Smenkare) and Smenkare's sister bore Tutankhaten and not Akhenaten and his sister.

Nebetah and Beketaten could have been sisters, mother and daughter, aunt and niece, or the same person. They largely are not referenced after they are young and are only found with the title of King's daughter, not King's wife, although a few speculate she (presuming Nebetah and Beketaten were one and the same) was in fact the wife of Akhenaten and mother of Tutankhaten.

Some speculate Akhenaten may have impregnated his daughters Meritaten and Ankhesenpaaten due to two children referenced late in his reign: Meritaten Tasherit and Ankhesenpaaten Tasherit, where Tasherit means 'the younger'. However, there is no conclusive evidence this is the case as they may have been Smenkare and Meritaten's daughters or Akhenaten and Kiya's daughters. Regardless, these two children were not included in *The Lost Pharaoh Chronicles*.

Nefertiti's parentage is unknown. Since she was part of the erasure executed by a later Pharaoh, little is known about her. This erasure of time is what inspired *The Lost Pharaoh Chronicles* as five Pharaohs were lost to time for almost three millennia. It is assumed Nefertiti was not entirely Egyptian and may have even been a foreigner or adopted into an Egyptian family. Temehu is the name the Egyptians gave to a tribe in Libya, and so the author named Nefertiti's mother,

Temehu, to depict her unknown heritage. Ay is speculated to be her father due to his title 'Father of the God"; however, no record ever affirms him as her father. Tey is most likely not her mother due to her title only stating 'governess' and never 'royal mother' .

From writings found in the Amarna letters, it is widely accepted that a plague swept through the entire region during Year 12 of Akhenaten's reign and killed Kiya, Tiye, and three of Nefertiti's daughters—Meketaten, Neferneferure, and Setepenre—because they disappear from the record after Year 12.

There is no evidence of a rebellion; however, if the cult of Amun was as powerful as records show, the author assumes a rebellion would have taken place when the premier god switched to the Aten. Furthermore, rebellions would not have been recorded in Egyptian history, due to the perception of civil weakness.

It is believed that Nefertiti died sometime between Year 16 and Year 17 of Akhenaten's reign. Some say she lived past Akhenaten's death and was in fact the Pharaoh Neferneferuaten who shows up a few years later after Smenkare, but some associate two separate individuals under the same name and attribute the later Pharaoh to one or two of her daughters: Meritaten, Ankhesenpaaten, or Neferneferuaten Tasherit.

A little peek into the author's mindset:

- There are only a handful of named fictional characters in the story. The majority of the main characters are based on and named after their real-life counterparts. She wanted to stay as close to the historical account as possible, yet still craft an engaging story. For example, Pawah was a lay prophet and scribe of Amun in the 18th Dynasty noted during the reign of Neferneferuaten, and although his quest to take the throne could have been a possibility, there is no evidence to support Pawah as the villain in *The Lost Pharaoh Chronicles* or as a leader in the fictional rebellion group, The People's Restoration of Egypt. The author is working on a prequel collection, and one of the stories is the character Pawah's backstory, ***The Fifth Prophet***, available on Amazon. Go even further into this series and unveil how Pawah transformed the naïve Nebetah into the conniving Beketaten in ***Exiled***, the first complement story to the series.

- The author used "Pharaoh" as a title in the story due to the mainstream portrayal of Pharaoh to mean "King" or "ruler." *Pharaoh* is actually a Greek word for the Egyptian word(s) *pero* or *per-a-a* in reference to the royal palace in Ancient Egypt, or, literally, "great house." The term was used in the time period this series covers; however, it was never used as an official title for the Ancient Egyptian kings.

- Ancient Egyptians called their country *Kemet*, meaning "Black Land," but because the modern term *Egypt* is more prevalent and known in the world today, the author used Egypt when referencing the ancient empire.

- The term 'citizen/citizeness' is similar to the modern 'Mr.' and 'Ms.'; Whereas, 'Mistress of the House' is what they called a married woman over her household.

- The phrase, 'in peace' was the standard greeting and farewell.

- Regnal years were not used during the ancient times, but rather used by historians to help chronicle the different reigns. The author decided to insert these references throughout the novel to help the reader keep track of how much time has passed and to have a better idea of the historical timeline.
- Additionally, the people of Egypt seemed not to celebrate or acknowledge years of life; these were included in the story for the reader's reference. The only "birthday" celebration was every month of Kaherka, which is somewhat equal to December in the Julian calendar. It was a symbolic celebration of the king's coronation, for the gods to renew his lifeforce. To read a free short story the author created as a winter gift for her readers surrounding this time for Amenhotep III, visit her website and download "King's Jubilee."
- *Amun* can be spelled many ways—Amen, Amon, Amun—but it refers to the same god. Likewise, the *Aten* has also been spelled Aton, Atom, or Atun. The author chose consistent spellings for her series for pronunciation purposes.
- Ancient Egyptians did not use the words "death" or "died," but for ease of reading this series, the author used both in some instances. Rather, they would use alternative phrases to satiate the burden that the word "death" brought, such as "went to the fields of Re," "became an Osiris," and "journeyed to the west."

The author hopes you have enjoyed this story crafted from the little-known facts surrounding this period, and is hard at work writing. Find out what happens next with

Beketaten and Pawah, Ay and Horemheb, Paaten, Nefertiti's daughters, and the rise (or fall) of Egypt in the sequel, Secrets in the Sand! Sign up at www.laurenleemerewether.com to receive the Reader's Guide and to receive alerts when new stories are on their way.

WHAT DID YOU THINK?
AN AUTHOR'S REQUEST

Did You Enjoy
Salvation in the Sun?

Thank you for reading the first book in **The Lost Pharaoh Chronicles**. I hope you enjoyed jumping into another culture and reading about the author's interpretation of the events that took place in the New Kingdom of Ancient Egypt.

If you enjoyed *Salvation in the Sun*, I would like to ask a big favor: Please share with your friends and family on social media sites like **Facebook** and leave a review on **Amazon** and on **Goodreads** if you have accounts there.

I am an independent author; as such, reviews and word of mouth are the best way readers like you can help books like *Salvation in the Sun* reach other readers.

Your feedback and support are of the utmost importance to me. If you want to reach out to me and give feedback on this book, ideas to improve my future writings, get updates about future books, or to just say howdy, please visit me on the web.

www.LaurenLeeMerewether.com
Or email me at
mail@LaurenLeeMerewether.com

Happy Reading!

EXCLUSIVE READER OFFER
IN CASE YOU MISSED IT!

Get the first story of
The Lost Pharaoh Chronicles Prequel Collection
for FREE!

Visit www.laurenleemerewether.com
to receive your FREE ebook copy of
The Mitanni Princess.

Her future is pending.

The Mitanni Princess Tadukhipa weighs her options: happiness in exile and poverty, death in prison, or a luxurious life of loneliness. Cursed to love a servant and practice a servant's trade, Tadukhipa rebels against her father, the King, for a chance to change her destiny.

ACKNOWLEDGMENTS

First and foremost, I want to thank God for blessing me with the people who support me and the opportunities he gave me to do what I love: telling stories.

Many thanks to my dear husband Mark, who listened to me drone on and on about the ideas that flew through my head and agreed to invest in me as an author.

Thank you to my parents, siblings, beta readers, and launch team members, without whom I would not have been able to make the story the best it could be and successfully get the story to market.

Thank you to Spencer Hamilton of Nerdy Wordsmith and Sterling & Stone, who put this story through the refiner's fire making this piece of historical fiction really shine.

Thank you to RE Vance, bestselling author of the GoneGod World series, who offered guidance in the series framework and structure.

Thank you to the Self-Publishing School Fundamentals of Fiction course, which taught me invaluable lessons on the writing process and how to effectively self-publish, as well as gave me the encouragement I needed.

Thank you to Magalí Torres for the wonderful book cover design.

Finally, but certainly not least, thank you to my readers. Without your support, I would not be able to write. I truly hope this story engages you, inspires you, and gives you a peek into the past. I've also created a detailed Reader's Guide to help you delve into the history and the story a little bit more—just sign up at www.LostPharaohChronicles.com to receive it.

My hope is that when you finish reading this story, your love of history will have deepened a little more—and, of course, that you can't wait to find out what happens in the next book of the series!

ABOUT THE AUTHOR

Lauren Lee Merewether, a historical fiction author, loves bringing the world stories forgotten by time, filled with characters who love and lose, fight wrong with right, and feel hope in times of despair.

A lover of ancient history where mysteries still abound, Lauren loves to dive into history and research overlooked, under-appreciated and relatively unknown tidbits of the past and craft for her readers engaging stories.

During the day, Lauren studies the nuances of technology and audit at her job and cares for her family. She saves her nights and early mornings for writing stories.

Get her first novel, *Blood of Toma,* for **FREE**, say hello, and stay current with Lauren's latest releases at www.LaurenLeeMerewether.com

facebook.com/llmbooks

twitter.com/llmbooks

instagram.com/llmbooks

bookbub.com/authors/lauren-lee-merewether

amazon.com/author/laurenleemerewether

goodreads.com/laurenleemerewether

Don't miss the Lost Pharaoh Chronicles Prequel Collection.

Order now on Amazon or stay updated at www.laurenleemerewether.com

The Prequel Collection

The Mitanni Princess

(The Lost Pharaoh Chronicles Prequel Collection, A Free Novella)

Her future is pending.

The Mitanni Princess Tadukhipa weighs her options: happiness in exile and poverty, death in prison, or a luxurious life of loneliness. Cursed to love a servant and practice a servant's trade, Tadukhipa rebels against her father, the King, for a chance to change her destiny.

Grab your copy for free at www.laurenleemerewether.com.

The Mitanni Princess sits alongside four talented authors' stories in an anthology, *Daughters of the Past (available on Amazon)*.

If you have read both *The Mitanni Princess* and *Salvation in the Sun*, use the password: ATINUK!

This unlocks the secret bonus ending of *The Mitanni Princess* at www.laurenleemerewether.com.

King's Jubilee

(The Lost Pharaoh Chronicles Prequel Collection, A Free Short Story)

A secret. A brotherhood. A father's sin.

Crown Prince Thutmose's auspicious future keeps his chin high. Striving to be like his father, Pharaoh Amenhotep III, in every way . . . until his eyes open to one of his father's biggest failures.

What will Thutmose decide to do when he takes the crown one day?

Grab your copy for free at www.laurenleemerewether.com.

The King's Jubilee, a short story, also sits alongside sixteen other authors' stories in a young adult multi-genre anthology, *Winds of Winter*, available on Amazon.

The Valley Iris

(The Lost Pharaoh Chronicles Prequel Collection, Book I)

A forbidden love within a sacred village haunts her mind and troubles her future.

Even the vision granted to her from the goddess Hathor keeps Tey from the man she loves. Tey doesn't understand why her mother won't fight for her. She can't see why his family doesn't accept her until it's too late.

Is Tey doomed to live a life with someone else or with no one at all? Can she pick herself up in the darkness of the starlit night and seek her own happiness?

Find out in this coming of age drama set in the New Kingdom of Egypt.

The Wife of Ay

(The Lost Pharaoh Chronicles Prequel Collection, Book II)

Temehu, the daughter of Nomarch Paser, is expected to live a certain life, marry at a certain age to a man of certain status, and have children.

But in her attempts to pursue want she wants for her life, she finds herself questioning the fate of her heart on the journey to the afterlife. Enduring the wrath of a new jealous step-mother and the nobility's harmful gossip and outcasting doesn't soothe her reservations either.

Is she reaping divine punishment for her deeds? Will she find peace for her eternal soul?

Find out in this coming of age drama set in the New Kingdom of Egypt.

Paaten's War

(The Lost Pharaoh Chronicles Prequel Collection, Book III)

Injured in war. Captured by the enemy. Sold as a slave.

Despite his situation, Paaten believes his future is not in enemy land. But as Paaten struggles to find his way back home, to his Egypt, he finds himself in an unforeseen battle waging the biggest war yet:

That of his heart . . .

Will Paaten return to Egypt to fulfill his destiny or renege on his oath to Pharaoh?

The Fifth Prophet

(The Lost Pharaoh Chronicles Prequel Collection, Book IV)

Power. Gold. Prestige. That's all he wants.

Young Pawah's life changes when he travels to Waset on his parent's hard earned savings to become a scribe at the temple of Amun. Facing discrimination in Waset for being the son of a farmer among the wealthy elite, Pawah discovers the ease of which he garners sympathy and subsequent pity gifts of gold with lies and deceit.

Growing into his own on the streets of Waset, how far will Pawah take his ever-expanding greed for gold and power that hides behind his charm and wit?

Dive into this coming-of-age thriller that chronicles the villain of *The Lost Pharaoh Chronicles*.

Egypt's Second Born

(The Lost Pharaoh Chronicles Prequel Collection, Book V)

Bullied by his brother and disregarded by his father, young prince Amenhotep seeks to belong. . . in some way. . . to some one.

Not expected to live as a babe, Amenhotep beats the odds only to find a life always in his brother's shadow and cast out from his father's glory. Turning to his mother proves a challenge and the noble girls seem to laugh save one, Kasmut.

Does Amenhotep succumb to the shadows of his father's great palace or does he rise above the ridicule to forge his own path?

Find out in this heartwarming tale of two royal brothers and their journey to love one another despite past wrongs and shortcomings.

Blood of Toma

Running from death seemed unnatural to the High Priestess Tomantzin, but run she does.

She escapes to the jungle after witnessing her father's murder amidst a power struggle within the Mexica Empire and fears for her life. Instead of finding refuge in the jaguar's land, she falls into the hands of glimmering gods in search for glory and gold. With her nation on the brink of civil war and its pending capture by these gods who call themselves Conquistadors, a bloody war is inevitable.

Tomantzin must choose to avenge her father, save her people, or run away with the man she is forbidden to love.

Lauren's debut work of historical fiction, *Blood of Toma,* won a Montaigne Medal nomination and a finalist award for the Next Generation Indie Book Awards in Historical Fiction and Readers' Favorite Award in Young Adult-Thriller.

Get this ebook for free at www.laurenleemerewether.com.

Made in the USA
San Bernardino, CA
07 June 2020